FROM WHERE THE SUN NOW STANDS

FROM WHERE THE SUN NOW STANDS

by Will Henry

Introduction by John Jakes

MADISON
PARK
PRESS™

NEW YORK

For Marie Richardson

Contents

Acknowledgments

For certain historic speeches of Chief Joseph, Chief Toohoolhoolzote and General O. O. Howard, the author is indebted to the following sources: "Chief Joseph's Own Story," *North American Review*, April, 1879, Harper & Bros., New York, 1879; *Northwestern Fights and Fighters* by Cyrus Townsend Brady, published by Doubleday, Page & Company, Garden City, New York, 1913; *The Nez Perce* by Francis Haines, copyright, 1955, by Francis Haines, and used by permission of the publishers, University of Oklahoma Press, Norman, Oklahoma; and "Chief Joseph of the Nez Perce" by C. E. S. Wood in the *Century Magazine*, May, 1884. Material based on *Yellow Wolf* by L. V. McWhorter, published by The Caxton Printers, Ltd., Caldwell, Idaho, copyright, 1949, by The Caxton Printers, Ltd., is used by special permission of the copyright owners. To them also the author owes thanks for permission to use the map that appeared on the endpapers of that book.

It would be impossible to list all of the sources consulted in the writing of this book but in addition to those already mentioned, grateful acknowledgment should be made to the following: *A Dictionary of the Numipu or Nez Perce Language* by a missionary of the Society of Jesus in the Rocky Mountains, St. Ignatius' Mission Printers, Montana, 1895; *The Indian Council in the Valley of the Walla Walla*, 1855, by Lawrence Kip, privately published; and his *Army Life on the Pacific, a Journal of the Expedition Against the Northern Indians, the Tribes of the Coeur d'Alenes, Spokanes, Palouses, in the Summer of 1858*, Redfield, New York, 1859; *Personal Recollections* by General Nelson Appleton Miles, Riverside Publishing Company, Chicago, 1897; *Howard's Campaign Against the Nez Perce Indians, 1877*, a report by Thomas A. Sutherland, Portland, Oregon, 1878; and *Life of Owhi, His own Statement*, a statement given by Owhi to Dr. Walter S. Johnston, agency physician, Nespelem, Washington, 1920. This manuscript is in possession of Judge William C. Brown of Okanogan, Washington, and a copy was furnished by Marie Richardson, with permission of Judge Brown.

The author especially wishes to thank Marie Richardson for her aid in research and for making important sources available to him.

Introduction

by John Jakes

Will Henry's novel of the nineteenth-century West is remarkable on several counts:

First is the conjunction of author and subject—a white, middle-class American ventured to write about a subject foreign to his ethnicity and upbringing. As any historical novelist does, Will Henry immersed himself in Nez Perce culture and history, but I suspect that today, some talking heads would say that he was poaching in a territory where he had no right to go, never mind that he did so with a wonderful, moving result.

From Where the Sun Now Stands is also unusual in its concept and execution. It considers American history as a two-sided coin. The side we never see directly is that of soldiers and settlers who fulfilled America's "manifest destiny," cannibalizing the continent out to the Pacific and converting it to a bastion of civilization for newcomers.

Will Henry turns the coin over, to reveal a portion of the same history from the viewpoint of one of the tribes, the Pierced-Nose people of Oregon and Idaho. (The Nez Perce didn't pierce their noses or decorate them with bizarre ornaments, however; historians tell us that misnaming the tribe was the error of an interpreter with the Lewis and Clark expedition.)

From Where the Sun Now Stands chronicles the 113-day, 1300-mile retreat of Chief Joseph and his people from Idaho to Montana, fleeing an impending return to a reservation. "The result," Henry writes in his foreword, "is intended as a tribute to a way of life and an ideal of freedom which have vanished with the war bonnet and the buffalo."

The Nez Perce were largely a peaceful people until threatened. They enjoyed enlightened leadership from Chief Joseph, a major player in the novel, and his father before him, also called Joseph. The elder Joseph had met Lewis and Clark on friendly terms.

The advancing tide of settlement wouldn't allow the Nez

Perce, or other tribes, to roam freely on what they considered their ancestral lands. But as Joseph observes, to pen up an Indian on a reservation is to "break his heart . . . to kill him. This the white man knew."

Chief Joseph is a remarkable character. He isn't a fierce warrior such as Geronimo or Sitting Bull; more often he's found tending to the welfare of the women and children of his tribe. Something of a mystic, he is described as "a strange, sad-eyed man who never smiled." He prided himself on persuasive oratory—"placing all the facts in a straight row." Joseph is credited with having the gift of seeing the future, though this talent is increasingly distrusted as the story progresses.

Joseph argues for restraint—retreat to Canada—rather than inevitable slaughter in the face of superior numbers of white men. His philosophy of defensive war is humane:

"We do not fight women and children and old men. We may die, they may kill us, but we will never harm their old people, their women and their little ones, as they have ours." Contrast this nobility with Kenneth Roberts's characters in an earlier selection in this series, *Northwest Passage*. Whatever Roberts's personal views, his pre-Revolutionary frontiersmen regard almost all Indians as drunkards and cowards; untrustworthy.

The moment for which Chief Joseph is best remembered is not a massacre such as that at the Little Big Horn, but his declaration in October 1877, when he saw the futility of continuing the long retreat:

"My heart is sick and sad. From where the sun now stands, I will fight no more forever."

You will discover how he was treated after his remarkable and touching concession.

The first-person narrator of the novel is Heyets, a young Nez Perce on the cusp of manhood and warrior status. His name means Mountain Sheep. You'll find a mingling of English and Nez Perce names throughout the book. This tends to be a little daunting, much like names in a Russian novel, but it isn't an insurmountable obstacle.

Using Heyets as his spokesman, Will Henry can show us the differences between the two sides of the historical coin. For example, Heyets tells us that at no time did his tribe consist of more than thirty to sixty braves armed for war. This is far fewer than the legions of blue-coated cavalry put into the chase by O. O. Howard—"One-Hand Howard"—the general who lost an arm in the Civil War and, later, founded Howard University. That imbalance, Heyets declares, was "Indian history"—unacknowledged by the other side.

But the foes of the Nez Perce are never merely cardboard opponents. More than once, Heyets takes pains to point out that the soldiers are just like the Nez Perce on the eve of a battle:

"Frightened. Sad. Lonesome."

But later, before a key engagement, he again stresses the differences:

"That is the way a white man remembers a battle—so many soldiers here, so many there. . . . The horses precisely here, the cannon exactly there. An Indian remembers where his mother fell bayoneted, or his little brother had his skull smashed. . . . The one way is history, and the other only Indian lies."

Through his narrator, Will Henry can give us vivid examples of tribal mores. Heyets describes essential battle preparations:

"First there was the matter of clothing. Before a big fight the Nez Perce always stripped to his loincloth. Bare flesh took a clean hole. Cloth on the body over the skin was driven into the body by the bullet and made a dirty hole. . . . Then there was the matter of food. No Nez Perce ate before a battle. An empty belly punctured clean. A full one burst like a rotten melon. . . . The third thing was more difficult, and so more necessary even, than the others. It was about women. About lying up with them, that is, the night before a fight. . . . Lying with a woman . . . took away much strength. . . . Of the three main laws, it was surely the most important and the most sternly observed."

In my first introduction for this series, I said that my choices were fine historical novels that have drifted into the literary shadows for a variety of reasons. In the case of Henry Wilson Allen, Jr.,

(1912–91), who wrote as Clay Fisher and also as Will Henry, his preferred pseudonym, we're dealing with a writer who saw himself obscured in the long shadow of a far more successful purveyor of "Westerns." During a lengthy interview with Jean Henry-Mead, Henry said, "I consider myself out of the mainstream of tradition-al Western writing. This fact, more than any other, has operated against my achieving . . . wide popular readership."

In whose shadow did he stand?

"The most effective writer in the business ever . . . Mr. Louis Dearborn L'Amour."

L'Amour's sales figures were spectacular while Will Henry's were only respectable. Henry for a time was part of the Western line published by Bantam Books but L'Amour was its star. Over the years I've repeatedly gotten pleasure from L'Amour's lively storytelling, but Will Henry stands apart, an artist. His skill refutes his own melancholy belief toward the end of his life that, forgotten, he was "the Snail-Darter of the Western Writing World."

Will Henry's father, Dr. H. Wilson Allen, Sr., of Kansas City, Missouri, was an oral surgeon who considered his boy too starry-eyed and introspective for his own good:

"You're unreliable, lazy, you lack true grit, and I don't want to recommend an honest living for you. I think you'd do better at a dishonest living. Why don't you become a writer?"

Dr. Allen's suggestion took.

Junior wrote a story when he was "eleven or twelve"—in long-hand—and submitted it to *Liberty* magazine, where it was quickly and understandably rejected. Many years later Henry discovered the manuscript, typed and re-titled it, and then saw it accepted and published.

Henry was largely self-educated. He survived three semesters at a junior college, but reading was his chief tutor. He devoured the ubiquitous pulp magazines of the 1920s and 1930s, as well as pop-ular literature—Kipling, Sax Rohmer, Conan Doyle. He said that his favorite author was Mark Twain, closely followed by Steinbeck.

Drifting west to Los Angeles, he survived on odd jobs, renting his strong arms and back to moving-van crews. He lived cheaply, as many Los Angeles newcomers do. A job he landed as a writer in the MGM short subjects department gave him both experience and a respect for screen writing—"a splendid art form in its own right." Chapter 19 of this novel describes a battle in pure cinematic language. Further along, when the Nez Perce are trapped by a horde of cavalrymen, Henry again visualizes it almost as we might see it on the screen:

"On the ridge, for the whole length of its crest and running to either flank, east and west, there swarmed a solid darkness of horse soldiers. As the people cried out in their heart-fear at the sight of them, officers' swords and bugles blew from one end to the other of the blue-coated line . . ."

As Will Henry and Clay Fisher, Henry Wilson Allen, Jr., published fifty-four novels and collections from 1950 to 1984. *From Where the Sun Now Stands* appeared in 1960, under the Random House imprint. By then the author already had a strong track record of sales to the movies—not too surprising, considering his MGM experience.

By the 1950s he'd begun scripting television Westerns, but books soon became more important. The Will Henry byline first appeared on *No Survivors*, in 1950. "Clay Fisher" debuted with *Red Blizzard* a year later.

Death came in 1991, in a hospital in Van Nuys, California. Henry is buried about twenty miles from his home in Encino. He is survived by his wife, Dorothy, who was very helpful in clearing the rights for re-publication of *From Where the Sun Now Stands*.

I hope two things are clear:

Will Henry wrote historical novels, not "cowboy stories." His novels often take the part of the underdog in a conflict. This is a grand example.

And he wrote as he did because of the powerful attraction of western history—indeed, the landscape itself:

"I've always loved the West," he said, "both as a land and an intangible mythology. I love the looks of the deserts, the skies, the mountains, the roll of the plains. . . . I can't to this day take an automobile ride in prairie country, or mountain country, or hill country, or canyon country, that I don't thrill to it, and feel its strangeness, and the pull of its mystique, and want again to write . . .

"Oh, yes, I love the West."

Foreword

From Where The Sun Now Stands is a novel based on the historic
one hundred thirteen-day retreat of Chief Joseph and his people from
White Bird Canyon in Idaho to the Bear Paws in Montana. It has
been told here through the eyes of an aging member of Joseph's own
Wallowa band, who made the thirteen hundred-mile march as a
young warrior.

Care has been taken to preserve historical facts and the utterances
of leading figures. Yet the interpreter is a Nez Perce Indian, and it is
precisely the differences between Nez Perce and white points of
view which heighten the eloquence of this tragic chronicle.

The result is intended as a tribute to a way of life and an ideal of
freedom which have vanished with the war bonnet and the buffalo.
May it serve, then, to dignify the Indian position and render justice
to the memory of Chief Joseph and his people.   W. H.

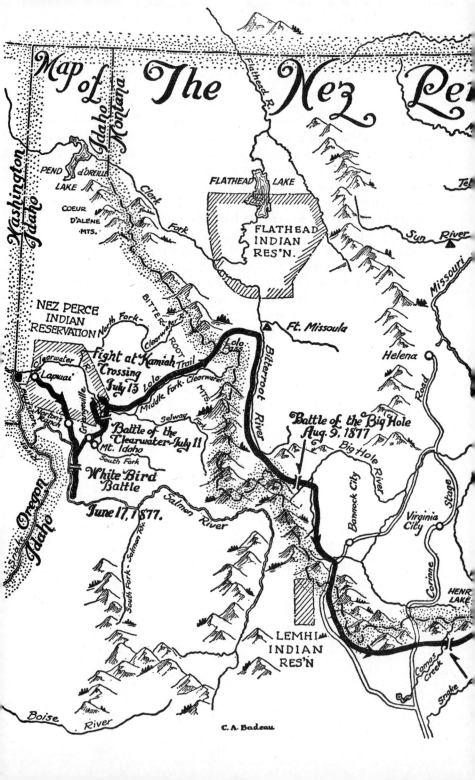

Map of The Nez Per...

Washington
Idaho

Idaho
Montana

Flathead R.

PEND d'OREILLE LAKE

COEUR D'ALENE MTS.

FLATHEAD LAKE

FLATHEAD INDIAN RES'N.

Tel...

Sun River

Missouri

NEZ PERCE INDIAN RESERVATION

North Fork

Clark Fork

BITTER ROOT

Clearwater River

Lolo Pass

Ft. Missoula

Helena

Road

Fight at Kamiah Crossing July 13

Clearwater R.

Lapwai

Lolo Trail

Lolo

Middle Fork. Clearwater

Selway

Bitterroot River

Battle of the Big Hole Aug. 9, 1877

Norton's Ranch

Battle of the Clearwater-July 11

Mt. Idaho

MTS.

Big Hole River

South Fork

White Bird Battle

Oregon
Idaho

June 17, 1877.

Salmon River

Bannock City

Virginia City

Stage

Corinne

South Fork - Salmon Fork

LEMHI INDIAN RES'N

HENR... LAKE

Camas Creek

Snake

Boise River

C. A. Badeau

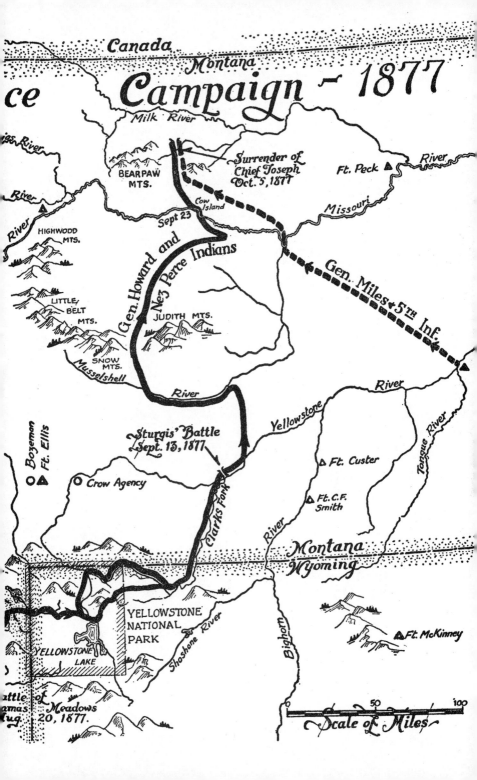

Book One
The Wallowa

1. The Appaloosa Pony

I remember the day as though it were but one or two suns gone. It had been an early spring. The weather in mid-April was already warm as late May. I was on the hillside above the village tending my father's horses when Itsiyiyi, Coyote, the friend of my heart in those boyhood times, came racing up from the lodges below.

Coyote's eyes were wild. His nostrils were standing wide with breath. His ragged black hair was tossing like the mane of a bay pony. He was always so alarmed by the least affairs. Now I wondered what small thing brought him dashing up the hill, and I awaited his news, very superior in the advantage of my fourteen years to his twelve.

But Coyote had the real news that morning. *"Eeh!"* he said. "We are going to the buffalo. Isn't that a grand thing, Heyets?"

It was surely a very grand thing. Well nigh an incredible one. Boys our age going to the buffalo? *Eeh* indeed.

The last time any of our band had gone had been several springs ago when Tuekakas, Old Joseph, the father of our present chief, had begun to grow blind and had asked Young Joseph to take him once more to the buffalo before his sight failed altogether and he could see no more the lonely grandeur of that brooding, vast stillness where dwelled the Crow, the Sioux and the Assiniboin, and where the eye could run to the end of the world. That previous time only Joseph and the other of the old man's sons, the younger one, Ollikut, the Frog, together with a chosen few hunters, had gone with the aging chief on the journey of his last bidding. When they had come home again Tuekakas was chief no more and the elder son, Heinmot Tooyalakekt, Thunder Traveling to the Mountain—our Joseph—was the leader of the Wallowa Nez Perce.

So it had continued to this very day of Coyote's great news in the spring of 1874. Now we were all of us going many suns across the Idaho mountains to hunt the curly cows and shaggy

3

bulls on the plains of far Montana. Only an Indian boy—really only a Nez Perce Indian boy—could know the full, fierce joy of that.

In the end, of course, there were a good many of the Nez Perce who found one reason or another for staying home. The world is simply made up of people who will go to the buffalo and people who will not go to the buffalo. Still, our small group made a rather impressive sight as it gathered for the departure.

For our horse herd, the most important part of any Indian journey, we had brought up only the best animals owned by the various families going along. The total number of these would average at least six or seven horses for every one of us, and each animal carefully selected for a special purpose either of work or play.

First to be counted—that is to say poorest in overall quality—were the pack and travois beasts. Next upward in the scale was the traveling horse, the one to be ridden on the trail. Then came what the Christian Nez Perce, the treaty Indians, called the Sunday horse. This was always a show-off animal chosen by us free-roaming nontreaties for important social events, the most important of which was riding into Lapwai to make the treaties unhappy with their fenced fields and little white man's farms, to remind them of what they had paid for giving up the fine wild life we still enjoyed. They were the Nez Perce people who had not listened to Old Joseph when he tore up his Bible and stalked out of the thieves' treaty council of 1863. They were the people who stayed at that evil meeting with old Chief Lawyer and signed the bad paper which gave away all our lands in the Wallowa which the true treaty of 1855 had guaranteed us forever. That was why we called Lawyer's people treaty Indians, and why we used the Sunday horse to make them feel sad.

So the Sunday horse was always one of very flashing style and no real bottom. But the buffalo horse and the war horse, ah! They were the back fat and the hump ribs of all horseflesh, the *boudins*, the real intestines of the matter. And the greatest honor which could befall a Nez Perce boy was to be allowed to lead by hand upon the trail a grown man's buffalo or war horse. In this direction I was to have my second surprise of that April morning.

When I left the breakfast fire at sunrise of that day not one word had been suggested about going to the buffalo. Some minutes after I went up on the hill, Ollikut came up to our fire and sat down. He thanked my mother, Takialakin, for the helping of camas root and steamed beef fat which she offered him, ate a little of it with his fingers in the polite way, then said to my father, "Well, Wiyukea, what are you thinking of doing this morning?"

My father, whose full name was Wiyukea Koos, Elk Water, thought a moment before he spoke. Indians have that habit. It is why they do not talk as much as the white man. But presently my father waved his hand and replied to Ollikut.

"*Eeh*, neighbor, it is early yet. I have no thoughts."

Ollikut nodded as though to admit that was a reasonable answer, then asked my father how he would like to go to the buffalo if he had no better thing to do.

My father glanced at him and said, "Do you mean today?" and Ollikut looked up at the sky all around and answered, "Well, as far as I can see, it is going to be a good day."

That was the entire planning right there. By the time the idea had spread from our fire to the last one in the village, the ponies had been run in and packed and we were ready to go. There remained, however, that matter of my second surprise.

The present summer was the eighteenth of my uncle Hemene Moxmox, Yellow Wolf. Among the Nez Perce a boy becomes a man at seventeen. So, in the ceremonies which mark this time of life, something wonderful had just happened to him.

I saw him coming toward me leading a horse. It was a four-year-old of that rump-whitened Appaloosa breed made famous by my people. Yet even among that noble strain this one was a very special horse. I drew in my breath and stood like a sand-crane in the river, struck motionless by such impossible beauty.

"Well, what do you think of him?" asked my young uncle, halting a little way off and letting the horse go out on the rope to show his spirit.

I shook my head, unable to answer intelligently. Finally I said, "I have no words, but you may trust me, uncle. I will keep your secret. Tell me what warrior has let you lead this great horse which I have never seen before."

"No warrior," he answered quickly. "He is my own horse."

"No, I won't believe it. How ever is that?"

Yellow Wolf grew impatient with me.

"See here," he said, "do you deny that Joseph is my uncle? That I am his nephew?"

I shook my head. "No," I said. "I don't deny it, but how does that explain the horse? And what is his name, how do you call him?"

"Tipyahlanah Weyatanatoo, Sun Eagle," he replied. "How is that?"

"Lovely. Exquisite. But why do you have him?"

"I have him as my first buffalo horse, a gift from Joseph himself."

"Never! From our chief himself?"

"I will say it three times—he is mine and Heinmot Tooyalakekt gave him to me this day."

I blinked hard. A Nez Perce may tell a story which is not true two times only. The third time must be the truth. It is our law. That beautiful horse belonged to Yellow Wolf, a man could stake his life upon it.

But before my envy could weaken me further, Yellow Wolf said quietly, "Here, take him; he is yours to lead from this place to the Land of the Buffalo."

It was too much. I could not reach out my hand to take the rope. A skinny pony-herd boy being allowed to care for the buffalo horse of Joseph's own nephew? Ah, I could not bear the honor of it. The tears of gratitude came to my eyes and spilled beyond them down my cheeks.

Yellow Wolf did not see the tears. He looked away even though he did not move his eyes. A man does not see another man cry. He may look squarely at him but he does not see. It is *simiakia*, the Nez Perce way, our inner pride of Indian manhood.

"Take the horse," repeated my young uncle, and put the rope

gently into my hand. I clenched it tightly and he walked off
straight and unbending as a Crow lance haft.

2. Going to the Buffalo

The dew was yet upon the meadow grass when we set out across
the valley, bound for Kamiah Crossing of the Clearwater. Here
we would strike the great Lolo Trail, the ancient Indian road
across the Bitterroot Mountains into Montana. Everyone was
laughing and singing spring songs or calling out cheerful words.
That was the way it was with my people in those happy days of
1874, following the returning treaty of 1873; the good paper by
which President Grant gave back to us our ancestral valleys of
the Wallowa and Imnaha Rivers. There were no problems, no
real fears remaining. All was as it had been before the thieves'
treaty of 1863. One Indian said to another, "Let us go to the
buffalo," and, quick as that, down came the tipis, in came the
horse herd, off went the happy people.

It was a grand time. Every sunbeam which smote the dew
dazzled my eye. Every stir of pine smell coming from the hills
hurried my blood. Every bird song struck my heart like a sweet
arrow. And why should it not? Was I not astride my good blue
pony, Tea Kettle? Was I not leading the magnificent Sun Eagle?
Was I not the proudest of all Nez Perce boys from Oregon to
Idaho? Ah, those times, those times.

In a little while, riding north, we came to the Snake River.
We rode down to it at the regular place just below the mouth
of Salmon River. The Snake was in flood. It was like meeting
hohots, the angry grizzly bear, upon a narrow ledge. Yet we
could not turn away from it; we had to go over it at this place.

Joseph and the men sat their horses studying it for some time.
The problem was the women and children and old ones. Had the
men been alone, they would have swum it of course. Now things
were different.

Joseph held up his hand. "Unroll the pack covers," he told
the women. "There will be a boat-building."

At once all was activity, all was hard work. These pack covers with which we made the boats were buffalo hides cured with the hair on, not soft-tanned with smoke and oil like the tipi cowskins. They would turn the water as shiny as the gloss feathers of a drake's vent. When the green willow withes were cut and bent into frames, to be sprung free inside them, we had an Indian transport which would float like a corked soldier canteen. "Bullboats" the white men called them, and they never did capture our Nez Perce secret of building them, which allowed us to ferry any freight, even to a small wagon, across the main Snake in spring flood. Those round, hairy craft bobbed like ducks yet did not ship one droplet in the wildest current.

As for me that morning of the boat-building when my mother seized the bridle of Tea Kettle before I could turn him to escape and ordered, "Get down, loafer, you are not a warrior yet; go help cut the willow sticks," I would gladly have sold our tribal secret of construction for three rifle shells, or a good piece of mirror glass. But that was before I actually went down to the river with my camp ax, and it was certainly before I surprised that Asotin girl at her morning bath.

Did I say there were two young girls with our small band? No? Well, one of them I knew. She was Coyote's sister. All elbows and long leg bones and two big teeth in front. We called her Beaver and she would have made a better boy than Coyote. But the other one I did not know. She was visiting our band from the village of Chief Looking Glass's Asotin people, on the Clearwater near Kamiah Crossing. I had not seen this other girl for I was training myself to be a warrior, or at least a horse racer. Oh, I will admit I had heard she was a *palojami*, a fair one. Yet I had also heard, loftily from Yellow Wolf, that she was no more than a *tekash*, a cradle-board baby; that she had not yet been out on the mountain, had not yet menstruated.

The Nez Perce were very strict about such things. We adolescent boys were not even supposed to look at a girl who had not yet come to maturity, much less talk to her or be seen alone with her. But that law was not made for this Asotin girl. No Indian boy could see her standing unclad there beside the river,

slender and willowy as a water reed, and turn his eyes away from
her. Or his heart, either.

She felt a little something, too.

We stared hard at each other and I got mad with myself for
what I was thinking and I said angrily to her, "You are nothing
but a *tekash*. Put on your dress."

She made a strange face at me and said, "Why?"

"Because I order it. Do as you are told."

"I don't know if I will or not. What is your name, boy?"

"Heyets. What is yours?"

"Meadowlark."

"Very well. Put on your dress, Meadowlark."

She hesitated a moment, blushing a little, then smiled. "All
right, Heyets, I am putting it on. Don't watch me."

Of course I dropped my eyes and she slipped the deerskin
camp dress over her dark head. Then she came up to me and put
her fingers under my chin. "Now look at me, Heyets," she said.
"Here is your woman waiting for you."

"My woman, did you say?" I demanded, lifting my gaze. "Do
you think to make a laugh on me? We are only children."

"What is the difference? Did you not command me to do a
thing and did I not do it?"

"Yes, you did it."

"Do you think I obey every boy like that?"

"I don't know. How would I know what you do?"

"Don't worry about that. I will show you." Meadowlark
smiled and took my hand and gave it a long squeeze. Then she
said, "Come on," and turned about and led me into the willow
clump behind us. When we were in there where it was safe and
dark and close, she said, "Now kiss me on the mouth as hard as
you can; I want to feel how that is."

I stood awkward and very frightened. I wanted to do what
she said but could not make my arms move. She found my other
hand and pulled me in toward her. When I touched her body
with mine we were suddenly kissing with our mouths and I was
grown weak and full of evil. In that same bad moment Meadowlark gave a quick laugh, twisted away from me, bounded out of

our willow clump and away up the river trail to the place of the boat-building. She did not give me one backward glance. It was as though what we had just done had never been done at all. It was a very foolish feeling.

Suffering it, I made to move out of the willows and pick up my bundle of boat sticks where I had dropped it. As I bent down, a familiar yellow-topped moccasin trapped my reaching hand against the bundle. I looked up fearfully and saw above me the scowling face of my uncle, Hemene Moxmox.

"Stand up straight," said Yellow Wolf. "You know what I must do." He stepped back and I did as he bid me.

It was a hard beating. He gave it to me with a rabbit-throwing stick he was carrying in a walk down the river. I held my place and did not move, as Nez Perce manhood rules demanded. But my mother was right; I was not a warrior yet. On the seventh or eighth blow I fell down.

Yellow Wolf stopped and looked at me severely. "You were wrong," he charged. "Do you admit it?"

I nodded that I did.

"What were you thinking?" he went on. "You never looked at girls before."

"No, I didn't. But this girl was different."

"She was no different."

"Very well." I grimaced, feeling the pain of my welts. "Have the girl any way you want her, but what about the horse? What about leading Sun Eagle now?"

"Naturally you cannot lead him any longer." Yellow Wolf shrugged. "I will give him to Coyote."

"Do not do that, uncle," I pleaded. "Coyote is a *meopkowit*, a little baby. What will people think of me?"

"They will think you got off lightly if I ever tell them what I saw in those bushes just now. Isn't that so?"

It was, indeed, and I nodded again.

"Never mind," said Yellow Wolf, "we will forget all about it. Do you want to go rabbit-hunting with me now?"

"Yes, uncle, but I have no throwing stick."

"Use mine. I will do the stomping out."

"Thank you. How about my boat sticks here? My mother is waiting for them."

"Let her wait. She had no right to send you on such squaw's business. Leave the sticks. Some woman will pick them up. Come on."

"My mother won't like me tonight."

"Stay the night by our fire. My mother likes you."

"Thank you, I believe I'll do that." I took the throwing stick from him, hefting it as a boy will to get the feel of something joyful and exciting. "It has a good balance, a lovely balance," I said. "Let's go."

We went away down the river together. After a while, when there were no rabbits, we took off our shirts and pants and went into the water. There was a big pool at that place, eddying with a safe, smooth whorl behind a fine black rock. The water was all sun-flecked and foamy and full of spring warmth, and we swam and played in it like young otters. Presently we crawled out on the rock and slept in the sunshine and dreamed of being warriors and of hunting the buffalo when we got to Montana.

3. Up the Wild Tahmonmah

Next morning we got across the Snake with no trouble. Yellow Wolf's grandmother fell out of their boat but Seekumses Kunnin, Horse Blanket, Yellow Wolf's father, just sat there and watched her go bobbing away down the river. You see, she was not the mother of Horse Blanket but of Horse Blanket's wife, Swan Woman. The law of our people forbade the son-in-law to speak to the mother-in-law, or to put his hand upon her. So Horse Blanket obeyed the law. When the old lady kept screeching at him to jump in and save her, he only turned to Swan Woman and said, "It serves the old fool right. Next time she won't try to make water over the side of the boat in a current like this one. Let her go."

Fortunately Yellow Wolf was swimming his pony with the horse herd being crossed below the boats. He got his rope on the poor old thing and towed her on across and stranded her up on the far side like a humpback salmon half drowned from fighting upstream.

I was able to see all of this because I was riding in the boat with Yellow Wolf's family. I had spent the previous night by their fire for fear my mother would not be joyous about the boat sticks. Word came to me by my father that it would be just as well if I were to stay with the Yellow Wolf family a few more days. My mother, who was a Christian, had been telling him she had had enough of such Indian nonsense as going to the buffalo, and that she was certainly going to send me into Agent Monteith's church school at Lapwai the coming winter. My father hoped that my staying with Yellow Wolf would protect me from the dangerous turn of my mother's mind these latter days. I stayed in the tipi of Swan Woman and Horse Blanket all the way to the Clearwater.

On the other side, in Idaho country, it was decided to make a detour along the Tahmonmah, the Salmon River, so that we might visit other relatives on the way to the village of Looking Glass. Naturally I became very excited when I heard this. Up the wild Tahmonmah lived the two most famous fighting chiefs of our people. These were Toohoolhoolzote, Harsh Sound, leader of the Salmon River band, and Peopeo Hihhih, White Bird, chief of the White Bird band. The country in which these Idaho Nez Perce lived was called Land of the Seven Devils. It was the most remote, rough and spectacular, altogether mysterious region imaginable. I could scarcely contain myself. It happened that I had not seen either of these great warriors before that time, and there were two reasons for this. First, the Salmon River and White Bird Nez Perce were small, wild-living bands. They had no great wealth of land or livestock, nothing to make them tame. They clung most closely to the old ways and in result we saw less of them than of the other bands, like the Asotin. Secondly, Toohoolhoolzote and White Bird did not entirely trust Joseph and were so intractable in their hatred of the white man and his ways that some of us feared them more than we did the missionaries and agents.

Our Wallowa band had been the traditional ally of the white man in that country since the time of Lewis and Clark. The grandfather of our own Joseph had guided those two great white friends of the Nez Perce down the Big River to the Western Sea. Many of the Wallowa, even in that present spring of 1874, were still Christian converts, educated to read and write and speak good English in the school of old Agent Spalding—the true agent—at Lapwai. My own mother was one of this group.

Our vast lands lying between the Grande Ronde River on the west and the Snake on the east had been given back to us by President Grant only the past year of 1873. This had made the wild bands uneasy. It had made their hearts a little jealous, too. Joseph's people numbered but fifty-five grown men, yet they were the owners of a million acres of the choicest Nez Perce pasture. The wild bands thought we had been given this favor because Joseph listened to the white man. They would not believe he could listen and still do as he liked. For their part they would not listen at all and claimed they were unfairly treated because of this, and because they were honest where we Wallowa were sly.

So there was the explanation of how I could come to fourteen summers not having seen the famous Toohoolhoolzote and White Bird. And, as well, the probable reason Joseph now took thought to visit them before going on to the Asotin. Our chief never gave up trying to unite his entire people. He believed, always, that if the nontreaty Indians were to save any of their land from the settlers, gold miners and whiskey-sellers who were stealing it from them, they must resist as we had in the Wallowa —peacefully.

But no matter. With sunrise of that second morning we were off up the Salmon to see the wild Nez Perce. The prospects sent my heart soaring.

It was spring. A fine shower during the night had washed the sky clean as a river stone. The sun was warm and sweet. Above us on the steepening hillsides the pine jays scolded with a good will. Below us along the rushing green waters of the river, the redwing reedbirds whistled cheerily. Tea Kettle, my dear mouse-colored pony, tried to bite me in the leg and buck me off. Yellow Wolf, my young uncle, who was as fierce as any fighting Indian, jogged by on his traveling mare and gave me a friendly sign. Even Joseph, that strange, sad-eyed man who almost never smiled, brightened to nod and wave at me as I passed him where he sat by the trail, watching, to be sure all his people were safe across the Snake.

I looked all about me at that lovely pine-scented country and at those handsome, good-natured Nez Perce people riding up Tahmonmah River, carefree and noisy-throated as the mountain birds about them. Doing that, I thought to myself that a Nez Perce boy might well take such a moment to offer up some thanks to Hunyewat, our Indian god. The trouble with the white man was over. Our ancestral homes had been returned to us, and in all the Nez Perce world there was nothing to be seen but blue sky, nothing to be heard but bird songs.

Sitting there on my little gray pony, I bowed my head to the morning sun and said the proper, humble words to Hunyewat.

4. The Guns of Kamiah

When we got to White Bird Canyon, where the first village of the wild bands was located, I am afraid I did shame to my fourteen years. Neither White Bird nor the savage fighting Indians we had come to see were at home. There were only the wrinkled old people and the mothers with young children. The truth was that when I saw this was the case, I cried. Fortunately no one saw me save Coyote, and him I fooled by saying that I had been struck in the eye by a low branch beside the trail. But it was a very great disappointment all the same.

Always alert, Joseph halted our band a little way out from the quiet village. "Wait here," he ordered, and rode on in with his tall brother Ollikut to see what the trouble might be. He came back in a short time, and it was real trouble he had to report.

That same morning word had come that the Nez Perce herds being driven to higher country for summer pasture had been halted at Kamiah Crossing of the Clearwater by white men. These men all had guns and were from Kamiah Valley where they had their homes and through which went the way to the summer pastures. When the Indian herders rode up to the river these men showed the rifle to them and said roughly, "Stop where you are with those animals; you are not driving them to Kamiah or through Kamiah. You have your own country which has been given you. Stay on it."

When White Bird heard of this he became very angry. At once he had ridden off with his warriors into the badlands back from the river to gather up old Toohoolhoolzote and his fighting men on the way to Kamiah Crossing.

Joseph's face grew stern as the mountain rock around us, as he told us this. It was true, he said, that the Nez Perce had moved their herds into and through the Kamiah grass every summer since the grayest chief could remember, and it was a wrong thing for the settlers to have closed the Indian road like that. But it would be even more of a wrong thing for the fighting Indians to start any shooting. White Bird and Toohoolhoolzote must not be allowed to come up to those white men at the river.

"Ollikut, Elk Water, Horse Blanket," he said in a low voice, "you three come with me. Go get your best horses."

"Certainly," answered Horse Blanket. "But I have a favor to ask. My son Yellow Wolf is seventeen just now. He should be given some experience riding with grown men on serious business."

Joseph nodded without hesitation. "Yes, let him come. A young man must learn." He turned to my father. "And how is it with you, Elk Water?" he asked, eyeing my father keenly. "Do you not have a problem also?"

"Well, yes," my father said, frowning. "I would like to see my son go along, too. He is only fourteen summers and no warrior fit to ride with grown men, but his mother was several years in the church school at Lapwai and she thinks soft on the white man. She is spoiling this boy. I want him to see how the white man really is. What do you think?"

Joseph took several seconds with his answer.

"Yes," he finally said, "that was in my own mind. Does he have a good horse?"

My heart, leaping the moment before, dropped like a stone. But in the silence following Joseph's question Yellow Wolf stepped forward and said quietly, "Yes, Heyets has a good horse. He has my horse, Sun Eagle. I will stay home. Coyote, bring that horse up here for Heyets."

I could not believe my ears, yet I had to believe my eyes, for there came Coyote leading up the Appaloosa pony. As I stood dumbfounded, Joseph said to Yellow Wolf, "That was a kind thing to do, nephew. Do you know that?"

"No, uncle," replied Yellow Wolf shortly. "I only know that it is true what his father says; his mother is ruining this boy with white talk. We Indians must stay to our own ways. He is welcome to the horse."

He was very fierce with the way he said it and Joseph shook his head reprovingly. "Your spirit is wrong," he told him, "but who can deny your heart? Come, I will give you another horse. Go, take my six-year-old black, the one with the bobbed tail. Hurry. We must all hurry. *Koiimze* . . . !"

At his words, they all dashed off to catch up their fastest horses, and that was a very lucky thing for me. In my excitement to be up on the dancing Sun Eagle, I tried to make a leaping war mount and dived clear over his back and fell down his far side into the dust and horse droppings of the trail. Talk about a thing like that has followed many an Indian to his grave, but happily in this case our band was interested in watching the men change horses and no one save Coyote saw me fall. With a boost from him I managed to get back up on the Appaloosa and stay there, before the others got back.

I was not small with my gratitude, either. I said, "Thank you, friend Coyote. One day I shall return the favor." But Coyote only shook his head soberly. "It will not be necessary," he said. "Only show me that wonderful trick of jumping clear over the horse. That was amazing, Heyets. No one but you could have done it."

"All right," I agreed hastily, "I will teach it to you when I return. Only keep it our secret, do you hear? One word of this to anyone else and you are no longer my friend."

I didn't hear his answer for at that moment Yellow Wolf came racing up on Joseph's black, and yonder came Joseph, Ollikut, Horse Blanket and my father from four directions at one time, whipping their horses with shouts and whistles of encouragement. They came by me on the whoop, never hesitating; Ollikut in the lead, the others seeming to run right up his roan's rump, yet somehow, after the miraculous fashion of Indian mounts, never bumping or touching or throwing one another offstride while still galloping so close you could not have slid a lance blade down between their lathered hides. For myself, I had all I could do merely to hang onto the Appaloosa. He went off after the others like an arrow from a war bow. In twenty jumps he had me running knee-and-knee with the mighty Ollikut.

Joseph's brother, six feet three inches tall and the handsomest Indian who ever lived, looked over at me as I came up, and said, "That's a fine horse you have there, boy. I particularly admire the way you handle him."

That was the proudest moment of my life thus far. Ollikut was the hero of my boyhood; he was the hero of all the Wallowa boys. I felt ten feet tall when he spoke to me like that. "Thank you, my chief!" I called to him, and sat so proud and vain upon Sun Eagle that I did not see the pine tree standing just beside the trail ahead.

"*Eeh-yihh!*" Something struck me in the stomach like the ball from a cannon soldier's gun. The next moment Sun Eagle was still running with Ollikut but I was not. I was sitting in the middle of the trail, paralyzed on the end of my backbone. The last I saw of the Kamiah Crossing party was the sweaty rears of its mounts, along with the runaway, Sun Eagle, disappearing into a cloud of dust down the Clearwater Trail. And that is the way it came about that I did not actually lie to Coyote about that low branch beside the trail, after all. At least not very much.

Now with a real reason to cry, there was no thought of such a thing. I was mad with myself like a true Indian.

I got up and was dusting myself off when who should appear but Coyote leading my gray pony. He was on his scrubby brown colt and he had a pudgy White Bird boy with him. The boy had his own horse, a paint and a poor one.

"Well," I challenged them, "what do you want?"

"This is Peopeo," replied Coyote. "His real name is Young White Bird but they call him Little Bird and he is the son of old Chief White Bird, the great fighter."

"The near-son only," corrected the sober-faced one. "My mother was his sister. But he raised me in his tipi and gave me his name. What's your name?"

"Heyets," I answered shortly.

"Very fine name," he said. "It means Mountain Sheep."

"That's quite smart of you, boy. And you only seven or eight summers, too."

"Seven summers," he said unsmilingly. "Ten more and I will be a warrior like you."

I watched him narrowly but he was not making a joke on me. He actually thought I had seventeen summers.

"Well," I said, cheering up, "what shall we do? Ride down the river and stone the potholes for mallard hens?"

At once the chubby White Bird boy was scowling at Coyote. "I thought you said he would want to go over to the Clearwater and creep up on the meeting at Kamiah Crossing," he said.

"I did," protested Coyote. "But with Heyets you can't tell. He changes his mind like a woman. Very strange mind."

I did not care to stand there listening to a simpleton like Coyote explaining the workings of my thoughts to a seven-year-old White Bird Indian. I grew angry.

"Be quiet!" I ordered. "Of course I would like to go and hear the council. But what is the use of such talk? It will be over before we can get these poor crowbaits of ours halfway around the mountain." I took pause, getting madder. "Coyote," I said, "from here where I now bid you farewell, I will speak to you no more in this life. I warned you. *Taz alago*, good-bye . . . !"

"Well, all right, good-bye," agreed Coyote. "But I just thought you would like to beat Joseph and the others to Kamiah

Crossing. That's why I wanted you to see Little Bird. He knows a way we can do it. The secret way of his people over the mountain instead of around it. He says we can get our poor horses to the crossing before any of them. Before Horse Blanket, Yellow Wolf's father. Before Elk Water, your own father. Before Ollikut, Joseph's brother. Before even Yellow . . ."

"Enough, crazyhead!" I cried. "Is this true, Little Bird?"

Little Bird lifted his chin. "I am a White Bird," he said. "Would I lie to a Wallowa?"

I made as though I did not understand the insult, and said, "*Eeh-hahh*, there has been too much talk. Let's go."

"Yes, that's right," spoke up Little Bird. "We have a tall mountain to get over. Follow me. And when we get up high, let your ponies have their heads. There are some places up there you will not want to look over. *Eeh-hahh!*"

Coyote and I understood that kind of talk. We gave a happy laugh, hit our ponies with our buffalo-hide quirts, went charging off after Little Bird's shaggy paint. We were gone as quickly as the men before us.

5. How the White Man Really Was

That was a wild track up over that mountain but it was a good one. We got to the Clearwater before Joseph and before even White Bird and Toohoolhoolzote.

Little Bird led us off the mountain down a creek bed which had a cover of timber all the way to its joining with the river. This was below the crossing, near which we could plainly see and hear the white men sitting around their campfire making loud talk of the easy way they had run off the Indian herders that morning.

The day was well gone now. Whippoorwills were crying on the mountain. The sun had dropped from sight beyond the western hills. Only its last shafts were striking the face of the cliffs above us. North and east, heavy clouds were threatening rain. The river was beginning to drift a chilly mist.

I shivered and suggested we circle the white camp and go on up the river to the village of the Asotin. Up there we could get a warm sleep in a dry tipi, also some good hot meat for our supper. But Little Bird had not come over the mountain to visit the Asotin. "No," he said, "I won't go up there. My father says Looking Glass's people take the white man's way. *Kapsis itu,* that's a very bad thing."

"Well," I grumbled, "it's going to rain. We'll get wet and lie here shaking all night. That's a bad thing, too."

"*Eeh!*" he shrugged. "You Wallowa are all women."

"Not this Wallowa!" cried Coyote. "I fear no rain. I fear no white man. I fear no fat White Bird boy. *Ki-yi-yi!*"

He threw back his head and burst into the yelp before I could move to stop him. My stomach closed up within me like a bunching hand. Only one thing saved us. Coyote made such an excellent imitation of his namesake that the white men were fooled. One of them picked up his rifle and shied a shot our way. The bullet slapped though our cover at the same time my hand took Coyote across his mouth. He gave a startled yip and shut up. The white man laughed and put down the gun and said, "By damn, I must have clipped the little varmint. How's that for luck?"

We didn't answer him, letting him think what he wished. It got pretty quiet. Presently Little Bird said respectfully to me, "What I suggest, Heyets, is that we creep up the river bed and listen to the white man's talk. Coyote said your mother went to the school at Lapwai and has taught you their language. You can tell us what they are saying up there. How's that?"

I started to give him some reason why we should not attempt this riskful thing but was spared the need.

"*Eeh!*" I whispered, "it's too late. Look up there!"

I flung out my arm, pointing to the mountainside beyond the white man's fire. Everything became very still.

Up on the crest of the last rise before the crossing, sitting their horses like so many statues carved from the Idaho granite, were two craggy-faced war chiefs and half a hundred unfriendly-looking, eagle-feathered fighting Indians.

"Nanitsch!" hissed Little Bird, filling the silence with the fierce pride of his words. "It is my father, White Bird, and his friend Toohoolhoolzote, come to kill the Kamiah white man! Watch what happens now, you Wallowa!"

The fighting Indians came down the hill. They came very slowly, giving us time to slip up through the river brush to be close to it all when it happened. As they rode forward, the white men left their fire and took up their rifles, walking out on foot to meet the mounted Indians in the way such things were done. Both parties stopped about one arrow shot apart. For the Indians, White Bird and Toohoolhoolzote rode out. For the white men, it was a lanky fellow with no whiskers and a foxy eye, and a long-faced man with a wide forehead, straggly whiskers and a drooping, pale eye. We knew them both, and well. They were Ad Chapman, called Narrow Eye by us, and Lapwai agent John Monteith.

The talk began but did not go far. Neither White Bird nor Toohoolhoolzote spoke a word of English. Monteith knew our tongue but little, and had to wait for interpreter Chapman to explain every small thing for him. Chapman was a squaw man living with a Umatilla woman. We Indians knew him a long time and took him for our friend. But the talk kept stopping because of Agent Monteith. Toohoolhoolzote, famous for his harsh temper, began to grow angry. He glared at the Lapwai churchman and growled at Narrow Eye Chapman.

"Sumbitch!" he rasped. "I will not stay here and listen to any more of this delaying. We know why we are here. You know why we are here. Why do we argue? I am going to ride back a ways and return with my gun cocked for firing."

"No, no," the squaw man pleaded. "Wait now, old friend, don't do that. You haven't heard the whole story yet."

Toohoolhoolzote looked at him hard.

"Do you deny these men stopped our cattle?" he asked.

"No, I can't deny that. But . . ."

"Never mind. I only want to know if they stopped the cattle. Now I will ask it of you one more time. Can the cattle go over the river into the Kamiah grass or not?"

Chapman looked around like a rabbit caught by dogs in an open meadow. Then he spoke rapidly to Agent Monteith. The agent got very dark in the face.

"You tell that Indian," he ordered Chapman, "to bring his cattle and come live on the reservation as the other Nez Perce. Tell him there is plenty of grass at Lapwai. Tell him I will send for the soldiers if he doesn't do as I say."

But Narrow Eye knew better than that. He shook his head.

"No," he said quickly, "we won't do that. I will ask him to wait until morning with his decision. That will give us time to send back for more men. We will need every gun in the Kamiah if we stay here. Those Indians are mad."

Agent Monteith peered at the painted faces of the fighting Indians and of a sudden his own stubborn face changed. Even from as far away as our river bushes we could see him get pale above his whiskers. At once he agreed to the squaw man's plan and Chapman turned and told the lie to the Indians.

Toohoolhoolzote was for war right then. But White Bird looked up at the sky and said no. The morning would be time enough. The light would be better for shooting then, and they could make sure they got every one of the white men.

For a moment I let out my listening breath, thinking everything was going to rest quiet at that point, giving Joseph time to get up and prevent the fight. I finished translating what had been said, for my two friends, not thinking how they might take the white man's treachery. I had still much to learn about fighting Indians, even very small, fat ones.

Little Bird, the moment he heard of Chapman's deceitful words, burst from our cover like a cottontail. Bounding through the twilight toward the Nez Perce, he shouted for them to beware, to fight right then, that Narrow Eye Chapman was sending for more guns, maybe even for the horse soldiers, that all would be killed if they waited for morning.

When Little Bird did that—jumped and ran—I didn't know what to do. But crazy Coyote, he knew what to do. He jumped and ran, too, yelling, "Wait for me! Wait for me . . . !"

One of the white men, a heavy one with dirty red whiskers,

cursed, using his god's name, and called out to the others. "Come on, boys, we had better beat through them willows. Might be a whole litter of them red whelps in there!"

With the yell he leaped on his horse and plunged him into the brush where I was running around in senseless circles trying to decide which way to go. He reached down and seized me by the back of my hunting shirt.

"Lookit here, by cripes!" he bellowed. "See what I've found. Damn me if it ain't a little red swamp rat!"

Well, it was no little red swamp rat, only the fourteen-year-old son of Elk Water, the Wallowa Nez Perce. But there was no time for Indian pride. Before the red-whiskered man could bring me back to the campfire and before the fighting Indians could form their line to charge upon the traitorous white men, a single rifle shot rang out upon the mountainside.

The lone bullet splashed a whining mark of lead on a big rock which stood midway of the meadow, and a deep voice rolled out saying, "Do not fight. Stand still. The first man on either side to ride beyond the rock will be shot."

We all fell silent, looking upward toward the cliff down which wound the Clearwater trail.

There, fiery red in the reflected light of the disappeared sun, tall as giants on their beautiful buffalo horses, were Joseph and Ollikut, with my father and Yellow Wolf's father and Yellow Wolf himself. All save Joseph had their rifles pointed toward the midway rock and there was still smoke curling from Ollikut's gun, showing it was he who had fired the one shot. For himself, Joseph did not even have a gun. He was commanding the stillness with his upheld hand alone. It was a strange thing. All the Indians and all the white men likewise did his bidding. Not one man made to move himself or his horse or his loaded rifle in all the time it took our Wallowa chief to ride down from the cliff.

It was the first time I had seen the power of Joseph's hand. It was the first time I knew that he possessed this *wyakin*, this personal magic to command other men. I think that many of the Nez Perce had not seen it or felt it before this time, either. It was

as though they did not know this Joseph, as though he was a
stranger among them.

The stillness hurt the ears as he made his way across the
meadow toward the white men from Kamiah.

Joseph talked straight with the white men. The other Indians
stood at the edge of the settlers' fire. But they did not talk; only
Joseph talked. In his patient way he went back to the beginning
of the agreements on paper between our two peoples. He reminded Agent Monteith of the Walla Walla Council of 1855 in
which only the Nez Perce stood faithful to the white man, and
in which all the other tribes, the Yakima, the Umatilla, the
Palouse, Spokane, Coeur d'Alene—all of them save the Nez
Perce—spoke against peace and would not sign the paper.

Always, Joseph said, the Nez Perce had abided by that treaty.
Only when the thieves' treaty took away their lands in 1863,
after gold was discovered at Orofino, had the Nez Perce faltered
in their friendship, and even then they had made no war but only
stayed apart from the white man, asking nothing but to be let
alone. Now had come President Grant's good paper returning
the Wallowa country to the Nez Perce. Now all should be as
it was in the old friendly days. But here was the white man trying to steal the Indian's grass again. The Kamiah was Indian
country. There was no treaty keeping Nez Perce cattle away
from it. Yet here was the white man standing at Kamiah Crossing, showing the rifle and saying hard things to Joseph, who was
trying to keep the peace.

Was it not enough, cried Joseph, throwing wide his arms, that
the white man had torn the gold from the Indian earth? That he
had taken the best farmlands for himself? That he had built his
whiskey stores along the Indian trails? That he had lured the
Indian children away from their parents into his Christian
schools? Had taught them to pray to Jesus Christ and to sneer
at the old Indian gods? Had made them to forget the ways of
their own fathers and mothers, and led them to think their own
people were lower than dogs and the white man the lord of all
on earth? That he had lied to, stolen from, cheated the poor

trusting Nez Perce for seventy snows? Were not all these things
enough? Did he now also have to starve the Indian as well? To
stomp in his water and stale in it, too? Must he not only take
what grass he needed, but also that small amount necessary to
the Indian's poor few cattle? What did such a situation leave
Joseph to say to White Bird and Toohoolhoolzote? What could
he tell his angry brothers to keep them from fighting in the
morning? If any of the white men had an answer to that question, he had better give it to Joseph right now.

There was a long silence then, while Chapman translated and
the white men talked it over. Then Agent Monteith showed his
stumpy teeth and stood forth to talk, unfriendly.

It was time, he said, for the Nez Perce to realize they could no
longer move themselves and their cattle about the land as they
pleased. They were going to have to keep themselves and their
herds in one place from now on, even as the white man did.
There was no choice. If they would not do it, the soldiers would
come and make them do it. Was that perfectly clear to Joseph?

Joseph was a wise man. He did not answer yes just to make
good feeling. He shook his head and said, no, he did not think
it was perfectly clear to him what the churchman from Lapwai
was saying. It seemed there was possibly more meant than had
been admitted. Would the agent try again, he asked Chapman,
and this time try with his tongue uncurled?

Chapman winced and said to Joseph, "I hope you know my
heart is with you, Heinmot. I think much of my wife's people.
But I am white. What can I do?"

"Do nothing," answered Joseph, "that I would not do."

"I will try," nodded Chapman, and went back to Monteith.

The latter proved quite ready to repeat his meaning in straight
words. He did not like Joseph because he could not fool him,
so he took refuge in hard talk.

"All right," he scowled, "here is precisely what I mean. . . ."

He then told Joseph that he and our people were not to go to
the buffalo any more. Such things, he said, only stirred up the
young men and made them wild. Moving around as in the old
days, going here to smoke the salmon, there to dig the camas,

hither to visit friends, yon to fight enemies—all this had got to stop at once. Our people were away on such journeys six months of the year. Because of that the children were kept out of school and had no chance to learn the way of life which would allow them to dwell in harmony with the white people. This was a wrong thing. A start must be made with the children. They must be put in school and made to stay there. There must be a common god and common ways. Only through the children might this be.

When Joseph heard these words he asked only what putting the children in school had to do with showing the rifle at Kamiah Crossing. Monteith answered him at once, and fairly.

Peaceful Indians, he said, were Indians who stayed in one place. Moving Indians were fighting Indians. And the day of the moving Indian was all done. From this time forward the Nez Perce must do as Indian agent John Monteith said, not as White Bird said, not as Toohoolhoolzote said, not as any other fighting chief said. And what Agent Monteith said was that the Wallowas must now stay in their level valley, the White Birds in their deep canyon, the Salmon Rivers behind their big mountain. To guarantee this obedience there was but one sure way: stop going to the buffalo and put the children in the reservation school and raise them as white boys and girls. It was up to Joseph to make this clear to the other Nez Perce. Did Joseph understand that?

Our chief nodded slowly. The hurt in his face would have made a stone weep. Yes, he said, for the very first time he did understand. Now it was revealed to him what the white man really wanted of the Indian. It was not to live at peace with him, as brother with brother. When the agent talked about not going to the buffalo, about the cattle not going into Kamiah, that was only an excuse. The white man knew that to pen up the Indian in a small place was to destroy his spirit, to break his heart, to kill him.

If that was what Agent Monteith now wanted Joseph to tell the other chiefs, he would do it. He would tell them that either they went home and stayed there, or the horse soldiers would come and drive them upon the reservation. He would tell them that in any case their children must soon be sent into Lapwai school and made to live there. He must tell the agent, though, that this was a very dangerous thing. With this low-voiced warning, Joseph turned away from Monteith and told the fighting Indians what had been said.

I had a very good look at this last, sad part of the meeting. It was being held in the campfire tent. The red-whiskered man was in there with me, holding his bad-smelling hand across my mouth the whole time. But I could see between his fat fingers and through the slight parting of the tent flap. Of course none of the Nez Perce knew I was in there. They all thought I had got away down the river.

When Joseph told the others about not going to the buffalo any more, about the horse soldiers putting them on the reservation if they moved around, about Agent Monteith demanding the surrender of the children as the earnest of their good faith, the fighting Indians did a strange thing. Their faces grew not angry but very hurt, and when Joseph had finished the last word they moved away and went back up on the mountain without a sound. Only old Toohoolhoolzote stayed with Joseph, and with him he now went toward the white men.

Coming up to Monteith, Joseph said, "I have told my people what you said. Now Toohoolhoolzote will tell you what my people say." He stood back, giving over his place to the old Salmon River chief. Toohoolhoolzote stared at all the white men for a long time, then he nodded.

"I will talk short," he said in Nez Perce to Chapman but fixing his fierce gaze upon the Lapwai agent.

"Tomorrow, if you are still here, there will be shooting. We are going to the buffalo. We will graze our cattle where we wish. We will not bring our children into Lapwai. Joseph is a good man and he is your friend. Toohoolhoolzote is a bad man and he is not your friend. When the sun comes up, remember that. *Taz alago*, agent. Sleep light."

For a time the old man stood there, the firelight making a spider web of seams and dry canyons in his face skin. His mouth was set in a line wide and ugly as a war-ax cut. His eyes burned like a wolf's eyes. His expression was unmoving. Suddenly I was as afraid of him as the white men. The sight of him braced there, lean and dark and strong as a pine tree for all his sixty-eight winters, staring down all that bitter talk and all those menacing white rifles with nothing save his Nez Perce *simiakia*, his terrible Indian pride, put a chill along my spine from rump to neckbone. When he finally turned to follow his warriors up onto the mountain, it was even more quiet than when Joseph came down the cliff trail.

Now there was only my own Chief Joseph left. He told Chapman in Nez Perce that he was sad that Agent Monteith had done this dangerous thing to the spirit of the wild bands. He promised he would yet do what he could to prevent the shooting in the morning but begged Chapman to try and get the white settlers to leave the crossing when it grew full dark, and to be far away from it when the sun came over the Salmon River mountains next day. Then he, too, turned to go. In the last breath, however, Agent Monteith requested him to wait. Wearily Joseph did so, and the agent wheeled toward the camp tent and called sharply. "Bates, bring that boy out here."

Redbeard Bates grinned and spat and shoved me stumbling from the tent. Outside, he pushed me forward into the firelight to face my chief. Joseph's face softened when he saw me, but Agent Monteith's face grew hard.

"Joseph," he said, "tell your people over on the mountain that I don't trust them. I will hold the boy with me until we see there is no shooting and no following us away from here. The boy will be well cared for. After a time you come into Lapwai and we will talk about him. I know this boy is of your own blood and I have an idea for him which you would do well to listen to. It may be that we can use him to lead in the others. Do you understand such an idea?"

Joseph understood it perfectly. But to Agent Monteith he merely nodded without words, while to me he spoke ever so gently in his deep voice.

"No harm will come to you, Heyets," he said. "Go with the agent and do not fear. I shall come for you. As you wait, think

well upon what you have seen and heard here. Think about why
your father wanted you to come with us, and about why I
agreed with him that you should. Then when you have thought,
remember it, always remember it. It is a lesson about the white
man that you will never learn in his school at Lapwai."

I drew myself up, standing like a Nez Perce.

"Yes, my chief," I said, "I will always remember it."

"Good," said Joseph, and put his two hands on my shoulders
to give me strength to go with my pride. Then he smiled, touching me softly on the cheek with his fingers. "*Taz alago*, Heyets,"
he said, and turned for the last time away from that fire by the
Clearwater.

"*Taz alago*, my chief," I called after him into the deepening
twilight, and was glad he did not look back to see the tears that
stood in my eyes though I was fourteen summers and would be
a warrior soon.

6. September Wind

I had never been to Lapwai longer than one day, as on a Sunday to watch the treaty Indians pray, or on a Saturday when
they drew their agency beef and might favor a visiting relative
with a bit of fat meat to take home at the white man's expense.
Accordingly, as I now rode toward the mission school with the
agent, I began to recover from my fright and to wonder how it
might be to live on the reservation for a longer while—perhaps
two or three days or a week. But I never found out.

We had been riding most of the night, having slipped away
from the crossing as Joseph advised. Now, as the sun come up,
we stopped to boil water and make coffee. Before the water
started to roll, five Nez Perce came out of a brushy draw and
rode up to our fire. They were Joseph, Ollikut, Horse Blanket,
Yellow Wolf and Elk Water, my own father.

"Well, Joseph," demanded Agent Monteith at once, "what is
this? Have you tricked me? What do you want here?"

Joseph looked at him steadily.

"It is not my way to play tricks," he said. "Last night I gave you the boy so there would be no trouble with those White Birds and Salmon Rivers. There was no trouble. Now I want the boy back, that is all."

"Give them the kid!" I heard Ad Chapman whisper to Monteith, but the agent said no, he would not do it.

Ollikut saw him shake his head. He pushed his roan buffalo racer forward and cocked his gun.

"Agent," he said, "we want the boy."

"For God's sake," pleaded Chapman to Monteith, "give them the kid and get shut of them. That damned Ollikut will kill us. We're not fooling with agency Indians."

Agent Monteith stuck out his straggly beard and bared his many small teeth like a cornered cave bat, but he gave in.

"Joseph," he said, "I am charging you with this matter. I want this boy in school this winter. You know why. It is the only way in which he can learn the white man's way."

"Yes, agent, but he should have his say in what he will do."

"No, he should not. That is one of the worst troubles with you Indians. You raise these children to be wild. You never say no to them and you never punish them for doing wrong. Children must be taught to do as they are told."

"We teach them, agent. But what has that to do with striking them and saying no to everything they want? There are other ways to show them wisdom."

"Joseph, I won't argue with you. I leave it to your own mind whether this boy is going to grow up Indian or white. You and I are grown men; we will not change our ways. I have one god; you have another. My father taught from the Holy Book; your father tore up the Holy Book. We are as we are, you and I, but the boy can be anything which you and I agree he can be. You are the head chief of the Wallowa, the most powerful band of the Nez Perce. If you send this boy of your own blood to go to school at Lapwai this winter, you will have said to all the wild bands that you intend to take the white man's way, to obey your agent, to learn to live the new life. It will be a powerful thing for peace, an important thing for your people. What do you say? The decision is yours. You alone can make it."

It was strong talk. I could see that Joseph was thinking much on it. I held my breath, badly frightened now. Of a sudden I lost all my bravery about going to Lapwai for a few days. They were talking about the whole winter, perhaps about several winters. This could be a fearful thing. I had heard many stories of Indian boys dying at the white man's school because of broken hearts and bad food and lonesomeness for tipi smoke, boiled cowish, dried salmon, roast elk and horse sweat, saddle leather, gun oil, powder smell and all the other grand things a nontreaty Nez Perce lad grew up with in his home village and his native hunting lands. Joseph, too, knew of these poor boys. The thought of them weighed heavily on him and made him take such a long time that Ollikut threw him a sharp glance and said, "Come on, Heinmot, make up your mind. I have sat here long enough with this gun cocked."

Joseph nodded to him and sighed very deep.

"All right," he said to Agent Monteith, "give us the boy now. When the grass grows brown and the smell of the first snow lies like a knife in the wind, I shall bring him to you at Lapwai."

In May, in the land of the Nez Perce, the spring sun comes first to the southern slopes of the hills. Here in the warm, sandy soil the cowish plants break through the mountain loam even before the last snows are gone. To these cowish patches in that month of May would come my people, eager in their hunger for the taste of fresh vegetables after the long winter months of dried camas roots and smoked salmon. Yet in the May of that year we did not go to the buffalo. I sang no gathering songs, danced no thankful dances, ate no cowish at the great Feast of the First Eating. I sat apart and thought only of September and that first smell of snow in the sharpening wind.

June was the time of going to the camas meadows. In that month my people took up the tipis and journeyed to the upland plateaus where, out of the flooded meadows, would come the

fabled blue camas, the water hyacinth or Indian lily of the
Northwest. At this glad time my people were camped in the
cool pines above the meadows laughing and singing and waiting
for the camas to "come ripe" and dry up for the digging. But I
did not take part in this good feeling. I stayed out on the mountain alone and thought of September and the snow wind.

Under the mellow sun of July the shallow waters of the camas
fields evaporated, the rich muck dried, the great Indian harvest
began. Now while the men sat at their gambling games or raced
their famous Appaloosa horses, and while the children played
at stick-and-hoop, or fished and hunted the summer away, the
women took out the digging tools with their stubby wooden
handles and pronged elkhorn tips, and pried up the ripened
bulbs of the blue lily. After that came the cooking. As many as
thirty bushels of the bulbs were covered with wet meadow grass
and steamed over heated stones. Then the bulbs were mashed,
shaped into loaves and sun-baked into a nourishing Indian bread.
With the meat of the salmon, the elk, the deer and the mountain
sheep this bread fed us through the deepest winters, and so July
was the month of gratitude for the camas root. But I did not
join in the thankful sing. I only wandered afar with Tea Kettle,
my small gray pony, and looked with aching loneliness out
across the blue peaks, hazy canyons, lapping waters and lofty
pines of the homeland I would see no more after the grass was
brown beneath the autumn wind.

In late summer, in August, after the high spring floodwaters
had fallen and all the rivers were running low and clear, it was
the time of silver water, of the great Columbia salmon run from
the Western Sea to the headwater creeks of our Nez Perce country. This was the end of the Indian year, the highest time of
thanks for my people, and the hardest time of work for them.

When the salmon came the men would strain from dawn to
dusk with spear and net at every falls from the mighty Celilo
upward to the least spawning creeklets which fed the main forks
of the Salmon, the Snake, the Clearwater, the Grande Ronde,
the Wallowa and Imnaha Rivers. The sandy beaches would soon
be heaped to a small child's waist with the great humpbacked fish.

Then the women would work like pack horses to split, clean, rack and smoke the bright slabs of that blessed red flesh which provided nine of every ten Nez Perce meals around the year, and which made my people the strongest in all that Northwest country. Yes, August was the month of highest prayer to Hunyewat. Yet even then I could think of no gratefulness, no contentment, no happiness, but only of Joseph and Agent Monteith and after them only of the brown grass and snow smell of September and of the log-walled prison waiting for me in the school at Lapwai.

At last the Moon of Smoky Sunshine, September, was but three suns away. In that brief space it would be Sapalwit, Sunday, and Joseph would ride up to the tipi of my father and call out in his soft, deep voice, "Elk Water, where is the boy? Where is Heyets, our little Mountain Sheep? The grass is grown brown again, the skies have turned the color of gun steel. I smell snow in the wind. It is the time to keep our word to Agent Monteith."

I let two of those last three suns torture me. Then late on the final night, when the chilling winds had blown out all the cookfire embers and no one stirred in all that peaceful camp, I crept beneath the rear skins of my father's lodge. Moving like a shadow I found my faithful friend Tea Kettle where I had tethered him in a dark spruce grove that same afternoon. He whickered and rubbed me with his soft nose and I cried a little and loved him with my arms about his skinny neck. It was a bad time but I did not think of turning back. I only climbed on his back and guided him on into the deepening shadows of the timber, far away from the camp of my father's people there beside the salmon falls of the Kahmuenem, the Snake River, nine miles below the entrance of the Imnaha.

I was bound for the land of our mortal foes, the Shoshones. My reasoning was that if I could take an enemy scalp I would no longer be considered a boy. I would be a man, a warrior, fourteen summers or no, and they would no more think of sending me to school with Agent Monteith than they would my fierce uncle, Yellow Wolf.

As for equipment, I had Tea Kettle, who could barely come up to a lame buffalo calf at his best speed; a *kopluts*, which was not a true war club at all but only a rabbit-throwing stick cut off short to make it look like a *kopluts*; a rusted hand ax with a split haft and most of the sharp part of the blade broken off; and a boy's bow-and-arrow set given me by Horse Blanket on my tenth birthday. Then I had also a much-mended gray soldier blanket marked U.S. in one corner and stolen for me by my father from the big fort at Walla Walla. And I had three loaves of camas bread and a side of dried salmon and my personal war charm, a smoked baby bear's foot cured with the claws and hair left on. And, oh yes, I had my knife. No Nez Perce would think of leaving his tipi without putting on his knife.

So there I was on my way to kill a Shoshone, a Snake Indian warrior far over across the Bitterroot Mountains in the Wind River country. I might, in addition, steal a few horses.

Meanwhile there were more immediate problems. I had left home in good spirit if weak flesh. Now, however, after a long time of riding through the dark forest, the balance was beginning to come even. It occurred to me that I had ridden many miles. Perhaps I had better stop, make a fire, roast some salmon, warm a slice of camas. When I had eaten I would feel my old power. Then, although I had already ridden a great distance that night, I would go on yet further before lying down to sleep.

I got off Tea Kettle and gathered some moss and small sticks, which I laid properly in the shelter of a wind-fallen old pine giant. With my flint I struck a tiny flame and fed it into a good little Nez Perce fire. I cut a spitting stick and propped a piece of salmon and one of camas over the flames. Then I put the soldier blanket around my shoulders and leaned back against the big log to consider my journey plans. The next thing I knew, a shaft of sunlight was prying at my eyes and two very familiar Indians were crouched to my fire eating my salmon and camas bread.

"Good morning," nodded Chief Joseph. "This is fine food, Heyets. You had better come and have some of it with us."

"Yes," said my father. "It is a long ride to Lapwai."

"What day is this?" I mumbled, my mind still spider-webbed with sleep. "What has happened to bring you here?"

"This is Sunday," answered Joseph in his kindly way. "And what has happened to bring us here is that we have come to ride with you to Agent Monteith's school. You must have left very early, Heyets. That showed a good spirit. Probably you did not wish to bother us to rise so soon."

"Yes," agreed my father. "Surely that was it. Heyets is a fine boy. He wanted to let us sleep. Is that not the way it was, Heyets?"

My mind had got more clear and it was in my heart to lie to them, to say yes, that they were right about my thoughtful actions. Yet I could not bring myself to do it. To my father I might have lied, for he was a simple man and would not have guessed the difference. But Joseph, ah, Joseph was entirely another matter and another man. His great calm face, deep voice and sad dark eyes touched me with a faith which would not let my tongue wander.

"No," I replied, low-worded. "That is not the way it was at all. I was running away. I was going to the Snake country to take a Shoshone scalp so that you would think I was a man and would not send me to Agent Monteith's school. My heart was like a girl's. I was weak and sore afraid. I wanted only to stay with my people, with my father and with my chief."

There was a silence then, and my father looked hard at Joseph. He turned his head away from both Joseph and me, and I could see the large swallowing bone of his throat moving up and down. Still he did not say anything. He waited for Joseph to speak.

At last my chief raised his eyes and said to me, "I beg your pardon, Heyets. The wind was making such a stir in the pine trees just now that I do not believe I heard what you said. Did you hear him, Elk Water?"

"No," answered my father, "I don't think I did. What was it you said, boy?"

I looked at Elk Water, my father, and at Joseph, my chief. Then I looked beyond them up into the pine boughs above us.

There was no wind moving up there, no wind at all. I shook my head and got to my feet.

"Nothing," I said, untying Tea Kettle and kicking dirt upon my little fire. "Let us go to Lapwai and keep the word with Agent Monteith."

7. Lapwai Winter

It will not take long to tell of that Lapwai winter. It was not a good thing. The memory of it turns in me like a badly knitted bone, and like a badly knitted bone it will not let me forget.

I was sick much of the time, homesick all of the time. It was a heavy winter, very cold, with a lot of hard-crust snow and deep river ice the whole while. Some of my little Indian friends who sickened at the school did not grow well again. They were not watched over by Hunyewat as Heyets was. They lay down in the night and did not get up again in the morning. When we saw them the others of us wept, even we big boys.

If they were Christian Indian children they were buried in the churchyard. Their mothers were there, their fathers were there. All their many friends and relatives were there to stand and say good-bye to them, and to sprinkle the handful of mother earth on them as was the old custom. Agent Monteith read from the Holy Book at graveside, and the proper songs of Jesus were sung over them.

But if they were wild Indian children, as myself, their bodies were left to lie out and freeze solid like dog salmon. Then they were stacked, as so many pieces of stovewood, in the open shed behind the schoolhouse. There they waited, all chill and dark and alone, until such time as their parents could come in over the bad trails to claim them for the Nez Perce ceremony of putting to the last sleep.

It was not a happy or a kind place for a boy raised in the old free Indian way. It made my heart sad and lonely to stay there. In consequence, and although I knew I was being closely watched because of my kinship with Joseph, both by the agency and my own people, I grew all the while more determined against Lapwai and the white man's way. Naturally I learned but little at the school.

I already knew how to speak the white tongue from my mother. But I did not let this help me. I would not learn to write, and in reading I was as a child of but six or seven. This blind pride was my father's blood, the *simiakia* of my untamed ancestors entering into me. I was not a wicked boy but neither was I willing to work. I was like a young horse caught from out a wild herd. I knew nothing but the longing to escape. The only chance to teach me anything was to gentle me first, and there was no chance at all to gentle me. I thought, of course, and many times, about Joseph's faith in me. I wanted to do what was right for the sake of my chief's hope that I would serve as an example to the other wild bands, so they might send their children in safety, and with profit, to the white man's school at Lapwai. But my own faith was no match for my chief's. Daily I grew more troublesome to Agent Monteith. Daily he grew less certain of my salvation.

When I had been with him five moons—through the time of Christmas into that of the New Year—it had at last become plain to him that I was not settling down, and Joseph was sent for. When my chief arrived I was called in and stood by while talk was made about me through the reservation interpreter. Joseph began it with his usual quiet way of getting at once to the point.

"This boy's mother," he said, "reports to me that she has visited him here at the school and you have told her that her son is a bad boy, that he will not work, and that he is as bad for the other children as for himself."

He paused, looking steadily at Agent Monteith.

"Now I do not remember that Heyets is a bad boy. Perhaps my memory has failed me. But since I am also of his blood, I think you had better tell me what you told his mother."

Agent Monteith grew angry, his usual way when challenged.

"Now see here, Joseph," he blustered, "are you trying to intimidate me?"

"Excuse me. I do not understand your meaning."

"Are you trying to frighten me?"

"Never. What I want is the truth. Should that frighten you?"

"Of course not! This boy simply will not study as he should. He will not work with the others. The class is told to draw a picture of our Lord Jesus humbly astride his lowly donkey, and this boy draws a lurid picture of an armed warrior on an Appaloosa stallion. I ask him, 'What picture is that, Heyets?' and he says, 'Why, that is a picture of Yellow Wolf on Sun Eagle going to the buffalo.'

"Now I put it to you, Joseph, is that a decent way for a boy to behave before the others? A boy upon whom we have all placed so much hope? A boy the other bands are watching to see how he fares at Lapwai? Answer me; say what you think."

My chief frowned and pulled at his chin in thought.

"I don't know," he said carefully. "Does he draw well?"

"He draws extremely well, easily the best in the class."

"He draws a good horse? A proper Indian?"

"Very good, very proper," scowled Angent Monteith. "Perfect likenesses, especially the horse. He puts all the parts on the animal and when I reprimand him he offers to take me to the Wallowa and show me that Sun Eagle is indeed a horse among horses."

Agent Monteith blew out his cheeks, filling them like the gasblown belly of a dead cow.

"Now you listen to me, Joseph. You promised to bring this boy here and to make him behave and work hard to learn the white man's way. This has since become a serious matter. Heyets is creating a discipline problem for me among the older boys. Some of them are beginning to draw pictures of spotted Nez Perce ponies in their study Bibles. I insist to you that this is no way for this boy of your blood to carry out our bargain."

Joseph shook his head in sober sympathy.

"You are right, agent," he said, "providing that what you tell me is true. But before I make my decision I would like to have you tell me one special thing Heyets has done—show me some one example of his evil ways—so that I shall know what it is you and I are talking about."

He hesitated a little, then said quietly, "Sometimes, you know, the white man says one thing and actually means several others. It becomes difficult for an Indian to be sure."

Agent Monteith's wispy beard jutted out like a bobcat's whiskers, but he kept his voice reasonable.

"Joseph, you are the most intelligent Indian I know. You are a shrewd man by any standards, red or white. You have been to this same school yourself. You were the best pupil they ever had here before Old Joseph tore up the Bible and took you away. You understand exactly what I mean and you do not have to ask me for any examples."

Joseph only nodded again and said, "Nevertheless, show me one special bad thing this boy has done."

The agent turned away quickly and picked up a study Bible from the desk of James Redwing, a Christian Wallowa boy of my own age and my best friend among the reservation Indians. He opened the book and handed it to Joseph.

"Very well," he snapped, "look at that!"

Joseph took the book and studied it with great care.

"Let us see," he said. "Here is a picture of a very young baby being carried in his mother's arms. She is riding a small pack mule led by her husband. They are leaving an old town of some sort in a strange land, and they are not going very fast with such a poor beast to take them. Nevertheless they are in a great hurry. There is fear in their faces, and I believe the enemy must be pursuing them. Is there something I have missed?"

Agent Monteith stamped his foot.

"You know very well that is the Christ child fleeing Bethlehem with Mary and Joseph!"

"Oh, yes, so it is. A fine picture of all of them, too. Much better than in the book they had here before."

"You know equally well," Agent Monteith continued with a

cold eye, "what else I am talking about, and what else it is that you have missed. What is the title printed under the picture of the Christ child?"

Joseph squinted, then held the book up for me to tell him the words. I did so and he turned back to Agent Monteith and said, "The words are 'Jesus Fleeing the Holy City.'"

"Exactly. And what has some heathen pupil scrawled in pencil beneath that sacred title?"

My chief's face never changed. Again he held the book up to me and again I whispered the words to him. Looking back at Agent Monteith, he shifted the Bible as though to get a better light on it and answered gravely, "Ah, yes, there is something else here, sure enough. It says, 'If he had used an Appaloosa pony his enemies would never have caught up to him.' Is that what you mean?"

"That is precisely what I mean, Joseph."

The agent took time to get a good breath and to let some of it puff back out of his cheeks.

"That additional writing—that desecration of the Lord's Book—was done by James Redwing, a Christian Indian of your own Wallowa band and a very fine boy who until these past months has been our foremost pupil. James is nearly fifteen years old and I have worked with him a long time, Joseph. He had become a white boy in his thoughts and in his actions. I had saved him. He prayed on his knees every day and had given over his life to the service of our Saviour. Now he writes things such as you see there, and the other boys all laugh."

"That is not right," said Joseph softly. "But they are only boys, all of them. Boys are full of tricks, Agent."

"Indeed they are!" cried Monteith, swelling up again, "and I will just tell you about one of those tricks. This past Christmas we celebrated the birth of the Master by making our own stable scene with the manger as it was in Bethlehem. There was a small mule which we used as the faithful ass tied beside the sleeping babe, and do you know what some monstrous boy did to the innocent brute?"

Joseph shook his head wonderingly.

"I could never imagine," he said. "Tell me."

"He took," began Monteith, "some of the mission's whitewash and dappled the rear of that poor animal to simulate a Nez Perce Appaloosa, and marked in bright yellow paint on the two halves of its rump the name Sun Eagle. Now what do you think of that for your fine boy? He admitted it, you know. It was his work."

My chief put his chin down to his chest. He seemed to be having some trouble with his swallowing. It was as though he had caught a salmon bone crosswise in his throat and was trying to be polite about choking on it. But after a bit he was able to raise his head and continue.

"I think it is very unfortunate," he answered the agent. "It is true my own father tore up the Bible and that I have followed his way, but I will not tolerate Wallowa boys making laughs about your god. What do you suggest we do?"

"Heyets must be punished severely."

"In what manner?"

"An example must be set. He should be flogged."

"Have you flogged him before, Agent?"

"No. Frankly, I've been afraid to try it. The rascal told me that if I touched him he would have his uncle Yellow Wolf come in and kill me."

"His uncle Yellow Wolf is but a boy himself, agent."

"You do not need to tell me of Yellow Wolf. I know him very well. He has the eye of a mad dog. I would not trust him ten feet away."

"I see. How else have you thought to punish Heyets?"

"He must be made to say the school prayers on his knees in front of the other boys."

"All alone?"

"Yes, all alone."

"Has he prayed like this before, Agent?"

"Not once. He says he believes in Hunyewat. He says he did not come here to study Christianity. He tells wild tales of the power of Hunyewat to the Christian boys and has them believing that anything Jesus of Nazareth did in 'ten moons' Hunyewat could do in 'two suns.' He asks them such sacrilegious questions as, 'Did you ever see a picture of Hunyewat riding a pack mule?' and he has the entire class so disorganized they spend more time learning the brave songs and scalp chants from him than they do the Sunday School hymns from me. I will not tolerate it a day longer, Joseph. The matter is your complete responsibility and you must take the final decision on it right now."

Joseph moved his head in understanding and raised his hand for the agent to calm himself.

"Very well, Agent," he said. "Do you know what my father told me about this same school when he came to take me away from it many snows ago?"

"I can very well imagine what the old heathen may have said," agreed Agent Monteith. "But go ahead and tell it your way. You will regardless. That's the Indian of it."

"It is," replied Joseph, "and here is how my father told it to me in that long ago time.

"He admonished me, 'My son, always remember what I am about to say. A school is a good thing when it teaches school thoughts from school books. But the place for God and for God's book is in the church. Pray in the church and choose what god pleases you. But in the school do not pray; in the school, work hard all the time at the printed thoughts of reading and writing and of the white man's way of figuring with numbers. Do that six days and on the seventh day go to church and pray all you want.' "

"Your father was a very wise man," admitted Agent Monteith, "until he left the church."

"He was a very wise man after he left the church, too," said Joseph, "and here is the rest of his wisdom which you did not allow me to finish just now. The old chief finally said to me, 'But, my son, when the time comes that they will not let you learn your lessons except at the price of kneeling to their god, when they demand of you to become of their faith before they will give you a schoolbook, or feed you your food, or allow you your decent shelter from the snow and cold, then that is the time to tell them that they do not follow the way of their own Lord Jesus which he taught in the Holy Land two thousand snows before our little time here upon our mother earth. I once believed on the Saviour myself,' said my father, 'and I know his words as well as any agent. It was not his way to ask for payment, neither before nor after he gave of himself, or of his food and shelter.' "

"In heaven's name," fumed Agent Monteith, breaking in on my chief, "what are you trying to say, Joseph?" And Joseph answered him very quietly, "I am only saying that it is not my way, either," and after that both men stood a considerable time staring straight at one another.

It was Agent Monteith who at last grew nervous and broke the stillness.

"Well," he laughed uneasily, "that is scarcely anything new. You have not been in church since your father tore up the Bible on this same spot eleven years ago."

"That is not what I mean, Agent."

"All right, then, what is it that you do mean?"

"I am speaking about the boy. I am doing with him as my father did with me when they would not teach me unless I prayed."

"Joseph, I warn you!"

"It is too late for warning. All has been said. It is you and I who have failed, Agent, not this child. There is nothing he can do here. In his way he is wiser than either of us. He knows he is an Indian and cannot be a white man. I am taking him back to his own people, Agent. You will not see him again in this place. *Taz alago.*"

I could not have been more stunned. Since I knew the importance of my position at the school, I had been waiting to learn what kind of punishment would be agreed upon as the price of my staying there. Yet, instead, here was my chief taking me proudly by the hand and leading me out of that log-walled schoolhouse there at Lapwai, Idaho, in the severe winter of 1875, without one more spoken word or parting, rearward glance of consideration for powerful Indian agent John Monteith.

I will say that it was a strange and wonderful feeling. Thrilling to it, I got up behind Joseph on his broad-backed old brown traveling horse and we set out through the falling snow toward the snug tipis along the Imnaha River where, since the most ancient among them could remember, our Nez Perce people had spent their winters.

In all the long way home Joseph and I said not a word to one another and that, too, was the Indian way. All had been said back at Lapwai. Now was the time for riding in rich silence and, if a grateful Nez Perce boy remained of the old beliefs, for offering up an Indian prayer to Hunyewat.

So it was I bowed my head behind Joseph's wide back and said my first humble words in five moons. So it was I ended my Lapwai winter.

Book Two
White Bird Canyon

8. The Vision of Smoholla

The rest of that winter went swiftly. Spring came again to the Northwest land, and my people left the snug shelter of the Imnaha and went back out upon the warming, open meadows of the Wallowa. All was peace. In the cedar brakes and side canyons our mares had foaled and our cows had dropped their calves. Many another April and May had gone by without so good a crop. The grass was the best it had been in eight seasons. The snow in the high mountains melted evenly. There was no flooding, no real trouble of any kind in our herds or among our people. Then June came on and the sweet stillness of the meadow was shattered, as though by the startling crash of a rifle in a narrow, rocky place. With no warning and no reason, President Grant took back his treaty word. He reopened the Wallowa to white settlement. The Nez Perce were stunned.

Looking back after so many years, I remember, as if it were only two moons ago, the events which brought on all our trouble. Everywhere among the nontreaty bands war councils were called. But Joseph would not yield. He stood like a great rock against the wild current in the river of war talk. Night and day he rode the trails cajoling, threatening, imploring our people not to fight, not to take the bloody road from which there could be no turning back. His best argument was that everything would be made all right as soon as a Nez Perce group could travel to President Grant with the truth. He promised that such a group would go to Washington that same summer. Gradually, he won over the tamer chiefs. They in turn talked down the dangerous chiefs such as White Bird and Toohoolhoolzote. By mid-July it seemed certain there would be no war. But the peace was not real; the war talk among the wild bands went on secretly, and there were some hard arguments in that talk which the soft answers of Joseph could not turn away.

During the two years of President Grant's good treaty there

were over one hundred crimes against Indians, of the like of rape, cattle theft, barn- and fence-burning, murder and whiskey-selling, committed by white men who were then captured to be taken before their own law councils. Of that number only twenty-seven appeared to explain themselves to the judge chief or the Indian commissioner. The others all just stayed away and laughed. The Indian might be weeping over the body of his raped woman, or the body of his brother shot down for his horses, his rifle, or his little piece of land, or whatever it was that the white man wanted, but the white man only stayed away and laughed at the law councils.

Under such conditions the fact that Joseph could stop the wild bands, even for one summer, was a great thing. But for him, there would have been an Indian war in 1875.

Still, even with that peculiar power of his to command, Joseph failed to convince the nontreaty Nez Perce. He only persuaded them to wait that "one more summer." And even in this risky matter he had been forced to take a bad chance, to depend on the good hearts of the agents and commissioners to back up the word he gave the wild bands about going to see the White Father in Washington. As usual, the white man repaid Joseph's loyalty with shallow lies and delays.

No Nez Perce went to Washington that summer. Nor did any go that winter. Nor any the following spring. Joseph's name grew weaker still among a considerable part of our people. That second June—of 1876—began with as mean a temper as the one before it. Then, with things strung tight as a drawn buffalo bow, terrible news came west from our friends the Crows. Sitting Bull, Gall, Hump and the great Crazy Horse had caught Yellow Hair Custer and his cavalry soldiers on the Little Big Horn River and killed them all. It was a wild spark in the dry tinder of that Northwest Indian summer.

More and more openly White Bird and old Toohoolhoolzote, beginning now to be joined by Hahtalekin and Looking Glass in their hard talk, spoke against Joseph and those among the Wallowa who still obeyed him. Because of Joseph, they said, the Nez Perce had lost their last chance to win back their ancestral lands from the white invaders. The Nez Perce would not forgive Joseph that, they promised. They would not forget it. They would make Joseph remember it when the time came.

So, in bitterness, doubt, despair, blustering talk and anxious indecision, passed that second of the bad summers.

The winds of September soon stirred out of the north. The gun-steel chill of October blued the dimming sun. The icy breath of Old Enim, the Winter Lord, frosted the land, froze deep the streams and stilled the pulses of life throughout the meadow, mountain and forest land of Aihits Palojami, the Fair Land of the Nez Perce people. When at last the third spring came, it was not like the two which had gone immediately before it. There was something in the March air. From the Tahmonmah and the Kahmuenem to the Imnaha and the Wallowa, fearful Nez Perce raised their wary heads and sniffed that something in the spring air and knew it for what it was—the smell of old trouble. It was what the wrinkled elders of the inner council called *hattia tinukin*—the death wind.

Now many things happened very fast.

It was the tenth sun of March, 1877. Old Chief Lawyer was at last dead. To succeed him as head of the Nez Perce, that is, as the white man's head of the tribe, an agency Indian, Reuben, was appointed by Agent Monteith. This was an exceedingly foolish decision.

Old Lawyer had been a fighter. In his day none stood before him in battle. He had a Nez Perce heart and the highest Nez Perce breeding; no matter that the nontreaty Indians would not sign the 1863 treaty with him and no matter that they would not come on the reservation at Lapwai with him, they respected him. But Reuben was a farmer. He had never fought. They sneered at him and they would not accept him in Old Lawyer's place. The control over the nontreaties, which the old man had been able to hold in some reasonable part, now went back over to the wild Indians. In this way the real leadership of the tribe was needlessly surrendered by Monteith and it now came onto the shoulders of three powerful antitreaty chiefs who could be

trusted to lead the people as far away from Lapwai as Old Lawyer had kept them close to it.

Two of these chiefs are already known to this story: White
Bird and Toohoolhoolzote. The third was Looking Glass, leader
of the important Asotin band, a man in his middle years and full
powers, a renowned fighter and avowed anti-Christian. Looking
Glass held his people to peace and to the plowing of their farms
along the Clearwater only because of his great friendship with
Joseph. But the Nez Perce knew that in his heart Looking Glass
was for war.

Next in line of authority to these three chiefs stood four
younger men. These were Hahtalekin, called Buffalo Hunter,
and Husishusis Kute, called Naked Head, of the Paloos band,
and Joseph and Ollikut of the Wallowa band. All of these save
Joseph were warriors of reputation and, in addition, Naked Head
was the Chief Dreamer of the new Indian religion of Smoholla,
the prophet. Joseph at this time was thirty-seven, Ollikut thirty-
three. Hahtalekin was forty-nine, Naked Head about forty-five.
The age of Looking Glass is uncertain but he must have been
over fifty. White Bird, of course, was past seventy; Toohoolhoolzote, sixty-eight. White Bird and Looking Glass, beyond
their influence as tribal chiefs, were both fanatical subpriests of
Smoholla's new religion.

Smoholla was a Shahaptian, a Priest River Nez Perce. A broad
barrel of a man with a huge round head, he was no chief, no
fighter, had no reputation of leadership whatever among our
people. Even his band was of no standing among us, not being of
pure blood and living toward the sea in the Columbia drainage
in a country not fit for high-caste Indians. But Smoholla had
something more powerful than pure blood. Many years before,
he had a dream. And thereby he became immortal among
haughty Nez Perce fighters and leaders who would not, otherwise, have lent him a worn-out horse to ride home on.

Smoholla's being of an impure breed did not affect the quality
of his mind. He had the cunning of a brush-land coyote, the
brightness of a river-bottom fox. He was impressive because of
his enormous head, and the white men remarked upon his start-

ling likeness to their great orator and chief, Daniel Webster.
This proved to be more than a sameness of the outside flesh.
Smoholla had the tongue of a sorcerer. Even while a young man
he became known up and down the Columbia as a medicine man
and speaker of frightening gifts. Our band had heard of him as
far up the Snake as the forks of the Salmon. But then, in 1860,
he had a fight with the powerful Nez Perce fighting chief,
Moses, and his fortunes changed.

Moses believed Smoholla had the magic to send sickness and
even death where he desired. And Moses had the thought that
Smoholla desired to send him some portion of these gifts. He
henceforth told his subchiefs that he felt it wrong for any man
to have such a *wyakin*, and set out down the river to find Smoholla and kill him. He did catch the Shahaptian medicine man
and had a historic fight with him upon the banks of the Columbia. The battle lasted until dark. At that time Smoholla fell down
and Moses, thinking him dead, left him there and went back up
the river to tell his people that the evil one had been destroyed,
that there would be no more bad sickness sent by him to harm
the up-river Nez Perce.

But Moses had done his people the most terrible favor in their
history. He had brought them the greatest sickness ever visited
upon the poor Nez Perce—the Dreamer religion of Smoholla,
the prophet.

Recovering consciousness in the dead of night, the wounded
medicine man stole a canoe and floated downstream through the
dark hours. His power as a sorcerer had been destroyed by his
defeat in the fight with Moses, and he well knew that his life
would not be worth a broken string of Shahaptian water shells
should the victorious chief hear he still lived. He must go away
for many many moons and travel afar through many foreign
lands. This he did.

It was not until after an absence of five winters and a fantastic
wandering of five thousand miles through the great cities of the
Western Sea, far south into the land of Mexico and back up
north through the Indian lands of the Apache in Arizona, the
Wasatch in Utah, the Paiute in Nevada, that he again, and with

magic suddenness, appeared in the midst of his home village in Nez Perce Oregon.

To his surprise, he was received as a man returned from the dead. His fellow Shahaptians would not believe that he was still ordinary flesh and blood. They insisted he was a spirit-man. This gave Smoholla his great idea. His smart mind perceived the simpleness of his fellows and pounced upon it like a hunting cat.

He told a story of a wondrous journey to Akunkenekoo, the Land Above, after Moses slew him beside the Big River. There he had met the Great Chief—he was careful not to call him Hunyewat—and had been given the command by him to return to his mother earth and instruct the Indians in their new religion, which he, the Great Chief, would send to Smoholla in messages from above. The idea of the new religion was very simple—the killing off of all whites as the only way of making Indian paradise in the land of the Nez Perce. Another part of the idea was that at a certain time, which Smoholla would announce, all the Indians who had ever died or been killed would be resurrected to help the live Indians do the job of killing the whites. Also, to feed all of these dead Indians come back to life, all the animals which had ever been slain in times past would be resurrected right along with the Indians. The Great Chief was also and finally opposed to mining and farming, which changed the surface of the sacred Indian earth and which were also, incidentally, the only ways white men could make their living in that country. The first time I heard Smoholla preach, in later years, he explained it this way. (And so well, too, that he very nearly convinced me despite my Christian mother's strong instruction to me that only fools would believe such heathen nonsense.)

"My young men," Smoholla would shout, "shall never work! Men who work cannot dream, and all wisdom comes to us in dreams. You ask me to plough the ground. Shall I then take a knife and tear at my mother's bosom? You ask me to dig for stone of gold. Shall I therefore dig under her skin for her bones? You ask me to cut the long grass and make hay to sell and become rich like the white men. But how will I dare cut off my own mother's living hair?"

It may be imagined what effect this sort of harangue had been having upon the nontreaty Nez Perce during the past two springs of the breaking of the President Grant treaty. Yet even so, the tradition of friendship with the white man was so strong in the majority of the Nez Perce people, that Smoholla's religion had gained no dangerous following until that third spring, of 1877. In that latter time, however, the teachings of the Too-ats, the Dreamers, fanned by the death of Old Lawyer and the unjust succession of fat Reuben, spread like prairie fire in dry grass.

The Nez Perce began "turning Too-at" by the hundreds. They took their children out of the boarding school at Lapwai —had not Smoholla said the place was cursed?—by the dozens and the scores. The fever grew.

Before that time many had said Smoholla was crazy. Even up to the last moment many stayed with Joseph in denying the central curse of the Dreamers that all the whites in Oregon and Idaho must be killed before there could be Indian paradise once more in that country. Yet whether or not these cool heads could have delayed the Too-ats' bloody dream must remain among the secrets of our mother earth, for upon the twelfth sun of that same March, Agent Monteith sent to Joseph his notorious order for him to have all the nontreaty Nez Perce upon the reservation at Lapwai by April 1st, and the last chance to stomp out the Too-at fire was gone.

That order was no accident of ignorance. Monteith knew the country. He knew the problems of the Indian way of life within it. He knew we could not find our cattle and our horses—no, nor even all of our people—and move them all to one single place in nineteen suns. We would need, in fact, three moons for the job. To command a crossing of the mighty Snake—which must be effected to reach Lapwai—in the midst of an unseasonably early melt such as that one of 1877, was a deliberate order of destruction. Joseph refused it with flat anger.

As angrily, Agent Monteith sent his final reply: "Very well, then; instead, be at Walla Walla on April 1st, to meet with General Howard; come prepared for agreement on the removal

of all the Nez Perce from the Wallowa and for their subsequent
delivery, with all their herds and other possessions, upon the
reservation in Idaho upon the day and minute of the soldier
chief's decision."

When Joseph revealed this order to his council of elders on
the night of the thirteenth sun, the grizzled chiefs only looked
at one another and nodded and said quietly, "Let us talk more
softly now, brothers, so that the women and little ones will not
be distressed by the sound of this evil wind from over in Idaho."

But it was not the sound of that bad wind they were thinking
of. It was the smell of it. And now, at last, they had a deadlier
name for that smell than even *hattia tinukin*. It was General
One Hand Howard.

9. One Hand Shows the Rifle

When the time came, Joseph did not go to Walla Walla to
meet One Hand Howard. Instead, he sent his brother Ollikut in
his place. He had heard that One Hand meant to humble him by
luring him to come to the fort, then not being there himself but
rather making him talk with one of the smaller soldier chiefs.
This turned out to be a true report. When Ollikut arrived at the
fort One Hand was "away on soldier business" and there was
only a young man, Lieutenant Boyle, there to talk with Ollikut
and the five warriors Joseph had sent with him.

Ollikut scowled and told Boyle they had better try another
time. Boyle said that General Howard would be there the next
time, and Ollikut went home satisfied.

Joseph, however, thought One Hand was still trying to trick
him into looking small. So once more he did not go to the fort
but sent his brother again. He was no match for One Hand in
the ways of such cunning. This time One Hand was there, and
it made Joseph look bad, as though the soldier chief's heart was
good and our chief's heart was not good.

Yet, One Hand showed a friendly spirit. "Tell Joseph," he
instructed Ollikut, "to come see me at Lapwai on the first day

of the next month. We will set no time for moving now. We will talk about it then."

Ollikut brought this message home, and Joseph took heart from it. "All right," he agreed. "It sounds as though the soldiers have more sense than the agents. Tell One Hand I will be there with my chiefs."

The few suns remaining in April shone swiftly. On the morning of the first sun of May, Chief Joseph appeared at Lapwai. Hearing that he was there, the other chiefs came in quickly from the places where they had been waiting to see what he would do. The feeling was good. One Hand Howard was cheerful and smiled a lot. Our courage grew.

There was a very large soldier tent with all sides rolled up, pitched not far from the schoolhouse. It had a long piece of canvas coming out over the entrance. It was a "sick tent," the kind the soldiers used to put their wounded men in after a fight. It was the biggest kind of tent they had. Our courage grew some more. We knew they placed value on this meeting because they used that big tent. Our chiefs sat down in front of it with much hope.

The others of us—I was along as a special favor, this being my manhood summer—all sat or stood on a little rise of ground in front of the tent where we could see each sign made by our chiefs and hear every word spoken by the agents and commissioners.

It was the third sun of the month; we had been there three days waiting for all the chiefs to come in and for all the first talk and the handshaking to get done with. Now all of that was over and we were all sitting there expecting One Hand to make the beginning speech.

But it was Agent Monteith who got up. A bad sound ran through the Indians. They had not come to hear the agent; they had heard him too maany times before. They had come to listen to One Hand Howard, the soldier chief with his best arm gone, high up by the shoulder. As the sound the Indians made was not a friendly one, I expected Monteith would grow angry, but he did not. Rather, he smiled. Soon enough we found out why.

The Lapwai agent's long wait was over. For the first time in his six years in our country he was speaking to us with the power to make us listen. Here is what he said, addressing Joseph:

"I sent out Reuben and some others to your camp and invited you to come in. Now you must come in and there is no getting out of it. You and White Bird can send your Indians to pick up all their horses and cattle and come on the reservation. I have land for all of you. Joseph can pick the place he wants if he will come at once. General Howard will stay until matters are settled."

The Nez Perce were caught with nothing to say. They had no plans for such orders. They had come thinking One Hand was there to help them, and not the agent. Unable to decide what to do, the chiefs asked General Howard if they might have a little time to think. To their surprise he told them they could have all the time they might require. At the moment they thought nothing of this generosity, talking among themselves several days and going back and forth in a friendly way to General Howard for advice.

But the wind changed direction quite suddenly when the council resumed once more. One Hand became very stern. His cheerfulness broke away like honeycombed shore ice, showing the cold gray water of his true face underneath. Agent Monteith got very brave at the same time. He started to talk mean to us.

When he did this, Joseph turned away from him and spoke to General Howard.

"I have been in a great many councils," he said, "but I am no wiser."

"What do you mean?" asked General Howard.

Joseph spread his hands.

"Always it is the same in the end. Always it is the Indian who must do this and must do that. Why?"

"You will have to speak more plainly," insisted General Howard. "Your meaning still does not reach me."

Again Joseph spread his hands.

"We are all sprung from a woman," he said, "although we are unlike in many things. We cannot be made over again. You are

as you were made, and as you were made you can remain. We
are just as we were made by the Great Spirit, and you cannot
change us; then why should children of one mother and one
father quarrel? Why should one try to cheat the other? I do not
believe that the Great Spirit Chief gave one kind of men the
right to tell another kind of men what they must do."

One Hand became most excited then.

"You deny my authority, do you?" he shouted. "You want
to dictate to me, do you?"

Joseph shook his head and his face grew sad. When One Hand
turned angry like that, it was time to let someone else talk for
the Nez Perce. Joseph stood back and let old Toohoolhoolzote
come forward, exactly as he had at Kamiah Crossing when I was
a little boy of fourteen.

Toohoolhoolzote acted like a man with his mouth full of buffalo gall. Joseph, he said, had spoken for peace. One Hand and
the agent had not heard him. Toohoolhoolzote would speak for
something else. Maybe they would hear him better.

"The Great Spirit Chief," he began, fierce old eyes flashing,
"made the world as it is, and as He wanted it, and He made a
part of it for us to live upon. I do not see where you get authority to say that we shall not live where He placed us."

General Howard drew back as though he had been struck
across the face with a *kopluts*.

"Shut up!" he roared. "I don't want to hear any more of such
talk. The law says you shall go upon the reservation to live, and
I want you to do so, but you persist in disobeying the law. If
you do not move, I will take the matter into my own hand, and
make you suffer for your disobedience."

One Hand paused for an angry bite of air, then went on. "If
you continue your rebellious ways, stirring up the people and
making them ugly with all this Too-at talk, all this talk of the
Dreamer religion, I will have you sent to the Indian country, to
Oklahoma, the Hot Place, and I will send all of the bad ones
down there with you. Now do you understand that?"

This, of course, was the wrong way to talk to a fighting Indian. Toohoolhoolzote's face turned dark as night.

He walked up to General Howard and he put his jaw out toward him and spoke in a voice deep as a growling bear's.

"Who are you, that you ask us to talk, and then tell me I shan't talk? Are you the Great Spirit? Did you make the world? Did you make the sun? Did you make the rivers to run for us to drink? Did you make the grass grow? Did you do all these things that you talk to us as though we were boys? If you did, then I understand how you have the right to talk to us as you do."

Strangely, General Howard held his temper. "You are an impudent fellow," he replied to Toohoolhoolzote very quietly, "and I will put you in the guardhouse."

Wheeling about, he waved to two soldiers standing by with loaded rifles. "Arrest this man," was all he said.

The soldiers moved to seize Toohoolhoolzote but he pulled away from them, hissing like a snake. "Do not put your hands on me!" he warned. "I am a chief; I do not need to be led like a small child. I will go with you, do not worry."

He then turned back to General Howard, broad chest expanded, head high, fine old eyes unafraid.

"Is that your order?" he asked. "I don't care. I have expressed my heart to you. I have nothing to take back. I have spoken for my country. You can arrest me, but you cannot change me or make me take back what I have said."

The soldiers were very uneasy now, and they had good reason.

As they marched the fighting chief away, White Bird looked at Joseph and said, "Heinmot, shall we let them do this shameful thing to our brother?"

Joseph knew that if he said no to White Bird's question, all the white men at that tent, including One Hand Howard, would be dead on the ground before the soldiers got Toohoolhoolzote around the corner of the school building. So he answered White Bird carefully.

"Wait," he said. "Do nothing yet. I will speak."

Then he stepped forward, raising his hand, and all the Indians ceased their muttering and fell silent.

"I am going to talk now," he told General Howard. "I don't

care whether you arrest me or not. The arrest of Toohoolhoolzote was wrong, but we will not resent the insult. We were
invited to this council to express our hearts, and we have done
so."

With those few simple words Joseph began his farewell speech
to the white men at Lapwai.

"You are asking us for the last time," he said, "to give up our
Valley of the Winding Water, our beautiful Wallowa country.
Many snows since, you asked this same thing of my father, Tuekakas, the Old Joseph. My father had become blind and feeble.
He could no longer speak for his people. It was then I took my
father's place as chief. In this council I made my first speech to
white men. I said, 'We have never accepted presents from the
Government. Neither Lawyer nor any other chief had authority
to sell this land. It has always belonged to my people. It came
unclouded to them from our fathers, and we will defend this
land as long as a drop of Indian blood warms the hearts of our
men.'"

Joseph shook his head at the memory, went on quickly. "Soon
after this my father sent for me. I saw he was dying. I took his
hand in mine. He said, 'My son, my body is returning to my
mother earth, and my spirit is going very soon to see the Great
Spirit Chief. When I am gone, think of your country. You are the
chief of these people. They look to you to guide them. Always
remember that your father never sold his country. You must
stop your ears whenever you are asked to sign a treaty selling
your home. A few years more, and white men will be all around
you. They have their eyes on this land. My son, never forget my
dying words. This country holds your father's body. Never sell
the bones of your father and your mother.'

"I pressed my father's hand and told him that I would protect
his grave with my life. My father smiled and passed away to the
spiritland.

"I buried him in that beautiful Valley of the Winding Waters.
I love that land more than all the rest of the world. A man who
would not love his father's grave is worse than a wild animal.

"For a short time we lived quietly. But this could not last. White men had found gold in the mountains around the land of the winding water. . . .

"I labored hard to avoid trouble and bloodshed. We gave up some of our country to the white men, thinking that then we could have peace. We were mistaken. The white men would not let us alone. We could have avenged our wrongs many times, but we did not. . . . When the white men were few and we were strong we could have killed them off, but the Nez Perce wished to live at peace.

"If we have not done so, we have not been to blame. I believe the old treaty has never been correctly reported. If we ever owned the land we own it still, for we never sold it. In the treaty councils the commissioners have claimed that our country had been sold to the Government. Suppose a white man should come to me and say, 'Joseph, I like your horses, and I want to buy them.' I say to him, 'No, my horses suit me, I will not sell them.' Then he goes to my neighbor, and says to him, 'Joseph has some good horses. I want to buy them, but he refuses to sell.' My neighbor answers, 'Pay me the money, and I will sell you Joseph's horses.' The white man returns to me and says, 'Joseph, I have bought your horses, and you must let me have them.' If we sold our lands to the Government this is the way they were bought.

"Through all the years since the white man came to Wallowa we have been threatened and taunted by them and the treaty Nez Perces. They have given us no rest. . . . I have carried a heavy load on my back ever since I was a boy. I learned then that we were few, while the white men were many, and that we could not hold our own with them. We were like deer. They were like grizzly bears. We had a small country. Their country was large. We were contented to let things remain as the Great Spirit Chief made them. They were not; and would change the rivers and mountains if they did not suit them.

"Year after year we have been threatened, but no war was made upon my people until General Howard came to our country two years ago and told us that he was the white war chief of all that country. He said, 'I have a great many soldiers at my back. I am going to bring them up here, and then I will talk to you again. I will not let white men laugh at me the next time I come. The country belongs to the Government, and I intend to make you go upon the reservation.' "

Joseph paused for his first moment of long silence. His eyes found the eyes of One Hand Howard. One Hand's face was gray again. He did not look happy. Joseph said no more to him, but addressed himself to us, and what he told us brought every Indian sitting under that tent roof up to his feet and looking around for his pony.

"Now those two snows are gone," our chief said. "I remember One Hand's promise, but I do not think he does. I will tell you why. While we have been his guests here, taking our time while he smiled and told us to do so, he has been marching his soldiers behind our backs. *Eeh!* You will see now why Agent Monteith went back to his hard talking; why One Hand lost his smile. When we began to talk, his soldiers needed more time to get into position around us. When word came to One Hand that there was no more need to delay, that his men were all where he wanted them to be, then he changed his face, then he stood up and showed us the rifle.

"But go slowly, my chiefs. It is too late for anger. There is no use looking toward your horses. This morning, very early, young Yellow Wolf rode in from the home camp to tell me there were suddenly soldiers on all sides of the Wallowa. We are surrounded. There is nothing to do but to go look at the lands they offer us here at Lapwai."

With those last words Joseph turned his back on One Hand Howard and walked away from the big tent. When One Hand showed the rifle to Joseph, he lost the best friend the white man had in all that Indian country.

The next day Joseph rode out with General Howard and with White Bird and Looking Glass to inspect all the good land which Agent Monteith had told about having for him and the other chiefs. They found nothing. It was poor land there at Lapwai, the best of it having been taken up long ago. Joseph said he

would have none of it. White Bird and Looking Glass would not
even talk to Howard or Monteith after they saw the first two
or three scrubland places the agent offered our proud people.
Everyone rode back to Lapwai with an angry mind.

The following day the final talk was made. It was ugly from
the start. One Hand warned us abruptly that our people had
thirty days to go back home, collect all their stock, and move
onto the reservation. He told Joseph, "If you are not here in that
time, I shall consider that you want to fight, and will send my
soldiers to drive you on."

Our chief thought this over a moment. As he did, I turned to
Yellow Wolf, who had come up to stand with me on the little
hill by the school building.

"Uncle," I whispered, "do you think there will be a war
now?"

He shook his lean head.

"Not while Heinmot speaks for us," he said. "But look at the
eyes and faces of old White Bird and Looking Glass. Think
what is in the mind of Toohoolhoolzote, staring out of the bars
of the guardhouse over there. Do that, and then see if you need
to ask me the question again."

I looked at White Bird and Looking Glass, and their eyes and
faces were fastened on One Hand Howard like those of crouching buffalo wolves outside the herd circle of the old bulls' sharp
horns. I could read their hearts. They were waiting only for the
white man to look the other way, to be off his guard one minute.
I looked across at the guardhouse. I could see old Toohoolhoolzote's face pressed against the iron bars of the one window,
could even see his gnarled hands gripping the bars like the
throats of white men. I turned back to Yellow Wolf.

"I do not need to ask the question again," I said, and we both
fell silent as Joseph now answered General Howard in the spirit
Yellow Wolf had indicated he would.

"War can be avoided, and it ought to be avoided," said our
chief. "I want no war. My people have always been the friends
of the white man. Why are you in such a hurry? I cannot get
ready to move in thirty days. Our stock is scattered, and Snake

River is very high. Let us wait until fall, then the river will be low. We want time to hunt our stock and gather our supplies for the winter."

Then it was that General Howard stood up and pointed his finger at Joseph.

"If you let the time run over one day," he said, "the soldiers will be there to drive you on to the reservation, and all your cattle and horses outside of the reservation at that time will fall into the hands of the white men."

Joseph seemed to know that this was so. Life went out of his shoulders. "I believe you," he said quietly to the unfriendly one-armed soldier chief. "I will go and tell my people."

To us Indians, after the white men had taken up their chairs and desks and papers and gone away, and we were mounting up our ponies to leave, he spoke with a terrible weariness.

"I said in my heart," he told us, "that rather than have war I would give up my country. I would rather give up my father's grave. I would give up everything rather than have the blood of the white men upon the hands of my people."

Again he sighed with the heaviness which lay upon his breast, again went on with deep sadness.

"But General Howard has refused to allow me more than thirty days to move my people and their stock. He goes, even now, to prepare for war. Where we go I know not. We can only pray that Hunyewat will guide us. We had better pray very hard, too. The road I see ahead is dark; our time to travel it is very short."

He turned his tall gray buffalo horse away from Lapwai with those sorrowful words, and we followed him, each silent with his own thoughts. There was no laughing, no talking. There was only the clinking of bit rings and the squeaking of stirrup leathers as we rode along. All the talking had been done. Only one question remained. We all knew what it was.

10. The Whiskey Talkers

When we came home from Lapwai there was a great council of war in our village. All the wild chiefs came in. Fighters I had never seen, famous ones like Wottolen, Eagle from the Light, Peopeo Tholekt and Naked Foot Bull, were there. To the last one of them, they were in the same mean temper. They only wanted to hear hard words and promises of white killings. It was a time to make an Indian boy's blood run in his veins like hot lead, to set a red youth's heart on fire for war and the talk of war.

This time it seemed Joseph must fail. White Bird talked for war. Espowyes, Light in the Mountain, talked for war. White Bull, Yellow Long Nose, Bad Man, Rattle on a Blanket, Hawk Heart, Bull Second Boy, Mean Person, Red Scout, Bowstring, Dead Bones—famous fighters every one—talked for war. Naked Head, the prophet of Smoholla, said that this was the time the Shahaptian Dreamer had foretold. His two medicine helpers, Kahpots and Tahomchits, danced and made prayer smoke for a great killing of whites. Even old Fire Body, the uncle of that little Asotin girl Meadowlark whom I had never forgotten, got his pants off and danced in the circle with the young men till the sun came up. It was a night like no other.

Some mixed-blooded Indians from the half-breed town across the river from Lewiston (the white man's village where the Clearwater came into the Snake) came down with three barrels of trade whiskey for sale, and we bought them out and got drunk. This was a big time. I felt taller than a mountain. There were lights in my head and fire in my bowels. I had the strength of ten men, yet I could scarcely stand up to walk. It was wonderful.

Warriors fought with clubs and knives and hatchets. One man killed another by splitting his head with a Lapwai shovel, and the dead man's wife stabbed the shovel-hitter with a camas hook through his liver. Hohots Elotoht, Bad Boy Grizzly Bear, tried to lift his horse with one hand to win a bet of two tin cups of whiskey against his skunkskin loincloth. He got angry when he looked up from his straining and saw that his friend Lepeet Hessemdooks, Two Moons, was sitting on the pony to make it heavy. He dropped the horse on purpose, without warning, and Hessemdooks fell off and had three ribs cracked when the horse stepped on him in running away.

Right in the middle of all this I came face-to-face with my uncle Yellow Wolf and offered him a taste from my soldier canteen of whiskey. He took the canteen from me and struck me over the head with it. The seams burst and the whiskey was wasted. I had forgotten that Yellow Wolf did not use strong drink or tobacco, and I was very lucky to get off with only a sore place on my head and losing a little whikey. Besides, I knew how to get more whiskey. There was an old warrior, a friend of mine, called Dookiyoon, the Smoker. He had a bullet hole in his belly and claimed he could swallow smoke and make it come out of his navel. My Lapwai friend, James Redwing, who had run away from the school to come home and go to war with me, would not believe this. Three times that night he bet me that no Indian could blow smoke out of his belly. Dookiyoon did his trick each time (for trick it was of course), and I won two cups of whiskey each time. All it cost me was my friend from Lapwai and a shag of wormy tobacco for the old man. The last I saw of James Redwing he was going to get his gun and shoot himself in the stomach so that Smoker could show him the trick.

Ah, that dance was something. It was altogether the wildest I ever recall. The greatest part of it all was old Toohoolhoolzote showing up just ahead of sunrise, freed from his five days in the guardhouse at Lapwai and come growling down to the war council to make the most stirring talk for killing whites in Nez Perce memory. Otskai got so excited he pulled out his short gun and shot his own right big toe off. But it was no loss. Wookaw- kaw, Woodpecker, a good friend of his, offered him two good mares in foal for the toe, so that he could put it on a string and wear it around his neck for a new *wyakin*. Otskai took the mares and was going to shoot off his other big toe for two more mares, but somebody got the gun away from him and hit him over the head with it and Woodpecker saved the other two mares. After that, and while Toohoolhoolzote was still talking, the third barrel of whiskey was broken open. I remembered nothing more until the sun was shining straight up in the middle of the sky and I had a taste in my mouth like the smell of house-cat droppings. Yellow Wolf was standing over me with a face cold as snow-ice and kicking me in the rear as though I were a settler's pig asleep in the street mud and telling me to get up and go put some cold water in my face, that Joseph was going to speak at last.

11. Across the Angry Snake

Joseph stood tall before us in the morning sunlight and talked with words which touched the hearts of all. Even the young men, big for war, grew still and heard him out.

"This is our land," he said, sweeping his long arm from the east to the west over the green hills and meadows of the Wallowa. "Here we were born. Here we have put to sleep our loved ones. Here we had hoped to be put to sleep in our own times.

"But a man does not decide these things for himself. There is some god above us all, who says yes and no, and we cannot decide against him, we cannot order our lives as we would.

"Now we have been told to gather our cattle and to come upon the reservation at Lapwai. How can we refuse?

"Last night there was much whiskey, much loud and vain talk for war. Now the sun is shining. We can see out across this fair land of ours. The grass is green, the water is blue, the rocks are tawny brown, the pine trees blue and silver upon the hill. Would you then darken all this with the blood of our white friends?

"Remember, when you talk for killing, that many of the white men *are* our friends. Many others have treated us bad, have shamed and cheated us, have stolen our land and cattle and been evil with our women. But remember this, my brothers. When you start a killing, you cannot stop it when it comes to the house of your friend. You cannot say to the killing, 'Wait, do not go in there, that man is my friend.' The killing will not hear you. It will go in the house of friend and enemy alike.

"There are white men in this land, in the Wallowa, the Kamiah, at Lapwai and Lewiston and Mount Idaho, whose food I have eaten, under whose roof I have slept, whose women I honor as I honor my own women, and whose children I love as I love my own children. Do you ask me to go with you when you kill those white men? When you shoot down their women? When your stray bullets pierce the bodies of their little children? Think about it, my chiefs."

As though to give us the time to do as he bid, Joseph now waited before us motionless and still. White Bird bowed his head and would not look at him. Espowyes stared off toward the hills. Even Naked Head turned his eyes away. It was the same with all of us. We were half of us sick with whiskey, nearly all of us sick with the ways of the white man. Yet not one voice spoke out against our chief's shaming of us. It was the same from simple-minded Otskai to cunning old war talker Toohoolhoolzote. We were feeling Joseph's power. Not an Indian made a sound, and our chief raised his hand, commanding us to listen again.

"We are camped here," he said, "at the mouth of this friendly little stream where many times before we have met and been happy.

"Yet it is not this shining little stream we have to cross. It is not even the Grande Ronde, the Wallowa, or the warm-breasted Imnaha over which we must get those poor little calves and colts swum safely. It is the Snake.

"And listen, my brothers, can you not hear the thunder of that dark water calling to us? Aye, it is like the cry of a ghost in a bad dream, my chiefs, but it is no dream. It is the Snake River in spring flood, and we must go and gather up our herds and cross over it. There is no more time for the women to weep, no more time for the men to talk. We must do as One Hand Howard has told us. Thirty suns, he said. Not an hour more.

"Remember that the eye tells what the tongue would hide. You all looked into General Howard's eye. You know what it told. If we do not go upon that reservation, if we cannot get our cattle up and across the river within his hard time, he will come and kill us.

"I will not wait for that, I will not have the white man's blood upon my hands. Come with me, those of you who feel the same way. I will say no more."

Joseph was true to that last promise. He did not say another word but walked through all those hundreds of angry and sick and hopeless Indians toward his tipi and his tall gray buffalo horse. We all watched him. He got on the horse and turned him out of the village, south to the meadow where we knew he had his herds. Now all eyes swung back to White Bird, Toohoolhoolzote, Hahtalekin and Looking Glass, the other four main chiefs.

Looking Glass, small, slender, dark as the smoked hide of a black buffalo, looked after Joseph a long time, then turned and walked up to White Bird and Toohoolhoolzote.

"What can I do?" he said to the old warriors. "He is my friend." He went quickly then and got his own horse and guided him south out of camp, following Joseph. The old chiefs looked hard at one another, and at young Hahtalekin. "He is a fool," said the young chief, "but I, too, love him. I am going to get my horse."

White Bird and Toohoolhoolzote were left alone, with all the Indians watching them.

"*Eeh!*" said fierce old Toohoolhoolzote, after a moment that seemed long enough to build a bullboat. "We are all fools, and us old ones the worst of any. Come on, Peopeo, let's get our horses, too. We can't fight a war all by ourselves. Not at our age."

"It's a true thing," answered his friend, White Bird, and the two of them went off, side by side and walking straight as rifle barrels, to get their horses and ride off after Heinmot Tooyala-

kekt, chief of the Wallowa Nez Perce, to collect the cattle and
the horses and to turn them, every one, toward the terrible Snake
River.

It is a fact, written even in the white man's grudging records,
that Chief Joseph made the gather of the Nez Perce herds in
three weeks. He did not get all the livestock, and some that was
left behind was our good stock. But he did obey General Howard's order and he did have the better part of our animals got
together and moving in good order toward Snake River and the
old Indian crossing at the mouth of the Imnaha by the last sun
of the third week.

The council at Lapwai had broken apart May 15. It was now
June 4. When Howard had said thirty suns he had been using
the Indian term, or the Indian meaning, of one moon, one
month. Therefore, we had now eleven days remaining of the
original time to get our herds up to and over the river, and on
north to Lapwai.

But many of the people now lost heart. Looking at that
swollen ugly river and at their prize saddle, pack, breeding and
beef stock, especially listening to the nervous lowing and neighing of the mother animals and the frightened blatting and whick-
ering of their new babies, a large number of the people wanted
to turn the herds free and go back to the Wallowa. Yet Joseph
held them together once more. He reminded them they must go
across and lose some of their stock, or not go across and lose all
of it. Again, they could see there was no choice. Most of them
knew in their hearts that Joseph was right, that they could not
turn back, that the bones of their fathers lay forever behind
them. It was shortly after first sun-up that we put the lead animals into the back eddies of the Oregon side.

There followed ten hours as evil as any our people had known.
We went into the water of the mighty Kahmuenem, at the
foaming mouth of the Imnaha, with five to six thousand head of
the finest Indian horses ever bred. We came out of that water in
the late afternoon with three thousand head. The Snake had
eaten the rest of them.

Some Indians say we had four thousand cattle, losing as many as one in three head of them. I do not remember myself. My eyes were too full of tears at counting the tens and scores and, finally, hundreds upon hundreds of noble Appaloosa and lesser mounts swept away in the hoarse-throated hours of that great herd-swim over the flooding Kahmuenem.

We did our best. Yet to me, as to many another hard-eyed Nez Perce that tragic day, the best was still very bad. White Bird and Toohoolhoolzote spoke the thoughts of a goodly number of us when they rode up and confronted Joseph after the last survivor of our battered herds had staggered up and out of the snarling river to stand trembling and panting on the Idaho shore.

With a dramatic outflinging of his arm, old Toohoolhoolzote commanded the eyes of all of us there on that rocky point above the crossing, to turn downstream.

"There you are, Heinmot!" he cried. "See what your words have done. Count those bodies. The poor things had no chance. The little babies went under. The old ones went under. Many of the best and strongest were swept away. But you said we had no choice, no other chance. Now look down that dark river. Look as far as your eye can look and your heart will let you look. Tell us what you see!"

Joseph said nothing. He only stared off down the river. Below the booming entrance of the Imnaha, down there where both rivers straightened out to run together with their full fury, the snagging teeth of the canyon rocks were black with the wet and shining carcasses of the dear friends and pets of us all. Even little Tea Kettle, the small blue-gray companion of my happy boyhood, aging now and unable to stay with me all the way across, had gone down in the last pony-lengths from safety. He lay now somewhere in the spray-wetted ranks of the dead on those distant bank rocks, or had been swept on downstream out of sight to be spat out into the quiet waters of some side pool a mile, or five miles, or ten miles along the twisted canyon. Sun Eagle, the great and glorious, had been torn from beneath Yel-

low Wolf and sucked down the black throat of the Snake. Old
Brown, Joseph's faithful traveling mount of nearly twenty
years, was gone. Ollikut's famous roan buffalo runner had disappeared. All the Indians had lost some of their horses and some
of the Indians had lost all of their horses. Joseph knew this. It was
in his heart like the barb of an enemy arrow. That was to be seen
by the dullest of us, as we watched him now and waited for his
answer to Toohoolhoolzote's question. At last he was ready
with it.

"A man comes to you with a gun and you have no gun," he
said. "He puts the gun to your eyes and says, 'Toohoolhoolzote,
I will give you a choice. You have five horses. If you will give
me two of them, you may go away with the other three, and
with your women and children unharmed. If you will not give
me my two horses, I will use the gun and take all of your horses
and cannot say that my bullets will not hit some of your family
standing behind you. Now what do you say? I am cocking the
gun.' "

Joseph stopped and put his hand on the old man's shoulder.
"How would you have answered the man?" he asked.

"I would have knocked aside his gun and fought him for my
other two horses," replied Toohoolhoolzote. "I would rather be
dead than to let a man rob me without a fight."

"What good would it do you to be dead?"

"I would not have to look down this river of sorrow."

"Life is a river of sorrow, old friend. You cannot come to it,
you cannot cross over it, without knowing some sorrow. You
cannot look up the river only to the sunrise; you must look down
it toward the darkness, too."

"We should have stayed and fought for our land," said Toohoolhoolzote.

"Yes," agreed his friend White Bird, moving his pony forward. "That is right."

"No it is not," Joseph answered both of them. "We have lost
some cattle and many horses. What we have saved is a far more
precious thing. Each should thank his chosen god that we have

come safe across the Kahmuenem with all our people. Do you understand that, Toohoolhoolzote? Will you pray with me?"

Up to that moment none of us seemed to have thought of ourselves, or of our loved ones. We had all been too heartsick about our horses. Now Joseph's words struck the tone of truth. It was indeed a remarkable thing that we had got across the Snake with not even a *tekash* baby or a toothless grandmother being dragged under and drowned.

But the two old fighting chiefs were Too-ats. They were not believers, with the rest of us, in the old peaceful Nez Perce god, Hunyewat. Their new religion brought them always around to the same answer: the blood war against the white man.

Toohoolhoolzote's ancient face grew bad to look at.

"I will not pray with you, Heinmot," he said.

"Nor will I," said White Bird.

"What will you do then?" asked Joseph.

"For myself, I don't know," White Bird answered him. "I am still too sick from looking down the river."

"And you, Toohoolhoolzote?"

"I don't know, either," replied the other old chief. "I am also still too sick. One thing alone I do know, Heinmot. I will never listen to you again. That is my word, that is my warning. *Taz alago*, my chief. Good-bye."

As was his way when he knew the talk had outlasted itself, Joseph said no more. We all sat and watched White Bird and Toohoolhoolzote ride away. When they were gone down off the lookout point, Joseph bowed his head and said a prayer. Those of us who were still with him there bowed our heads, too. But I don't think any of us were praying or thinking with Joseph. Even the lips of Ollikut, his trusted brother who worshiped him, were not moving with Joseph's lips. But beneath the cover of our bowed heads the eyes of all of us were moving. They were moving down the river, just like the eyes of the two old fighting chiefs. And our thoughts were far more with the old chiefs than with Joseph.

There was only one answer to the still, slack forms of our beautiful horses crushed on the cruel rocks down there where

we were looking. It was *Shoyapee,* the white man. No prayers
to any god would change that. Joseph might pray there until the
sun went down, or until a hundred suns went down. He would
pray alone.

We were Nez Perces. We would pray no more. *Kiuala piya-
kasiusa.* It was time to fight.

12. The Camp at Tolo Lake

At Tepahlewam, the old camp at Tolo Lake where the Nez
Perce people came together after the crossing of the Kahmuenem, Joseph called an immediate council to see what the wild
bands were going to do.

But neither White Bird nor Toohoolhoolzote were ready to
speak yet. They had tried to interest Looking Glass in going out
with them against the white men then and there, and the Asotin
chief had refused. Hahtalekin, the Paloos chief, had likewise told
them he would abide by his word to Joseph, that he would go on
into Lapwai with his band. So the two old fighters had drawn
back a little to think about things.

Joseph, on the other hand, knew better than to try to talk of
either war or peace when his people were still bleeding in their
hearts for their lost livestock and grieving deeply in their memories for the silver waters and empty tipis of the Wallowa.

Instead, he went through the great camp telling the people
that here they would rest. Messengers would be sent advising
One Hand that they had crossed the Snake and would be at
Lapwai in a few days. One Hand would understand. He would
make them no trouble over a few extra days. As for the Nez
Perce, let them use those last days to make a camp all could remember in their hearts for the rest of time. This struck the right
feeling.

After the first day of mourning the people began to pick up
their spirits. Not that the camp was happy. It could never have
been that. It was more that my people wanted to believe Joseph,
and did not want to believe White Bird and Toohoolhoolzote.

As Joseph had told Toohoolhoolzote at the Snake crossing, people always wanted to look up the river at the sunshine; they never wanted to look down it at the dark.

But while the people were working so hard at being light-hearted, Joseph was being deceived by his own blood. It was on the third night that Yellow Wolf came to the tipi of my father and asked to see me outside. When we had gone a little ways off, he stopped and said, "Heyets, I have been sent to tell you something. The young men are talking war. If you want to go with us, you will have to go out on the mountain right away."

I looked at him, my heart beginning to pound.

"What is it?" I said. "What do you mean?"

"In a few days White Bird will get Joseph to go with him to kill some beef for their families from White Bird's cattle which he had to leave behind over in the canyon. While they are over there the young men are going to do something about all this."

"This is not an honest thing," I started to object, but Yellow Wolf waved me down.

"Listen," he said. "We are not trying to be dishonest with Joseph. We are trying to be good to him. If he is not here when the trouble starts, then the white men cannot blame him for it. Isn't that a true thing?"

"In a way perhaps."

"Of course it is. Now if you want to go with us, say so. If you don't, just be quiet about what I have told you."

"I don't know, Hemene." I hesitated. "Have you thought hard about this thing?"

"Ever since Sun Eagle was swept from beneath me at the river."

"Aye, that was a sad thing. I lost my little Tea Kettle, too. Yet they are horses, not men. If you go out with the others, you will not be making war on horses."

"You don't have to tell me such things, Heyets. Be careful. I am losing my patience."

I nodded and fell silent, thinking very hard.

"No," I said to him at last. "I will not do it. My heart is with my chief."

Yellow Wolf's face grew mean.

"My heart is with him, too!" he cried angrily. "I love my uncle. This is nothing against him."

"How can you say that it is not?" I asked him. "He has spoken for peace. He has given his word to One Hand that we will come onto the reservation."

"He cannot speak for us all. That is the Indian law."

"Yes, it is," I admitted.

"For the last time, then, you will not go with us?"

"No, I will not."

"All right then, Heyets. Do not say anything to our chief. He cannot stop us and it will only make him unhappy to hear what the young men are saying."

"I agree," I said. "He has enough sadness already."

"*Taz alago,*" said Yellow Wolf. "Good-bye."

"*Taz alago,*" I answered him. "*Kuse timine,* go with a good heart."

Yellow Wolf did not answer me. He had already faded away into the night. I waited there a few moments trying to decide in my mind whether to go to my father or to Joseph with what he had told me. But my thoughts would not come together. I could see right on both sides. Finally I, too, turned away into the night. I would let it go, I would do nothing. Probably it was just talk. The young men had been talking for three years. Why add uselessly to my chief's troubles? Why stir up the camp just when he had got it quiet? I nodded my head, walking along. I was growing up. I was getting some good mind-power. I was learning to think in lines of peace, like my chief. Talk trouble and there will be trouble. Say nothing and the spirit will be soothed. I went into my father's tipi and sought my warm buffalo sleeping robe. My father heard me come in and called out softly, "Is that you, Heyets? What was it? What did Hemene want?"

"Nothing, Father," I answered him. "Only to talk about me going on the mountain. He thinks it would be a good idea."

"Oh? Well, it might be so. Good night, Heyets."

"Good night, Father. Sleep quiet."

"Aye, my son, the same to you."

"Good night."

"Good night . . ."

We said no more. Presently my father was snoring. I lay awake, staring up out of the smoke hole at the Idaho stars twinkling high and bright over that peaceful Tolo Lake camp at Tepahlewam, the old Nez Perce Place of the Rocks. Pretty soon I, too, was snoring. Yellow Wolf and his talk of war seemed as far away as those fat white stars above the smoke hole. In my mind no thought remained that I had done wrong. What my chief did was the business of my chief. What my uncle did concerned no one but my uncle. What Heyets told his father was a matter for which Heyets must answer only to Heyets. It was the Indian way.

And it was an ignorant, a willful, and a fateful way.

I had a chance to stop the Nez Perce War that night, and did not take it.

13. The Salmon River Raids

Tipyahlanah Siskon, Eagle Robe, was a fine old Nez Perce man living on his Salmon River farm back in the summer of 1875. He had one young son, a handsome youth born to him and his wife late in their lives, when they had thought Hunyewat would never answer their prayers for a man-child. Wahlitits—it meant Shore Ice in one translation—was seventeen that summer, and away on the mountain, taking his manhood time alone, when this thing happened to his aged father.

The old man had a white neighbor with a poor piece of land next to his rich bottom acres. Eagle Robe wanted to go once more to the buffalo that summer, so he asked his white neighbor to watch over his place while he was gone. For doing this he gave the white man a nice corner piece of his rich land as a gift. The white man's name was Larry Ott. He told Eagle Robe he would be glad to watch over his place and keep the deer and elk from eating his planted crops, and that he was very grateful for the fine piece of land for such a small service. The old man went away happy and had his last hunt. When he came back that fall he was given to understand Ott's gratitude. His white neighbor had moved into Eagle Robe's house and taken his whole farm. He would not let the old man set foot on his own property and when the latter asked to come in the house and get some of his clothes, Ott took up the rifle and shot him through the chest.

Young Wahlitits came home that night and found his father huddling under a rail fence, dying from the great hole in his breast. The old man prayed his son would not seek revenge upon Ott for his death. He ordered the boy, as a dying promise, not to take up the rifle, and Wahlitits, crying in his heart, agreed that he would do as his father asked. He went away from that place with his father's body, and did not come again to it.

Now two snows were gone, another summer come, and Wahlitits was with us in the great camp at Tolo Lake. In such dark ways moves the will of Hunyewat.

After Yellow Wolf visited me that third night I watched very carefully for signs of trouble in the camp. I saw nothing. A week passed. The eighth day, the twelfth sun of June, drew to a lingering, sunlit close.

As dusk came on, the camp stirred itself with excitement. Joseph had given the word for a big dance that night. In two more suns it would be time to pack the lodgepoles and go into Lapwai. Therefore, let all be happy in that last free camp of the Chutapalu, the Pierced-Nose People.

This word was very fine as far as it went. But it did not go as far as the burning heart of a certain young man with a long and waitful memory. That night, when the fires were leaping and the drums booming, when the trade whiskey which always seemed to find its way into our celebrations had been passed around too many times, Wahlitits mounted his finest war pony and rode into the circle of the dancers. If he was not drunk, he had had some whiskey. I know he nearly rode me down in the circle. And I was still watching him when his horse, being frightened by a swirling blanket, backed into the side of old Fire

Body's tipi and stepped all over the family's supply of kouse-root.

Old Otstotpoo came roaring out of that lodge as though his body truly were made of fire. "Loafer!" he yelled at Wahlitits. "Crazyhead! *Meopkowit!* You young fools playing at war make my bowels sick. See what you have done; stepped on my woman's hard work; ruined all her kouse-roots. *Eeh!* You call yourself a warrior? For half a pound of wet powder I will pull you off that spotted wolfbait and give you a taste of my *kopluts!*"

"Shut up, you old fool!" Wahlitits yelled back at Fire Body. "What would you know of war? You haven't been in a fight since you chased after the Cayuses that burned Waiilatpu."

"*Eeh!* Talk!" shouted Fire Body disgustedly. "If you want to do something like a warrior, why don't you go down on the river and kill that white man who shot your father? Eh? What do you say, big mouth? Why don't you do something to make yourself proud? Don't answer me. I know. You would rather go raiding kouse-roots in some old woman's tipi. Heh! Warriors indeed! There are no more warriors today. Bah! *Ukeize! Enimkinikai!*"

Wahlitits grew pale as a man who is shot through the body. The whiskey color went out of him and all in a moment he was talking quiet and straight.

"Old man," he said, "you have told me something. I am sorry about those kouse-roots and I will pay you for them when I come back. Tell your woman not to worry."

Those were his words. I was standing there and I heard them exactly. They do not sound like much now. They did not sound like much then. But they were the words which started the Nez Perce War. Within thirty minutes young Wahlitits had got his two cousins, Red Moccasin Tops and Swan Necklace, and with them had ridden south and east away from Tepahlewam. All night they pushed their horses across the rough country and when the sun came up they were sitting them atop a naked ridge half a mile above the Salmon River. Below them, peaceful in the early summer dawn, lay the bottomland farm where Wahlitits had known his happy boyhood.

The Nez Perce youth took his eyes away from that sight of

dark and bright memory. He worked the lever of his new Winchester rifle, pumping a shiny brass shell into the loading chamber.

"Come on," he said to his two friends. "Let's go down there and see that man who shot my father."

Larry Ott was not at home. He had fled the country when he heard the Nez Perce were crossing the Snake and coming toward Lapwai on the Idaho side. Some say that Joseph sent a friendly treaty Indian to tell him to get out of the way, that we were coming and the young men were angry. I do not know. There were so many stories of everything that happened then. Wahlitits, for instance, always said that Ott put on the clothes of a Chinese miner and hid in the Chinese camp up the river, and that is why they could not find him though they went twenty miles up the Salmon looking hard everywhere. I only tell what I know, or what someone I trusted like a brother told me.

What I know about that first day of raiding on the Salmon— the thirteenth of June—was that the three Nez Perce boys found some other white men while they were looking for Larry Ott. They killed one bad man who deserved to die. That was Richard Devine, an Englishman who lived up above Slate Creek. This man was mean and old and kept a fierce pack of dogs trained to chase Indians only. One time he had set those dogs on young Wahlitits when he was fishing up the Salmon as a little boy of twelve. Now Wahlitits remembered. He turned up the narrow canyon where Devine lived. When searchers found Devine a week later, he was not a pleasant thing to see. We Nez Perce never mutilated the dead, but sometimes the living got hurt very bad before they died.

Now the boys turned back down the river. There was a man down there, Henry Elfers, who had held a gun on some Indians while his partner, Mason, whipped one of the Indians with a bull-driving leather. Swan Necklace remembered that man Elfers because he had been a boy with the Indian party. After the three Nez Perce went by the cabin of Elfers that day, the memory became less bitter. I will name no names, but one of the boys took his cinch off his saddle, with the iron ring in it, and while the other two held the arms of Elfers he flayed the living skin off the white man's back. When his head dropped to his chest, they let him fall to the ground and then shot him through the head with their rifles.

Still farther down the river they found two more white men, Bland and Beckroge, harmless prospectors. By this time their senses had left them. By this time they were telling themselves the war had started. They killed Bland with a hand ax and Beckroge with his own pitchfork.

Turning back toward Tolo Lake late in the day, they headed for White Bird Creek where Samuel Benedict, the whiskey seller, had his cabin and store place. Now their heads were hurting from the past night's whiskey, and their hearts were beginning to bother them about that day's fearful ride down the river. They began to talk around for somebody to blame. They did not have to talk far before they came to Benedict. He had sold the whiskey that made them do those killings up the Salmon. It seemed that he should be made to pay for their crimes.

But Benedict had Indian friends. Always the white whiskey sellers had Indian friends. He was ready for the boys. There was a gun battle which wounded Benedict and one of the treaty Indians who had warned him, but night came on and Wahlitits and his two friends went on up the canyon to the mesa. They camped out on Camas Prairie, safely away from the main camp. They were all cured of the whiskey and the blood hate for one day and after they had made a fire and talked, they knew what they had done and what a terrible thing it might be for the rest of their people. It was decided that Swan Necklace, the youngest of them, should ride on in and tell Joseph what had happened, so that all in the camp who wanted to stay out of the war could leave in the night and be far away when the sun came. That way, only the fighting Indians would be involved. The peaceful ones, the women, the children, the old grandmothers and grandfathers could get out of the way and stay out of the way and the soldiers would not shoot at them.

This was the message that Wetyetmas, Swan Necklace,

brought into our camp that early evening of the thirteenth sun. I was there and I heard him. But like all the other Nez Perce in reach of his voice, I knew he was too late. Joseph was not there. The plan of the war talkers had been carried out smoothly. White Bird had convinced our chief that he should accompany him over to his canyon to kill out that beef before going into Lapwai. To make the matter as bad as it could be, White Bird had invited Ollikut to go along also. The younger brother had accepted. The premier chief left in the camp when Swan Necklace rode in was old Toohoolhoolzote. The hand of Hunyewat was moving again. Joseph could have stopped the killings, and the war, right then. There were six hundred Indians in that camp. Not over thirty or forty of that number were ready for killing in that minute. But Toohoolhoolzote was one of those thirty or forty, and he did not lift a finger to stop what then went forward.

Lepeet Hessemdooks, Two Moons, that whiskey drinker and angry talker, one of the few Nez Perce men of middle years who were for war, got on his horse and started riding up and down, shouting for warriors who were not afraid of the soldiers to mount up and make themselves known.

At first, he did not get many. Only about five young men from Toohoolhoolzote's own Salmon River band. But then, in rode Wahlitits and Red Moccasin Tops, and at once things took fire. In a few minutes there were seventeen men ready to ride back to the Salmon with young Wahlitits and his two original raiders. That made twenty warriors. They were all nontreaties, anti-Christians, white haters. Most of them were of the Salmon River band. Not one of them was a Wallowa. Not even my fierce uncle, Yellow Wolf, would go with them and thus betray his word to Joseph. But the others went. They elected Two Moons as their leader and they swept down off the mesa in the dead of that night and within the following twenty-four hours howled up and down the Salmon River settlements like *hattia tinukin*, the Nez Perce death wind.

To begin the second raid they went back to Benedict's whiskey store on the White Bird and got crazy drunk. To pay for the whiskey they burned down the store and shot Benedict. On down the main valley of the Salmon they caught and killed at least fourteen or fifteen white men. That was the white man's own number. For myself, I think it was more than that. Who knows what bodies were never found? Even one woman and one child were killed. It was exactly the thing that Joseph had said it would be. No man could start a killing and then tell it which houses to go in and which houses to stay out of. Every single case of true crime done by Indians in Idaho in that war of ours, was done in that one day of the second Salmon River raid. They even burned out their old friend Ad Chapman, the Umatilla squaw man living on White Bird Creek, and chased him in a wild horseback race all the way into Grangeville near Mount Idaho. This was a fateful thing, too, for in his anger at his Indian friends turning against him, Chapman went to General Howard and said he would serve him as chief scout until the last Nez Perce was brought in and punished. A strong friend, Narrow Eye Chapman made a terrible enemy, and no honest Nez Perce ever blamed him.

With dark of that fourteenth sun, Two Moons and his drunken killers rode back to Tolo Lake. Joseph and Ollikut were there to face them. Our chief put his hand on the bridle of Two Moons' horse and said to the Salmon River man, "You have struck a knife into my back while it was turned. The three boys might be excused. They started out to revenge a personal matter. This I could explain to General Howard. But what am I to say of seventeen grown men who will drink whiskey and shoot down women and children? You know the answer to that; you knew it before you started out. I will send to General Howard and try to tell him that these were all bad men, like Benedict the whiskey seller, which you shot and stabbed in your madness. But I know what One Hand will say back to me. Everyone listening to me knows what he will say. Those were not all bad men that you killed. They were not even all *men*. One woman and one child are dead. When One Hand now comes with the soldiers, who can say that we did not send for him ourselves? That is your question, Hessemdooks. Let us hear your answer to it."

Two Moons sat his horse, face turned away from Joseph. There was but one answer to that question. Two Moons knew it. Joseph knew it. Every one of us nontreaty Indians of the Salmon, the Asotin, the Paloos, the White Bird and the Wallowa, who were standing that moment within range of Joseph's voice, knew it.

Two Moons jerked his bridle from Joseph's hand and turned his horse angrily away. He and his men rode off, back out into the darkness from which they had come, saying no word to Joseph nor to any of us. After a while Joseph turned from watching them and said wearily, "Go and strike the tipis; the sun must not see us here. . . ."

14. Flight to Sapachesap

Joseph said we would go and hide in Sapachesap, a huge cave in the wall of Cottonwood Creek's canyon.

Sapachesap meant Ride In, or Drive In, and took its name from the fact it was big enough to take a man on horseback or even a team and wagon. It was an old tribal meeting place thought to have magic powers for good, and the older Nez Perce believed we would be safe there. I can remember my surprise at Joseph making this order, for I would not have believed he felt so strongly on the old ways. But I was just beginning to know him.

We reached the cave with no trouble. That was on the fifteenth sun of June. With us were Looking Glass and most of the Asotin people, all of the Paloos with Hahtalekin, some of the White Bird and Salmon River Indians. Missing from our number were Toohoolhoolzote and White Bird and the war talkers from both their bands. These fighting Indians had gone on to the old White Bird camp where Coyote and I had met Little Bird three summers ago. We made camp there on Cottonwood Creek and Joseph said to keep the horses herded up close until we heard from the scouts he had sent out from the Tolo Lake camp, and from the messengers he had sent to General

Howard at Lapwai. It was early dusk when the first of these riders began to come in.

The news was bad. One Hand was talking up a real war. At Lapwai the troops were assembling. In a little time, when the soldiers who had been set to watch the Wallowa could come up, he would have four hundred men there ready to march after us. And he meant to march after us. He would not even talk to Joseph's peace messengers. He would not even let them come into Lapwai. He did not want them to see what he was doing. But our nontreaty friends got the word to us. One Hand had made a declaration of war. By the middle of that same afternoon, he had sent word to Mount Idaho, Lewiston, Grangeville, Cottonwood and the other white settlements that the war against the Nez Perce had begun, that from that time the hand of every white man in Oregon and Idaho was to be set against Joseph and his people. As soon as the troops could come together at Lapwai, One Hand would march against Joseph and would pursue him until the last nontreaty Nez Perce had been killed or captured. Meanwhile, there were other soldiers than those coming to General Howard at Lapwai to be feared and watched out for. White Bird had sent a rider to say that one bunch of soldiers was coming up the Salmon toward his camp. His scouts had counted two hundred of them. Another bunch of soldiers was somewhere over near the Clearwater, with about the same number. Counting the regular soldiers and the settlers who always gathered up to fight with them, we had seven hundred or eight hundred enemies to worry about.

At this same time our scouts from Lapwai told us that One Hand was saying we had three hundred to five hundred warriors, that this was why he had to wait for more soldiers before he came after us. This was white man's history.

There were only six hundred of us Indians, counting every squalling baby and wrinkled grandmother among us. Of that number there were but one hundred twenty men of war age, seventeen to fifty years, and of these no more than fifty-five or sixty were trained warriors. The tribal count of all men, in all bands, at the time One Hand declared his war upon us, should be known. It was sixteen men in the Paloos band, thirty men in the Salmon River band, forty men in the Asotin band, fifty men in the White Bird band and fifty-five men in our own Wallowa band.

The white history tellers talk with many tongues and they are not all straight. They have never told how few we were, how many of us were women and children, how tiny was the number of real fighters who stood against their soldier armies in every battle that was coming then. We never had more than thirty to sixty men fighting in the first line of rifle fire against all those hundreds of soldiers who chased us the one hundred thirteen days and thirteen hundred miles from Tolo Lake to the Bear Paws. *That* was Indian history.

We were huddled in Cottonwood Canyon then, at the entrance of Sapachesap, the sacred cave of our ancestors. The last rider from Lapwai had come in. The men from White Bird's camp had come in. All the back scouts from Tolo Lake, Snake Crossing and our abandoned homes in the Wallowa had ridden over Buzzard Mountain and were with us there at Sapachesap. All that was to be known of the enemy was known. It was time to decide the last movement.

Joseph called the chiefs together at his fire in front of the cave. The council lasted almost no time. Looking Glass led the way. He said he was going to take his Asotin and go home to their permanent village on the Clearwater. This would show the soldiers that he did not want war. Whatever Indians went with him would be safe. There were plowed fields and houses with log walls at his village. Agent Monteith knew that the people of Looking Glass did not move around. Therefore, the soldiers would not dare attack them.

This talk had a great effect. Most of the nontreaties gathered there on the Cottonwood did not want to fight; the fighters had gone on to the White Bird camp. Quickly Hahtalekin said he would advise his little band to go with the Asotin. What would Joseph do? he wanted to know. But as the Paloos chief asked, he was not watching Joseph; he was watching Ollikut, the warrior brother. So, too, was Joseph.

Our chief then arose to answer Hahtalekin's query as though he were lifting the snows of eighty winters on his tired shoulders. But, as always, his voice thrilled us with its deep, rich *simiakia*, its pure tone of Indian pride.

"I will advise my people as you have, Hahtalekin," he said. "I will say to them, 'Go with Looking Glass. Go with Aleemyah Tatkaneen, my old friend, to his peaceful village on the Clearwater. There you will be safe, there the fences and the fields will protect you.' "

He paused at this point, a sound of sadness coming into his voice.

"As for myself," he continued, "I have prayed all the afternoon, asking my heart what to do. The answer has come to me with our scouts from Lapwai, who tell us One Hand Howard has said that Joseph is to blame for this war. Because of this blame, I cannot go with you, but must go with Ollikut and the young men to the camp of White Bird. Pray for me, my people. If we must, we will fight the soldiers over there. *Taz alago*, good-bye."

He turned and nodded to Ollikut, and the two of them made their way through the people toward the tethering place of the horses. About twelve of our young men followed them. Then a few, not so young, moved away from the fire, following the young men. I saw Horse Blanket, Yellow Wolf's father, go. I saw Elk Water, my own father, go. Then Smoker and Fire Body, two really old men, got up and went for their horses. I felt a burning in my stomach and a shakiness in my legs. Then there was a familiar hand on my shoulder and a well-known voice speaking to me, and Hemene Moxmox, my uncle Yellow Wolf, was saying in my ear, "Well, Heyets, will you go to war or will you go with the women?"

My throat hurt so that I could hardly answer him. But I was suddenly feeling my seventeen summers. I was seeing Joseph, my chief, and Ollikut, our fighting leader, sitting on their war horses, waiting out there beyond the leaping firelight. And I was seeing all the other Indians around us watching Yellow Wolf and me—watching to see what Heyets, the son of a fighting father and a white-talking mother, would do.

I drew myself up and made the war sign of our people. I took a rifle bullet from the belt I wore around me, and I bit the lead from it and emptied the powder into the fire before me. It hissed and flared and gusted orange-red, as the flames struck it into life. Its puff of white smoke was still rising in the war sign of the Wallowa when I turned to Yellow Wolf.

"*Uako ues timine*," I said to him. "I will go with you."

Together we made our proud way across the camp. The Indians stood back for us, touching their fingers to their foreheads in respect as we passed by. Only one of them did not do that. She was a fine-looking woman of middle age, straight and graceful as a mountain fir. As we went by her, she said to me, "You fool! you fool!" and spat in my moccasin tracks behind me. I did not look at her; I could not.

It was Takialakin, the Antelope, my mother.

15. One Hundred Horse Soldiers

We reached White Bird's camp at sunrise. All was quiet there. It did not seem like a camp that expected to fight soldiers that day. Only White Bird and a few of his friends—old Toohoolhoolzote was there—were up and out of their tipis. They were squatted around the breakfast fire in front of White Bird's lodge waiting for White Bird's women to get the fresh-boiled kouse and elk liver ready to eat.

When we rode up, some of the fighting Indians looked at us pretty unfriendly. These were mostly White Bird Indians. But old Toohoolhoolzote knew Joseph better than they did.

"Well, Heinmot," said the old man, pleased. "I see you have decided to be a true son to your father."

"I am here," was all Joseph said, and did not move to get down off his horse.

Ollikut was another matter. He stepped down from his pony and walked over to White Bird.

"I am here, too," he said, "and I don't like what I see. What is the trouble here? Why are you not ready to fight? What are your horses doing out there on the hills? Last night your rider told us there would be a big fight here today, two hundred soldiers coming up the Kahmuenem, a real chance to ride and shoot. What has happened since last night?"

"A very good thing has happened since last night," replied White Bird. "Seeskoomkee is here."

At once Ollikut's handsome face grew stern.

"Seeskoomkee?" he said. "Why is he here? What does he want? I don't trust that *neksep*. Where is he?"

Neksep was the word for foreigner in our tongue, and we all knew why Ollikut used it on Seeskoomkee.

Seeskoomkee was not a Nez Perce, though his name was Nez Perce and meant No Feet. He was a California Indian who had been sold into the treaty Nez Perce bands as a slave. Ollikut distrusted him not because he was a foreigner or a slave but because he worked for the white man at Lapwai. And the rest of us were just as suspicious of him as was our chief's young brother. So we waited, still not getting off our horses, until we should have White Bird's answer.

"He is here, as I said," replied the latter, after giving Ollikut hard look for hard look. "He is resting in my tipi, getting a little sleep. He rode all night."

"From where?" said Ollikut.

"Lapwai."

"What does that mean?"

"Let him tell you. He was the one who saw it. Come out, Seeskoomkee. Ollikut is here and does not trust you."

There was a stir in the tipi and the slave Indian hobbled out. I winced, as I always did when I saw him.

All his toes, both heels and a good part of the foreflesh of both his feet were gone. They had fallen off from freezing. No Feet was also an evil-looking person in his face and body. He moved back-hunched like a crippled weasel, his mouth twisted into a snarl by the pain and effort it took him to get about.

While I did not know him even well enough to nod or exchange hand signs, I did not have to be told he was a *cultis*, no good, Indian. It is strange how much a boy knows when he is seventeen and how little a man has learned when he is seventy.

When Ollikut now challenged No Feet as to his reason for riding all night from Lapwai, the slave Indian answered him in a voice as unafraid as any war chief's.

"There is only one reason I am here," he told Ollikut. "The white man treats me like a dog. The Indians at Lapwai treat me like a packhorse. You treat me like a man."

"There must be more," said Ollikut.

"Yes, there is. In all the times I have visited the wild bands I have never heard the word *asueleye*. No nontreaty Indian has ever called me slave. Look at me. My feet are twisted, my body turns like the back of a snake run over by a wagon wheel. But I have pride. I am a man. Nothing else matters to me."

Ollikut gravely nodded his understanding of that.

"What then?" he said.

"When I heard that you were in trouble, that One Hand was going to drive you in, my heart was glad because I knew I could help you."

"Yes?" said Ollikut. "How is that?"

"This way," said No Feet. "All spring I have worked as a packer with One Hand's supply mules. I have seen much, forgotten little. When I saw what I saw yesterday at Lapwai, I knew it was time to ride out here and help you people."

Joseph now got down from his horse and came forward. "There is much danger for us all in this time," he told Seeskoomkee, "but I believe you. I will listen to you."

"Yes," said White Bird, getting up and motioning to the rest of us still on our horses, "those are good words. All of you get down and come to the fire. There is food enough for everyone. While we eat, this Indian can tell you Wallowas what he has already told us. You will see then why I say there is no hurry."

It had been a hard ride over the mountain in the dark. We were glad to get down and join the breakfast circle. But while they were still passing the food No Feet began to talk, and in a few seconds we were not hungry at all.

It has occurred to me many times since, that Otskai was not the only crazy Indian among the nontreaty Nez Perce. Consider

White Bird's present advice to be calm. Think about it as I was forced to think about it, a boy seventeen years old, a boy who had never fired a gun in anger at the enemy. A boy who had only an old Springfield soldier musket, which sometimes went off and sometimes did not go off, when the trigger was pressed. Listen in that way to what Seeskoomkee had to say about the soldiers at Lapwai. And think, at the same time, about old White Bird sitting there dipping up kouse with his fingers and telling us there was no need for hurry.

At four o'clock in the afternoon of the day before, a white settler from Mount Idaho had galloped into Lapwai with the news of the second Salmon River raids. In three and one-half hours from that time, One Hand Howard had ordered one hundred soldiers to take the trail. At dusk they had started toward our old camp at Tolo Lake. Each soldier had cooked food for three days in his pack. He had forty rounds of ammunition in his bullet belt. There were five heavily loaded pack mules going along with them carrying more food and more ammunition. Seeskoomkee even knew the companies and the officers. They were Company F and H of the First Cavalry, and the officers were Captain Perry and Captain Trimble and Lieutenant Theller and Lieutenant Parnell. It is funny how a man remembers things which mean little to him. What difference to us Nez Perce that one white man was named this and one named that? Yet perhaps it is not so strange. When you look at a man through a rifle sight, his face stays in your mind.

But there was even more to No Feet's news. Two other companies of cavalry soldiers were coming from the new camp which One Hand had sneaked in behind our backs while we talked peace to him in Lapwai. There were also many foot soldiers coming on a big fireboat up the river from the fort at Walla Walla. More foot soldiers had been sent for from as far off as Fort Vancouver. *Eeh!* The trouble was all around us. No Feet could tell us nothing more than he had up to this point, but what he had told us was already enough. This time One Hand Howard was not going to show us the rifle, he was going to shoot us with it.

Ollikut was on his feet and moving for his horse even before Seeskoomkee got the last word well out. Yellow Wolf was directly behind him, and I was directly behind Yellow Wolf.

Others of our Wallowa fighters stopped eating to come with us, but Ollikut waved them back.

"Heyets and Yellow Wolf are all I want," he said quickly. "The rest of you stay with Joseph and do as Joseph says to do. Don't follow us. We have a risky way to ride and small numbers travel with the least dust. *Taz alago,* be careful. We will return tonight."

That was all of it. Ollikut never was a talker like Joseph. The next moment we were up on our horses and running them north and west toward the rocky badlands of the Lapwai plateau. It was still but a little after sunrise. There was plenty of time to find what we were looking for, even in such a rough and many-canyoned place. It is not easy to hide one hundred horse soldiers and five pack mules from three Nez Perce scouts.

We found the soldiers about the time the sun was straight above us. We tied our horses downwind, where they would not get the scent of the soldier horses and whinny to them, and we went on in close to the trail and hid beside it to study the soldiers when they passed by.

We lay so close to them in the narrow place Ollikut had chosen that I could see a mole on the nose of Captain Perry and could count the buckle holes of his horse's bridle.

Those soldiers were scared. A man could not miss that. They were not talking much and only two or three of them in the whole line laughed. All of them were watching the country all around, keeping their eyes high up in the rocks on either side of the trail, looking for Nez Perces. They were not smoking as they rode and Ollikut, who had spent much time down at their fort at Walla Walla when he was a boy, and knew a great deal about soldier ways, whispered to us that this was a sure sign that they were on war orders. For one, I didn't care what their orders were. I knew they were scared plenty to be out there looking for Joseph's people and that made me very proud.

When they had gone by, we got our horses and hung onto those soldiers all day long. They never quit riding. At Tolo Lake they only rested their horses, then went on east, toward Grangeville. In the late afternoon it came on to rain heavy. It got a little cold, too. By dark they were at Grangeville, sixty-five miles from Lapwai. The trail had been mud to a horse's fetlock the last ten miles. Those soldiers and their horses were tired; we thought surely they would stop at Grangeville. But Ollikut shook his head and said to us, "They don't think the same way we do. One of us will sneak in on the town and make sure. It will be you, Hemene. Be careful."

Yellow Wolf left his horse with us, going off into the night on foot. The rain drove down as though it were angry with us. We couldn't see Yellow Wolf after the first three steps.

We were waiting in an old hayshed. It had only two walls and a piece of roof left, but it was better than standing out in that settler field at the edge of Grangeville and drowning. After a little, I thought to talk with Ollikut and see what he thought of the way ahead for our people.

"I don't want to talk about it, Heyets," he said, when I had asked him.

"Why not, my chief?"

"You saw the soldiers. Seeskoomkee was not lying. They are coming to kill us."

"How are you so sure?"

"That is why they are frightened. They know they are going to fight."

"I thought you wanted to fight," I said.

"I don't know now," he answered. "I don't feel happy. I don't like to see men frightened like those soldiers."

"Why?"

"Because they are frightened of me, and it makes me think something is wrong with me. It makes me feel like a bad man. I don't want to kill those soldiers. Why won't they leave us alone?"

"I don't know, my chief," I said, and let the talk go. Ollikut was strange in his way. He was a lonely man. He thought a great deal but he did not have Joseph's mind-power. He could not answer his own thoughts and it made him uneasy. I think that's what made him such a great fighter, being uneasy like that, like an animal.

The rain helped cover up the quiet that grew between us, and I was glad. After a long while I felt a hand shaking me by the shoulder and it was Yellow Wolf and he was back from his scout of the soldiers at Grangeville. He had been very lucky, being able to get close in under such a rain. He said he had stood only a few feet behind some treaty scouts from Lapwai, who were with Perry, and they had thought he was one of them.

His news excited us. The white people in Grangeville had refused to let the soldiers sleep there. They had insisted they go on and take the White Bird camp by surprise. They were going to go with Captain Perry and show him where the camp was. Yellow Wolf had heard Captain Perry say they would rest until nine o'clock, then march on. That way they could be in position to attack our camp at daylight, and we would be beaten before we could get out of our beds.

"Do you think they will do it? Will go on tonight?" Ollikut said doubtfully.

"That's one thing," answered Yellow Wolf, "we won't have to think about."

"What do you mean?"

"I mean they have already gone on. They are riding this minute. And guess who their main scout is."

"Some Indian you mean?"

"No Indian. Narrow Eye Chapman."

"That's bad."

"Yes. I had my rifle on him in the dark. I thought to kill him—we were not four barrel lengths apart—but then I worried that they might shoot me, too, and you wouldn't know about those soldiers riding on."

"You will make a warrior," said Ollikut. "Let's go."

"I am already a warrior," said Yellow Wolf, "and I am already gone." He hit his horse with the butt of his rifle. Ollikut grunted something in reply to him, and jumped his horse, too. Neither of them said anything to me nor made any move to wait for me. I scrambled after them through the mud and rain, understanding their treatment of me and accepting it. I had a little way yet to ride before I could count myself out loud in the company of such as Ollikut, the Frog, and Hemene Moxmox, the Yellow Wolf.

Three hours later the rain had thinned away and the stars were out. We three Nez Perces were sitting our horses on a rocky ridge, high above White Bird's sleeping village. A few hundred feet below us, uncertainly seen through the patchy wisps of rain fog hanging to the hillside, Captain Perry was moving his horse soldiers into line at the crest of a steep slope which plunged downward three miles to the banks of White Bird Creek and the first of the Nez Perce tipis. We could not make out how many of the settlers from Grangeville had come with the soldiers, nor could we wait for the summer daylight to see. When that daylight came, those soldiers and those settlers would be firing into our tipis down there on the creek, and it would be a little late in the morning for sitting up on our hillside counting their rifle flashes.

The same thought was in the mind of Ollikut.

"Come on," he said softly to Yellow Wolf. "Let us go down and tell the people."

"Yes," said my dark-faced uncle, "there is particularly something I want to tell that old fool, White Bird."

"What is that, uncle?" I asked him, turning my pony after theirs, and asking the question mostly to remind them Heyets was along with them.

"I want to tell him there is no need to hurry. I want to see him trying to put his pants on with one hand and fire his Winchester with the other, when those soldiers come down off that hill to-morrow morning. I want to tell him to take his time when Narrow Eye Chapman is fanning his shirttail with the wind from that five-hundred-yard buffalo gun of his. You think that's a good idea?"

"Very good," I agreed. "I would like to go with you when you tell him. All right?"

"All right," said my uncle. "Now shut up. You talk too much."

"It will be light in a little while," said Ollikut, looking toward the east.

"Yes," nodded Yellow Wolf, "and a very warm day, one with little wind, I think."

"Very little," said Ollikut. "A good day for long shooting. How do you feel, Hemene?"

"Strong. And you?"

"*Uakos titokan,*" answered Ollikut. "Big as a giant."

16. Valley of the White Bird

We got down the hill into our camp just a little after the middle of the night. There was a little excitement at first, then Ollikut and the main fighting men held a council and talked everything out straight in a very short while. There was no confusion as some have said; never believe that. Toohoolhoolzote and White Bird kept quiet and Joseph was not even there. He had sent Ollikut to do his talking for him, and he said he would abide by what his brother thought best.

In this regard Ollikut had some ideas. He said he thought it would be wise to go slow in the first moving up. With soldiers you never knew whether they wanted to fight or parley. He thought these soldiers had been sent out to fight but had lost their heart for pushing us too much. Therefore, he suggested, it might be a good thing to send out four or five Indians with a white flag first thing in the morning to see what Captain Perry really wanted to do. It might be that we could get out of a fight here, where we had so few men, and save ourselves for a later time when there would be either not so many of them or more of us. What did the others think of that?

Old Fire Body answered at once and said he did not think much of it. What had happened? The last thing he had heard, it was all agreed that we were to fight.

Ollikut only nodded carefully. "Exactly what we said, yes. But now there could be as many as two hundred white men,

with good guns and plenty of bullets, up there on that mountain, and because I have had no whiskey my heart is not as big
as yours."

"Bah! I will kill the first one of them. And I have not had any
whiskey, only a little, only two cups full."

"Shut up, you old fool," said Two Moons. "Ollikut is right,
and it was four cups full you had. If you take one more we won't
even let you go out with us in the morning. Go ahead, Ollikut.
You counted their horses, you saw what kind of guns they had.
What do you say to do?"

"I say be careful. Move out slow. Send some men with a truce
rag on a stick. Follow behind them on both sides of the valley,
out of sight, dividing your guns the best you can. The thing to
do is to let them come down into the valley. You know how that
land is over there where they must come down. There is that
draw they will follow off the mountain, then nothing but rolling
grass, not too steep, and only small rocks to hide behind."

"Well, yes. Of course there are the two big rocks."

Two Moons was talking about the twin buttes of White Bird
Valley, sitting between our camp and the soldiers.

"Of course," agreed Ollikut, "and that is good. We can keep
them between us and the soldiers as we go forward behind our
men with the white flag. What do you say?"

"I say I don't understand all this," broke in White Bird. "In the
old days we just rode out and had a fight. We didn't need any
plans."

"Yes, and besides," said his friend Toohoolhoolzote, "who ever
pays any attention to a plan? Plans are no good. I will fight by
myself."

Ollikut touched his forehead. "Do what you wish, old friend
of my father," he said politely. "And you also, White Bird. Who
could tell such warriors how to fight?"

The old chiefs liked that and there was no more heard from
them. I thought to myself that this was the first touch of Joseph's
cleverness I had seen in his brother, but I was wrong. Ollikut
was not meaning to be clever. He knew those leathery old fighting men from the bygone days. Ollikut was thirty-three. He

knew several things I did not. I could not imagine that one man sixty-eight years old and one man more than seventy years old ought still, in all honesty, to be called warriors. But years are funny things. Some men are old at thirty, some young at eighty. It is a thing of the spirit. White Bird and Toohoolhoolzote were warriors. They had the spirit. And they were not fools. They knew Ollikut meant what he said. Two Moons knew it also. I was the only one foolish enough to feel sorry for the old chiefs.

I was given little time to suffer my ignorance. Tipyahlanah Kapskaps, Strong Eagle, a young man of great strength and fiery manner, stepped out to talk. "I have yet to make my reputation in war," he said, "but it seems to me that everybody is saying a different thing here. We will fight, we will not fight. We will go slow, we will go fast. We will all go together, we will all do what we like. Will one of you kindly tell me what it is that we will do?"

"What do you want to do?" asked Two Moons quickly.

"I want to fight. My friends and I, we want to fight."

As he said that, Wahlitits and Red Moccasin Tops stepped up and stood with him. It was the first I had noticed that the three of them had on gorgeous red blanket coats of identical kind. They made a thrilling sight standing there in the firelight with their dark eyes glittering and the dull metal of their rifles gleaming in their hands. I began to get that warm feeling in my belly and that shakiness in my lower legs. All of a sudden I was very excited about how Two Moons would answer Strong Eagle's reply.

"Well," he said, grinning now like a man very pleased with what is in his mind, "if you want to fight, go with me in the morning. If you want to talk, go with those who will ride out with the white flag. If you want to wait and see what will happen, follow Ollikut. Does that sound all right to you?"

"Yes," said Strong Eagle, "that sounds good. Or we may go by ourselves, we may not follow anybody, we may just ride out as the three red blankets."

"Then we are agreed," announced Ollikut, standing up.

"On what?" asked Two Moons.

"We will send out a white flag."

"Yes, we are agreed on that."

"It's the best way," said Ollikut. "If we can get out of a big fight here, it will be better."

"Yes," nodded Two Moons. "Or, if we can't, we will all fight. We will all kill as many soldiers as we can."

"Good," said Ollikut. "Now we had better go and bring in the horses we want and tie them by our tipis. Make sure, too, that all your friends with rifles are with us when we ride out in the morning. *Pinimse eleuz,* sleep light, my chiefs."

The council was over. Everyone got up and went away quickly. All were satisfied. All understood the plan. To a white man listening in the dark outside the fire's light it might have sounded as though we did not know what we were going to do, but we did. It was the Nez Perce way, much superior to white arguing. We were going to do exactly what we wanted to do, each of us. On that we were completely agreed. There was no confusion at all.

Even so, I could not sleep. After a time of trying, I left my blanket to wander through the camp. This would be the first time I had faced a soldier with a gun in my hand. I needed some reassurance. It would be a good thing to go about the camp and see how the older men were carrying out the war rules, how they were following the Nez Perce laws to ready themselves for combat. As I went along, I thought of the main things we did before a fight, those warrior rules which were so proud a part of our tradition and in which we were so much wiser than the white man.

First there was the matter of clothing. Before a big fight the Nez Perce always stripped to his loincloth. Bare flesh took a clean hole. Cloth on the body over the skin was driven into the body by the bullet and made a dirty hole. That was a simple fact. Then there was the matter of food. No Nez Perce ate before a battle. An empty belly punctured clean. A full one burst like a rotten melon and let a man's life out on the ground with his guts. That, too, was a simple fact. The third thing was more difficult, and so more necessary even, than the others. It was

about women. About lying up with them, that is, the night before a fight. The Nez Perce never did this. Lying with a woman
made the thighs weak, and took away much strength from the
loins and other body muscles. Yes, of the three main laws, it
was surely the most important, and the most sternly observed.

So it was that I wandered the camp that night to learn the
proud ways of our people before a fight. And so it was, indeed,
that I learned them.

Moving quietly so as not to intrude a boy's awkward lack of
battle knowledge on his elders, I came along, unseen, to the side
of Fire Body's tipi. There was the old man sitting by a little fire
with his woman roasting elk meat and eating of it as though it
were a moon ago and we were all happy beside the Wallowa. Going on, I came to the fire of Chuslum Moxmox, Yellow Bull, an
important warrior. There he slept on the ground with his rifle in
his hand and his horse standing on tether over him, and yet he
was not war-dressed in any way. There he was all ready to fight
and he had not even taken off his pants!

I went on. I felt bad but it would be all right. I would go now
and see Two Moons. He would straighten out this confusion.
He was the next in leadership to Ollikut and, although he drank
too much whiskey, he was a real warrior. He would make my
mind right.

But when I came to the tipi of Two Moons I stopped very
suddenly; I moved back into the shadows and stood very still.
It was a warm night. The sideskins of Two Moons' tipi were
rolled up to let in the air. Unhappily, they let in my eyes as well.
He and his woman were moving together on the same sleeping
robe in there. They were groaning and panting hard. I knew
what they were doing there and went away quickly.

I tried my best to put out of my mind what I had seen and
heard. Yet I could not. Either my people were not so proud as I
had been taught to believe or they did not honestly think there
would be a fight tomorrow. A long time later, back at my bed-
ding spot, I was still puzzling over the matter when a noble form
loomed through the dark and Ollikut said softly, "*Paize*, Heyets,
kusem. I have work for you to do. Come along." Then, even

more softly in his deep voice, "I am glad to see that *you* know how to behave like a warrior; I am glad to see that you are ready."

How I loved Ollikut in that moment! What pride he gave me! What shame he put on the others! I never knew that man to do or say a wrong thing. Others talked. He *did*.

"Yes, my chief," I said, getting up and pulling my pony's tether rope from its peg, "what is it you would have this Nez Perce do for his people?"

Quickly then he told me. With Swan Necklace and four other youths of my age, I was to go up to a lookout place which Swan Necklace knew about, and which gave a long view of all the land between our camp and the place where the soldiers waited on the high ridge above the creek. We were to send one of our number back down the hill at the first move from the enemy. Then we were to continue sending down a rider every few minutes until the soldiers were far enough down into the valley so that our warriors, hidden on both sides of it, could see them for themselves. Swan Necklace was to be our leader but I was named second to him.

It was a little while after that when we six boys started up the hill. The sky was beginning to gray a little in the east. By another little while it was getting pink. Then the top rocks above the hiding place of the soldiers over on the western ridge grew rosy with the dawn. A few minutes after that we saw five officers, a scout and a bugle soldier ride out and look down the long slope to our village. I knew the scout and I said to Swan Necklace, "*Eeh*, that's Narrow Eye Chapman." He said back to me, "Yes, send down the first rider to Ollikut." In that quiet, easy way the Battle of White Bird Canyon began to move.

The one hundred horse soldiers came down the hill. We watched them, our hearts pounding. The first thing we saw was that there were only a few white men from Grangeville with the soldiers. There were not a hundred or half a hundred. There were only eleven of them. Eleven and Narrow Eye Chapman. Down the hill to Ollikut went our second rider.

We watched the rider until he reached our people below us, wanting to see their happiness when they heard about those soldiers being all alone except for a few men from Grangeville. We knew this would make a difference to the Indians down there. The moment our second rider got down there, things began to move.

Ollikut and Two Moons had been gathering to the north of the village and, after the Indian way, were starting to make talk about what they should do today; as against what they had agreed to do last night.

But when our second rider came up to them, all doubt was put away. At once we saw Ollikut, with about twenty men, dash toward the western butte. Two Moons, with fifteen men, galloped toward our butte, the eastern one, taking up his position right below us. We could see his party well enough to call names and faces. We saw old Otstotpoo, old Fire Body, for one, and we laughed. What did that old fool think he was going to do? He was full of elk meat and whiskey and flatus. Was he going to blow the soldiers down? That was my question and my friends all laughed at me and I thought I was pretty funny. But there were others with Two Moons who were not jokes. He had most of the "bad boys" with him. The bad boys were the ones the chief warriors like Ollikut could not control. For instance, we saw the three red blankets with Two Moons, and we thought of the council last night and of Two Moons saying to Strong Eagle, "if you want to fight, go with me." We knew, right then, when we saw those three bright blankets burning in the morning sun below, that there was going to be a fight today whether Ollikut wanted one or not.

Now our eyes went back to the soldiers. They were about a third of the way down the hill. They had got down the steep part, down the draw which let onto the broad grassy slope of the creek valley. Now they had less than two miles to go before they would be in our tipis. And the ground was much better. They began to trot their horses, forming up their lines.

"*Inayiaza,*" said Swan Necklace sharply. "Send the third rider."

In a few minutes now the soldiers would be out where Two Moons could see them from the eastern butte. They came on, holding their horses four abreast, one-half of them coming ahead of the other half, with a space of ground between the two bands. As we watched, Ad Chapman and his eleven settlers separated from the soldiers and started over to the east, over toward Two Moons and toward us, riding to get where he could look down the valley around the bow of the big ridge and see the village which he knew to be around the bend of the creek and the mountain. "*Koiimze!*" ordered Swan Necklace to the fourth rider, and away he went, sliding his pony down the trail to warn Two Moons that Narrow Eye was coming his way.

Now the soldiers were only one mile from the village. They were out in the broad place of the valley. An officer and eight men started around the eastern butte. It looked as though they did this because Narrow Eye had lost his nerve and led his eleven men back toward the main soldiers, the ones which were coming cautiously with Captain Perry around the bow of the mountain where Ollikut waited for them behind the western butte. Those eight soldiers were pretty brave to ride out alone like that. They were a lot braver than Narrow Eye and the white men with him. But we no sooner thought that than Narrow Eye came galloping back up to be with the officer who was leading the eight brave men, and we knew that it was not Narrow Eye but only the cowards from Grangeville who had grown weak in their hearts. We felt better after that, for we never had thought Narrow Eye was a coward.

Suddenly many things began to go on below us. We saw Ollikut send a blanket signal across the valley toward our side, and saw Two Moons answer it. A moment later our five-man band rode out from our eastern butte with the white flag. Their leader was a good fighter. He was one of the bad boys. His name was Wettiwetti Houlis, which meant Mean Person, and I thought it very strange that Two Moons would send such a one out to talk peace with a white flag.

"Listen," I said to Swan Necklace, "do you see who they are sending out to talk to Narrow Eye and those eight soldiers?"

And he said back to me, "Yes, and I don't like it. We had better get out of here. There is going to be trouble right away."

Down in the valley Indians were beginning to move everywhere. Some were leaving Two Moons to go over and be with Ollikut—we saw the three red blankets dash across the creek away from Two Moons—and others were leaving Ollikut's side to come over on our side. That was a sure sign. Indians always did a lot of riding back and forth, crisscrossing like that, just before a fight.

"All right," I answered my companion, "let's go."

We went for our horses. Just as we got them to the head of the trail to start down, we heard two shots. Looking toward the soldiers we could see the smoke still rising from the place where Narrow Eye Chapman sat his horse ahead of the eight brave soldiers. He still had his gun to his shoulder and we could not believe what he had done. But it was true; our eyes did not lie. Below us the Indians with the white flag were racing their horses back toward us. One of them was riding knee-and-knee with another, and he was holding the other one up on his horse. Out on the grass behind them lay the white flag where it had fallen when Chapman shot the Indian who was carrying it.

As we watched, motionless for one breath, we saw a third puff of rifle smoke rise up. But this was from an Indian gun, answering Chapman. And away out across that open grass, a long, long way out across it, we saw the bugle soldier who was riding with Chapman and the brave officer and his eight men, throw up his arms and slide off his horse. It was so still in that moment that, from our high place above it all, we could distinctly hear the distant tiny sound of his trumpet clanging among the rocks where he flung it in his death fall. And it was a death fall. There is something about the way a man goes off a horse that tells you such things. I had never seen it, yet I knew it. In the same breath Swan Necklace, who had seen these things, and not long ago, was saying to me, "*Koiimze*, my brother, we had better hurry. That man is dead. And did you see who shot him? Did you see who it was that made that quarter-mile killing?"

"No," I answered, "who was it?"

"Your friend full of elk meat," he said. "Old Otstotpoo. He said he would do it, that he would kill the first soldier, and he has done it. *Eeh!*"

I looked up the valley toward the other horse soldiers.

"He has done a little more than kill a soldier with that shot," I said, my words as tight as the drawing of my belly within me.

"Eh?" said my friend. "What is that?"

"He has started a war with it," I answered him, and kicked my pony away from there and down the rock-ledge trail to the floor of White Bird Valley.

Two rifleshots up the valley from our twin buttes, the main soldier chief, Captain Perry, got his men down off their horses and behind what rocks he could find for them. The horses he sent back to his rear with ten men to hold them. Out in front of him Lieutenant Theller, the brave one—we got all the names from Seeskoomkee, who was with Ollikut—had his men down off their horses, too. But it was a little different for him. We could reach him with our guns. Yet we were waiting a little while to see how it was all going. In the quiet, which went on for perhaps ten minutes, I rode over to be with Ollikut. Many more men were with him by then.

Now all around me Indians were finally stripping for battle, finally getting their clothes off so the wounds would be clean. Only the three red blankets refused to do this. They kept on their bright coats to show their great courage. But the others, even Ollikut, were naked; save for loincloths, moccasins, cartridge belts and war charms hung around wrist, arm, neck or belly.

The soldiers did not keep them waiting. Over toward Two Moons' side Captain Perry sent Narrow Eye and his eleven cowards from Grangeville to lay up in a strong nest of rocks where they could fire into the Indians behind the east butte. He thought those settlers were fine shots and would drive those Indians out of there. But Two Moons knew of a shallow draw which went out around that rock nest. Up that draw he went on the gallop with his fifteen bad boys. They burst out on the flank of those Grangeville whites, riding their horses right up into the rocks, yelling and firing straight into the men's faces. They shot two of them bad and three or four more not so bad. The others got on their horses and ran away. Two of our scouts followed them all the way to Grangeville. They told us those white men did not get out of a gallop until they were home.

When the settlers ran away on the soldiers' left side, we struck at them from the right. The three red blankets gave a yell and led the attack. Behind them came Ollikut and the rest of us, half a hundred or more, with about twenty-five guns and the same number of bows and arrows. Out from behind our western butte we charged, straight into the main soldier line.

Seeskoomkee yelled to Ollikut that it was Captain Trimble there ahead of us. By that time Joseph's young brother would not have cared if it was General Howard himself. His *simikia* was on fire. He wanted blood. And he got it. We all did.

Trimble's men were still on their horses, not afoot like Captain Perry's men in the middle of the line. The sight and sound of those fifty wild Nez Perce Indians running their horses over those rocks and draws like antelope, firing their rifles one-handed and yelling their war cries as they came, was too much for those soldier horses. They began to buck and pitch and scream in fright, and their riders were thrown off, dragged, kicked or stomped into the ground. Before a single Nez Perce pony cleared the last gully and rode into them, those soldiers were beaten. It was like a buffalo shoot; short, hard run, with much dust and yelling. One heard firing and cries of stricken, dying things. There was a swirling drift and stink of powder smoke in the nostrils; blood and the hot, squirting bowel movements of terrified horses. Then came a big and sudden quiet, a standing still of mounts and men all over the field, while the smoke and the dust still lifted and the wounded cried for water or for death, and the dead cried for nothing.

Over on Two Moons' side eighteen soldiers, including the brave Lieutenant Theller, lay dead in a rock hole where they were trapped and shot out like cornered coyotes. On our side, on the right, fifteen soldiers were dead, most of them shot out of Captain Perry's middle band fleeing on foot for their horses when Captain Trimble's horses stampeded. In all we killed thirty-three soldiers. They wounded two of us Nez Perces. From the time I crossed over to be with Ollikut—better say from the time the three red blankets yelled, "Let's go!" and jumped their horses out from behind the western butte to charge Trimble—five minutes had passed. It took me longer to ride across the creek from Two Moons to Ollikut than it did for us to kill those thirty-three horse soldiers from Lapwai.

It was still only sunrise when we killed those soldiers. The day was the seventeenth one of June in the summer of 1877; a very hot day with little wind. The place where we did it was called Lahmotta, the valley of the White Bird Canyon.

17. Redbeard Remembers

For a day or two we sat there wondering what to do, never touching the soldiers' bodies. From Lapwai had come some news which confused us; One Hand was still waiting there for more soldiers. He had sent to all the military posts—to Walla Walla, Stevens, Vancouver, Canby, Townsend, Klamath, even to Harney—ordering extra soldiers. Captain Whipple, who had started after us from his Wallowa camp, was told to turn around and come to One Hand at Lapwai. Some cannon soldiers coming home on a boat from Alaska were stopped and sent to Lapwai. Soldiers were sent from San Francisco. We could not understand this. Why was One Hand afraid of us? He already had four hundred men to fight with. We had sixty-five. Maybe seventy. *Eeh!* We began to tell ourselves that one more good fight—the one we would have with him when he got up his nerve to come out of Lapwai—and our war with Agent Monteith and General One Hand Howard would be over.

Our hearts grew very glad and very big, but Joseph talked against us. He said One Hand was not afraid; he was only smart. He said to go slow, to be careful, but by then we were not listening to him as we had before. In the big fight Joseph had not fired a shot. He had stayed back at the camp in charge of the old men who were to protect the women and children if the horse soldiers broke through us warriors at the buttes. That had weakened his name. None of the fighters said anything a white man would call hard. They only looked at one another and said, "Well, he is not like his father," and in an Indian way that was all that needed to be said. So the advice of Joseph was not taken from that camp forward. Toohoolhoolzote and White Bird were the chiefs in his place, and they just sat and waited for One Hand to come after us.

On the fifth day we heard he was coming. He was going toward Tolo Lake with four hundred men and one hundred scouts and settlers. They had many mules, much equipment, and were moving pretty fast. We got nervous. Toohoolhoolzote said, "Let's move up the river a little ways," and White Bird said, "Yes. Let's go up and camp at Horseshoe Bend."

So we went up the Salmon some miles to a place where there was a loop in the water like a horse's iron shoe, and there we camped, still pretty nervous.

The truth was, Ollikut told Yellow Wolf and me, that both White Bird and Toohoolhoolzote were getting too well on in their years. They could still fight but it took them too long to decide things. Some of the young men had come to him, Ollikut, asking that he make the decisions without saying anything to the old chiefs. He had agreed and he had come to ask Yellow Wolf and me if we would go out and find One Hand for him, so that he would know how to advise the young men.

We set out at once and had no trouble, reporting back to Ollikut on the seventh night. One Hand was at White Bird battlefield, we told him, burying the dead soldiers. We had caught one of his scouts, who was an old friend of mine. It was Redbeard, who had held his dirty hand over my mouth that day at Kamiah Crossing when he had caught me in the river bushes. Yellow Wolf and I had made a little talk with Redbeard, reminding him of those good old times. We had talked pretty hard to him. Not that he wouldn't be well by the next summer. Just a tap, here and there, with Yellow Wolf's rifle butt to jar loose his memory. It worked. He talked back to us. One Hand was

going to the Salmon River from Tolo Lake. He was going to
come up the Salmon on the east bank to try and cut the Nez
Perces off from going over the Clearwater and getting on the old
Lolo Trail out of the Idaho country, over into Montana.

Ollikut had some news for us, too. While we had been away
Rainbow and Five Wounds, surely two of our most famous warriors, had come back from the buffalo country to join up with
us. Even Yellow Wolf was impressed. Wahchumyus and Pahkatos Owyeen—those were their Indian names—had reputations
among the Nez Perce to equal such as Hump, Gall and Crazy
Horse among the Sioux. Yellow Wolf and I had never seen these
two, and so we were very eager about going along with Ollikut
to hear how they would advise taking care of One Hand
Howard.

Like most great fighters, Rainbow and Five Wounds were
simple men. They had a simple idea for humbling General Howard and for taking the spirit out of his four hundred new men.
"Listen," they said at once to Ollikut, while Yellow Chief and I
stood by, breath held, "there is really nothing to it; here is the
way it will go. . . ."

That night it came on to rain hard. It had been raining up-
country for three days. The river was beginning to growl. But
to us Indians it was a soft growl, like a dog will give his master
when his ears are being scratched.

Pretty soon General Howard came marching up on the other
side from us. We insulted him. We rode our horses back and
forth, daring his soldiers to come over and get us. One Hand had
been in that country a long time but he had learned nothing of
Indian ways. He ordered his soldiers to cross over the Tahmonmah and attack our village, which lay just out of rifleshot from
his side of the river. We waited until he had half his soldiers on
our side and half on his side. Then we yelled to our women,
"*Teueze inpeze*, take down the lodges!" and they laughed back
and struck the tipis to the last lodgepole, loading all the pack and
travois ponies and driving them out of there, in the space of
thirty minutes.

Thus the plan of Rainbow and Five Wounds began. We simply slipped away down the river on our side, easily keeping ahead of the soldiers in the rain and mud. It was a very bad trail on that Indian side of the Salmon, even in dry weather. It was up and down all the way, cross gullies coming in constantly across the trail, and every gully holding a side creek, now up and foaming with flood water. To us Nez Perce, "half-wolf, half-horse, half-otter," as the white men used to describe us, it was nothing to travel over such land in such weather. To the soldiers from Lapwai, many of them strange to the country and even to soldier life, it was a bad dream. We hung them up on high ridges where they could find no trail to follow us down. We lost them in deep ravines where they had to backtrack to get out again. We took them into steep places where their pack mules could not stay on the narrow ledges. We led them into mud traps where their fat cavalry horses could not pull themselves out. They lost mules, horses, equipment, and even some men sick with coughs from the cold rain. Then, when we had them torn apart—I think it was five days we deviled them—we turned straight for the river again, coming onto it at a deep and dangerous place called Craig's Crossing.

To Indians who had crossed the main Snake at full flood this going over at Craig's Crossing of the Salmon in only moderate high water was nothing. We would take the pack covers from about six horses, stretch them over a few willow sticks, to make bullboats and pile in our women, children and camp goods. We put four strong swimming horses with towing ropes on each boat, and away over the water we would go, safe and dry as ducks. But One Hand was helpless. There was nothing he could do but turn around and go back all the way to Horseshoe Crossing through the mud and rocks of the west bank. While he did this, as indeed Rainbow and Five Wounds had known he must, we packed up our people once again and headed across the clean open going of Camas Prairie.

Our course was now clear. General Howard himself had given us the idea with his fears that we would try to get away into Montana. All the chiefs except Joseph picked up interest. Why not do what One Hand had suggested? In Montana we had no white enemies. The settlers over there had never fought us. The soldiers over there had never shot at us. *Eeh!* Once we lost One Hand and got over to a dry fresh camp on the Clearwater, we could make plans.

It was with these feelings and with this new hope of escape from One Hand Howard and from all those white people in Oregon and Idaho who hated us, that we turned away from the Salmon River at Craig's Crossing in the last days of June. Across Camas Prairie lay Kamiah Crossing, the Lolo Trail and far Montana.

I looked up ahead and saw the rain clouds thinning to the north and east where we were bound; saw the sun making rainbows above the distant hills; looked about me and heard that my people were laughing and talking in the old way again, as they had these three summers gone when we had started up the wild Tahmonmah to see if White Bird and his band would come with us on the great adventure. Perhaps, after all, we were going to the buffalo!

Book Three
The Lolo Trail

18. Where Is Captain Whipple?

We made a last camp before striking the Clearwater. It was on the upper drainage of a small tributary stream. Cottonwood Creek is the name I remember. It was a happy camp. We were all well, we had outwitted One Hand Howard, and we were near our many friends and relatives who had gone with Looking Glass to his village above Kooskia. We were anxious to see our people. I, particularly, was eager to do so. I wanted to talk to my mother. She was heavy with young and I was sure she had not felt herself when she had spit in my tracks that night at Sapache-sap Cave. It was one of those late babies—I had no other brothers or sisters—and she had not been well with it. So my concern could be understood.

Since we were so close, one day only, I consulted with Ollikut as to riding on ahead. I told him I wanted to see my mother before she saw my father, since she was sure to get in a fight with him for leading me out with the Salmon River "bad boys." Ollikut saw the wisdom of this. One of his own two wives was a sister to my mother. He was well acquainted with the family temper.

I tried to get Yellow Wolf to go with me but he was restless. He said he and Rainbow and Five Wounds were going to take a look around. They didn't trust One Hand. There might be some other soldiers on the hunt for us.

"How can that be?" I complained. "He had all of them with him back there on the Salmon. We counted four hundred. That's all he has."

"Is it?" said my uncle. "What about those soldiers of Captain Whipple's who stood behind us with the rifle to make sure we crossed the Snake and came into Lapwai? I saw those soldiers in the Wallowa. I was the one who scouted them for Joseph when he was talking to One Hand at Lapwai, and I remember them."

"Well?"

"Well, I did *not* see them with One Hand back there at the

Salmon. You know why, Heyets? I will tell you. They weren't there."

I nodded, once again impressed with my uncle's fierce cunning. He had only twenty-one summers then, but he had killed four horse soldiers at White Bird and already stood second only to Ollikut in war rank among our Wallowa band.

I felt good to have such a man watching out for me against our enemies. I felt good, too, because I was bound for the big village of the Asotin to see my mother. I got a little smart with Yellow Wolf. I grinned and put my hand on his shoulder, patting him as though he had done a bright thing, and said to him, "Good, good, that's very fine thinking, Hemene. Ollikut was right. You'll make a warrior yet."

His face grew dark. He struck my hand from his shoulder. "You are a fool, Heyets," he said. "You make me feel like a fool. Go and see your mother like a small boy. Be happy. Have a good time."

"Now wait, Hemene . . ." I began, but he would not wait.

"No," he said, "we are done, you and I. When you would not pray with Joseph over those dead horses at the Snake, I thought you had become a man. But you have not. You are seventeen summers, Heyets, and you are still looking for your mother. I am sorry for you."

He left me standing there, more surprised than hurt. This was because he was wrong. There were no other soldiers out looking for us. There would be no more war with One Hand. We were going to get our people who were staying with the Asotin and go live happily in the Land of the Buffalo. Why should I not be lighthearted? Why should I not be pleased that I was going to see my mother again?

I got on my horse and set off across country to strike the Clearwater at the village of Looking Glass. It was a sparkling day after the rains. I whistled to my traveling horse and kicked him in the ribs. He was full of fresh grass and sunshine. We skimmed over the ground like swallows. It was a glorious morning.

I sat on the hill above the river looking down on the village of the Asotin. I had not been there since I was a little boy. I remembered many fences, large fields, fine big barns of logs, houses with wooden walls, all such things. Now they were gone. I saw only three or four little patches of ground, a few ragged fences of split rails, three or four tumble-down sheds, and some gaunt milk cattle wandering among the many cowskin lodges and the five or six tiny log houses of the white man's kind. I knew, though, that nothing had changed. It was just the difference between the way a little boy's eyes remembered things, and the way things really were. Feeling a bit sad, I rode on down the hill and came to the river.

There was a girl there at the crossing—really a young woman —bent to the water's edge, her back to me, scrubbing at some battered old cooking pots. I thought to ask her if she knew which was the lodge of Takialakin, my mother. Riding up, I said, "*Taz meyui*, good morning. Are you of that village, there, across the river?"

She stood up and turned to me.

"Well, Heyets," she said, "don't you know me? I am Takzpul."

"You, Takzpul?" I gasped, and sat there like a stick of wood. I could do no more. In our tongue *takzpul* was the word for beaver, and Beaver was what we used to call Coyote's skinny sister. But Coyote's family had moved to live with the Asotin while I was in the Lapwai school three winters gone and I had seen none of them in that time.

"Of course I am Takzpul," the girl answered me, while I tried to get my mouth shut again. "Do you find me so changed?"

In my mind came questions like "Yes, where are your two big teeth in front?" and "Certainly, what became of all your bony elbows and knobby knees?" and "Of course, what happened to your ribs that used to stick out like those of a Salish pack mule?" but instead I said politely, "Never. I would know you any place. How is your brother? How is my old friend, Itsiyiyi?"

"Coyote is not well. He has been two years in the school at Lapwai and has caught the lung cough. How are you, Heyets?"

"Well," I said, "here I am. What do you say?"

She studied me carefully. Finally she frowned and shook her head.

"Don't worry about it," she said. "You have some time yet. How many summers are you now? Fifteen? Sixteen?"

I looked at her coldly.

'Did you ever hear of Lahmotta?" I asked her.

"I think so," she said. "There was a fight there two weeks ago. Is that what you mean? Where all those soldiers got shot?"

"Yes," I replied proudly. "I was there."

"Is that so? It must have been exciting. Where were you?"

"I said I was there."

"No, I mean what were you doing? Whose horse were you holding?"

"You are very funny," I said. "I shot three of those soldiers myself. One of them died. I was *there*."

"It must have been a good fight," she said. "I heard about Yellow Wolf and Two Moons and the three red blankets and old Fire Body and a few others."

I could see it was no use talking to such a fool.

"Well, *taz alago,*" I nodded, controlling myself. "Tell Coyote I will come and see him soon."

"Thank you," she said. "I will do that. He will be glad to hear it. He loves you like a brother."

I paid no mind to her nice words; they were too late. But in a minute she called after me, "Oh, Heyets, I am sorry—wait a minute!" and of course that was different and I stopped my horse and said, "Yes?" and waited for her to come panting up with her apology.

She stopped her pot-scrubbing and straightened up from the water but she did not come running after me. She only waved and smiled and said, "You didn't answer what I asked you. How many summers was it, fifteen or sixteen?"

I did not answer her. What need to do so? I knew how many summers I was. I knew how many horse soldiers I had shot. I gave her my back and rode on.

In the village I had no trouble finding the tipi of my mother. It was one of the first ones I saw, pitched down by the river. My heart warmed as I saw the familiar elk's head my father had painted over the entry flaps. But when I got up to it, I was afraid to get off my horse, and so I sat outside and called in a low voice.

"*Kaiziyeuyeu*, greetings. Who is here?"

There was no answer from within the lodge. I called again, a little more loudly.

"*Neiz kunu?* Are you in there, my mother?"

Now there was a stir within the lodge and a weak voice made a small sound. Instantly I was off my pony and through the entry flaps.

My mother was lying there, pale and thin. At her breast was a new baby, its ribs showing and its little buttocks blue and pinched. It looked like a young bird, naked from the egg. I dropped to the ground, taking my mother's hand which she held up to me with a smile.

"Well, Heyets," she murmured, "you will excuse me. A mother should be up to greet her son. The truth is I cannot rise without great effort, and I did not know it was you who called me. How is your father? How are you?"

"Mother, my dear mother." I pressed her hand hard. It was not strong as I remembered her hand. "What has happened here, what is the matter?"

"Nothing, nothing. It is the child, your little brother. I have him only four days. I will be up soon. It was a difficult time. He came like a stillborn colt, with his head where his feet should be. Had not Swan Woman been here to help me . . ."

I nodded, grateful that the faithful Swan Woman had not gone with Horse Blanket, her husband, and Yellow Wolf, her son, to the village of White Bird and the battle of Lahmotta. But I knew my mother was lying; I knew she would not be up soon.

"It was a gracious thing that my aunt stayed with you through your time," I said.

"She is of the old ways," said my mother. "She saw it as her duty, as the duty of one sister to another." Her weary face showed doubt. "In many ways," she said, "the old life is better for us. I have tried to see the white man's way, and I have tried to make you see it. Now I don't know. Now I hear they came to kill you in Lahmotta and that many of them died there. It seems to me they killed themselves. Yet blood will cry for blood. I should feel ashamed of you and your father; I should feel that Joseph betrayed us all when he led you away from Sepachesap; I should feel that I did right to spit in your moccasin tracks when you walked by me on your way to war. Yet I am a Nez Perce; I am an Indian. When I heard you had beaten the horse soldiers, when I heard you had taken One Hand and lost him over on the other side of Salmon River, I was not angry, I was not ashamed; I was proud."

"Mother," I said softly, "I am of the same feeling as yourself. I don't know, either, which way is right any more. It is one reason I wanted to come home. I wanted to talk to you. There is a great decision coming for us Nez Perce very soon."

"Yes? How is that?"

"The fighting Indians are in camp over on Cottonwood Creek. Tomorrow they will move down to where the creek joins the Clearwater. Then they will send down here to ask which of the Wallowa and the Asotin will go with them to the Land of the Buffalo."

"To Montana? They are going across the mountains?"

"Yes, Mother. One Hand will be across the Salmon soon. The chiefs do not think we need to fight him again. They say that if we go to Montana where the people do not hate us, there will be no more trouble. We can live as in the old days over there."

My mother looked at me.

"What chiefs say that?" she asked quietly.

I told her which ones they were and she said, "I thought so. What does Joseph say?"

"Nothing," I answered. "I went to him to ask his advice before the fight and he would not give it."

"No," said my mother. "I do not believe that."

"Well," I admitted, "he did say one thing. He said, 'My son, listen to no heart but your own. As it beats, so will you be. As

you are, so will your people remember you.' " I made a movement with my hand, finishing helplessly. "That was his answer,
every word of it."

"And you do not call that advice?" asked my mother.

"I didn't think so then."

"What do you think now?"

"I don't know."

"Did you shoot any soldiers up there?"

"Yes."

"Did you look in their faces after you shot them?"

"Yes."

"How did they look to you?"

"Frightened. Sad. Lonesome."

"Did you look in your heart then?"

"Yes."

"What did you see?"

"Nothing—I saw nothing."

"Nothing, Heyets?"

I hung my head. "I saw Joseph's face," I said.

"Why do you think that was, Heyets? Why do you think you
saw your chief's face when you looked in your heart after you
had shot the soldiers?"

"I don't know, Mother. Do you?"

"I think so. I think it was because you *knew* he did not want
you to listen to Two Moons and the other bad ones. That, instead, he wanted you to think for yourself, to listen to your own
heart; in that way being true to him, your chief, and to us, your
people."

Again I bowed my head.

"I think you are right, Mother," I told her. "Yet, if I did listen
to Two Moons rather than to Joseph, how can I know that I did
wrong?"

"I believe I can answer that also, my son."

"In what way?" I inquired frowningly.

"With a question," she replied softly.

She reached her thin hand for mine and when I took it she

smiled and let the silence grow a long time, and I could see that she was thinking far away. At last she looked up at me and was ready with her answer.

"When many snows have gone, Heyets," she said; "when you and I and the children of our children's children lie deep asleep within our mother earth, what name will be remembered by our people?

"*Will it be Two Moons, my son, or will it be Joseph?*"

19. The Village of Looking Glass

It was quite early when I spoke to Coyote's sister at the crossing. I had delayed overnight on the ride down from the Cottonwood to see if I could not get a fat doe to bring my mother. The liver, eaten raw, was very good for weakness after a loss of blood, such as in a child-bearing. But hunting luck had not been with me. Another kind of luck was with me, though. The Tooats must have given me that idea about the deer liver.

It was now, as I left my mother's tipi to go find my friend Coyote, still only a little after sunrise.

Habits of a lifetime are strange things. When a white man comes out of his house he will always look up at the sky, as though to make sure how the weather will be. When an Indian comes out of his tipi he looks around quickly to make sure no enemies are about. The white man does not realize he does this, nor does the Indian. But they do it, and I did it that early July morning stepping out of my mother's tipi there in the village of Looking Glass, the Asotin.

Without thinking, my eyes roved the country out around that big camp. East, first, into the sun; then swiftly around to the west, away from it. In the last flick of my glance, I saw the wink of that sun strike something familiar to my eye in the riverbottom timber just below the village. Again the habits of a lifetime. An Indian boy learns early to distinguish sun signs. There is a certain way sunlight will gleam on a copper breast ornament, a certain way it will twinkle on glass trade beads, sparkle on silver headbands or bracelets, or glitter from the blade of a buffalo lance. There is also a very certain way it will wink from the worn brown steel of a rifle barrel. Those trees down there below the crossing were full of soldiers.

A terrible thought of guilt took me. Before I had left the camp of my fighting friends on Cottonwood Creek, Joseph had called me to him and charged me with a message to Looking Glass. Do not alarm the other Indians, he had told me, but make the idea clear to Aleemyah that those of his people and of mine who want to go to Montana must leave and come up here at once. Tell them to meet us at Peeta Auüwa, the old campground. We shall be there tomorrow, and so should they who want to go to Montana. "Make that very clear, Heyets," he had said to me in parting. "Yellow Wolf is right when he does not trust One Hand. Tell the people down there not to delay. Each sun is now dangerous to those who think that freedom lies at the end of the Lolo Trail."

At the time I had heard his words with my ears alone. Now I was hearing them with my heart, but it was too late. Looking Glass was surrounded by soldiers and I had put them there by delaying on the trail one full day to get a deer liver for my ailing mother.

What should I do? I could not run, shouting, "Soldiers! soldiers!" through the camp, for the people might panic. Neither could I stand there knowing what I knew. Cautiously I reached for my horse's bridle. The camp was beginning to stir by this time and of a passing old woman I inquired, "Good morning, Grandmother. Which is the lodge of Aleemyah Tatkaneen?"

"*Eeh!*" she said. "I am not your grandmother, homely boy, and that is a good thing from my viewpoint. Nevertheless, that is Aleemyah's lodge over there." She pointed with her head slightly. "The one with the white smoke pouring out the vent. That is that crazy aunt of his. She throws on an armload of *pootoosway* every morning. One would think Aleemyah had the loincloth sickness, or something. That woman is crazy."

I was not interested to learn that Looking Glass's aunt lived with him, or that she had a habit of fumigating his lodge every morning with the wood of the Nez Perce medicine tree. "Thank you, dear little *Nakaz*," I said to her. "May all your grand-daughters miscarry."

"Thank *you!*" she waved after me. "And may your mother be forgiven for delivering you."

At the lodge of Looking Glass I got off my pony as naturally as I might, calling the chief's name in a cheery good-morning way. He came to the entry flap and stared at me in an unfriendly way. "Who are you?" he said.

"Heyets," I answered. "The second nephew of Joseph. I have a message from my chief."

"What message?" he asked, not moving to let me pass him. "Give it and be done."

Looking Glass was a big chief, a warrior of great reputation. He did not like being called out of his lodge so early in the morning by an unknown Wallowa boy. Yet there was no time to be careful with him.

"Joseph said to tell you to get out of here in a hurry if you wanted to go to Montana with the Indians from the Lahmotta fight. But it's too late for that, my chief. The soldiers are already around you."

"What!" he snapped. "Soldiers? Here? What soldiers?"

"The soldiers of Captain Whipple," I said. "The ones from the Wallowa. They are down there in the trees along the river. I saw them just now as I came out of my mother's tipi by the crossing."

"How do you know they are Captain Whipple's soldiers?"

"Yellow Wolf told me."

"*Eeh!* That war talker! He sees soldiers behind every bush."

I glanced behind me, down the village street toward the crossing, very nervous at the delay. What I saw down there sent my hand reaching for my horse's reins.

"Take a look beyond me," I told Looking Glass. "Down to-ward the river. Do you see a man on a horse riding this way? Coming from those trees down there? Does he look like a soldier to you?"

"Yes," said Looking Glass, dark face motionless but black eyes moving swiftly. "It's a two-bar soldier; a captain."

"Do you know him?" I asked.

"Yes," he said. "It's Captain Whipple."

We stood and heard what Captain Whipple said to Looking Glass. Redbeard was along to interpret for the soldiers and when he translated Captain Whipple's words to Looking Glass, saying that he wanted the Asotin chief to surrender at once and without any condition of good treatment or respecting of Indian property, we could not believe our ears. But Captain Whipple meant it. He had been sent up here by General Howard to see that the Asotin did not join the bad Indians who had defeated Captain Perry. General Howard had given him no orders as to good treatment or honoring of Nez Perce property.

We were at once alarmed. For me, personally, it was more immediate than for the others. While Looking Glass was replying to Whipple and while Redbeard was waiting for him to get through his speech, Redbeard turned unexpectedly to me and said in English, "I see you, Indian. Later on we'll have a little parley of our own. Just you and me, eh? You red son of a bitch. I'll learn you to put a knife at my kidneys while your friend belts me with a rifle butt." Before I could think to reply to him —brave words will never come until it is long past time to use them—Looking Glass had finished telling Whipple he would not surrender. Redbeard, who had been cocking one ear to what the Asotin chief said while he himself threatened me, now said fast in English to Captain Whipple, "We'd better back out of here, Cap'n. The blackskinned devil says he won't play. Says you have no right to order him about. He is at peace and his people have not left this village. He says he'll fight if that's what you want."

"You tell him," said Whipple quickly, "that we don't want any fight. Tell him General Howard just wanted to make sure he didn't go to the buffalo with those other Indians. Make it peaceful for God's sake. I don't like the looks of this."

What he was worrying about was all the hard-faced Indians who were coming up to stand around. But Redbeard was one of those white men who made the Indian wars what they were. He really did not fear Indians. He really believed that one good white man could beat any number of Indians in any kind of fighting. A man like this was as dangerous in the white camp as Smoholla in the Indian camp.

"By God," he said to Captain Whipple, "you're not going to let this little polecat bluff you just by throwing up his tail!"

"Tell him what I said," repeated Whipple. "The men are in position by now."

Redbeard turned with a sneer to Looking Glass and told him what Whipple had said. Looking Glass scowled and nodded his head.

"All right," he said. "You tell him we have no idea to go to the buffalo. Tell him Agent Monteith told General Howard a lie when he said we were going to run away to Montana. This is our home. Tell him to look about him here, at our fields and houses and fences. Is he a fool? Can't he see? Can't he think?"

Redbeard said a few words to Captain Whipple and they both climbed on their horses and rode off down the village street toward the river. When they got free of the tipis they turned toward the trees where the soldiers were. The minute they did that a bugle called softly and the waiting soldiers broke from the trees in a great yelling line. Horses neighing and rearing, guns blazing in a wild order of fire, they rode into the village of the Asotin. Those poor Indians had no chance. There were scarcely any warriors among them, since most of the young men were with the fighting band up on Cottonwood Creek. But there were a very great number of women and children and old people, and the fear that spread through them as the horse soldiers rode into the tipis was a frightening thing to watch.

There was no thought to get weapons, food, clothing or camp things. Everything was left. The people sought only to save their lives. The earliness of the hour added to the panic. Many tumbled out of bed naked, not even armed with the decency of clothing. I saw women running without a shred to hide them from the hot eyes of the soldiers. I saw oldsters ridden down as they struggled to get out of the way of the leaping cavalry horses. I saw children knocked spinning. Indian horses broke picket.

Wandering cattle bawled and stampeded through the lodges. The dust was like that raised in a buffalo kill, thick, dirty yellow, choking the throat, blinding the eye, and stinking with the sharp smell of wet manure and horse urine squirting everywhere.

Since I had my horse at hand when the first soldier fired his rifle, I was in better position than most.

My only thought, of course, was for my sick mother. I kicked my pony straight down the middle of the main street. I was perhaps halfway down it when I saw two soldiers coming out of a tipi, dragging a pale young boy by the hair. They had thought he was a girl, for as they came out in the light with him one of them said, "For Christ's sake, Bill, we must need spectacles. This here's a buck!" They threw the boy down and one of them kicked him in the ribs and said, "Get up and run, you little son of a bitch. I need some target practice." The boy struggled to obey, to get up to his feet, and in doing it he turned himself halfway toward me and I saw his face. It was Coyote.

I went blind then. I shot the first soldier and clubbed the other one with the butt of my empty rifle. Both were in the dirt of the village street, as I leaped down to kill them, to cave in their skulls, with my short-hand'ed *kopluts*. But I was spared from doing that murder.

"Behind you, Heyets, behind you!" Coyote was suddenly yelling. He had grabbed for my horse's reins and now was hanging onto the rearing animal, as I whirled in response to his warning. I was too late. As I came about, I saw Redbeard Bates and another settler from Kamiah riding down on us. The settler fired at me and missed. His horse took him by me before he could lever and fire again. Redbeard had a one-shot buffalo gun. He fired it from his hip at little Coyote, and I heard the bullet hit him. He spun three times around but he held onto my horse, even as his knees gave way and he went down.

Now Redbeard Bates, too, was off his horse. He was grinning and coming at me with his big Sharps rifle held like a war club in his right hand, and I knew he meant to kill me if he could. But I was a Nez Perce. And I, also, had a war club. I tightened my grip on my *kopluts*, crouching like a lynx. He roared at that, coming in on me with no care and no fear, exactly as a great bear would come in on a slender, tuft-eared bobcat. It was his mistake that he did not fear Indians.

When he raised his rifle to swing at me, I was there. When he came down with it in the killing sweep, I was not there. I was behind him. And my *kopluts* was behind him, too. I brought it into his head just as he tried to twist back around. It took him across the bones of the face and across the socket of the right eye. I felt the bones give in beneath the iron head of my weapon and I saw the eye, blue and staring as though still in place, spurt out and hang lifeless on his cheek by a gray shred of nerve and sinew from the crushed socket. He screamed like a woman in labor and fell to the earth, groveling and clutching about in the dirt and bawling low and sick as a gut-shot animal.

I left him there, wheeling about to face his friend. But the other settler had not turned back to help Redbeard. For the moment there was no enemy against me and I jumped toward Coyote and my horse.

Coyote was still conscious. I picked up his slight form and put him across my mount's withers and got out of there. I rode for the river and the tipi of my mother, hopeful the soldiers had passed her by in their hurry.

But now tipis were beginning to burn throughout the village, and when I came to my mother's place there were only a few smoking shreds of cowhide and burnt poles bent over and curled like matchsticks to show where the lodge had stood. My mother and the baby were gone.

I rode on down to the river, not hurrying so much now, for the firing and excitement had gone on past the crossing by then. As I came up to the stream there were still Indians all up and down it, struggling to get across and hide in the timber of the far side. Like the Salmon, the Clearwater was high. The weaker ones were having trouble making the crossing. But all were helping one another and it seemed to me that most were getting over and getting safely away. For myself, I held up a moment, searching the bank on my own side for any sight of my mother. As I did this I recognized an old woman sitting calmly down to roll up her dress before entering the water. Though our meeting had been brief and the meat of our little talk well salted, it was like seeing a friend of life's full journey. I guided my horse over to her.

"Good morning, grandmother," I said. "I will be honored if you will help me get this wounded boy across the water. You sit on the horse with him and I will hold onto the tail and swim after you. All right?"

"No," she said to me, "it is not all right. Why don't you mind your own troubles, homely boy?" She jerked a gnarled thumb at Coyote. "It seems to me you have enough of them. *Eeh!* That boy won't live. He's shot through the liver, can't you see that? Look at the color of him."

I did not want to look at Coyote, or to think about his color. His tongue was out between his teeth before we left my mother's tipi, and I knew where he had been shot.

"Listen, little mother," I said, "if you won't help me with my friend, perhaps you can do me another service. Do you know Takialakin, the wife of Elk Water, the Wallowa?"

"Eh? Antelope? Yes, I know her. Poor thing, poor thing . . ."

"Yes," I said. "I am her son and I am looking for her."

"You, Antelope's son? I don't believe it. Well, I'm sorry I talked to you as I did. A fine woman, a fine woman. Of course, she was a Wallowa."

I caught something in the way she said the last part, and a great fear clutched at my heart.

"What do you mean she *was* a Wallowa?" I said.

"Boy," she replied, "in the first rush to the water I saw a woman with a very young baby try to swim over down there at the bend where it is fast and deep. Some soldiers had set fire to her tipi with her still in it, and she was running with eyes wild, like a horse when the fire fear seizes it. I called to her not to go in down there, to wait and come up here where it was not so bad, but she did not hear me. I will not swear it was Antelope, boy. These eyes are eighty snows old. But it was Antelope's tipi she came out of, and she had a very small child at her breast."

"Mother," I said after a moment, "now will you take this wounded friend over, and let me go down there to look for Takialakin and the baby?"

"Don't be a fool, boy, you can't help them. But here, give me the horse. There is somebody going into those bushes up there that you can help. Look!"

She flung out her arm and my eyes leaped to follow it. Across the trail from us, two soldiers were dragging a young Nez Perce woman into the heavy brush where they could not be seen from the village. Even as they entered their hiding place, one of them was struggling to rip away his belt and to get his pants down.

Again my Indian rage blinded me. I was into those bushes growling like a wolf. Inside there was a little clearing floored with white river sand. On this bed the one soldier had flung the Indian girl. Her lower dress was already torn away, leaving her naked, and she was not resisting as she might first have, for they had used her very hard already.

I came up behind the one who was holding her, taking care not to hit him in the head. I did not want to kill him. I hit him with my *kopluts* across the spine, just below the shoulder blades. I knew, by the way he flopped when he let go of the girl, that I had struck him as I wished to. He might live a long time. But with a backbone broken as that one was, he would never walk again, nor ride a horse again, nor soil any woman, red or white, with his ugly seed.

The other beast did not even know his friend was gone, but as I raised the *kopluts* to break him as I had the first one, he gave a strange, squealing grunt and rolled away from the Indian girl with his hands grabbing his belly. It was then that I saw the knife in the Indian girl's hand and realized she had opened him up from his breastbone to his navel in the same moment I had crippled his friend.

And it was only then, when she came up off that bloody sand to seize my hand and gasp, "Come, warrior, run!" that the killing rage cleared from my mind and I knew her. It was Meadowlark.

20. Short Trail of Lieutenant Rains

My mother and her new baby were not seen again. Coyote died that same sundown. Those were all I knew that the Nez Perce lost in that stupid attack on the village of Looking Glass. A few more had bullet wounds, many more were hurt from falls, or horse collisions, or burns suffered trying to rescue something of their life possessions from blazing tipis. But the fact that so few were killed or critically injured proved of brief blessing to the shocked survivors.

As the sun now sank across the Clearwater from us, where we hid in the timber of the far side, the summer dusk was lit by the fires of the Asotin and Wallowa tipis piled up and set aflame by Whipple's order. Into these fires were thrown all the blankets, buffalo robes, pack covers, cooking things and housekeeping wares of the Nez Perce camped in that fatal spot. Almost the entire horse herd had been left behind and, naturally, all the other livestock. The poor Indians crouched all about us— Meadowlark and the old woman of the crossing were with me— were without food, weapons, horses, and in many cases without full clothing or, indeed, without any clothing at all. Mercifully, nighttime came soon. The Indians began to move under its cover.

All through that second night of July we traveled the river. By daylight we were at the mouth of Cottonwood Creek and with our friends at Peeta Auuwa. Our poor tired people thought they would rest then, but there was no more rest for any Nez Perce in Idaho. Yellow Wolf, Five Wounds and Rainbow had cut the trail of two scouts from Whipple out looking for the Indians who had beaten Perry and lost One Hand Howard on the other side of the Salmon. They had killed one scout but the other had got away, and we had to guess that he would tell Whipple where we were and which way we were going. A war party was right then making up to go out and look for the soldiers which Whipple would surely send out to find our camp.

Weary as I was, I knew I had to go with that party. My

people had much against me. Because of my delay in reaching the village of Looking Glass, the soldiers had been able to come up and take it. My only chance to redeem myself was to go out with that war party. I got a new horse, left Meadowlark and the old grandmother with Yellow Wolf's people, went up to the gathering place and offered myself.

In the wonderful way of my people, no judgment was spoken against me. I never heard a word in my life about being late to reach Looking Glass. My uncle Yellow Wolf only said, *"Eeh! Here comes another soldier killer,"* and that was all there was to it.

We set off in a westerly direction. With us were Two Moons, Five Wounds, Rainbow, Otskai, Wahlitits, Strong Eagle, Red Moccasin Tops, Swan Necklace and some others; about twenty-five of us. It was now about eight o'clock in the morning. The day was July 3rd. It was another fine day, with high white clouds, a little light wind and sunshine. We all felt pretty good.

Down there below us, starting to ride through a small valley we knew had but one outlet, we saw the ten horse soldiers and their chief. Five Wounds and Rainbow talked quickly with Two Moons, then sent for Yellow Wolf.

"Hemene," they asked him, "are those any of the Wallowa soldiers down there?" They meant Captain Whipple's soldiers, and Yellow Wolf, after a moment of shading his keen eyes, nodded his head. "Yes," he said, "I know that officer. He rides with Captain Whipple. Those are Wallowa soldiers; they are the ones we are looking for."

"Who is the officer?" asked Two Moons, peering. "I don't know him from here."

"I don't think you would," said Yellow Wolf. "He is a new one, very young, only a lieutenant. I don't know his name."

"I do," said Seeskoomkee, who was with us and had moved his pony up to the front. "That's Lieutenant Rains. A nice boy. I cut some wood for him this spring."

"Well," said Rainbow, "that lieutenant is riding a short trail. That's a bad place up ahead of him."

"Very bad place," agreed Two Moons with a grin. He took up his soldier canteen and drank from it, and I could smell the stink of the whiskey. "Let's go; we need those guns," he said. "If No Feet doesn't want to see that nice boy get hurt, he can stay up here."

"No," said Seeskoomkee, "I'll go along. I don't think I will be cutting any more wood for the soldiers."

Fifteen minutes later we were waiting in the narrow place of high rocks where the trail came out of the little valley. In a few minutes more we heard the clink of the iron shoes of the soldier horses coming toward us. The soldiers had no chance. Their guns were in their scabbards. We fired right into them, so close we could hear our bullets hit. Three or four of them got into a pocket of boulders and fired a few shells, but it was all over in five or six loadings. I caught Lieutenant Rains' horse and got the best prize of the fight—an officer's Winchester with a silver buffalo on one side of the frame and a mountain sheep head on the other. We left those soldier boys where they were in the rocks. We took only their guns and canteens and blankets and some saddles and bridles. We never took hair. No Nez Perce ever scalped a white man in memory of either side. But it was a hot day and the buzzards had smelled out that place and were already wheeling in the sky above it, so we quickly left with the soldier horses packed up with our prizes. It was not much of a fight. None of us were very proud of it. Even Two Moons threw away his empty canteen and said, "*Eeh!* I don't like to fight boys!"

Back in our camp that night we slept a few hours, took fresh horses and were riding again at daylight. Yellow Wolf and I slept out in the trees, away from the tipis. I did not want to see Meadowlark and he did not want to see Coyote's sister, who had her eyes cast on him. It was a smaller band of us which went out that second day, mostly very young men like myself. Yellow Wolf was the oldest. Our job was to scout for some of our people who were still on the trail from the Salmon River. We had to find these people and to guide them into the new camp. We never did find the people but we found a party of white settlers riding across Camas Prairie and we jumped them hard. They had better luck than the soldiers. They got onto high ground and we couldn't get them out. We killed two of them and they killed two of us. We were going to stay and send for help to kill them all but we captured a boy of only sixteen who was with them and from him we learned that we had better move on quickly. Captain Perry had rested his soldiers and had come out from Lapwai to join Captain Whipple. They were in camp across the prairie at a place called Cottonwood (on the same creek where we were camped). In fact they were so close to where we caught those settlers that they could have come over from their camp any time and chased us Nez Perce away. The white boy told us the settlers were from Grangeville and Mount Idaho and were going to help the soldiers. Imagine that! Seventeen settlers going to help two hundred soldiers! We felt so good about that, we let the boy go unharmed. All we needed to do to see the soldier camp at Cottonwood was ride up the rise of ground where we caught those Grangeville and Mount Idaho foolish ones; that was how close the soldiers were. So we got out of there about as fast as he did. Later, we heard, the army arrested that Captain Perry for being a coward and not coming after us that day, but they let him go. As the white man saw it, there were no cowards among the soldiers. The Nez Perce had a different idea.

That night, back in camp at Peeta Auüwa, we were treated like heroes and the fever from the Rains massacre and the nearness of all those soldiers at Cottonwood began to work in the Nez Perce. War talk was running all over the camp. Looking Glass himself led this talk. He did it with a speech at the council of the chiefs which was called upon our return. He talked as he looked, tough and mean and dangerous. And not quite true.

"Two days ago," he said, "my camp was attacked by the soldiers. I tried to surrender every way I could. My horses, lodges and everything I had was taken away from me by the soldiers we had done so much for. Now, my people, as long as I live, I will never make peace with the treacherous Americans. I did everything I know to preserve their friendship and be friends with the Americans. What more could I have done? It was because I was a good friend of theirs I was attacked. The officer may say it was a mistake. That is a lie. He is a dog and I have been treated worse than a dog by him. He lies if he says he did not know it was my camp. I am ready for war. Come on and let us attack the soldiers at Cottonwood. Many a man dies for his dear native land and we might as well die in battle as any other way."

That was a big camp by then; one hundred ninety-one men of all ages and four hundred fifty women and children. The noise they made shouting and crying out words in agreement with Looking Glass made the short hairs along a man's lower neck stand on end. But I saw something the others did not, and I quit my part of the noise-making as though some spirit hand had shut off my mouth.

It was Joseph standing alone far back in the shadows from the fire, and he was looking at me. I dropped my eyes, unable to meet my chief's eyes. I stepped out of the circle and went back into the shadows myself. Joseph said no word to me, or to anyone. He just kept watching.

The next day we heard that nearly one hundred soldiers were coming out of Mount Idaho looking for their seventeen friends we had surrounded the day before in full view of Captain Perry and his cowards at Cottonwood. These men were not regular soldiers but what were called "volunteers"; settlement men marching together in the manner of soldiers.

We knew their leader. He was an old eagle chief, a colonel, named McConville, known as a pretty big talker and not too good a fighter. So we began to gather up and decide what to do about him. While we were still arguing, an Asotin scout came in, very excited.

"Guess what?" he cried. "Those Mount Idaho men are riding many of our horses we lost down the river. I saw Moositsah, my best buffalo runner, among them. Come on!"

Looking Glass was out scouting to find the best way to come at the Cottonwood soldiers but Ollikut was there and he said to the man, "All right, let's go. We need those horses back."

"*Eeh!* I am with you." It was Rainbow, on his feet and angry. Right behind him, close and true as his shadow, his friend Five Wounds rose up. "Aye, and me too," he said. "We can't go after those Cottonwood soldiers with those Mount Idaho people to worry about. Let's take care of them."

I was standing there listening to all this but I was very tired. When Yellow Wolf said to me, "Well, let's go get our guns," I answered him, "No, you go on. I'm not going this time. You don't need me."

He looked at me in that way of his which was so hard to hide from. "No," he said, "we don't need you, but maybe that Asotin girl does, eh? Is that it, Heyets? You want to stay here and play soft-leg while we warriors go out and get back the horses which you—well, forgive me, Heyets, I keep forgetting you are only seventeen summers."

"Uncle," I said, standing proud, "you just keep forgetting that part of it. Remember one other thing though. I am still the nephew of Yellow Wolf."

"*Uataska,*" answered my uncle, grinning the way a wolf grins by lifting one side of the upper lip only. "Good. Now let's go get those guns."

So that was the manner in which I came to be with Ollikut's war party which went out to look for the stolen Asotin horses.

That was a famous morning in the history of our people. It was the beginning of the day which saw us catch McConville and his eighty men on that steep hill which the white men ever after called Mount Misery. It was the sunrise of the day upon which, after its night had fallen, we ran off McConville's picket line, culled from its number the forty-three prime Looking Glass horses we wanted, scattered the rest of them like flung gravel ten miles across Camas Prairie. It was the start of the day which saw thirty-three of us Nez Perce send almost a hundred white men walking home to Mount Idaho to lie about how they lost their horses, and saw us do it without one Indian getting hurt.

But all that is not what I remember. What I remember is a little moment when we were leaving camp. We were jingling along holding in our horses to make them bow their necks, step short, throw their rumps and show their pride. We came to the edge of the camp and there was a lone Nez Perce woman crouched before a poor quality tipi with the flaps drawn and the black sign of Tinukin scrawled in charcoal above them. Before the mourner was a bed of embers upon which she was burning branchlets of *pootoosway*, the medicine tree. As the smoke rose upward she was softly calling out the words of an ancient Nez Perce spirit song. Riding by, I saw that the tears of a real *timme-nekt* were running down her tired face, and I knew her sorrow was not for a stranger.

But I did not know the woman. To Yellow Wolf I said, "*Mana hayat?* What woman is that?" He shrugged to show he did not know, either, but an Asotin warrior riding behind us said, "That is the mother of Weësculatat. They are putting him to sleep this morning. It's too bad, too. He should have more reward than one old woman weeping over him. Bah! These are bad times. Consider the high honor which he brought upon himself yesterday."

"What honor was that?" I asked.

The Asotin man looked at me like a rattlesnake. "It is no more than I would expect of a Wallowa taught at Lapwai," he said. "But that is the trouble today. Nobody remembers the old ways. Nobody honors the old laws. Weësculatat was the first to die in our war with One Hand Howard. The first to die in a war should be put to sleep with all pride. It's a very unusual honor."

"That's true," agreed Yellow Wolf.

"Yes," said the Asotin. "Do you realize that up to the time of Weësculatat's death yesterday we had killed forty-five of the enemy?"

"Forty-six," said Yellow Wolf. "You are forgetting that Whipple scout I shot three days ago."

"Oh yes," nodded the Asotin man, and he and Yellow Wolf rode on together, leaving me to feel my ignorance of the old laws and to take my last look back at the mother of Weësculatat sitting the sunrise vigil over the still-eyed form of her only son, the first Nez Perce to die in One Hand Howard's war.

Uetu, no, my brother, it was not McConville's eighty men shivering all night with the fear of us, not the restealing of those forty-three Looking Glass horses, not the big dance held for us upon our return to camp, which I remember about that famous morning in the folklore of my people. It was that last look back at Weësculatat's little mother crying alone in the Idaho sunrise.

21. Ride Proud at Peeta Auüwa

There followed a strange five days in that camp at Peeta Auüwa on the South Fork of the Clearwater River at the mouth of Cottonwood Creek. What was strange about them was that the war held its breath, it stopped, it seemed to withdraw and fade away like a bad dream in those five days.

McConville, frightened and humbled, did not come out of Mount Idaho again. The men from Grangeville stayed close to their houses, too. Over by Camp Cottonwood the two captains sat inside their trenches which they had dug when they saw Looking Glass scouting them, and so no fight came about over there. Down to the south and west our last scouts from the Salmon came in to say that there was no sign of One Hand Howard on the back trail.

A day passed, then two, three. Our people began to laugh again as they talked. There was no hurry, they now said, about going to Montana. Maybe One Hand had given up. Maybe they could stay in Idaho after all. It would at least be a good idea to wait and see.

In this mood the fifth day was set aside for celebration and camp cleaning.

I took the occasion to see Joseph. I had been worrying about him, feeling sorry for him, ever since I had seen his face the night he listened to Looking Glass talk for war. He seemed to me to be a man who had lost his power and did not know it. That, I thought, was a very sad thing for such a proud chief.

I found him sitting under a tree outside his lodge, playing with his new daughter. The little one had been born at Tepahlewam, the Tolo Lake camp. Her mother, Toma Alwawinmi, Springtime, the younger of Joseph's two wives, was sitting with them, beading a buckskin shirt. Behind them the older wife had the lodge skins rolled up and was giving the tipi a fierce sweeping out. It was a peaceful, happy scene and made me feel better than I had on my way across camp.

Joseph waved to me, his warm brown eyes happy to see me.

"*Eeh!* See now," he said to Springtime, "it is little Heyets. We have not seen him for too long a time. Come, sit down, boy." He brushed a place for me with a pine branch he was using to keep the flies away from the baby. "Well, boy, how are things with you? You look well." He paused, shaking his head. "I was very sorry to hear about your mother, Heyets. A terrible thing."

"Yes," I said. "I never hated the soldiers until then."

"I know," he nodded. "In my own mind there has been no peace these many days. I have been asking my heart what to do."

"What does it say? Are we safe now?"

"I don't know yet; I will speak out when it tells me."

"Yes, surely, my chief." It was a lie. I was sure now that he had lost his power, certain that he did not mean to speak out ever again.

"Well," he said, "you shouldn't be here talking to an old married man with a baby in his lap. Do you mean to say you are not going to be in the big race? You should be out grooming your best horse now. How is it you sit here wasting time?"

"In truth," I answered, "I have no good horses any more. I had one shot at Lahmotta, rode out three more in losing One Hand, ruined the last one getting away from the Asotin village last week. I have been using Hemene's horses these past days. I haven't even a Sunday horse left of my own stock. Only this old broken-down traveler you see me on."

Joseph shook his head. "I don't like to see those White Bird and Salmon River boys win the race. Things have gone hard enough for us Wallowa lately. Besides, it's a *timei* race; maybe the last one for a long time."

I hadn't known that it was the big Nez Perce ceremonial race, run once every summer, in which the young men rode in the name of some special *timei*, some certain one marriage-age girl. But then I didn't have any *timei* of my own.

"Well," I said, "you can see what chance I would have. This old brown bonepile . . ."

"Exactly," interrupted Joseph with one of his rare smiles. "What chance would you have with such a poor horse?"

It was a direct question and I said, "You mean I do have some kind of a chance because of this horse?"

"Two chances," he said. "One to test your *timei*, one to win the big race."

"But I have no *timei!*" I protested. "What time have I had for girls?"

"Well, time enough I hear," nodded Joseph dryly.

"Yes," said Springtime, breaking in with that kind of a smile a woman uses to make you think she knows something she doesn't. "That's what I hear, too."

I began to feel a little foolish and a little angry.

"Why not speak straight with me?" I demanded. "Say what it is you mean."

"Why not trust your chief and do as he says?" Springtime asked me. "Enter the race. Ride that old brown horse in the parade for the girls' selection. See what happens. Listen to Heinmot for a change, Heyets. Or have you forgotten how to do that?"

I had earned that sharpness and I accepted it. "All right," I said, "I will do it. I will be down there at the race ground this afternoon with this old horse. But I don't see the sense of it."

"When we're young," nodded Joseph, "there is much we don't see the sense of. *Taz alago*, Heyets. Thank you for coming to see me. We know each other from better days. It's good you will still come to sit by Joseph a little while."

"*Taz alago*," I replied, standing up. "*Taz alago*, Toma Alwawinmi. The baby is beautiful. She looks like you. Very lucky baby."

"*Kaiziyeuyeu*, Heyets, thank you. I am glad you came to see Heinmot. His friends are very few these days."

"Not so few," I said. "There are many of us who still look to our chief. Believe that."

Joseph looked away, very far away.

"Perhaps in their minds," he said. "But in their hearts they have forgotten me. Heyets, you better go now. It makes me sad to talk about my people who have forgotten me."

"All right." I smiled for his sake. "I will see you at the race. But I wouldn't do it for anybody else, my chief. I will say that three times."

"Well," said Joseph, standing up and putting his hand on my shoulder, "here is something I will say to you three times: I wouldn't ask it of anybody else. Now get out of here and let me eat."

The people were in a very high spirit for that race. There was no more whiskey in camp and so no more trouble. All came up to the hour of the big *timei* race in good temper and loud voice. All except Heyets.

To begin with, it was that old brown horse. He was a poor joke of a mount and I was going to be hooted and made heavy with, even by my best friends, when I showed up on him to parade past the place where all the girls were waiting to pick their young man for the race.

But more than the horse, it was the girls themselves which had me shaking in my stomach. I was a small fellow—that's why I was such a good race rider—and not handsome. Like Yellow Wolf I had a skin the color of an old saddle—my family was very dark, not a lovely red copper color like Ollikut, for instance. Neither did we have the broad noble features of the Joseph blood. We were narrow between the eyes, hawk-nosed, salmon-jawed. Too, we were quick, nervous movers, giving an impression of fierceness which was sometimes true, as in the case of Yellow Wolf, and sometimes false as in my own case. Added to nature's mistakes in making me slight, homely and bad-colored, I had been kicked by a horse when four years old, breaking my nose and making my underjaw set crooked. Then I had been thrown by another horse when thirteen years old, smashing a hip and leaving me with a walk which was at once too injured to escape notice yet not injured enough to earn respect or to obtain dignity. So it can be appreciated that my luck with girls had been not famous.

But the sun had passed midday and the parade had begun. Moving my old horse out from behind the tipi where I had been hiding with him, I clumped up with him just in time to be last in line going by the girls.

At once a great cheer went up for me. Then a laugh.

There must have been five hundred Indians crowded around that race ground along the river, and I think every one of them saw me in the same instant. You never heard such noise. The Indian likes a good joke. Contrary to what the white man says, my people could find a laugh in almost anything. The nature of the Nez Perce is full of sunshine. He laughs easy and he laughs open. Those Indians thought I was making a joke that day. That's why they cheered so loud, laughed so hard.

But the girls didn't cheer and their laugh was not the same. They were all made up in their finest soft white elkskins, otter braidbands, copper bracelets, silver bells and trade beads, and they had not gone to all that trouble for some simple fool of a Wallowa boy to ride in on an old bearbait of a brown gelding and make a big joke of their selection parade.

I felt just like a pimple on the end of a sore nose. I was out there where nobody wanted me but everybody had to see me. I very nearly put my heels to the ancient brown plug and ran away, right there, but I thought of Joseph and so was able to straighten up just in time and look those girls in the eye as I rode past them.

And they were something to look in the eye! For the first time I realized what Joseph had led me into. Those *timeis* were gorgeous! They were entirely breath-taking. Of a sudden I wanted very much to have one of them call out my name when we came back and lined up our horses in front of them. Of course this was a foolish want. I was not there to be chosen by one of the girls, or there to win the race. I was there because Joseph had chosen this way to recall to me my lost humility, to remind me that to "ride proud on a poor horse" was the most difficult thing an Indian could be asked to do. Accordingly, I sat as tall as I could on my old shambler as we turned the course once around and came back to take our stand before the Nez Perce belles.

First it was Kaaunat, the Morning Star, a surpassingly lovely Paloos girl of Hahtalekin's band who raised her hand, stepped out and called the name "Peopeo Moxmox!" and made Yellow Bird her warrior in the race. Then it was White Feather, a slim, exciting girl said to be the second most beautiful of all our young women. She called out the name "Wetyetmas" and Swan Necklace rode out to answer her call and have her favor tied on his pony's mane. Then it was Halpawinmi, Dawn, White Feather's dear friend and the reigning Nez Perce beauty, coming forward to give the name "Sarpsis Ilppilp" and to smile like morning sunshine when Red Moccasin Tops dashed out of our ranks to rear his dazzling Appaloosa before her and to make the magnificent animal kneel down with his head outstretched on the ground so that she might fasten her charm to his shining red mane.

The great crowd of fathers, mothers and old ones cheered the handsome Sarpsis, his famous red blanket coat and unforgettably perfect horse as with one throat. And it was while this cheering of both a fighting hero and the most popular boy in all five bands was still sounding along the riverside that a small, fiercely proud girl with haughty, high-chinned head and swift, slender body movements appeared in front of the other *timeis* and called out clearly, "Heyets! Heyets, the Wallowa!"

I knew that certain voice, slender face and mountain doe's body on the instant. My belly shrank up in me like wet rawhide in summer sun. I could not make my breath work, or my muscles move. But I was there and my chief had sent me there and I was a Wallowa. I called on Hunyewat to send me the strength to show those Indians what real *simiakia* was, and He did it. I felt the power in me and I kicked that coarse old brown horse out from among all those slim Asotin, White Bird, Paloos and Salmon River racers and rode him up in front of the *timei* girls as though he were the returned spirit of the mighty Sun Eagle himself.

"*Zaain*," I said to Meadowlark, "I am here." Before that time, naturally, I had stayed away from her out of respect for the brutal shame the soldiers had done her, and which I had been forced to see. Now I knew that enough time had gone. Her laugh was clean and quick again. It had in it that same beckoning tone I remembered from the other time she had laughed at me in the bushes at Snake Crossing when she was no more than a *tekash* baby.

We paraded toward the starting place, Red Moccasin Tops first with his favored Appaloosa. Then came Yellow Bird with the second-favored horse, a tall bay pinto. Swan Necklace and the others with their various mounts, every one a Nez Perce-bred, running horse, followed in a noisy, jostling line, each maneuvering to be in a good position to watch whatever other horses he was most concerned with. The last horse in line was mine and I made no effort to put him any place else. I was happy enough to be back there in the dust where I could be forgotten. The sight of Meadowlark's charm—a silver cross stolen from some blackrobe's prayer school—dangling from the old brown's ratty mane did little to ease my embarrassment. The poor girl had been loyal to me and had shown great bravery and pride. This only made matters worse. She owed me nothing, as I saw it, and the fact she would humble herself to call my name only added to my misery. Above all, Joseph had forgotten his promise; he had said he would be there and to trust him beyond riding the old horse in the parade. I had trusted him and . . .

"Heyets, *kine! kine!* Over here! Behind the lodge!"

It was a cracked old voice, one I knew from somewhere, and I turned to see who it was calling to me as I draggled by toward the starting line. I saw her then, and it was the old crone who had led me to save Meadowlark from Captain Whipple's soldiers. She was crouched behind a dirty gray Asotin tipi near the edge of the encampment. With nothing to lose but my last place in line, I turned the brown plug her way, glad enough to see even so much of a friend in that unhappy moment. But when I got around the lodge, out of sight of the crowd following the racers, my eyes stood out like those of a bottom fish pulled from deep water. "In the name of Hunyewat!" I gasped, "where did you get that horse . . . ?"

He was a black Appaloosa, the only one of that exact color I ever saw. Muscled like a buffalo over the fine bones of an antelope, he was a throwback certainly to some ancient wild stallion behind the carefully selected blood of our red, bay and roan Appaloosas, and he was at once the most striking, sinister-looking horse imaginable.

I could only look at him and shake my head. My old Asotin friend, however, talked fast.

"*Koiimzi!* Take him! He's a Sioux horse, never been in this country before last night. He came here in the dark as a gift to Joseph from old Red Heart's band, just back from the buffalo country. They're camped up the Fork a ways. Hurry! Here, I trade you, a horse for a horse." She seized my frayed rope bridle. "Don't ask questions, you fool, there's a race to run. Look! They are almost to the line!"

I saw the other racers drawing away from me but still could not move to take the great horse.

"*Kapsisniyut!*" rasped the old grandmother. "Are you seeking to do an evil thing against Meadowlark? Go! Take this black and white devil and run those White Birds and Salmon Rivers into the stink of their own manure. Do you say you will dare deny that Asotin girl who honored you with this blackrobe cross?" She ripped the piece of silver from the old brown's mane and flung it at me. I caught it and with it I caught a memory picture of Meadowlark's face upturned to mine and her husky voice saying, "Here, warrior, carry this for me!" Something bright and powerful surged up within me and I was on that black and white horse shouting, "What's his name? What's his name?"

"Mankiller!" croaked the old grandmother gleefully. "That's what the Sioux called him; that's why they sold him to Red Heart. *Eee-yahhh!*" she screeched at the horse and struck at his crouching rump with her walking cane. The Sioux brute squealed and shot out from behind the tipi like the flash of a lance blade turning in the sun. He was up to the Nez Perce horses in twenty jumps, catching them just as they turned on the starting line and the race judges fired their rifles and yelled, "*Ueye! Kuse! Go . . . !*"

Mankiller did not run like a horse. He ran like a wild animal. Sitting on him was like sitting on an elk sailing over a deadfall; a buck deer jumping headlong down the mountain side; an antelope drifting over the prairie sage like a puff of wind-whipped rifle smoke. Inside the first turn he had me through the pack and charging the heels of the front runners. Ahead of me I saw only Yellow Bird's pinto, Swan Necklace's blue roan, Red Moccasin Tops' Appaloosa. Into the second turn we went and out of it into the final straight run of the U-shaped Nez Perce course. Through the dust loomed the straining quarters of the pinto and the roan running haunch and haunch a lance length from my mount's nose. The Sioux horse squealed like an angry bear. There was no time to go around those horses, no room to go between them, but Mankiller made room. He drove squarely into the rumps of Yellow Bird's and Swan Necklace's mounts, wedging them apart by brute force, hurling himself forward, splitting them away from him as though they were wood chips and he a smashing blunt-edged ax. The pinto went down, throwing Yellow Bird, and the roan bolted for the river neighing in pain from the great bite Mankiller's teeth had taken out of his rear. Four jumps up the course was Red Moccasin Tops and his Nez Perce Appaloosa. Forty jumps up the course was the finish line. We could not do it; there was no time left. The collision with the pinto and the roan had cost us the race.

Mankiller did not know this. He blew out a great snort of air, flared his nostrils, went after the other horse with a wild stallion whistle that had half the mares in the camp pulling loose their picket pegs. He was to his enemy's croup in three mighty bounds, to his flank in four, his shoulder in five, head-and-head in six, drawing free in seven, showering sods in his face in eight. He won going only half-speed, by seven pony lengths, having managed, as well, in the process of going by him, to bite the Appaloosa in the belly!

The cheers Red Moccasin Tops had received when his Nez Perce horse had pranced and bowed for Halpawinmi were as summer breezes to the storm of noise which went up when I guided the Sioux racer toward the *timei* girls, my purpose to pick up Meadowlark and carry her behind me. But through the crowd I saw Joseph standing alone, watching me, and I turned instead in his direction.

"My chief, my chief!" I cried. "I know you sent the old woman with this animal, and I did not trust you. I thought you meant only to punish me, to make me ride proud on a poor horse. Forgive me, forgive me."

"Heyets," he said quietly, "you did ride proud on a poor horse. Remember that. Now take this good horse and go to the girl. Lift her up with you. Ride tall with her like a Wallowa. And re-member this about her: she did not know of the Sioux horse any more than you. Think of that when your bodies are together. That little Asotin is a woman, Heyets, sixteen summers or no."

His words excited me with their reminder of the custom for the winner of the race to be privileged to take his *timei* with him, away from the camp, for the "time of being alone," a tra-ditional privacy which might not be inquired into or spied upon. Bidding Joseph *taz alago* and the blessings of Hunyewat, I started once more toward the place where Meadowlark, dark eyes shining, awaited her warrior.

But I never reached her. I never took her up behind me. Our bodies never met.

As I turned away from Joseph a sound like distant thunder echoed from the bluffs on the far side of the South Fork. There was a whooshing growl and swish of air high above the river; then a smashing shower of rock and dirt spurted up in the middle grass of the race ground and every war-age man among us was running for his rifle.

We Nez Perce had heard that noise before; we did not need to look up across the water to see who was making it. It was not Captain Whipple. It was not Captain Perry. They had no cannon soldiers with them. *Eeh-hehh!* Run in the horses. Strike the lodges. Get the old ones and the children back from the river.

Strip to the loincloth and stay away from the women. The five strange happy days at Peeta Auüwa were over. *Koklinikse!* Move out fast!

That was General One Hand Howard up there on that bluff across the Clearwater.

22. The Clearwater Fight

Sometimes bare bones make the best feast. These are the bare bones of the Clearwater fight.

We had captured sixty-nine new rifles from Captain Perry at White Bird, ten from Lieutenant Rains at Narrow Rocks. Some one hundred twenty men with good guns answered the rallying cries of the chiefs when One Hand's cannon shot boomed out from the cliff above Peeta Auüwa.

Of this number two dozen at once dashed across the river under old Toohoolhoolzote to close off One Hand's only way down to the water, a narrow steep slope leading from the bluff-top to the bottom meadows, flanked by a gully-washed ravine. Crafty old Toohoolhoolzote, his instinct for war as keen as the nose of a buffalo wolf for newborn calf, had sensed that the soldiers would not watch this ravine, since they would assume it could not pass a horse and rider. Also, he knew they would have to go around the head of it, up on the bluff, to get to the slope which led down to our camp. He was right and the soldiers were wrong. They found that out when the old Salmon River fighter passed not one, but twenty-four horses and riders, up that ravine. Three of those twenty-four were Wallowas: Ollikut, the Frog; Hemene Moxmox, the Yellow Wolf; Heyets, the Mountain Sheep.

We got hidden in the rocks at the top of the ravine just as One Hand started around it with his soldiers. Nearly all of us had Winchesters in that picked group. We had plenty of ammunition. The fire we put into those soldiers starting around the head of that ravine was like the blade of a four-horse reaper in a field of ripe wheat. One Hand immediately called back these leading soldiers and made a great square of all his troops at the head of the ravine on level ground. Here there was a nice low spot in the middle of the soldier square where he and his officers could hide in comfort, and that is exactly what they did. We lost respect for One Hand Howard at that place.

But his soldiers fought well. Before our main strength of warriors could secure the camp and follow us up the ravine, they had dug good rifle pits all around their square and we could not drive them out with the heaviest fire. We shot at them all afternoon and as long as there was light, into the summer dusk. During the early night a fitful fire was kept up by both sides but the Indians began to go back to camp after midnight, certain that the soldiers were already whipped enough and would make no trouble the next day. In vain Ollikut argued with them to stay and fight, claiming we had One Hand cut off from water and that when he moved to get it, we could make a great killing among the soldiers. Looking Glass, who I was beginning to dislike more each time he spoke, was his main opponent. As usual he talked with a big mouth and in result more warriors followed him back down the ravine than stayed with Ollikut and the rest of us at its head. Dawn found us with less than fifty men on our line where there had been twice that number at nightfall.

One Hand was not slow to see the opportunity. About ten o'clock his soldiers came on in their full numbers—hundreds and hundreds of them—and while we might delay, we could not hold them. But we could try.

In the following fight, rock-and-rock skirmishing of the hottest kind, we showed them how to shoot. And we made them leave blood on every step of ground they gained against us. Our best were still up there with us. Old Toohoolhoolzote, White Bird, Hahtalekin, Wottolen, Rainbow, Five Wounds, Two Moons, Peopeo Tholekt, Ollikut; all save Joseph and Looking Glass of our premier chiefs and fighters were up there in the rocks with us those last hours. Yet those two absences made a strange difference. And they were judged in a strangely different way. The failure of Joseph to come up as far as those front rocks at any time in the fight was taken as a shame which the other

Indians made us Wallowas feel most keenly. On the other hand, they did not seem to hold Looking Glass in the least disrespect for his action in going back to camp under cover of darkness, an action which Yellow Wolf and a few others insisted angrily was no better than simply running away. That, I think, was the beginning of the split between Looking Glass and Joseph, those faithful friends of the old days when their fathers had ruled in the Valley of Winding Waters and when no man alive could have destroyed the trust of Aleemyah Tatkaneen in the word and hand of Heinmot Tooyalakekt. But this was war, and a dangerous war. Men were dying and other men would die. This was the greatest test. From somewhere in my memory at that moment among the rocks of Peeta Auüwa ravine, I saw back to my days with Agent Monteith at Lapwai and I beheld in my mind some words of a saying from the black book—"all that a man has will he give for his life"—and I thought of Joseph staying in the camp with the women and of Looking Glass sneaking away from us in the night. I knew that one of them had betrayed his trust, yet I did not think that it was Joseph. I knew what my chief was doing—looking after the women and children as he had done at White Bird—but I did not know what the Asotin chief was doing. To me it seemed, as it did to Yellow Wolf and those few others, that Looking Glass had run away.

The firing from the soldier lines, meanwhile, grew to be like a heavy rain in October. It chilled us and made our spirits shiver. Then it began cutting into our bodies like lances of ice and we could not stand up to it any longer.

Ollikut passed the word to leave the spring. The water was what the soldiers wanted, he said, and we could not keep them from it with our few warriors. Especially not when those warriors were beginning to argue about Looking Glass and Joseph and to lose their hearts for a real fight. The other chiefs up there nodded their agreement to the suggestion—no Indian ever issued orders to another in battle or council—and we began to move on down the ravine away from the spring and the bullet-splattered rocks from which we had made our hard fight to keep One Hand Howard from catching our camp unpacked and unprepared, as the coward, Captain Whipple, had caught the Asotin down near Kooskia.

We started down with some concern for we knew that Looking Glass had left us, arguing that One Hand would fight no more at that place and there was no need for any hurry. But down on the bottom meadows we found a glad sight fortunately. Joseph had every cooking pot and buffalo robe loaded on the travois ponies. The rifle fire from above had been his whip and Looking Glass's halter. The whole band was ready to go, waiting only for us to come down off the bluff with the final word. Ollikut gave that word to his brother Joseph and in that quiet, orderly way, without leaving a tipi they did not want to leave, without losing a head of stock they did not prefer to lose, all those many hundreds of Indian women, children and old ones marched silently away from Peeta Auüwa, the last happy camp of the Nez Perce people.

There was still plenty of good light left in the afternoon of the second day, still time for the Indians to appreciate their great defeat in terms of a report paper our scouts took off the body of a dispatch rider they shot about an hour before sundown. One Hand was wasting no time getting the news of his tremendous victory back to the settlements, it seemed. He made a great deal of the few old tipis and lame horses we had left for him—"eighty lodges with all their belongings and a great number of their horse herd"—but the part which really impressed us was the terrible damage he had done us in the fight. "Fifteen Indians killed on the field," he said. "Eight more dead of wounds subsequently. Forty Indians wounded altogether, and forty more taken prisoner in the action."

Now this was remarkable. According to our own uneducated count we had lost but four warriors, Going Across, Grizzly Bear Blanket, Red Thunder and Whittling, and had six wounded, of which only Kipkip Owyeen was seriously hurt.

We understood, too, that not a single member of the entire camp at Peeta Auüwa had fallen prisoner to One Hand. We finally had that part of it cleared up for us, though, when we learned that poor old Red Heart and his peaceful buffalo hunters had stumbled onto the soldiers and been captured and that they were the "forty fighting Indians" taken prisoner "on the field" by the great General Howard.

There was another small matter which never appeared in any of One Hand's reports. This was the final manner in which we gained the time to move our women and children safely away. We Nez Perces always thought it was a pretty good joke.

When those four hundred soldiers and two hundred scouts and mule packers of General Howard's at last got their thirsts satisfied at the spring we had let them have, and then got ready to move on down the slope to capture our lingering camp, they ran into a little surprise we had left hidden for them in the rocks they had not thought to search after we departed down the ravine. That surprise was five Indians. Their names were Wottolen, Otstotpoo, Tomylinmene, Howallits and my own uncle Yellow Wolf.

Those five Nez Perce riflemen held back the advance of six hundred white men for one hour and a half, while four hundred fifty unarmed women and children and old ones of the Peeta Auüwa camp got out of the Clearwater Valley to escape toward Kamiah, Weippe Prairie and the Lolo Trail.

That was our little Indian joke on General Howard. Somehow, he never got around to telling it on himself. Maybe he didn't think it was funny.

23. Good-Bye, Fair Land!

We went a little way past Kamiah Crossing toward Weippe and made camp. One Hand was not pushing us. We now had the main Clearwater between him and us, and the people were worried, confused, wanting to know once for all what the plan was. The chiefs called a general council of all five bands for the third night. It was thought two days of rest would bring all concerned to the meeting with better minds. Scouts were sent out to watch One Hand. Others were sent into the Kamiah Valley to see how the settlers were acting. We had not forgotten the time those same Kamiah people had turned us back from going to the buffalo three years before. We were worried lest they now meant to show us the rifle again. With settlers who hated us in front, and soldiers who hated us in the rear, it was not a good camp and we knew we could not stay long in it.

I went with the scouts into the valley. We learned that the way was clear there. The houses were empty. The stock was turned out of the corrals. All the people had gone into the crossing at Kamiah, apparently to meet the soldiers. We got back at sunset of the third day. The other scouts were not back yet. That night we all went to the council wondering where those scouts were; wondering *when* they would find One Hand, *where* they would find him and *what* he would be doing when they did find him. We were not easy in our minds.

It was a solemn council, no dancing, no singing, no wasted speechmaking. Not one Indian arose to boast of the way we had handled the soldiers over on the South Fork. That gave the truth about the mood of the people. When an Indian will not talk loud about his part in delaying an entire army of soldiers for thirty hours, he is either dead or mightily discouraged. And when an Indian is discouraged he is like a sick dog; all the strength goes out of him in one day.

When I got to the council four of the five main chiefs were there. Only the chief of my own band had not yet arrived. Since Ollikut had seemed to assume the leadership of the Wallowa after we had joined the fighting Indians at Lahmotta, we all expected he would now be the one to take the vacant place at the fire and speak for us in his brother's stead.

Imagine our surprise then, when there was a stir and murmur of excitement at the outer edge of the gathered people and the crowd parted to let through a familiar, plain-dressed man. My own excitement joined that of the others. *Eeh-hahh!* Joseph had come to speak for himself.

We all knew what the other chiefs knew: that now Looking Glass and his old friend would speak against each other and that would be the end of it. When they had said what they would, there would be a vote of the council as to which of them was right and which of them would be the leader of the Nez Perce from that camp onward. Joseph made no move to speak first, and so Looking Glass arose and faced him across the fire.

"My chiefs," he said, "I will talk short. If we are in a bad place here it is because our leadership has been bad. If we have done wrong it is because we have been advised wrong. I am talking about Joseph. He said to trust the white man. He said to do as One Hand Howard told us to do; to come on the reservation and obey the orders of Agent Monteith. Doing as he said, we have been betrayed, and not one or two times but at every turn of the trail. That is not my old friend's fault. He only said what was in his heart, but his heart was wrong. We cannot help that. Our pastures have been taken from us, our stock has been run off and branded by the white men, our great herds were drowned in crossing the Kahmuenem when it was flooding. Still we obeyed Joseph.

"But we were wrong and he was wrong. Our tipis were left to rot along the Wallowa, the Imnaha, the Salmon and the Grande Ronde. Our young men were driven to war, our women raped, our children infected with sickness at Lapwai, our chiefs insulted and made fools of in first one, then another council. At last there was the worst treachery of all, my peaceful village attacked and set afire by soldiers who crept up through the trees while their leader was talking to me saying there would be no fight, saying he only came with a message of friendship from One Hand, that he was only there to make sure we were not going to the buffalo with the bad Indians who beat the soldiers at Lahmotta.

"My chiefs, I seek no anger from Joseph, my friend. I say to you only that his faith in the white man has blinded him and made him weak. We must listen no longer to the Wallowa; they are the ones who took us from our homes, who started us on this bad path. Now we must listen to ourselves, and I ask you to listen to me."

Looking Glass paused here, sweeping the silent Indians with

his glittering eyes. It was as though he were asking for some sign as to how he should end his speech, and the Nez Perce gave it to him. It was a low rumble of wordless sound accompanied by much head nodding and agreement grunting. "*Eeh*," they were saying, "go on; so far we hear you very well."

"All right," the Asotin chief nodded back to them, "here is what I propose. Five Wounds and Rainbow have just come from the Crow country. They tell me the Crows want us to come live with them and hunt in peace. If we go there on those plains of Montana we will leave the fighting behind us. Our war with One Hand will be over. We will be safe."

He stopped again, flinging an arm suddenly to the north and east. "Peace is that way," he cried. "There lies the Lolo Trail. It will take us to the land of our friends."

He spun around, throwing his hand in the opposite direction. "War is that way. Back there waits One Hand Howard. He will take us to Eeikish Pah, the Hot Place, to Oklahoma. What do you say? Do you want to go down there and die with those other poor Indians? Do you want to go with me to Montana and live like a Nez Perce? You want to run free like a man, or sit here like women and surrender to One Hand Howard? For myself, what can I say? I surrendered to that dog, Whipple, who was sent by One Hand, and he burned my village. I will never surrender to the white man again. I am going to Montana."

When he finished there was a rumbling among the people, much louder than before, and some scattered shouts of "*Tukug! Tukug!* You are right, you are right!" But most of the Indians were waiting for Joseph to answer the anger of the Asotin chief. This he now came forward to do.

He moved slowly, as though with twice the weight of his thirty-seven years. He waited a long, awkward time for us all to get quiet. During that wait I looked at him and felt sad in my heart. He was so ordinary, so humble, so simple. He wore no gaudy war dress to match the elkskin fringe, eagle feathers and dyed horsehair tassels of Looking Glass. He had no dark, striking face, no wild, piercing eyes, no fierce excitement in his words and movements to arouse the Indian pride as Looking Glass could arouse it. Yet when at last he raised his hand in that old way of his, there was a stillness in that place which made the ears ache.

"My people," he began, "it is wrong to think that I have ever spoken for the white man. If I have told you to obey the soldiers, to do as the agents say, it is because my heart told me to do that. Now it is said that I did wrong. Now many of you think I betrayed my people. You blame me for this trouble. I will not answer that. Each of you must answer it for yourself. I will say only this: you cannot run away from this trouble; you cannot run away from any trouble. A man is born to trouble, as a woman is born to sorrow. We must look in our hearts, that is all we can do. I have looked in mine these many days since our young men ran wild along the Tahmonmah. At last I have found what it is my heart would have me say to you, my people, what it is that I think we must do. When I have said it, dear friends, I will say no more."

He looked at them another long time, as he had before he began to speak. Then he raised his hand again and said those few soft words none of us ever forgot.

"What are we fighting for? Is it our lives? No. It is for this fair land where the bones of our fathers are buried. I do not want to take my women among strangers. I do not want to die in a strange land. Some of you tried to say once that I was afraid of the whites. Stay here with me now and you will have plenty of fighting. We will put our women behind us in these mountains and die on our own land fighting for them. I would rather do that than run I know not where. . . ."

There was no growl, no rumble, no response of any kind from the people. They stood back and let Joseph go out again through their ranks. They looked at one another. They did not know what to do. Looking Glass had made it seem so easy. Now, suddenly, Heinmot Tooyalakekt had said a few quiet words and it was not so easy any more.

While they hesitated, there was a shout from the southern edge of the camp and all in an instant the chance which Joseph had held forth for the people, to alter the fate which waited for them beyond the Bitterroots, faltered, faded and was no more.

The signal cry was from our missing scouts, returned at last from Kamiah Crossing. Their news was startling. One Hand Howard was at the Clearwater. He was coming fast. He might have his soldiers across already. There was no time remaining for argument; the decision must be made.

Quickly the chiefs called for the vote: *yes*, to go to Montana with Looking Glass: *no*, to stay in Idaho and fight with Joseph. Swiftly the voting sticks were passed around. Long stick for yes, short stick for no. The stillness was thick as mountain fog.

Toohoolhoolzote voted long stick for the Salmon River band. White Bird voted long stick for his band. Hahtalekin voted long stick for the Paloos. Naked Head, sitting in the circle for the powerful Dreamers of all five bands, voted long stick. Ollikut was asked to vote for the Wallowa, making it unanimous, but he would not. Joseph was then sent for and requested to cast his vote in the same way, showing the people there was unity among the chiefs, giving them good heart and spirit for the hard way ahead. Generously, if unwisely, Joseph agreed; and thus was the decision taken.

The people were relieved. They had a plan now. They were going over the Lolo Trail to the land of the curly cows and the friendly Crows. Looking Glass was to be their new leader for the long journey. *Sepekuse*, so be it. That was the vote, that was the end of it.

The camp slept uneasy that night, nonetheless. The cook fires were smoking very early next morning. Almost within an hour the ponies were packed, the starting word passed. The way lay north and east up steep timbered ridges to Weippe Prairie, the historic Camas Meadows where Old Joseph first met Lewis and Clark seventy-two summers before. The time was nearing eight o'clock. The day was July 16, 1877; a cloudy day, cool and with a threat of rain. There was little talk and no laughter among the people. Here and there I saw an old woman weeping, or an old man riding with bowed head and trembling chin. I felt the weight of their sorrow. I knew the keenness of their grief.

I remember stopping my horse at the top of the first ridge and turning him off the trail so that I might look back alone at that lovely place none of us would see again. I remember the tightness at my throat, the sickness in my breast, the tears which arose in my heart but would not fall from my eyes. I even remember the words which cried up within me like broken, injured things, yet made no sound and never passed my lips.

Taz alago, taz alago, Aihits Palojami. Good-bye, good-bye, oh dear Fair Land . . .

Book Four
The Big Hole

24. We Leave the Lodgepoles

After a little while on the trail the chiefs began to worry about One Hand. They decided, without consulting Joseph, that some scouts should go back toward Kamiah Crossing and see what the soldiers were doing. Maybe the scouts last night had been excited. Perhaps the main soldiers were still on the far side of the river. It wasn't like One Hand to come too fast, to push too hard.

Five of us, with Teminisiki, No Heart, as leader, were told to go back. I was picked because I had been to school in Lapwai and the white men knew me for a favorite of Joseph. This, the chiefs thought, would give them confidence in our words. Our instructions were to talk across the river to One Hand, if we found him ready to march after us. The idea was to delay him, if he had not already started, for the trail we were taking was difficult and we needed all the time we could have. We were to talk to him as though the people were ready to surrender if they could do so with terms and conditions as to their own safety and the respecting of their rights to their horses and other property.

By this time it was raining and the trail was getting treacherous even for Indian travel. We got our horses and left the meeting of the chiefs in a hurry.

At the crossing we found the soldiers were indeed getting ready to cross over and come after us. At once No Heart went into his speech. Shortly I could see why he had been selected. What a smile! What a warm, friendly action! What convincing humility! Yet what honest Nez Perce pride and dignity! He was a remarkable liar.

And One Hand took in his talk hungrily. Back and forth went the calls. On our side it was No Heart. On their side it was Narrow Eye Chapman. After half an hour No Heart told Narrow Eye that he would have to discuss what had been said with the rest of us. Narrow Eye said that was all right, and No Heart, who had been out alone at the river's edge, rode back to where we had been waiting.

"Listen," he said, "all the time I was talking One Hand was writing on a piece of paper. Just now he gave it to a rider and that rider started back toward Lapwai. Did you see him from here?"

"Yes," I answered. "He went by the old cut-off. Why?"

"I think we should know what is in that paper," No Heart persisted. "Remember how One Hand tricked us at Lapwai? How he sent for more soldiers while he talked to us of peace? I don't trust him. He is trying to trick us, I think."

"Well," I said, "what do you think we are trying to do to him?"

"That is different," he shrugged. "We are just joking. We are just having a good time with him. We're not trying to hurt anybody, just having some fun."

"Yes, I suppose that's so. What do you propose to do?"

"Well, it's only an idea. But I thought I would talk to One Hand a few more minutes, while two of you slip down and cross over and catch that rider. What do you think?"

Chasing that rider sounded like a good time and so I said yes, I would do it, and away I went with another boy down our side of the river while No Heart went back to talk to One Hand. We had agreed that when we got back I would fire one shot with my rifle from the trail rise behind our side of the crossing, and that would be the signal for No Heart to break off the foolish talk and for all of us to get out of there. We would have gained what time we needed to let the women and children get well up the trail, especially since One Hand was not across the river yet and it was raining harder all the time.

The soldier horses were never anything like our own. They were fat with grain and little hard use. They could no more run a distance of ground in that rough country against a Nez Perce-bred animal than a fat milk goat could keep pace with a Weippe antelope. We caught up with that soldier with the paper in only a few minutes. We jumped him with our horses from two sides of the trail at the same instant and shouldered him in between us as though he were a beef we wanted to throw. We did not hurt the soldier, only knocked him over the head with a *kopluts* and took the paper away from him. None of us with No Heart that day were of the bad boys.

I don't think it was much more than another half-hour before we were back at the crossing. Down by the river No Heart was still talking to Narrow Eye Chapman. They were arguing over which officers would sit in judgment on the Indian side of the trouble. We didn't trust some of One Hand's officers such as Captain Whipple. But it was clear to me that One Hand had already made up his mind and that things were going to be as he wanted them, not the Indians. It was just as Narrow Eye called back to No Heart, saying, "General Howard says you are not to worry about that; he will choose the soldier chiefs to hear your story" that I upended my rifle and pulled the trigger.

Those officers over there ran like rabbits. You would have thought Ollikut was charging them with three hundred warriors. One shot, fired up in the air, and they scattered away as young quail will do who have not learned the difference between the crack of a gun and the snap of a twig. Even Narrow Eye dived for a rock, but we understood that, since by this time he knew he was no longer our brother.

No Heart whirled his horse around. He raised up his loinskirt with one hand, pointing his bare buttocks at General Howard and his whole army. Then he slapped his other hand across his bottom cheeks and made a loud noise with his mouth like a passage of gas, and we all laughed very hard at those soldiers and loped off up the trail, thinking our work extremely well done.

At the first turn which hid us from the river, we stopped and I read the paper for the rest of them. It said:

> . . . Joseph may make a complete surrender tomorrow morning. My troops will meet him at the ferry. He and his people will be treated with justice, their conduct to be completely investigated by a court composed of nine army officers selected by myself. Colonel Miller is designated to receive Joseph and his arms. . . .

It can be imagined what a second good laugh we got out of that. We Nez Perce always saw this thing which No Heart did at Kamiah Crossing as a great joke. We never accepted the idea

that it was treachery and would be so regarded by General
Howard.

It has always been said that we abandoned the lodgepoles at
the Clearwater camp where No Heart slapped his bottom in One
Hand's face. We did not. We meant to make our last tipi camp
at Weippe Prairie, beyond which the old trail was so clogged
with down timber and so broken by sharp rocks and steep
switchbacks that it would not pass a travoisload of poles. So we
had the lodgepoles with us when we left the river. But when
we came up to the people with our paper about Joseph's surrender and the story of No Heart's big joke on One Hand
Howard, *that* was where we left the lodgepoles.

Most of the Indians thought the joke was pretty funny. But
not Joseph. When he heard about it and when I showed him the
paper with his name on it, it was as though he had been struck
in the back with a rusty-bladed lance. He looked at me and said,
"Heyets, you may thank our god that it was not you who did
this fearful thing. Go and get Ollikut and tell him to stop the
march and call the chiefs. We should be able to do it at Dead
Horse Meadow," he finished, no longer talking to me. "That's
not far now and it's the last level place before Weippe."

"Do what at Dead Horse Meadow?" I asked, turning to go.

He stared at me in a way as close to ugliness and anger as I
had ever seen him show. His voice was rough with feeling when
he answered me.

"Don't question me, boy," he said. "Do as you are told. And
when you have done it, stay away from my sight a long time."

I went and got Ollikut. He rode up to the chiefs at the front
of the march, and I could see him and Looking Glass talking
hard. Pretty soon we came to Dead Horse Meadow, a little
patch of grass plastered on the side of the mountain like an
eagle's nest, and I saw the Asotin chief raise his hand and turn
his horse aside from the trail. Toohoolhoolzote, White Bird and
Hahtalekin went with him. Ollikut stayed in the trail, directing
the people to follow the chiefs out into the meadow.

Some shelter from the rain was found under the pines on the

far side. Here a fire was built and the council of headmen gathered around to hear Joseph.

But Joseph did not speak; instead, it was Ollikut. He talked like a warrior, plain and simple. He said that the foolish action of No Heart had one side which was humorous, but another which was dangerous. He said One Hand was not a man who would take an insult like that and laugh about it. He knew One Hand, he said, and so did some of the rest of them there. Did they think One Hand would be laughing right now back there at Kamiah? After getting twenty-three of his men wounded and thirteen killed at Peeta Auüwa? No, he answered the question for the chiefs, One Hand would be sending out scouts and soldier patrols to follow us. The words in One Hand's paper did not sound as though he had meant to be harsh with the Indians in the surrender. Now it would be different. When a man offers his hand to you in good faith and then you spit in his face while holding onto his hand, what do you expect him to do, laugh at you?

By this time most of the council were frowning with thought. A few still wanted to argue, still wanted to insist it was only a joke. But these hard-headed ones did not sway the others. They still frowned seriously and told Ollikut to go on, that they were listening.

It was here that Yellow Wolf, who had posted himself as a lookout among the rocks which edged the meadow's open side overhanging the back trail, came dashing up on his horse to report that a cavalry patrol was coming up the mountain not five miles behind us.

At once the chiefs jumped on their ponies and followed Looking Glass over to the meadow-edge rocks for their own look at the horse soldiers. But the light was not too good, being confused now with sunshafts breaking through the slacking rain, and after a minute the Asotin chief growled out, "Where's that Wallowa boy with the long eye?"

"Here!" called my uncle, Yellow Wolf, and gave my pony a slap with his rifle butt.

I was not displeased to be called upon. I did have some little reputation for far seeing, which was the entire reason, I think, that I had been given so much scouting to do up till then. That, and my ability with horses. Certainly, it was not for my fame as a warrior. It was true that I had shot that soldier at Lahmotta, but he had already seized the barrel of my gun and would have got it away from me had I not accidentally pulled the trigger in fighting him for it. Ollikut had seen how it happened and while he never said a word to anyone about it, I knew where I stood as a Nez Perce hero. As for my fighting in the coward attack of Captain Whipple on the Asotin village, my only Indian witness, little Coyote, was dead and I was satisfied that Redbeard Bates, if he still lived, would not care to stand up at the fire and be counted among the testifiers for Heyets. So I came to the edge of the meadow high above the Lolo Fork of the Clearwater proud enough to have been sent for, but smart enough, for one time, to keep quiet about it and say only to Looking Glass, "*Mana he*, my chief. I am here."

"Yes," he said, "and the soldiers are down there. Use those eyes I have heard about and tell me what you see."

I lay on my belly at the very lip of the outside overhang. Making two little tunnels of my hands, like the tubes of a soldier spyglass, I squinted at the crawling dots far, far below. The distance, taken directly downward as by a fired rifle bullet, was not quite one mile. The air was pretty good, clearing fast and with a clean field of sunshine spreading out over the slope where the soldiers were. I nodded and made a little sign to Looking Glass.

"They're at the Bent Horn turn," I said. "About where Yellow Wolf said. About five miles back."

"You fool!" snapped Looking Glass. "We can see *where* they are. We want to know *who* they are, and *how many!*"

"All right," I said, and tunneled my hands again. "There's one soldier chief I can be sure of. I know him from the strange way he sits a horse. He's from Lapwai. Major Mason. You know the one I mean?"

There were several grunts behind me, answering my question, and Looking Glass said, "Go on, go on."

"Twenty-five, thirty, forty soldiers," I said. Then, quickly, "No, wait. Thirty-two soldiers only. The rest are scouts. Thirty-two soldiers, eight scouts. That's it."

"You know the scouts?"

"No."

"How do they ride? Good? Strong?"

"Very good, very strong. They are of this country."

"Kamiah people!" rasped old Toohoolhoolzote. "Depend on it. We will have to shoot some of them."

"Yes." It was Ollikut, moving for his horse. "And we will have to leave the lodgepoles, too. Let's go."

"Wait," said Looking Glass, holding up his hand. "We don't have to unload yet. We will get the scouts first, then worry about the lodgepoles. Come on."

Ollikut did not move.

"We will unpack the lodgepoles first."

Looking Glass turned around.

"Who said so?"

"Heinmot Tooyalakekt," said Ollikut.

"I am chief now," said Looking Glass.

"Not in my heart," answered Joseph's brother.

Looking Glass's face got dark. His hand twitched on his rifle. But Ollikut's hand was upon his rifle, too, and it was not twitching. His eyes were as scum ice. He watched the Asotin chief, powerful body tense and still.

"Listen, Aleemyah," said Toohoolhoolzote, "what does it matter who said it? I don't care if Otskai, the crazyhead, said it. It's right. We've got to leave the lodgepoles. Our votes which made you leader did not make Heinmot a fool."

"Aye," put in White Bird. "He's still the old man's son, you know."

"Yes," nodded Hahtalekin. "He may be slow with the rifle but he still has the power of his father to think for his people."

"*Tananisa!* Damn!" cried Looking Glass angrily. "What are you doing to me? What are you telling me?"

"We are telling you," Ollikut replied with careful attention to his words, "that as Heyets can see the trail behind, Heinmot

Tooyalakekt can see the trail ahead. I fight for my brother. My brother fights for all of us."

"Bah!" said the Asotin chief. "A real man fights for himself. Come on. Who is going with me to get those scouts and drive those soldiers back?"

"We'll all go," answered Toohoolhoolzote. "It may be a hot fight. Boy," he yelled at me, "go tell Heinmot to get busy with those lodgepoles. We're going down the mountain to give him a little working time."

Before I could think of a decent argument, the whole pack of them was gone across the rain-soaked meadow and off down the muddy trail beyond it.

So it was that I missed the Major Mason fight in the thick timber a mile above the Bent Horn turn in the Lolo Trail. And so it was that I was made to do a woman's work with Joseph in place of a warrior's ride with Ollikut. It was something less than I deserved, I thought. Especially when the very first woman I approached to help with getting her poles unpacked, stood up from behind her travois horse and laughed. "Aha! Heyets. I *knew* you weren't seventeen summers! Knew it all along. The men left you behind again, eh? Here, take the other end of this flap pole. Be careful now, it might strain you."

It was that fool, Beaver, of course. Coyote's sister. The one who had lost the two big teeth in front and gained the lovely curves behind.

"*Enimkinikai,*" I told her without any great excitement, "Go to hell," and picked up my end of the pole.

But my excitement was due to improve. While I was still standing there deciding where to drop that cursed flap pole, I was surprised by a second laugh coming from behind the travois pony's bulky load. That second laugh settled two things for me: where to drop the pole, which I did on my own foot then and there and never even felt it; and who was giggling with Beaver behind that lop-eared pack horse.

I had not seen Meadowlark more than to wave *taz alago* since the cannonshot hit the race-ground grass at Peeta Auüwa. Surely she was not a *tekash* baby any more. She was sixteen summers and she was a woman. When she came ducking under that old pack horse's neck to stand before me on my side of the load, I could see that. Her soft-tanned elk campdress was fitted to her by the wet of the rain, close and clinging as her own skin. I brought up my eyes from her body and she read what was in them, bowed her slim head and said to me, "Take my hand, warrior, I will go with you."

I took her hand, as she said, and we walked away from there into the soft fall of the summer rain.

We stole that hour at the place where Joseph left the lodgepoles, the slim Asotin girl and I, and it was all the wedding we ever knew. We stopped at the first turn of the meadow path into the pines, each taking the other's hands in our own. Holding steady our eyes we spoke the old Nez Perce words: "*Inepne hanisa*, I take you for wife; *hama hanisa*, I take you for husband." After that we stood close a moment in the *piinpt*, the traditional "taking of each other" caress of my people, a gentle embrace without kissing. When that was done Peopeo Tegpeem, the Bright Singing Bird of the Meadows, and Heyets, the shy Bighorn Sheep of the Mountains, were man and mate stronger than any blackrobe could have made them. With our promise given, we sought and found a hidden place for its redeeming.

It was a small dense stand of canyon spruce only minutes from the meadow but as separate from it as another land. With the instincts reserved to the she-animal, Meadowlark guided me to this cover, then led me burrowing on hands and knees into its centermost chamber, which was as warm and dry as a firelit winter lodge, flap-laced against the outer storm. Above and around us I could hear the drive of the rain, increasing under the whip of a rising wind. But where we were, no drop penetrated, no wind stole in. All about us in that forest den was a luminous twilight darkness. Over us was spread the blanket of the warm still air. Beneath us waited the deep bed of woodland mosses and dried sweet grasses.

Before me the lithe form of Meadowlark rose gracefully. Her slender arms made a gliding upward movement and the rainwet campdress was off over her head. She dropped it from her and curled down naked into the bed of moss and grass. We were frantic, I with a boy's brute will to show my manhood, she with a virgin's urgency to prove her womanhood.

Gradually the easing came. We lay a little apart, resting from our union yet not surrendering it. I took her dear head gently into the shelter of my shoulder. I kissed her forehead and her cheek, and she smiled and pressed my hand and moved against me, sighing in tired, full content.

Where the tiny meadow called Dead Horse clings to the mountainside high above Kamiah, we lay in one another's arms for that brief hour which is life's best. The hush and quiet of the forest stole over us. The wind and rain talked distantly outside the blue spruce walls and brown grass floor of our secret wedding lodge. Our breathing grew light, our smiles calm. We slept like children, trustingly and unafraid.

25. War Talk at Weippe Prairie

It rained as though Hunyewat had seen his children's sorrow and sent the water to deepen it for them. The people said they could not remember such a rain. It cut up the land and carved away the earth. It cascaded rocks down the mountainside, sent trees crashing into the canyons. It broke the hillsides loose and boiled the rivers through their landslid flanks. In the few miles remaining to Weippe campground the trail became more like a running stream of Idaho mud than a track of solid ground. The horses were swimming more than walking. The loose stock, of which we had two thousand head, became impossible to drive. When we stumbled and slid out onto the camas meadow at Weippe, the chiefs saw before them an unbroken sheet of water a mile wide standing where the grass had been the week before. The march was halted in the trees at meadow's edge and scouts sent floundering ahead to see about the trail beyond. They returned about nightfall with bad news. The Lolo Trail was nearly impassable. We could expect to make no better speed over it than the pursuing soldiers. If One Hand was to push us hard right now, we could not get away. There was one answer to that; pray he would not push us hard. So be it. The people were told to unpack only what they needed to feed themselves. Everything else was to be reserved in readiness to march with first light. There could be no fires until the fighters who had gone back to stop Major Mason should come up to us and tell us where One Hand was. Meanwhile, we knew what to do: rest where and however we might manage.

I found a fairly good place under a big old deadfall. But when Meadowlark and I stooped to crawl under it we discovered it was already occupied by wet, miserable Indians crowded together like cattle. We were about to despair of shelter when, as we passed a rocky ledge covered by a great shaggy sage bush, a voice I had not heard in many days stopped me.

"Heyets? is that you? In here, boy. Hurry. Don't let anyone see you. We're cramped enough already."

"Father!" I cried. "You are all right!"

"Yes, yes. But don't stand out there telling the whole camp about it. Get in, get in. Bring the girl."

I seized Meadowlark's hand and pulled her around the big sage bush. Behind it, hidden in a way that only a warrior as cunning as my father could have seen, was a break in the rock —not a cave, really, but a fine dry place all the same, and worth about three good horses on a night like this one.

"Father," I asked, "where are you? Who is here?"

"Old friends," he answered. "Horse Blanket and No Feet. We are back safe from Lapwai."

They had been sent to the reservation to learn what they could from friendly treaties inside the boundaries. It was dangerous work and we thought they might have been caught, even hung.

"Are you well, Father?"

"Very well." But I knew from his expression that he mourned my mother.

"And you, great-uncle?"

"Also well," answered Yellow Wolf's father. "Is Hemene all right? Has he worried about his old father?"

"He loves you," I said. "He only teases you about being old."

"I am old," muttered Horse Blanket. "Forty-six years this

snowfall. *Eeh-yahh*. I feel as though I had ridden to the moon and back. *Ukeize*, damn the years, they are not kind. Who is the girl with you?"

"Meadowlark, the Asotin," I said. "We are married today."

"Today?" said my father. "No ceremony then."

"No, Father. We said the words ourselves."

"It is all the same, Heyets, we will love her as our own daughter. Even more. We need a woman in our lodge now."

"Thank you, my father," Meadowlark told him in her low voice. "I am glad to have a home."

There was a little stillness then, while we all sat in the dark with our own thoughts. Presently I asked my father if he knew who was leading the march now.

"Well, I hope it's Heinmot," he said.

"Yes," I said, "it's our chief. There was almost some trouble back at Dead Horse Meadow. Looking Glass didn't want to leave the lodgepoles."

"He's a fool. He thinks bad."

"Aye," growled Horse Blanket. "A big head with a little mind in it. Bad Indian. You'll see."

"Where is he now?" asked my father. "He's certainly not in this camp with Joseph running it."

"No. He's back on the mountain above Kamiah. Some soldiers were scouting us close. Most of the chiefs went with him to drive them off and follow them a ways so we can learn where One Hand is."

"*Eeh*." It was the soft voice of No Feet, the slave Indian, breaking in. "We can do better than that, boy. We can tell you what One Hand is going to do. He is going to take most of his soldiers and go the long south way, around the Mullan Road, to Missoula. You know what that means, boy? Yes. They are going to block up the other end of Lolo Canyon before we can get out of it. Meanwhile, other soldiers will follow us up this side of the mountains. You know what that means? They'll have us. There'll be no place to go. How do you like that?"

"It's very bad, Heyets," said my father. "We were just deciding whether to quit or go on or what to do."

"We'll go on," grunted No Feet. "Those soldiers have orders to shoot us down like crippled coyotes now. We can't go back. There's no place left in this land for a Nez Perce. Not unless he is only looking for a place to leave his bones."

"We will just have to beat One Hand to the other end of the Lolo Trail," sighed my father.

"Yes," I suggested, "unless we beat him before he gets started for the other end."

"What do you mean, boy?"

"I was just thinking of something. You remember how the settlers came running for One Hand when Two Moons took the bad boys up the Tahmonmah on that first raid? And you remember how One Hand came running with the soldiers the minute the settlers cried out for him?"

"Yes, what of it?"

"Just this. Why don't we raid the Kamiah the same way the bad boys raided the Salmon? We don't have to do all that killing. All we have to do is ride through the valley making a lot of noise. The settlers will start yelling and One Hand will have to come running and we will have a good start on him to get over the mountain. What do you say?"

There was a little wait, then my father cleared his throat and spoke to me as warrior to warrior for the first time since my growing up.

"You are a true son of your father," he said. "Let's go talk to Joseph."

Looking Glass and the other fighting chiefs came in at the same time I went with my father to see Joseph about the Kamiah raid. They were wet, hungry, angry and scared. They had beat Major Mason and followed his soldiers all the way back to One Hand's big camp and they had seen a lot of soldiers getting ready to go somewhere—not after us up the Lolo Trail. In fact, some of the soldiers were already leaving the Kamiah camp, marching the opposite way from the Lolo Trail. A smaller bunch had crossed the Clearwater and *were* coming our way. Looking Glass and the chiefs had ridden hard to get around them and come up to us in time to gather all the fighting men and go back and stop those soldiers coming our way. There were not a great many of them; about the same number as with Captain Perry at Lahmotta. It ought to be an easy fight. After it, we could take our time getting over the trail into Montana.

"*Tananisa!*" said Looking Glass angrily. "There you are!" He glared at Joseph, then swung around to ask of the rest of us, "Did I not tell you we should wait and make one more fight? Did I not argue with Heinmot back there at Dead Horse Meadow? Now see what has happened."

"What has happened, Aleemyah?" asked Joseph quietly.

Looking Glass turned back to him, dark face scowling. "One Hand has given up. He is going back to Walla Walla. We have beaten him and you have abandoned the lodgepoles for nothing. Our people sleep in the rain; they can thank you for that. If they had listened to me they would be safe and dry under their own tipis this moment."

"And do you know where they will be in a few days if you go back and make this last fight you are so anxious to make?" Joseph said. "They will be back at Lapwai on their way to the Hot Place, and you and I and all the chiefs here will be with them. We know that, Aleemyah; I do not say it to anger you or to make you look awkward. We know where it is One Hand is going and what he means to do. He has gone to close the other end of the Lolo Trail, old friend. Seeskoomkee has found that out from the Indians at Lapwai, and we have no choice but to believe him for he also has told us of this other soldier column coming behind you. Hear him yourself, Aleemyah. You are the leader now, it is for you to decide. I only say my part for my own people. It is for you and all the people to say if I left the lodgepoles too soon."

Quickly then No Feet repeated his story, and my father and Yellow Wolf's father supported it, saying they had sat by and heard the treaty Indian tell it to Seeskoomkee. There was no arguing against such witnesses.

Ollikut stood up. "Heinmot is right again. What good will it do to fight those few soldiers behind us, when One Hand has gone over the mountain with all the others? The only question is what to do about One Hand."

"We can beat him over the mountain," answered Looking Glass at once.

Joseph nodded calmly. "Better yet, we can beat him before he goes over the mountain."

"What?" snapped Looking Glass. "Do you make small of me, Heinmot? Do you joke?"

"Don't ask me," said Joseph with soft pride. "Ask this boy, Heyets. It is his idea."

"A boy? A wet-nosed Wallowa who has shot one soldier? *I* am to ask *him?*"

"Try it," said Ollikut.

"Never!" growled Looking Glass.

"Wait a minute," said old White Bird, limping forward to peer at me. "I know this boy. He's the one Heinmot sent to school at Lapwai. The one Agent Monteith says is *cultis cultis*, no good twice. That's enough for us. Speak up, boy."

Quickly then I told them my idea of raiding the Kamiah. It was very well received, too.

"Listen," said old Toohoolhoolzote, "the boy is right. Those settlers have just gone back to their homes from the soldier camp at the crossing. They are thinking the Nez Perce are chased over the mountain. We can slaughter them like beeves."

"Better yet," said Ollikut, "we can run off all their horses. They have not had time to gather them up again."

"That's right," agreed Hahtalekin. "They turned them all out when they ran into the soldiers at the crossing."

"Well, I don't know," put in White Bird. "Just taking a few horses might not be the thing. Nothing like killing a few whites to get the soldiers to come running back."

"The horses will do it," argued another chief. "Why start killing again?"

"Yes," said still another. "We don't want to fight the soldiers, we only want to fool them. That was the idea the boy had."

The argument began to get pretty hot. Everybody was wet, hungry and unhappy. But Joseph turned them off short of trouble. "Aleemyah," he said quietly to Looking Glass, "it is for you to decide. You must tell us what to do. You are the leader now."

The Asotin chief liked that. It was just the right thing to say on Joseph's part. The little dark-faced fighter stood up and made one of his long war talks. At the end of it all the chiefs were very enthusiastic about Looking Glass's great idea of raiding down into the Kamiah to keep One Hand from going over the Mullan Road to Missoula. Starting time was set for first light tomorrow. It was to be a horse raid with as little killing as possible. The chiefs filed away from the council well satisfied with their new leader and confident that the Kamiah raid was a stroke of purely superior Nez Perce mind-power.

For my part, how could I fail to agree?

26. The Lolo Trail

Four hundred eighty-six horses, that is what we ran off from the Kamiah raid. With what we had, it started us over the Lolo Trail with very nearly twenty-five hundred horses. That is not all. The raid set those settlers to yelping like stoned dogs. The soldiers behind us held up to protect them until One Hand could come running back from his start for the Mullan Road. And back he did come running. For ten days he had to sit in the valley with his main force of soldiers, waiting for still more soldiers who were coming up from Walla Walla. And in those ten days we got our start on him up that dangerous Indian track over the Bitterroot Mountains to Montana.

At that point it looked well for the Nez Perce. We had behind us only the same small force which had trailed Looking Glass and the Major Mason fighters back from their scout to Kamiah Crossing. These soldiers were few and very careful. They stayed far back and were really only scouts, keeping us in view for One Hand, making sure we did not leave the Lolo and double back into Idaho. Really they were just herding us, and we did our best to give them some honest work. In this direction we had a good and true friend; the Lolo Trail. She was a hard mother to us, but she was a mother.

I have promised not to put down here what I did not see with my own eyes, or hear from a companion whose honor was beyond all doubt. But that trail was such a devil that the word of an Indian is best supported by that of a white man in telling of the hardships we put upon those poor soldiers when we led them over it. Listen, then, to one of General Howard's own men, Captain Farrow, telling it for the white man's history.

"The trail ahead being obstructed by fallen trees of all sizes and descriptions, uprooted by the winds and matted together in every possible troublesome way, a company of forty 'pioneers' with axes was organized and sent ahead to open the trail, wherever possible. It is true that the Indians had gone over this trail ahead of the troops; but they had jammed their ponies through, over and under rocks, around, over and under logs and fallen trees and through the densest undergrowth, and left blood to mark their path, with abandoned animals with broken legs or stretched dead on the trail. . . .

"The following, from the record of August 2nd, will serve to show the nature of these daily marches:

"'The command left camp at seven A.M., artillery at head of the column. The trail led through the woods of the same general character; a "slow trail" owing to the mountainous country and fallen timber. The summit of the hills was covered with rough granite boulders, making the path quite difficult. . . . We march sixteen miles and encamp on a slope of the mountain. Poor grazing; the only feed consists of wild dwarf lupine and wire-grass. Several mules were exhausted and some ninety packs of bacon were abandoned along the way. Dead and broken-down Indian ponies very numerous along the trail. Camp made about four P.M.'"

That was how hard the whites found our friend and mother, the Lolo Trail, that rainy summer of 1877. And they were soldiers, carrying only supplies and weapons for themselves, concerned only with eating so much food and riding so many miles each day. Imagine what we Indians found for handicaps along that same road, burdened as we were with twenty-five hundred horses, four hundred women, children and old people, all the heavy baggage of a moving tribe leaving a homeland they expected never to see again, and bearing along with them every necessary thing for starting a new life in a new, strange country. Add to that the nearly unbelievable problem of transporting our wounded from the hot fights with One Hand Howard at White Bird Canyon and along the Clearwater, plus the old ones getting sick from the hard travel and long bad weather, and some idea may be had of what an Indian might have written for his people's history of those difficult days along the Lolo. Yet they were nothing, those Lolo days, to what lay waiting beyond them.

Driving hard for five suns after leaving Weippe, we reached the first good grass and stock water on the trail at Lolo Hot Springs on the sixth night. Looking Glass ordered all animals unpacked and turned out, explaining proudly from the back of his horse why this should be.

"We have left the soldiers far behind," he said. "It is even as I told you it would be. Where is One Hand, I ask you? He is over there." He pointed west, back toward Lapwai. "And where are we, I ask you?" he went on. "Here, right here." He pointed down to the ground beneath him. "It is just as I said it would be. We are safe. The way, from this place forward, lies all down the hill. The land before us is friendly to us, the people here like and trust the Nez Perce. We won't hurry the old ones or the injured any more now. Meanwhile, let prayers be spoken to the Great Spirit for our guidance out of Idaho and our deliverance into Montana. Pray to the old gods and be grateful."

It was a pretty good talk for the Asotin, I thought, not as vain as most I had heard from him, even though he did praise himself a trifle strong here and there along the way. However, the others seemed to like it well enough and in a spirit of agreement Joseph was moved to make a little speech in which he reminded the people that this spot was the place that Lewis and Clark had named Traveler's Rest, and which they had felt to possess some magical power to heal and refresh the weary in both spirit and flesh.

"Let us now forget our war with the Idaho and Oregon people, and with One Hand Howard's soldiers. Let us think, instead, of this old friendship for the white man which our fathers handed down to us and which we have lost. Indeed, my dear friends, let there be prayers of thankfulness as Aleemyah has said. Let us think only of the new land and the new life which lies ahead, and let us go forward to face it as with one heart beating in one body."

This, too, was a good talk. Now everything was all right. Not only was One Hand left behind but Heinmot and Aleemyah were friends again. Wasn't that a wonderful thing? Everybody here safe and well. The horse herd in good condition. Weather clearing. Trail drying out. Blue sky ahead. Buffalo ahead. Crow friends and white friends waiting to help us along our happy way. *Eeeh-hahh!* Wonderful, wonderful.

Those were four fine days we spent there at the hot springs. Kipkip Owyeen was up and walking around, recovering from his bad wound in the breast at Peeta Auüwa. Three women had new babies with no trouble. Dookiyon, my old friend, The Smoker, decided he wasn't going to die of the joint fever after all and that if Montana was going to be this good for his aching bones we should have moved here long ago. The other old people cheered up, too. And of course that cheered the young ones in turn, putting us all in better mind and spirit than we had been since the Kamiah people had turned us back at the Clearwater in the good old days of the President Grant treaty.

This was the feeling, then, when on the fifth day we resumed the march into Montana. It was, I believe, the twenty-seventh sun of July. Our way led down the high-walled, lovely path of Lolo Canyon. Beyond its narrow rock-bound issuance onto the plains below waited Bitterroot Valley and the new life in the Land of the Buffalo. All about me I could see the people lifting their faces as they rode along. I could see their lips moving, and I did not have to hear them speak to know what they were saying.

The words were in my own breast, too. *Inimnig ues timine eneke.* I am again the master of my heart. *Imene kaiziyeuyeu.* Thank Thee.

27. The Bitterroot Treaty

We came around the last turn in the canyon and there they were waiting for us, those friendly people of Montana. There were about two hundred of them, and a captain and thirty soldiers. They waited for us behind a barricade of big logs they had built across the Lolo Trail. All had rifles. All were dressed for war. They looked at us above the logs of their fort, and we looked back at them. A big stillness grew on both sides.

Looking Glass, White Bird and Joseph rode forward. Yellow Wolf and I, who had been riding with Joseph, stayed with him and went forward, too. There were only five of us, but you could see we made the Montana people very nervous, even though we had on no feathers and rode our poorest traveling horses.

Looking Glass was hot with anger and led us up to the muzzles of their guns, very nearly, before he stopped his horse and demanded in Nez Perce to know who those people were and why they sought to block the way of his people.

There was quite a scurry of talk among the settlers and the soldiers, several of them trying to answer Looking Glass at the same time. But none of them spoke our language. One tried Salish, another Chinook; a third tried some very poor hand signs, which we recognized as Sioux but which we could not be sure of, and so could not reply to. Joseph nodded to me that I was to follow him, and he pushed his horse up beside that of the Asotin chief. Making the truce sign to the soldier captain, he pointed to me and made the talking sign, indicating that I would be the interpreter.

It will be said by many that Joseph did not speak English. Some have written that he did not speak a word of English. That is not quite true. He had been to school with the good agent

Spalding; he was one of the brightest Indian pupils they ever had at Lapwai, and the school records will prove this. But after so many years he was not comfortable in the tongue and, like most Indians, found it convenient to let the white man think he was what they liked to call "a heathen savage" or "dumb Injun." He always preferred to have one of us talk for him and in this case it was me, because I was at hand and because the one thing I had learned at Lapwai was to command the tongue my mother had taught me from my first words as a *tekash* toddler.

Now the white soldier returned Joseph's peace sign. He did it in a clumsy way which showed he was not old to that country, and our talk began.

He was Captain Charles Rawn, he said to me. He and his thirty men were from Fort Missoula, where they were a guard for the workers then building that place. The other men were all from Missoula and the Bitterroot Valley, and they did not want us to go through their land. His orders, he said, were to turn us back over the Lolo Trail into Idaho. I told this to the three chiefs, and Looking Glass said, "Ask him who gave him the orders. I don't believe him."

I asked the question of Rawn and he replied, "General Howard." I told this to Looking Glass and he cried out, "That's a white dog's lie! One Hand is back in Idaho! How could he say this to a captain clear over here?" When I asked this of Rawn, he quickly said, "By the telegraph."

That was a simple thing but we had forgotten it. However, it didn't worry us. Looking Glass said that we had no fight with Rawn, only with General Howard. All Rawn had to do was give us free passage into the valley. We would harm no one. We would travel peacefully as we had always done in going to the buffalo. Each of our chiefs would guard the conduct of his own band. What did the white captain say?

Rawn replied that it was impossible; that he was acting under direct orders from General Howard and could not accept any terms. He would fight, he said.

But now the settler volunteers from Missoula began to talk. They knew many of our people, nearly all of our chiefs. Joseph,

Looking Glass and Eagle from the Light had been through here two years ago, going to talk with the Sioux about fighting the white man in eastern Montana. Looking Glass had been in Missoula only the very year before this one, having his eyes treated by a white doctor. We had friends back of those logs after all. A lot of them now told Captain Rawn to let us go through as we asked. Rawn would not do it.

The settlers held fast. If they could protect their valley homes by a treaty with us, why should they start an Indian war? They told Rawn we would stand to our words; that we were Nez Perce. Rawn still said no. Then it was that most of the settlers picked up their guns and went home. They told Looking Glass, "Chief, we take the treaty," and they got on their horses and left. About thirty of them—always there was that certain number who wanted to kill Indians any way they could—stayed with the soldiers. That made about sixty of them altogether.

Much lying has been done about what then happened. This is what we heard. Looking Glass said to Rawn, "You look hard up the north way. We are going this way, around the south end of your logs. You look where I tell you, you will not see us do it. One Hand cannot blame you then." And Rawn said helplessly, "What can I do? What can I do?"

Some of the Indian killers behind the logs were very angry, but that soldier captain agreed to let us ride by and we did ride by. There were a few shots fired by the settlers and a few by the soldiers. That we understood. They were keeping up their pride. But we had the word of the white captain and no Nez Perce touched his rifle that day. We knew those pride bullets would fly high, and they did.

Once all the people were around the logs in the trail, we waited to see what those soldiers and those Missoula people were going to do; whether they were going to honor their word or not. They left their logs right away and rode off in a hurry toward Missoula. We took it from that that they understood us as we understood them. Looking Glass said, "*Taz taz*, all is well. We will go south up the valley for a ways, camping near Carlton in the old place. Come on, we will talk when we get there."

So we left the place of the logs, thinking we had gained safe passage of the Bitterroot. We called that spot in our history the Place of the Lolo Treaty. The white man had a better name for it in his history. He called it Fort Fizzle.

That night in the council at Carlton camp, the chiefs debated the best course to take over the mountains which remained between us and the buffalo. At that time the idea was still to join the Crows and live with them; a good idea it seemed to most of us. The Crows hated the Sioux, who were our traditional enemies, and would help protect us from them while we got started in our new life. They were also the friends of the whites and would serve to let us, too, become friendly with them. No one up to that camp had said a word against the plan of going to live with the Crows. But now things changed. Some of the people were starting to worry.

There was something wrong with that easy way he had walked past Captain Rawn. The afternoon march had given us time to think, and a few of us were not so sure we had a treaty. Talk went around. The chiefs heard it and listened to it. The council argued with growing anger.

Joseph sat aside and did not join in. Ever since seeing the logs across the trail he had been quiet and sad. It was as though he saw something up there the rest of us had not seen. Now, as the other chiefs argued, he looked far away, back down the valley from where we had come, and even farther than that, back across the Bitterroot to the Kamiah, the Clearwater, to the Wallowa and home.

The other chiefs ignored him. It would have been a good time for all those who have written how Joseph led the Nez Perce all the way, to see him sitting there alone that night. It would have made small, too, those others who have written what a great military mind he had, what a great commander of his "red troops" he was, how the Nez Perce adored him and leaned upon his every wish and word. *Hahh!* A few of us loved him, yes. We of his blood kin, like Yellow Wolf and me. A good many of the older Indians honored him, too, and listened to him as the son of Tuekakas, Old Joseph, the *real* Joseph. But at that camp, and from the time they had stood upon the Lapwai bank of the Snake River staring down its rocky throat at all their horses smashed and drowned in the black water, most of those Indians had closed their hearts and covered their ears against the chief of my people. So the debating of the course went on without him.

There were two old-time ways to go. The short one led up the Big Blackfoot River, over Cadotte Pass and down Sun River. The long one led down the Jefferson River to Three Forks and over Bozeman Pass to the Yellowstone. Both these routes were now thought to be too dangerous. Fort Shaw and the town of Helena crowded the first one; Fort Ellis and Virginia City threatened the second. The chiefs believed it wise to avoid both army forts and mining camps in order to make the best time and be sure of peaceful traveling.

The council was thrown open to other suggestions. White Bird and Red Owl had one. Why not swing to the north? The rivers west of Missoula could be got past either by night marching or by a new treaty like the one today. Go straight north then, through the Flathead country to the top end of Flathead Lake. Everybody knew the easy trail which ran from there, by Marias Pass, to the plains beyond. What was wrong with that?

Looking Glass and Five Wounds had a better idea, they said. Go south through the Ross Hole country to the headwaters of the Jefferson. Then, don't turn east to Bozeman and Three Forks by the old trail, but swing far, far south, following the Great Ridge of the Big Mountains to the white man's new reservation, Yellowstone Park. Go past the park until they struck the Stinking Water, and down it into the land of their friends, the Absoroka, the mountain Crows. Was that, or was that not, a craftier plan?

Toohoolhoolzote and Naked Head, the Too-at prophet, stood with White Bird and Red Owl. Hahtalekin, Peopeo Tholekt, Rainbow and some others of equal rank stood with Looking Glass and Five Wounds. It was the White Bird and Salmon River bands against the Paloos and Asotin. Joseph was called up to cast the deciding vote for the Wallowa. It was then we learned why he had been looking back all day. He dropped his answer like a thunderbolt among us.

"My people," he said, "some of you have believed that I have a gift for seeing the trail ahead. If you truly believe this, listen to me now. The trail ahead is dark and full of sorrow. Turn back, my friends, turn back. If One Hand will still let us go home, I beg you to think about it. You ask me, should we go north or should we go south? Here is my answer. Go west. Go back to the Wallowa, to our beautiful Valley of the Winding Water. It is our home. We should never have left it, we should never have come here."

The people were struck silent.

There were not many there who did not know that Joseph had the power to see ahead. They might turn away from him because he had talked them into obeying Agent Monteith's order to come in to Lapwai. Or because he would not ride and fight in the first line, as at Lahmotta. Or because when the bullets were thickest he seemed always back with the women and children, as at Peeta Auüwa. But only the fiercest Too-ats, only the hardest-believing Dreamers among them, did not admit that Heinmot Tooyalakekt had a "power" to see beyond the eyes of ordinary men. So they fell still, and in that moment of hesitation they might well have taken a different direction than that which led them to that dark place which Joseph saw ahead.

But Looking Glass was of the Too-at thinking. And he was a warrior. "Heinmot," he said, "we are friends, but I don't trust your visions any more. The white man has put clouds in your eye. You saw wrong back there in Idaho. Why should we listen to you now?"

"I cannot answer that," said Joseph, dropping his gaze. "It is true I failed my people. What do you suggest?"

"That you listen to me; that you tell the people to listen to me."

Joseph accepted that.

"All right, Aleemyah. I have spoken. What is it you would say?"

"A question, Heinmot. One question of you, as chief to chief."

"Ask it, my brother."

"*Tasnig*," rasped the dark-faced Asotin fighter. "Did you, or did you not, with the other chiefs, elect me for leader through this country, because I knew it and the people, and did you not promise me that I should have the whole command to do as I pleased?"

Joseph sat for a little time, his head bowed. We could not see his face. But I watched his hands where they were clasped in front of him, and in their very stillness they cried out to us who loved him, louder than the loudest words. At last he raised his tired brown eyes and said very softly to Looking Glass, "You are right, Aleemyah. We did elect you head man of the camp. Go ahead and do the best."

28. The Council of Tinukin

Having now twice tested the leadership of Looking Glass and twice failed to find support for his own instinctive fears of leaving the homeland, Joseph accepted the will of the Asotin to go forward into Montana.

For his part, Looking Glass showed no uncertainty. He continued to insist, as he had since the hot springs camp, that there was no need to hurry. He ordered the people to keep their promises of the Bitterroot Treaty—to pass in peace up the valley—and that was all he asked of them. He even permitted a stop at one town, Stevensville, which the more nervous among us considered very risky indeed.

Still, we needed flour, coffee, sugar, salt, tobacco and tea, very important things to Indians used to living almost as white men. And it developed that the merchants of Stevensville were happy to take our trade, accepting either our gold or our fine horses with equal eagerness and at wickedly unfair prices. Yet there was no trouble, and the leadership of Looking Glass took on new strength.

As the Asotin had assured the settlers at the fort of logs, each of our main chiefs watched his own band and was responsible for its behavior. If a man did a wrong thing, he was to be disciplined at once and not gently. On this, Looking Glass was very severe, setting his own examples.

One of his Asotins grew loud with a storekeeper over the terrible charges made us, and Looking Glass threw the fellow out of the store into the street, ordering him back to camp under a six-man pony guard. Another time, half a dozen young Salmon River troublemakers, led by that old rascal Toohoolhoolzote himself, broke into an empty ranch shack taking some moldy flour, a little coffee, a rusty horseshoe rasp, three patched blue shirts and a handsome white vessel kept under the bed for urinating at night without going out in the grass. When word of that wrong reached Looking Glass, he made the Salmon Rivers pick seven good horses, one for each of the men who had made the break-in, and turn them into the rancher's fenced field in payment of the theft. The most remarkable part of this seven-horse command of his was that old Toohoolhoolzote obeyed him in it.

That was when I took my second look at our little Asotin leader who never smiled. When he later succeeded in keeping all of us in and around Stevensville for the rest of our stay there, with not one other white man complaining of any goods or stock stolen, or any of his family disturbed by an Indian, I took my third look at Aleemyah Tatkaneen. With that look, I decided Joseph may have been more right, than righteous, when he had bowed his head and told Looking Glass to go ahead and do his best.

Plainly, the Asotin's best was better than I had been prepared to believe. Not that I liked him yet. I didn't. But I still had to grant, by the time he had us safely away from Stevensville, that he was a pretty good trail chief.

We still went too slow, I thought, no more than fifteen miles a day. But Looking Glass kept saying, "No hurry, no hurry," and riding his gray traveling horse on south up the valley of the Bitterroot, sitting straight on him as a little brown twist of trade tobacco, his black cavalry soldier's hat with the Nez Perce otter-fur tassels pinned on the front of it perched square on his head, his Winchester under his right leg, his buffalo bow in his left hand, his fierce eyes never looking anywhere but ahead. And behind him the people said, "*Taz, taz,* that is good," bobbed their heads and followed where he led them, showing neither fear nor hesitation.

In that spirit we climbed out of the valley across the spine of the mountains, which we called the Big Ridge and which the whites called the Continental Divide. On the other side we went down the hill along the banks of the Big Hole River. Presently Looking Glass told us that we would camp by the river and cut lodgepoles. He thought that would be good news, and it was. By then we were all plenty tired of living without our tipis to cover us. "*Taz, taz,*" smiled the people again, and those last miles along the trail saw a great many kind words said for the leadership of Aleemyah Tatkaneen.

What few whites we passed gave us a lot of riding room, and we did the same for them. None of us dreamed that those whites might be spying on us. None of us thought of Joseph's warning. None of us remembered the telegraph.

But the telegraph remembered us. Up the valley of the Bitterroot, hard upon our rear, it called an enemy we had never heard of. He was an eagle chief, coming swiftly from Fort Shaw beyond Helena. He had with him one hundred sixty-three men. Of these nearly one hundred were his own soldiers from the fort. They were old soldiers, some time in the country, not afraid of breaking a hard trail or an honest treaty. The others with him were Captain Rawn's thirty cowards from the log fence across the Lolo Pass, and the thirty or thirty-five of the white Indian-haters from Missoula who had stayed with Rawn at the logs.

That eagle chief was smart. And he was hungry. He was smelling a great fame for himself if he could come up to Joseph's people. He ran our trail as though we had left hot blood on it. His men, riding in wagons taken from our settler friends in the Bitterroot, were rolling up behind us at a speed of thirty-five miles a day. They were blowing up behind us like a deadly cyclone; and we all the time smiling and nodding to one another and saying "*taz, taz*" and listening to Looking Glass calling out "no hurry, no hurry" and thinking only of getting down the hill to Iskumtselalik Pah, the Place of the Ground Squirrels, our old tribal gathering spot where we would cut the lodgepole pines which gave us our tipi frames, and set up the first real camp we had known in twenty-seven suns.

Oh yes. The name of that colonel who ran our trail with the blood hunger of a hunting weasel? It was Gibbon. John Gibbon. The one the Sioux called Red Nose. The one who came too late to save Custer. The one who thought he was in treacherous time to kill Joseph at the Big Hole.

Where thick timber covers all the hills and ridges of a land, the small pines standing close and stiff as hairs on a growling dog's back, the open places where the rivers spread out to wander more slowly are called "holes" by the white men. *"Tegpeem"* is the Nez Perce word. It means "meadow," or "flat place with grass." But whether meadow or hole, the word was a happy one in either tongue. It was where both white and Indian found the grass and water and wood lying all together, and so was where the very best of camps and memories were made.

These meadows were sometimes called after the men who first found them, as with Ross Hole, or after the stream which watered them, as with Big Hole, where we Nez Perce pitched our tipis late in the first week of that August, 1877. It was a lovely place, believe that. And we made a good start in it. The hot summer sun gave us good help to get in and dry the poles, and in no time we had the lodgeskins stretched over the frames and our village laid out along the river in the regular V-shaped plat used by our people. By the stream, pretty clumps of water willow grew light and yellow green. Back from it, tall single pines dotted the rich meadow with their red bark and gray-blue needles. After the long flight from Idaho, reaching that Big Hole camp in Montana was like reaching Ahkunkenekoo, the Nez Perce Land Above. The sound of the people laughing and singing once more, the sight of our beautiful horses again feeding on fat grass, the familiar smell of fire smoke mixed with lodgeskin cowhide, the splashing, cheery calls of the bathers from the

river, all these long-absent things filled our hearts with thankfulness, invaded our minds with peace and contentment. Yet something lay uneasy beneath it all.

On that last afternoon I lay lazy with Meadowlark for a while
around our lodge. She had driven my father's four pack horses
with all my mother's homekeeping things and our family tipiskins
the whole way over the Lolo, and I was very proud of her.
But after a while, kissing her and leaving her to chatter with
Beaver, who had come by to see how we were getting along in
our first home, I set out through the camp to seek out what was
the matter with it, why it did not lie altogether easy.

I knew, of course, that most of the people would not realize
what I was worrying about. For the most part, they were of
cheerful heart now. They worked, played, talked of little but the
new life waiting in the land of the Crows. It was not my purpose,
either, to diminish their fine spirit. Yet there were others in that
camp who, like myself, were not so restful in their minds.

The first of these, I was sure, would be Joseph. I had put our
lodge close to his, between his and Ollikut's, which was just
along the stream a ways, so I did not use my pony but walked.
In truth, I did not even have a horse up from the herd and
staked. This alone should have warned of our carelessness at the
Big Hole. No one had ponies up and staked that last afternoon.

Joseph was not at home. Springtime, the young wife, told me
he had gone up to talk to Looking Glass about moving on.
"But," she said, "Ollikut was just here and you can go see him.
There's a meeting over near his lodge to talk of the same thing.
Some of the men are uneasy. You know how that is; there are al-
ways a few like that."

"Yes," I agreed, "always a few. I wouldn't worry about them.
Uneasiness comes into the world with some of us. It runs heavy
in the blood of Joseph, as you know."

"*Eeh!* Do I know? Any woman who sleeps with Heinmot
Tooyalakekt knows! He paces the tipi floor by night. He sits out
by the fire long after the embers are cold. He looks up the trail,
he looks back the trail, he will not lie down, he will not close
his eyes. Always and always he thinks of the people. *Hahh!*

Sometimes I wish he were of an empty mind like Otskai's. I will tell you, Heyets, it is not easy being a chief's wife."

"I know, I know. How's the baby?"

"Fine. Fat as tallow. Strong like her father."

"Yes, and beautiful like her mother."

"You always say that."

"It's always true. *Taz alago*."

"*Taz alago*, Heyets. If you see Heinmot, tell him to get home. The supper is almost ready." I waved to her and walked away.

It was nearing dusk now, the sun down behind the Bitterroots to the west, the late summer day shortening swiftly. All over camp the cookfires were being lit and that stillness which comes with eating time in a happy village at a perfect day's end lay all about our lodges in that lovely place. There was not even a horse guard out; not even any of the young boys were out watching to see that their family's stock fed where the grass was best, as Coyote and I used to do on the hills above the Wallowa. What a scene of peace. Or was it?

At the tipi of Joseph's brother I found Ollikut's second wife, the older one called Fair Land, nursing his new infant son, Tewatakis. She looked up as I drew near and before I could say a word she nodded toward the trees.

"They're over there in the pines, nephew. Ollikut didn't want anyone to take alarm from seeing them gather."

I looked at her curiously.

"How did you know I came here about that meeting?"

"*Eeh*, you're of the blood, aren't you? All alike, all of you. Ollikut the very worst of the lot. Your uncle Hemene next. Go on now, boy. The baby's watching you. He won't suck."

"All right, thank you. You say Hemene is with them?"

"I didn't say it, but he is. And why not? He's your uncle, isn't he? And Ollikut's nephew? *Hahh!* To be honest with you, Heyets, I sometimes wish I had married a coward or an old man. It's not easy to be the wife of a warrior."

"*Ipselpise lammatiz kuse*," I laughed, "trouble doesn't pick any of us up with gentle fingers. *Taz alago*."

"You talk like your grand-uncle, Heinmot," she called after

me. "Like a threshing pony walking in circles."

I made her no answer. Indeed, I had none for her. Over in the pines I came upon the men squatting in the growing darkness, smoking hard, talking the same way. One following another, they testified to the *zeuzeu*, the uneasy spirit, which had brought them there.

Wahlitits, that savage boy who had started the war with One Hand by his Salmon River killings, said he had dreamed a death dream three nights gone. Lone Bird, a noted warrior, said that a voice had come to him out of the clear sunshine two days ago, saying not to linger there at the Big Hole, that it was a place of death, that all must hasten on from there. Wottolen, Hair Combed Over Eyes, one of our most honored men and a terrible fighter, trembled like a woman in labor and said that the first night of this camp he had seen the face of his father in the smoke of his woman's cookfire and that the old man had cried out to him, "Scout back! Scout back! Death is coming behind!"

Poker Joe, a half-breed Nez Perce who had met us on his way home from the buffalo and who had joined us in the march up the Bitterroot with his six lodges of people, now spoke and told us that the hearts of the Montana settlers were not as good for us as we thought. He also warned us that we must stop thinking One Hand Howard had all the soldiers there were. There were other soldiers, said Poker Joe, scattered all over that Montana country. We had better keep wide awake and not stay here too long.

Owhi, a wandering Yakima of high blood who had also fallen in with our march, got up and said that he, too, had just come from the buffalo and that Poker Joe was right—there were a lot of soldiers in that country.

The last man of exceptional reputation to speak was another half-breed of our own blood, also a late joiner of the retreat, a bad-eyed man with a temper to match his ax-blade face and ugly mind. His Nez Perce name was Heinmot Tosinlikt, Bunched Lightning. The white men in Montana knew him as Henry Rivers. He called himself Tabador, a word of no meaning in our tongue. By any name he was a bad Indian.

"I won't talk to you much," said Tabador, "so you better hear me pretty good. This camp stinks of death like a horse swollen six days in the sun. I don't mind to die, but I don't care to sit around with the smell of it in my nose. It makes me nervous. I say we go now, *amtiz!*"

After that, others of almost equal name as brave ones added their stories. Some were not so full of death but all held warning, in one way or another, of uneasiness about the Big Hole. When the last had spoken, the men in the pines took a decision to call a meeting of the Council of Twelve, our intertribal headmen, whose rulings were asked only in the most serious matters. It was agreed, upon Ollikut's request, to await the return of Joseph in the event he had been able to persuade Looking Glass through his own power.

But Joseph soon came up out of the twilight dusk and said to Ollikut, "It was no good, brother, he would not do it," and Ollikut said, "All right, we had better call the council, then. Come on."

We got up and went our separate ways to await the meeting and ruling of the council. I started home to Meadowlark but as I came up behind our tipi I heard her saying to Beaver, "I don't know, sometimes it is not so easy being the wife of a young man with no reputation; perhaps I should have married a warrior, or an older man with a lot of horses," and that made me mad enough so that I went on up to the council lodge and did my waiting there.

I was in time to see the last three members go in—Eagle from the Light, Yellow Bull, Naked Head—and was lucky to find a spot near the sideskins of the lodge where I could plainly hear what went on inside.

The talk was hard and it was hot. The vote came and it was nine to three for moving on, with four votes for making a back scout that night, as proposed by Wottolen.

Looking Glass then grew angry. His *simiakia*, his great Indian self-pride, would not let him change his mind. He stood up and told the chiefs that if they wanted to move on, they would have to elect a new leader to do so. As long as he, Aleemyah Tat-

kaneen, was leader, the camp was going to move only when he
said it might and not one-half sun sooner.

There was grumbling but no agreement was reached as to a
new leader. Once again Looking Glass had his way. The twelve
headmen went back to their lodges and their late suppers, still
arguing but with little spirit. Some of the ones who had called
the council admitted their dreams had not always been right;
most of their companions shrugged and said, "*lolikug, timmiuze*,"
they guessed the same was true for them. Wottolen did try for a
little while to get some of us to scout back toward the Bitterroot
with him, but we all had different things to do, and pretty quick
he went off and bedded down with his wife and forgot all about
the face of his old father in the fire.

I, too, my short anger at her forgiven with the sudden thought
of her soft body which came to me as I went toward our lodge,
sought the warm willingness of my wife's bed. We were, all of
us, no different from Wottolen. None of us was lacking in blame
that murky August night.

It was the fault of every Nez Perce who sat in the pines with
Ollikut, or waited outside the lodge of Looking Glass, or said no
to the urgings of Wottolen to scout back, that the gathering of
the twelve chiefs at Big Hole came to be called what it was in
the history of our people : *Piamkin Tinukin*, the Council of
Death.

29. Battle of the Big Hole

The dark hours passed and I could not sleep. By my side
Meadowlark breathed quietly. Many times I drowsed, myself,
but each time awakened with a start as though I had heard something in my half-sleep. After a long while it came to me what
was the trouble—I *had not* heard anything.

This was the time of morning when, back in the hills, the
coyotes should be crying as they trotted home to their dens after
the night's hunting. Down among the potholes of the river a
mud hen or mallard ought to be giving the early feed call. In the

alders away from the stream a mourning dove or rain crow ought to be talking. Actually there was no sound beyond our lodge save the soft swirl of the water flowing against the willow roots.

I moved carefully away from the trusting body of my young wife. I thought of getting my rifle, then did not do it. Outside, it was getting gray. During the night a mist had grown on the river and crept in among our tipis. Here and there were breaks and clear spots in its dripping wall; here and there its long stringers of blind gray fog blotted everything from sight. I shivered and peered about me.

Of a sudden, out of one of the fog banks on our side of the river, I was startled to see a horseman come riding. I crouched, ready to go for my rifle and give the alarm. Then I quieted myself. He was a man known to us from the Stevensville camp and before; a half-breed Scot by the name of Bostwick, a Montana man and a friend. I lifted my hand to him as our eyes met, and he smiled and waved back and made the hand sign for "coming to visit" and rode on into the mist, down-river.

Naturally I thought he was coming to see some family among us. Yet as a matter of habit I kept listening to the clip-clop of his horse along the riverbank, and it did not stop at any lodge but continued right on through the entire camp and back across the river by the lower ford. With that exquisiteness of sound which such a still, foggy morning provides, I could even hear his horse blow out his nostrils as he went into the water, and the clink of his ironshod hoofs striking the rocks coming out on the far side. I thought about that a moment, then shivered again and decided I would go back in and see if Meadowlark still loved her new husband. But I could not do it. No, I said to myself, your spirit-voice does not lie to you. You are not easy about this thing and you had better go and see Yellow Wolf.

Quickly I slipped off through the fog. At his lodge I found my uncle squatted over a tiny warming fire he had just fanned out of last evening's cookfire coals. He looked up at the sound of my foostep and said, "Hello, Heyets. I know what you are going to tell me—it's too quiet."

"Yes," I nodded. "And isn't it?"

"Sure. You know that. Did you see Bostwick go by on his gray horse?"

"Yes."

"Did you hear him stop?"

"No, he went on all the way out of camp. I heard him cross back over the river down below. What do you think?"

"I don't know. Probably nothing, probably he was just traveling. This is his country. But yonder comes old Nahtelekin. His horses are down that way. We'll ask him to look around down there. Ho! Nahtelekin, come over here."

"Eh? Who says my name?" queried the old warrior.

"Hemene Moxmox," Yellow Wolf answered him. "You going out to your horses?"

"Oh, Hemene. Yes, I am. Why do you ask that?"

"We just saw a white man ride by looking at our camp in a careful way. It was Half-breed Bostwick. He gave Heyets the visiting sign but he didn't stop. He went on toward your horses. Look out for him down at the ford. All right?"

"All right. What do you want me to do if I see him?"

"Nothing. Just come back and tell us. We'll go up the river, meanwhile. That's where he came from. We're not nervous, just thinking a little."

"A good idea," said the old man. "You never can tell."

"Yes. Well, *taz alago*, old one." I smiled. "Have a good day."

He shrugged off my hand as I reached to touch his shoulder, scowling unhappily.

"Come on," said Yellow Wolf, "let's go up the river."

That is how close some things happen. Who is to say what turn the war may have taken had we gone to follow Bostwick instead of sending poor blind old Nahtelekin to do it?"

Yet we did not go. We started off the other way and had not gone ten minutes, walking slow and stopping to listen a lot, when, from down by the lower ford, there broke a small crackle of thirty or forty rifles followed by such a crashing roar of other gunfire as to sound like five hundred rifles and a thousand soldiers. Our hearts stopped. Without a word we wheeled and raced for the lodges. But we were too late. History had already happened behind us.

Nearly sightless, old Nahtelekin, peering hard through his glazing cataracts to follow the hoofprints of Half-breed Bostwick's horse down to the water at the lower ford of the Big Hole River, had blundered into the hidden gun muzzles of Captain Catlin's thirty-four Missoula volunteers, and the treachery of Red Nose Gibbon was begun.

Yellow Wolf and I ran like deer before a forest fire. He reached his tipi and got to his gun, but I did not. As I sped past him toward my own lodge, a soldier on horseback leaped out from between two tipis firing down at me with his revolver. I twisted to leap behind a third lodge and was trapped by two soldiers on foot. My life was saved because their guns were empty. One yelled, "Grab him. I'll brain the son of a bitch!" and the other lunged at me. I got my knee hard into his genitals and he screamed and fell down writhing on the ground. The first soldier ran, and so did I.

I was almost at my lodge then. The camp, everywhere, was thick with soldiers firing at Indians who were running helplessly without guns. I saw no more than twenty Indians in that first terrible part of the fight who had guns to fire back at the soldiers. Most of the people had been caught still naked and sleeping. They were driven to run for their lives without weapons, without clothes, without any knowing of how many the enemy were, where he had come from, or how they were going to rally and fight him. My poor friends fought him as did I, with knee, tooth, foot, club of driftwood or rock of riverbank, anything to which we could lay hand that might do harm at arm's reach. The soldiers were in there to kill us. They shot at man, woman and child alike. The panic among us was fearful.

Nearing my lodge at the lower center of the camp, I saw, just beyond it, about ten Indians in a thin circle defending Joseph's lodge. They had six or eight guns among them and the ground out around them toward the river was already piled with soldier bodies. Behind the circle Joseph was standing like a rock, his deep voice saying, "Shoot low, shoot low, don't waste your bullets, we must hold here," and as he called out the calming orders, other Indians were beginning to come up, to stop and stay their wild running, and to join the circle at the lodge of Heinmot Tooyalakekt.

I no more than saw this before the gun smoke closed in and I was turning the last lodge short of my own. As I did this, I grew sick in the belly. There were two soldiers just ripping aside the flap, their faces ugly with anger and hate. But those two soldiers did not enter my lodge. Instead, I heard two shots. One of them grabbed his face and the other his chest, and both staggered back and slid to the ground. Then I saw Meadowlark appear in the door of our lodge with my Winchester still smoking in her hand.

She saw me at the same time. I leaped forward calling her name. She began to run toward me, holding out the rifle and crying, "*Koiimze! koiimze!* Hurry, hurry, Heyets! I am hurt." Then I saw the third soldier coming out of the lodge behind her with his rifle bayonet running red to its muzzle guard, and my heart and my whole life died within me even as Meadowlark ran crying toward me.

I caught her as she fell. The third soldier saw me with her limp form in my arms and thought I was without a weapon. But Meadowlark had brought me the Winchester and I held it in one hand now hidden beneath her poor wounded body. As the soldier charged me, yelling as though his mind were gone, I shot him in the mouth at about five feet.

the long soft grass and feathery branches would screen her. But

I could not wait to see him die. I slid and stumbled into a willow clump with Meadowlark, hoping to leave her there where as I burst through the scrub I heard an Indian voice croaking, "Here, boy, give her to me," and it was the old woman who had helped me so much before. But I did not want to give up my Meadowlark. I held her against my breast and for a moment her dark eyes fluttered open and she knew me. She smiled and murmured, "It is all right, now. I feel your arms strong about me; you are not hurt, you have your gun. *Taz alago*, Heyets . . ."

"No, no!" I cried. "Don't say that, don't close your eyes!"

But she had closed her eyes, and for the last time. The old woman took her from me and said, "She is right, boy. You have your gun. Go on, kill soldiers! I will watch this little bird for you. Go! Kill! All is done here."

"All the gods bless you, grandmother," I told her, and stood up and crashed out of those willows, levering my rifle and screaming hoarse and wild as an animal shot to his death deep in the bowels.

The fighting and the firing, because so heavy and so close in among the lodges, and because my grief-rage blurred my mind, as well, became confused for me from that time.

I could see and hear things, each by each, but I could not bring them together into one fight. They were like separated things in a sick man's dreaming, and I ran past them and into them and out of them and around them, not knowing how long I ran, nor where, nor even why.

First it was a broken voice crying somewhere off in the gun-smoke, "Wahchumyus is dead, they have killed Rainbow!" and I thought, no, that cannot be, they cannot have killed such a famous one so soon and easily. Then it was the bellow of Poker Joe's famous big voice lifting above the rifle crashes, telling the people, "Pick up the soldier guns! Pick up the soldier guns! Do not let one rifle get away!" Then, fleetingly, through a brief clearing of the mist and powder smoke, it was the deep voice of my chief again—and I looked and I saw Joseph still standing where the fight was greatest in the village street before his tipi, now with one small child held in his arms and two more clinging to his side. "Stay away from the tipis," he was saying. "They are burning the tipis, keep clear of them. Go to the river. Lie up in the willows. Scatter out, stay down in the grass, don't run wild here and there. Stay as close to us, here, as you can. Keep the women and children coming this way. We are holding here. Come on, come on, it's all right here with me."

At that sight the angry idea came to my mind to wonder if Looking Glass were still somewhere in that gun smoke calling, "No hurry, no hurry." The thought came also that I would have shot him if he were. But I did not see him anywhere and I ran on with only the picture of Joseph and the three children in my mind.

Strange, unreal things come to pass in a mixed battle. I saw Kowtoliks, Dead Bones, gather ten warriors at the riverbank and drive forty soldiers back over the water with only buffalo lances, war clubs and two or three guns.

I saw many bodies of both Indians and soldiers and men from Missoula bobbing dead in the river. I saw a Nez Perce I knew, Kahwitkahwit, Dry-land Crane, young enough to fight and not yet hurt, slip into the water with his two wives. He made them lie on their backs as though dead and he got between them, also as dead, and they all floated off down the current around the meadow bend and got away like that. But he was the only coward among us that day.

I saw the great Wahlitits helping his wife toward the willows through a storm of soldier fire. She was heavy with young and could not go fast. Six soldiers came out of the trees in front of them and the first one shot Wahlitits through the heart. His wife seized up his rifle and killed that soldier but she was herself shot down in the next instant and fell the way she was later found, with her body across that of her mate, shielding him from the soldiers.

Jeekunkun, John Dog, an Asotin uncle of Meadowlark, came by me dragging his shattered leg in the dirt. I wanted to help him find a hiding spot in some high grass but he cried, "Go on! Kill them! I saw them murder Illatsats, that handsome boy of Light in the Mountain's! They rode him into the shallows, shot him, rode their horses over him to drown him while he still struggled. Horrible!"

I knew the boy. He was no more than fifteen. I left Jeekunkun, running and dodging through the smoke toward my chief's lodge. I was like a coyote now. My bullets were gone and I ran like a shadow, so that I might not be shot. But my eyes saw much and my belly turned several times within me, and not for fear of my own life.

There was a child of ten who ran out of a tipi crying, "They shot Grandmother, they shot her in the head!" I knew the boy.

He was Samuel Tilden and his grandmother was Martha Joseph, close blood kin to my chief.

There was Tumokult, the mother of About Asleep, who came running naked down the street with a soldier after her. He got his hand in her long hair, threw her to the ground, stabbed her in the breast with the bayonet of his rifle, pulled the trigger in the very moment she arched her back and screamed to the pain of the blade.

There was White Feather, that lovely girl, knocked down before my very eyes by the blow of a soldier's fist, shot in the back as she fell, kicked when down until her ribs protruded through her side flesh, and rifle-butted in the face smashing out her front teeth and leaving her nose so that she would breathe through her mouth for the rest of her days. And there was her friend Halpawinmi, Dawn, our uttermost beautiful one. I saw her helping her little brother, who was sick, down toward the river. A horse soldier and three Missoula men chased her and shot the boy. She crouched down in the trail with him and they shot her, too. She rolled forward, with arms flopping loose like a medicine doll. I knew they couldn't hurt her any more so I ran on toward Joseph.

When I reached my chief's side there were nearly fifty fighters there with guns, most of them taken from dead soldiers. I was able also to get some bullets for my Winchester from Yellow Wolf, and so to get back into the shooting myself. Most of the chiefs were there. Ollikut. White Bird. Toohoolhoolzote. Hahtalekin. I did not see Looking Glass, but then I had little time to search for him.

The soldiers came at us strong three more times in that place. They had to break us there and they knew it. But we held, giving them shot for shot, curse for curse, and while the struggle went thus I saw through the powder flashes and the gun smoke five things that I will remember all my life.

The first thing was Otskai, crazy-headed Otskai, suddenly taking by the nape of his neck a prisoner Ollikut had made. Holding the soldier with one hand, he began making a speech about our nonwarrior dead, the innocent women and children

and elder ones who had been killed like animals with no chance
to fight back. In his free hand he held a horse soldier revolver.
The tears ran down his cheeks, his voice shook, his words broke
—and every time they did he would pull the trigger and shoot,
and the soldier's body would jerk and spin in his hand as the
heavy bullets bit into it again and again and again.

The second thing was Pahkatos Owyeen, the great Five
Wounds, bloody brother of mighty Rainbow, sitting out on the
bare sand of the riverbank in front of us under full fire from
the attacking soldiers, holding his dead friend to his breast and
crying over him like a woman with a dead child.

The third thing was Pahka Pahtahank, Five Fogs, eldest son
of Hahtalekin the Paloos, putting on his best white King George
blanket and walking straight out into the guns of those more
than one hundred soldiers against us there, firing at them only
with a bow and arrows and walking on and shooting until he
was to his knees in the river and the blood from his body was
staining the water all around him and he sank down out of sight
and was gone.

The fourth thing was Yellow Wolf seeing some soldiers break
into our Nez Perce sick lodge, where the wife of Sun Tied had
borne her baby in the night, and he then giving a Wallowa growl
and leaping to run for the tent and save the new mother. But
there were shots and screams inside the sick lodge and the soldiers were back out and gone away before he could come up
to them. Then it was Yellow Wolf looking quickly inside the
lodge, ducking and dodging his way back to us and telling Sun
Tied, who had not seen the soldiers, what had happened in there.
It was his wife shot and killed with powder marks on her face
to show the gun's muzzle had been thrust into her pleading
mouth; and his sister, Granite Crystal, sitting with her and the
baby as nurse through the night, stabbed and rifle-clubbed to
death; and the little baby dead with its tiny head crushed in
beneath a hobnailed soldier shoe.

The fifth thing was only a small thing, but strong in its Indian
way, too. It was a very aged man of our people, Wahnistas As-
wetesk, a white-haired, dignified old fellow, who came out of

his tipi when the soldiers first dashed into the village, spread his robe in his doorway and had sat upon it to that moment smoking his pipe and completely disregarding the fact that he had been shot at least twenty times through the body meanwhile.

Such were the things—slight things—an Indian remembers.

I never knew where all the soldiers came from, how they crept up on us in the night, how they ordered their fighting line, or anything like that. That is the way a white man remembers a battle. So many soldiers here, so many there. Such a captain here. Such a lieutenant there. This colonel in one place. That major in another. The horses precisely here, the cannon exactly there. But not an Indian. An Indian remembers where his mother fell bayoneted, or his little brother had his skull smashed, or his big sister cried for mercy and was shot in the mouth. Still, the one way is history and the other only Indian lies.

I do not know how long we fought the soldiers at Joseph's lodge before they began to give back and go away in retreat. It was not so long, nor so late as noon. Yet it was not all at once, either, but with hard fighting still going on in separate places up and down the river. In the shifting there was time, certainly, for any young warrior to add to his reputation and to his people's pride.

For myself, I followed Yellow Wolf as well as I might. Once we had the soldiers on the drive and had put them back across the river, so that Joseph could get about the business of moving the camp, I imagined my best chance for a daring act lay with my uncle. And I was right. For that is the way I came to be with the six Nez Perce who captured Gibbon's cannon and three thousand rounds of rifle ammunition.

We got around behind the soldiers and they never even knew we had the big gun and the bullets until it was too late. We killed the main cannon man, the one who aimed the gun, and wounded two three-stripe soldiers and ran off three others who were there. Poker Joe, who had come up to help us with Red Scout, took the cannon and dumped it down a hill into a sand bog of the river. Red Scout grabbed the pack mule with the rifle bullets and away we went with not even a brush scratch among us. Excusing myself, the others who took the gun that day should be remembered. They were Dropping from a Cliff, Sun Tied, Calf of Leg, Stripes Turned Down and Yellow Wolf. It is a nice thing for their families to remember.

There were one or two other things not good for Nez Perce memories. Like Bowstring and Owhi, that Yakima with the busy tongue who told so much in later times about his great heart in that fight, standing off to one side safe behind a ledge of rock and never firing a shot first to last. And like Burning Coals, a miserly old rascal who had a fortune in gold and horses, refusing to let the dismounted warriors use any of his fine saddle animals for fear "they would sweat them up and not cool them out properly." Yet the brave things were of the greatest number and deepest feeling.

When we returned from the cannon raid it was wearing into afternoon and Joseph had the village on the trail moving away from there. The soldiers had dug in on their side of the river and were scared. We had them pressed in pretty close and didn't think many of them were going to get away from us. But we had paid a terrible price for listening to Looking Glass—a price those frightened soldiers could not possibly know about—and so we were not as hungry to come in after them as they thought.

First it had been Red Moccasin Tops, leader of the three red blankets, killed in a hot fight with holed-up Missoula men. Then Quiloïshkish and Tipyahlanah shot very bad trying to bring in his body. Chief Gray Hawk was dying. No Heart, the happy fool who slapped his bottom at One Hand Howard, had been shot and killed by his best friend firing in excitement and thick smoke. Circling Swan, a huge warrior, one of our finest, was dead. Wookawkaw, Woodpecker, was dead. Sun Tied had disappeared, going to bury his dead wife and child, and had not come back again. Elk Water, my own father, was missing. Others of reputation had died, or were down with bad injury. The list seemed endless and its final harsh name was entered when Five Wounds, unable to withstand his grieving for Rainbow and sworn to keep a vow he had made with his friend to die on the same day in the same battle, mounted his favorite war horse and rode him, unarmed, across the river into the soldier fire until the whackings of the bullets, which we could plainly hear striking into his bare flesh, jolted his body off the proud mount and slid it mercifully beneath the passing current.

So by sunset the firing on both sides had dropped to where it was only a mutter, saying, "We are still here, we are still watching you, don't try anything," and the battle had come down to the time of last decision for both Red Nose Gibbon and the Nez Perce who had driven him back to his rifle pits only by running the Big Hole red with the best blood of Joseph's people.

30. Rescue of Red Nose

That night there was a council held on the field, and since so many were dead or missing, or wounded and sent on with the women and children, any of those still there were allowed to sit in the circle. It was my first council.

After some very short arguments—there was no fire, we sat in the dark and talked fast—Yellow Wolf got up and in his blunt way put the chill of truth on any big talk which might have followed.

"Here is the way it is," he said. "We lost only twelve warriors here today, but they were our best. If we kill one soldier, a thousand spring to take his place. If we lose one warrior, there is no one to take his place. Who will take the place of Wahlitits? Of Rainbow? Of Red Moccasin Tops? Of Five Wounds? Nobody. I say it again—we have left our best blood here. We are like a dog with a broken back. We can still snarl but we can't fight. We will be lucky if we can drag our body away up the trail."

Ollikut nodded. "The best we can do," he said, "is hold these soldiers here a little while tomorrow, giving the people all the start we can. It is foolish to talk of anything else. Look around you. How many of us are left here? Thirty, I think. And some of those not grown men."

I glanced around to see if any of them were looking at me, but they were not. It is a true thing that when the guns go off some boys become men, and some do not. I was still there. I was very proud of myself.

"Now," Ollikut went on, "think what has happened to us here. Over half a hundred of our women and children killed. Most of our lodges burned. Many of our weapons and much of our ammunition lost. A great many wounded—we don't know how many yet—for us to carry along and to care for and feed. I can think of perhaps twenty good fighters who have gone on with Heinmot and the village. Here we have thirty. That's fifty fighters left. And as my nephew has said, they are not our best— our best sleep out there tonight, along the river."

He paused, looking at us all, giving any who would the time to speak against him. Then he finished quickly.

"All right, I am leader here. We will divide the night in three pieces, ten of us to each piece. I will take the first piece. We will watch the soldier lines while the rest of you sleep. *Taz ziketin.*"

After he and his men had gone, Wahwookya Wasaäw, Lean Elk, that great fighter with the small body and giant's voice who had the nickname Poker Joe among us, spoke out of the darkness and said, "I will take the second piece. Who wants the third?"

"I will take it," answered my uncle Yellow Wolf, and so it was decided.

Naturally I stayed with Yellow Wolf, going a little apart from the others to sit with him and talk of our own fears and sadnesses and sick hearts.

Yet how will one talk of a thing like little Meadowlark stabbed and dying in a willow bush? Or of Sun Tied's tiny baby with its head crushed like a bird egg? Or of lovely White Feather with her face all smashed and broken by a steel rifle butt?

I told Yellow Wolf of my loss in naked words and then sat silent. He put his strong hand on my shoulder and squeezed hard with it, then patted me twice only and said, "Get some sleep, Heyets. Try to lie down and close your eyes. I will be here."

I shook my head and said no, that I could not sleep. But the next thing I knew it was very early in the morning and I had slept and Yellow Wolf was shaking me and saying, "Come on, nephew. It's getting gray as a fish belly over there in the east. We better hurry."

We got up and went over to where the soldiers were. Ollikut was still there, having stayed awake all night. When he saw Yellow Wolf he said, "Come here, Hemene. I want you to listen to something."

Yellow Wolf went over to him and crouched by his side, listening. I did likewise. It got very still. Then we heard it, from over in the soldier lines. It was a fearsome sound and at first we could not make it out. Then Ollikut said, "Hear that? There are no women over there, no old ones, no frightened children. Those are men crying over there. Those soldiers are bad hurt, and they are scared to death."

We listened some more and it was true. We could even hear words and I told the others what they were saying. Those men wanted to quit, they wanted to run away in the dark. They thought we were going to finish them when it got daylight and they were almost ready to defy their officers and to get out of there by themselves. Fear is a bad thing, it is the worst wound of all. Those soldiers were hurt worse than we thought and there was suddenly growing in all our minds the same new hope.

"Listen," said Ollikut, "we caught a scout earlier—you know Blodgett, the one who got away from us this afternoon, the one who was leading the cannon men? Well, we caught him down by the river getting water. We let him go but we didn't do it for nothing. We traded him his life for a little talk."

"*Eeh*," said Yellow Wolf, "what talk?"

"We killed twenty-nine soldiers today, and forty were wounded. We got a bullet into Red Nose himself. Blodgett says they won't fight. He says there are only about a hundred of them left. We have thirty. That's only three against one. What do you think, Hemene?"

"I don't know. What does Lean Elk say?"

"I just sent for him. He'll say yes, though. You know him."

"I'm not so sure. He's pretty careful. He doesn't act wild like that crazy Asotin. He's no fool like Looking Glass. I think he'll say to go slow. You remember he warned us about those other soldiers in Montana. He told us to look out for them."

"Yes, that's true. We better wait and see what he says."

But we did not get to hear what Poker Joe would have said. As we were waiting for him, we heard a sudden drumming of ironshod hoofs on the back trail from the Bitterroot, and Yellow Wolf said, "That's a white man, let's get him," and we all jumped to our feet. But Ollikut said, "No, wait. Let him go through. That way we can tell if he's a message rider from One Hand."

"What?" growled Yellow Wolf. "How can we tell what he is in this light?"

"We don't tell from him," said Ollikut. "We tell from how those soldiers act when he gets to them. Down, down! Don't anyone shoot. Let him ride through."

By this time the rider had gone on past us and was splashing across the waters of the ford. "Damn," said Yellow Wolf. "We should have shot him. I don't see the sense of letting him go."

"You won't see it," Ollikut said, "you'll hear it. If those soldiers are silent when they hear the rider's message, it is a bad message. We know they are low on bullets and need help, so if they don't make any noise we can stay another day and try to get them all. We will know, as well, if we hear a great shout go up over there, that help *is* coming and that we cannot hope to get them all. Does that make sense, Hemene?"

Yellow Wolf nodded that it did, and we all sat there waiting to hear what the soldiers of Red Nose Gibbon would do when that message rider from the Bitterroot got to them.

In that strange way that men will talk about small things when big things are about to happen, Ollikut said quietly to Yellow Wolf, "Can you imagine what Blodgett told us tonight? He said that Red Nose was telling his men that they had killed eighty-nine of us, and he said that Captain Catlin, the one from Missoula, was telling his men that they had killed two hundred eight of us! Now isn't that something?"

"Well," shrugged Yellow Wolf, "isn't that always the way the white man counts in an Indian fight?"

"Yes, sure. But imagine? I can't understand why they have to lie. We lost ten women, twenty-one children and thirty-two men, a terrible, terrible thing, and they can't even tell the truth about it. Why is that?"

Yellow Wolf shrugged again.

"Because they are white men. Do you need another answer than that?"

"No. That's it, I guess."

Silence came in on us once more.

"My uncle," said Yellow Wolf to Ollikut after a time, "I was told that Aihits was hurt today. Is it bad?"

This was the first I had known that Fair Land was injured and I leaned forward anxiously to catch Ollikut's reply.

"Quite bad," he said in a low voice. "Shot three times while running with the baby."

"Can she ride?"

"No, she must be carried."

"What about the baby? Is he all right?"

"Yes, he's all right."

"She can't feed him though."

"No, she can't feed him. Springtime has him."

"Springtime? She has her own baby."

"Yes, but she is a Nez Perce woman. She took the little one from my wife's arms and said to her, 'Give him to me, my sister. I have but one child and two breasts.'"

The stillness grew again.

"I saw a funny thing late yesterday!" said Yellow Wolf. "There was a soldier standing straight up down by the river. He wasn't leaning on anything, just standing there with his rifle in his hand. I fired at him and he didn't move; he just stood there. Finally I went up to him and touched him. He fell over. He was stiff as a gun barrel. He had been dead a long time. I never saw anything like that."

"That's good, all right," said Otskai. "But we saw something funnier than that, didn't we, cousin? It was a captain shot by somebody before us. Hemene saw him first and we went toward him together. He was crawling around his dead horse and I shot him in the chest. He just looked at us and shook his head and wouldn't die. So Hemene hit him with his *kopluts* right in between the eyes. And you know what?"

He paused as though to give Yellow Wolf his chance to deny having been with him on such a bloody business, then grinned delightedly at the memory of it and went on.

"That captain's teeth flew out of his mouth and lit on the ground. I mean all his up-side teeth and all his bottom-side teeth together. Now wasn't that funny? I could not believe it but Hemene picked them up and put them back into his mouth and they went in there as if they had grown there from little baby teeth just like anybody's. To make sure, I put my three fingers of one hand in his mouth and with the other hand I pushed up under his jaw, and those teeth bit me. I never saw anything like that; a soldier who could take all his teeth in and out. Real teeth, too. Now what do you think of that?"

"I think you're crazier than we thought," one of the warriors told him. "I saw you and Hemene sitting out there by that dead horse playing with that soldier's mouth. There were more bullets humming around you than bees blistering a bear in a honey tree. *Eeh!* You have no mind at all."

"Aye," grinned Otskai happily, "but I've got plenty of teeth. Look at this. Hemene let me keep them."

With the words, he reached out in the warrior's direction and we heard something clicking together. The warrior cursed, jumped back and snapped, "*Tananisa!* Damn! Don't touch me with those dead teeth . . ." Ollikut said, quick and sharp, "*Saus! Talig!* Be quiet, both of you. Listen over there toward the soldier lines."

Otskai grumbled a little under his breath, complaining that it was hard to have fun any more, but no one answered him, so he went off a ways and sat down by himself and then the only sound we could hear was the click-click of him playing with his soldier's teeth. That, and the breathing of the rest of us crouched there in the ground-dark of the new day, straining our ears to hear across the river.

A minute passed. Then another and another.

"He must be there now," said a warrior nervously from the shadows beside us. "I don't hear his pony running any more."

"It takes a little time," Ollikut explained carefully. "He has to talk to Red Nose first. Wait."

The words were scarcely from his lips when, out of the gray hush of half-light beyond the Big Hole, there arose a great glad sound of cheering and happy shouting from the soldier rifle pits.

We all looked at one another, and then at Ollikut.

That happy shouting could mean but one thing. Fresh men and ammunition were coming. We did not have to ask whose men they were, or where they had come from.

Ollikut stood up. He looked very weary. Picking up his gun from the log where it had been resting next to him, he stared a long moment across the river toward the rescued soldiers of Red Nose Gibbon. For a fleeting time his face had the same faraway sadness in it as his brother Joseph's. Then he was Ollikut again.

"Let's go," he said softly. "One Hand has caught up with us. This fight is over."

31. Camas Meadows

Takseen, the Willows, was the name of the first camp from the Big Hole fight. At this first camp death came to Aihits Palojami, Fair Land, the second wife of Ollikut. She left the infant boy, Tewetakis.

After our ugly surprise at Big Hole we Nez Perce believed all the white world was our enemy. We had trusted the Montana people and been betrayed. Now every person in our way was an enemy; now, as we fled toward Yellowstone, began the first killings and destructions since the Salmon River raids.

There was the Montague-Winter ranch killing, for an example. Two men, Montague and Flynn, were shot and war-clubbed when they refused us cloth for bandages, and when Flynn, who we knew to be an Indian-hater, threatened us with a shotgun he seized from behind a stove. Five other men were baling hay in a field beyond the house. By this time our young men were wild. The hayfield men ran and two of them were hit and killed. Three got away from us. One of them, a good man named Herr, later said that Flynn started it all with his hate. But four white men were dead, our fault or not, and the Indian fear began to run ahead of us through Montana.

On Birch Creek, the second day from Big Hole, our hearts still crying for our women and children which Red Nose had murdered, we caught a wagon train of supplies going to Salmon, Idaho. There were three wagons, each with trailers behind and drawn by sixteen-mule jerkline hitches; a big train and loaded with whiskey. We let two Chinese men and two eastern white people who were with the wagons go free. The others, the Montana people driving the wagons, we killed. But it was only after the whiskey had been opened that any of them were hurt. Several of our Indians got ugly-drunk in a few minutes and it was those who ran the blood. After three of the white men had been killed, Peopeo Tholekt and Yellow Wolf did a brave thing. At the suggestion of Ketalkpoosmin, they took axes and smashed all the whiskey barrels and let the last white man escape with his life.

Now there was big trouble. That white man would carry the news of this killing to the settlements. The soldiers would know where we were. It was all Yellow Wolf's fault. So shouted the drunk Indians, and they got very mad and began to fight among themselves. Coyote With Flints stabbed Lame John. Ketalkpoosmin was shot by Five Snows. Everybody was fighting and cursing.

"Come on, Heyets," said my uncle quietly. "This is no place for us. Here, help me with Ketalkpoosmin." He and Peopeo Tholekt and I got our wounded friend on his horse and, holding him up between our horses, we got him and ourselves out of there. Three days later we left poor Ketalkpoosmin in the trail to die—a thing he asked us to do for him—and that was the end of the Birch Creek massacre, and the end of the brave Indian who tried to stop it. It was also the end of any small last chance we might have had to get help along our way from the Montana people. They might have forgiven us the first killings, for they knew Flynn hated Indians and had a hard mouth. But the second-day killings of helpless captives by Indians who were full of whiskey and were even shooting among themselves was more than white blood could forget. Most of us never blamed them, either. But the hunt was closing in now. We were no longer in the control of our good people but of our bad ones. When the cry of the hound grows near, the soft voice cannot be heard and the harsh one rises up. As they ran now, the people were listening for the baying of One Hand Howard behind them. While they listened, bad voices like those of Teeweeyownah and Henry Tabador rose around them, and no white life within our path was safe from that time.

Kamisnim Takin, Camas Meadows, was the tenth-day camp from Big Hole. Here the people rested and repaired their trail gear, treated their lame horses, tended the bad wounded, buried the brave ones who would never see the buffalo. And here Yellow Wolf and I made the scout which saved us at that place, and which confirmed my proud name, the Mountain Sheep. It was a back scout to make sure the soldiers of One Hand, which we were certain we had lost by twisting our traveling line, had not found us again. It was a very small thing from which I made my reputation—from a high lookout peak I saw the soldiers in the far distance where Yellow Wolf had looked and said, "All right, there is nothing"—but that is the way Indians are; make much of nothing and nothing of much.

So my long eyesight was of service to the people that day, and we packed the camp hurriedly, hoping to keep One Hand from killing us in Camas Meadow, as Red Nose had done at Big Hole.

But One Hand had the scent now. He came up so fast that day we could not believe it of soldiers. Their night camp was only over the ridge from us, and we knew we could not get out in time in the morning, if they came for us as Red Nose had done.

A council was called. Lean Elk, or Poker Joe, sat at the head of it. The chiefs had voted him the leader after the Big Hole fight. Looking Glass had few friends now. Too many of us could still hear his voice in our ears saying, "No hurry, no hurry." But

Lean Elk had shown himself a careful and crafty man. He had been chosen mostly because he had a loud voice and the chiefs thought he would be easy to hear above the rifle fire of a fight. But now he was showing them he was smart, too.

"Listen, my brothers," he told them, "we've got to do something about those soldiers, and I think I know what it is. Black Hair has had a dream. I want him to tell you about it. I think it's a good one. If you agree, we will have some fun."

Black Hair told his dream, that he had seen in his sleep a vision of all of One Hand's horses surrounded and run off, and he and his soldiers left to walk home to Idaho all the way from Montana.

It was a pretty wild idea. We were beaten down very bad and One Hand had hundreds and hundreds of soldiers. As of that night, with deaths from wounds on the trail since Big Hole, and with warriors still too deep wounded from that battle to fight, we had exactly fifty-eight men of an age and in a condition to do hard riding and fighting. And of these fifty-eight half had slight wounds like cracked bones or shallow bullet holes.

The poor women, a good part of them hurt on the trail, or hit by bullets, or weak from no time to rest and scanty food, many of them carrying young in their bellies and nearly all of them caring for small children at their sides, had not had enough time to pack the ponies in the few hours after Yellow Wolf and I had come back from the lookout peak.

So there was no choice. It was stop those soldiers or surrender, and no voice was raised for surrender, not even Joseph's.

"You must give me tomorrow," my chief told the council, "to get the people safe away; the morning I must have at very least. Otherwise there is little chance to live."

Lean Elk looked hard at the council and said, "Well, you heard Heinmot. What do you say to him? How about it? You want to go after those horses?"

Ollikut stood up. I stood up beside him. Yellow Wolf followed me. Otskai followed him. Looking Glass, always fearless to fight, no matter his bad pride, stood up. Other older ones came to their feet: Toohoolhoolzote, Hahtalekin, Naked Head, Smoker,

Otstotpoo, old Fire Body. It was like calling out the best we had left, to see them come standing, one following the other: Wottolen, No Feet, Rattle on Blanket, Peopeo Tholekt, Kowtoliks, Light in the Mountain, Yellow Long Nose, Naked Foot Bull, Whittled Buckskin, Bare Legs, Going Fast, Curlew, Kipkip Owyeen, Sun Necklace, Wounded Head, Lone Bird, Calf of Leg, Grizzly Bear Blanket, Swan Necklace, Ten Owl—ah, they were the good ones. But the bad boys stood, too. Tabador, Teeweeyownah, Two Moons, Coyote with Flints, Five Snows, Wettiwetti Houlis (Mean Person), White Bull and Howallits. All were brave, all were ready to die. They didn't speak, they just stood up. *Eeh!* That was the way we voted for what the white men called "another stroke of red military genius" at Camas Meadows on the Yellowstone trail the night of August 19th.

We left the warriors with slight wounds to guard the camp. The other twenty-eight of us got our night horses up from the pony herd and went to say our *taz alagos* to our families. Since I had no family left, I sat alone on my horse at the edge of camp waiting for the rest to get done with their good-byes and come along. My heart was going over the back trail there in the darkness. I was crying inside for my mother and Meadowlark and my missing father, and I did not hear the soft step come up beside me. The girl's voice startled me.

"Heyets . . ." it called me gently. "It is I, Takzpul, come to say *taz alago*."

"Beaver!" I said. "What are you doing here?"

"I told you," she repeated quietly. "I am here to say good-bye to you. Is that all right, Heyets?"

There was a strange humbleness in her voice, not like the Beaver I knew. Somehow she sounded as lonely as me. I slid off the horse and stood before her.

"I am very glad you are here," I answered her. "I am alone, you know."

"Yes, I know. I, too. My mother was put in the earth this morning. Her wound opened two days ago. We could not stop the blood."

"I am sorry," I said. "I had not heard."

"She went away very quietly; smiled and said my name and died. She was very tired."

"We are all tired, Beaver. There is no rest for any of us."

"Heyets . . ."

"Yes."

"Did you ever know my real name?"

I felt guilty and bad, for I had in truth never thought about her other name.

"No. That's a strange thing, isn't it?"

"No, you never looked at me. Why would you care?"

"What is the name?" I asked.

"Meyui," she said.

"Morning Light," I nodded. "That's a pretty name."

"Thank you, Heyets," she said, and stood a moment with her head down. Then she brought up her eyes, looking at me. "Heyets," she asked, "can I be your woman? I don't mean to lie with, or make love to. I mean to cook for you and mend for you and watch your horses, do the things a woman should do for a warrior."

This was not an unusual thing in the Indian way, except that the one who offered to do it was usually an older woman, or a relative of some distance.

"I couldn't ask that of you," I told her.

"You didn't ask me," she answered softly. "I asked you."

"But," I said, "you are a young woman, beautiful, surely you have . . ."

"I have no one, Heyets. Only the old Asotin woman; I am living with her."

"But Yellow Wolf? I thought you followed him with your eyes. I don't understand."

"You never did, Heyets."

"I never did what?"

"Understand who my eyes followed."

Even that late I did not have sense enough to know what she meant, and I had to ask her. And, even in asking it at all, I was only being polite.

"Well," I said, "who *is* the lucky one then?"

"You, Heyets," she said simply. "My eyes have never sought another. I have loved you, as Coyote loved you, all of my life."

I had no answer for that. Fortunately, I was not required to have one. Toward us now I could see some of the other warriors coming up through the night gloom. "You showed a good heart in coming here," I said. "I am glad you did, too. I am not so lonely any more. But I don't think you better talk about being my woman. *Taz alago*, Meyui. Here come the others."

I swung up on my horse but she was at my side again, this time her slim soft hand resting on my naked thigh.

"Heyets," she said, "you'll need your best horse in the morning. Which one do you want me to bring up?"

There was no time to go on against her. "The black Appaloosa," I snapped. "The old grandmother knows which one. Mankiller, that Sioux horse Joseph gave me. Where will you be?"

"Our spot is two fires from Ollikut's."

"All right," I said roughly. "Good-bye."

In the dark she took my hand and kissed it before I could pull it from her.

"*Taz alago*, warrior!" she whispered, and stood back.

I gazed down at her a moment, then whirled my pony.

"*Taz alago*, woman," I said.

We went over the ridge to One Hand's camp, all riding bays and browns and blacks, night horses, ones with no white marks on them, and we came down on those soldiers with such speed and quiet and Nez Perce skill they could not know there was an Indian nearer to them than Camas Meadows.

We got around their picket line, four hundred horses, mostly saddle mounts, good ones, fat, strong, ready to go a long chase and give us much trouble if we did not run them off. We were then within two or three minutes of taking all of One Hand's horses there beyond the Camas Meadows camp. We even had them starting to move quietly away, taking them on their picket lines like strung fish, with not one soldier guard the wiser, not one sleeping soldier awakened. Then suddenly the night was torn apart by the blast of a rifleshot, almost in my ear, and I twisted in my saddle to see crazy Otskai with his gun up to shoulder and still smoking.

"I saw something move! I saw something move!" he yelled in his great bull's voice, and would have fired again had not Yellow Wolf driven his pony into Otskai's and seized the smoking rifle from him.

The horses, of course, were now lost to us. We could not get them away on the picket lines and we could not cut them loose in time. In a minute the camp would be full of awakened soldiers. Their rifles would be too many for us.

"Let's go!" shouted Toohoolhoolzot. "We can't get the horses now! Move away, move away . . . !"

"No!" Ollikut yelled back at him. "We can still get the mules. Let the horses go. The mules are grazing loose. While the soldiers are quieting the horses, we can get around the mules and run them off!"

So it was that we lost One Hand Howard's horse herd but ran off his entire herd of one hundred seventy-three wagon and pack mules. Our leaders in that night raid over the ridge from Camas Meadows were Ollikut and Toohoolhoolzote for one half the band, Espowyes and Teeweeyownah for the other half. The Asotins always said that Looking Glass was one of the leaders. He was not. He was there and that is all.

We nearly got One Hand's horses that night; we nearly turned him back. Had we done so, it might have changed the war. And we would have done it, too, save for Otskai's crazy head which did not work so well. Yet the only word of reprimand I ever heard spoken out against him from our people was Poker Joe's question which went booming out in Nez Perce the moment after the big emptyhead's gun went off and our night raid on the soldier horses was ruined: "*Ise tanin kenek kun nawas kunya tim onina padkuta?*" Roughly, in English, "Who the hell fired that shot?"

Book Five
The Bear Paws

32. The Killer Scouts

With the daylight Joseph had the people moving. It was well that he did. Coming over the Lolo Trail had toughened One Hand's soldiers. Even with their mules gone and their horses scattered, they managed to come up to us that next morning, and we had to stop and fight them off. It was a hot fight, but in fairly open land where our great horses could show themselves and their Nez Perce breeding. It was the first time we had got a chance to really ride against the soldiers, and they could not equal us. A long time later I talked to one of them and he said of our fighting from horseback that day, "It was like swatting at a swarm of hornets with a willow switch. You knock down one and six more are biting you before you can get your hand drawed back. I must have fired a hundred rounds that morning and the only Injun I hit was old Captain John, one of our own treaties, and I didn't even get a solid into him but only skittered his hat off."

One Hand tried to make much of that fight, but it was not much. One soldier killed and eight wounded, that was all we did to them. We weren't trying to kill soldiers that day, only mix them up and let Joseph get away with the women and children.

A little after noontime we had them all down off their horses and dug in behind rocks, so we left them there and caught up with the people. The soldiers did not push us after that, and we did not see them for many days again.

We went on past Henry Lake, crossing over Targhee Pass into the Yellowstone Basin on the twelfth day after Big Hole. Our back scouts told us One Hand had stopped at the lake and made a "long camp," meaning a camp where he planned to stay a while, a rest camp. We knew from that that we had hurt him bad taking his mules. We headed on into the Yellowstone country, following the Madison River, certain now that we had whipped One Hand again, that our rear was safe, and that all we had to do was to "keep our front clear" and we would be all right.

Toward this end two things were decided: Looking Glass, who knew them the best of any of us, was to go ahead by himself and talk with the mountain Crows as to where we could camp in their land, and whether or not they would help us against the soldiers if they came on after us; also we were to keep out in front of us, from the pass onward, special bands of "killer scouts" to make sure no white man who saw us coming would get away to warn the soldiers where we were.

There were three main killer bands. Kosooyeen had one. Rattle on Blanket had one. Yellow Wolf had the other. The chiefs selected these leaders for a reason. They knew they could not keep the bad boys from going on the scout, so they chose good Indians to lead them; because they wanted no white women or children hurt, and they knew that Indians like Tabador and Tee-weeyownah would shoot anything they came upon.

This again was Joseph's work. He convinced the chiefs they ought not to kill or harm any person who could not kill or harm them, but only destroy such grown men as might look to be scouts or messengers for the soldiers. There was to be no scalping or marking in any way of the dead. "We are Nez Perces," Joseph told the chiefs. "We do not fight women and children and old men. We may die, they may kill us, but we will never harm their old people, their women and their little ones, as they have ours."

It is a fact, one of great pride to the Nez Perce people, that in all that terrible passage of Montana, not one white woman or child was so much as touched by our Indians.

There is no other record of such treatment of settlement families in any similar Indian war. But then the Nez Perce were not as any other Indians. We had lived too long as brothers of the white man. Even in our last hours we could not kill and mutilate his loved ones. It was too much like murdering a sister, or son, or daughter, yes, or beloved mother. We never felt about the white man as did the Sioux, the Cheyenne, the Arapahoe or the Blackfoot. Our good Indians—which were nine as to one of our bad Indians—never did want to kill any whites. We fought them as they made us fight them, and that was all.

The word of a Nez Perce does not need to stand alone, either, in this matter. A western newspaper printed in the very time and country through which we passed, tells the spirit of Joseph and his people for not killing on that march.

"As to their religious beliefs," the paper states, "he [Joseph] said that all of the good Indians of their tribe held to communion with the spirits of their deceased friends. That these spirits frequently came to them in the still hours of the night and conversed That this change in their mode of warfare, whereby they had with them, and gave them directions what to do and how to live. shown such kind and humane treatment to the prisoners, had been in accordance with the directions of their spirit friends. That these spirits told them to always do what was right toward everyone; that they must stand up for what was right, and if they should be killed while doing so, it would be all right with them. As the Indians expressed it, 'It would make no difference.' "

Still there is no use trying to say lies just because of an old newspaper which told the truth.

No one will ever know how many prospectors, hunters, travelers and others who were not scouts or messengers for the soldiers, died in the path of our march into and through the Yellowstone country. It was more than a few. And some of them I saw. One will tell the story of the others. I give it because when an Indian remembers something he remembers all of it. He isn't clever like the white man. He isn't able to forget what he would like to forget. So it is that I remember the McCartney cabin.

To begin with, I went as a member of Yellow Wolf's "killers." The others were Otskai, Teeweeyownah, Tabador. The first little while out, we were lucky and caught an old gold miner named John Shively, who knew the way to the Crow country. He said he did at any rate, and for half a sun he set us on the track. It looked right to us, judging by how Looking Glass had said to follow him, and so we sent the old man back to the main band to hold for a few days in case he was lying to us.

Meanwhile we were joined by Yellow Long Nose, Bowstring,

Whittled Buckskin and two others. Yellow Long Nose said he
had found a camp of whites with some women in it and he didn't
want to try anything with them because of what the chiefs had
ordered, but thought that if Yellow Wolf would come along
with them that would make it all right because he was Joseph's
nephew. Yellow Wolf didn't want to go but Tabador did. So
Yellow Wolf had no choice.

"Heyets," he told me quietly, "I will have to go along and
watch Tabador. He is bad with women. You go ahead without
me and I will catch up to you."

They rode off and I scouted on ahead with Otskai and Teeweeyownah. The next day or so Yellow Wolf was back and told
us they had caught the people. They were just Helena people
camping in tents in the new Yellowstone Park and didn't even
know they were in danger. Nobody had been killed, Yellow
Wolf said, but Tabador had shot one of the men who was a
loud talker and did not like Indians. There were two women,
sisters. Both were young and handsome according to my uncle,
especially the one who was not married. Yellow Wolf said he
had told this second woman to stay close to Joseph and she
would be safe, but that if she or her friends got around White
Bird or Toohoolhoolzote and their Indians, they would be killed.

"I told her," he said to me, "that some of those Indians were
double-minded; that they would first be all right with captives
and treat them well, then would suddenly turn on them and kill
them."

"Were they all right when you left?" I asked him.

"Oh, yes. Heinmot gave them horses for the two women and
turned them loose this morning. He only held them a short while,
because he could see the bad boys were getting ugly. I took them
out of the camp—back there on the Koos Kapwelwen, the Swift
Water—and told them what Heinmot said: 'Get away from
here quick and do not stop for anything.' Believe me, they went
fast. They weren't talking loud any more. I guess Heinmot was
right to let them go, but I don't blame Tabador for shooting that
one. He would not give us food when we asked him at his tent,
and he struck at my hand when I put it out and said 'friend.' If

he had been of this country, I would have killed him myself."

"Well, uncle," I said, "I am glad you didn't have to do that. So far we have kept our word to our chief not to kill anyone who is not a soldier. I hope we can keep that same word all the way. I don't want to kill anyone else, do you?"

"No," said Yellow Wolf. "Not unless they make me mad."

I looked at him and thought of what I knew about his temper, and I shivered a little for the whites who were still in front of Hemene Moxmox, the Yellow Wolf of the Wallowa. But to him I only answered, "*Tamtaiza uatiskipg,* tomorrow will tell," and then said, "By the way, did you see Beaver and the old Asotin grandmother?" and he said, yes, he had seen them and they were well and waiting to see me again, and that the old lady wanted to know how the horse was—meaning the Sioux devil, Mankiller, which I was riding all the time now—and that Beaver had said to tell me that she sent a special *wyakin* to protect me on the trail, and that he was to give it to me.

"Well," I said, "where is it? Give it to me."

He reached in the pocket of the blue soldier-coat he had picked up at Big Hole, and handed over to me a small, round piece of silver which I knew at once. It was a Lapwai missionary medal with a carving of Jesus on it, and it had been my mother's dearest treasure.

"How did she have this?" I asked my uncle.

"She said Antelope gave it to her, when she thought she was dying in labor with that late baby. She said to tell you your mother wanted her to have it, but that she can't tell you why this was until a later time, perhaps never."

"All right," I said. "Thank you, Hemene. I guess we better go on now, eh? We've been waiting for you. Naked Foot Bull, Shooting Thunder and Watyahtsakon are here with us and say they have found a cabin up ahead which they want to look at a little closer. They thought we might want to go with them. What do you say?"

Yellow Wolf waved his hand in the yes-sign, and we turned our ponies to join the others and go see what there was in that settler house.

It was a nice place set in a pretty clearing of mountain grass. The pines grew tall beyond it. The meadow flowers stood thick around it. The door of the little house was open and from it was coming a lovely sound of tinkling music. It was like the ringing of small bells, yet it had a deeper soft tone underneath it, too. None of us had ever heard anything of its kind before.

We stopped at the clearing's edge, cocking our heads. Even the ponies put their ears forward and were curious. As we sat thus, Watyahtsakon's mount saw the saddled settler horse that was standing tied in front of the house. He threw up his head and neighed very loud. At once the music stopped.

A small white man came into the open door. He was wearing a funny kind of long back coat, and he had eyeglasses on. He peered at us as though he could not see who we were very well, then waved friendly and called out something cheerful to us in a tongue we did not know.

Naked Foot Bull, who had turned mean since losing all three of his young brothers killed at Big Hole, put up his rifle. He fired fast and only hit the little man in the arm. Shooting Thunder, who was one of our best shots, laughed and said, "*Eeh!* Here is the way to do it," and fired without even raising his gun and hit the little man in the belly and knocked him spinning back into the house.

When we got over there, he was dying. He said a few words to us and shook his head in a bewildered way, as if to ask us why we had hurt him. Then he curled up and vomited a jet of blood and lung-froth on the floor and after that he didn't say any more words.

Naked Foot Bull and the others went in the house and ate some food and set fire to some things and tried to make the music box work as the little man did, but they couldn't find out how to do it. Otskai got mad at it and began hitting it with his *kopluts*, and knocked out all its middle teeth. Then it wouldn't do any-thing but make a very high peep on one end and a very low thump on the other. Otskai got madder than ever and went over and picked up the little man and began yelling at him and point-ing at the music box and saying, "*Zepelignikse! Zepelignikse!*" At that, Yellow Wolf got mad and went in the house and dragged the crazyhead outside and told him, "You big fool, he can't make it work, he's dead."

Otskai looked at him and said, "Oh, that's right, I forgot," and at once he was no longer mad but smiling, as happy as though he had a good brain, and saying to Yellow Wolf, "Well, cousin, what will we do now? You want to go look for somebody else to shoot in the belly?"

Yellow Wolf scowled hard at him.

"No," he said. "You come with Heyets and me, over in the trees. We're going over there to wait for the others to get through in the house."

"No," said his big slow-minded cousin. "I'll go back in there with them. They're going to start a fire in the floor and make some coffee they found in a tin box."

"I don't want you to go back in there. It's a bad place. Your mother wouldn't want you in there."

From earliest childhood, Yellow Wolf had been charged with the care of Otskai, since he was the only one the huge fellow would obey. But now Otskai didn't want to obey, and began to look ugly. He raised his hand angrily.

Yellow Wolf pointed at the bullet pouch where he knew his cousin kept the teeth he had taken out of the dead captain at Big Hole. "I will take away the teeth," he said.

Otskai seized the pouch and cried, "No! No!" and Yellow Wolf said, "All right, then, come along," and Otskai put his head down and followed us like a great child.

Over in the shade of the pines we sat down with our ponies grazing to hand and thought for a little while without talking. We were both feeling uncertain. Soon Yellow Wolf said, "I don't think that was a right thing for us to do, shooting that small man who made the music. What do you say, Heyets?"

"What can I say?" I shrugged. "It broke our promise to Heinmot. That's not good."

"No, I guess not." My uncle was much fiercer in his mind toward the white people than I, but I could see he was really ashamed about this one. "The trouble is that we were not mad at him," he said. "Neither did he talk loud, and the music was very pretty. I'm afraid Heinmot will not like to hear about it. Especially since I was the leader here. What do you think?"

I had no answer for him, of course, but while trying to think of one I happened to glance across the meadow past the cabin.

"*Eeh!*" I whispered. "Don't worry about Heinmot, worry about those soldiers over there in the far trees."

"*Soldiers!*" he rasped.

"Yes," I answered, reaching for my rifle and my pony reins. "And a good lot of them, too. Eighteen or twenty at least. Let's go."

"Wait," said Yellow Wolf. "First we must warn the others." With the words, he fired his rifle three times up in the air and yelled, "*Piuapsiaunat!* Soldiers!" to our friends in the settler house, and we got out of there.

The soldiers did not pursue far. They were brave, but also they knew a little something about Nez Perces. Only one warrior got hurt. That was Otskai. He got excited in jumping on his pony and forgot about the dead-soldier teeth. The bullet pouch got twisted around behind him and he sat on the teeth and they bit him in the rump. Otherwise, we came safely back to camp.

That is the story; the one I said would do for all the others. It is the true way that Yellow Wolf and I, together with six others of our chief's wild young men, made poor the word of Joseph in Montana.

It is, as well, the way in which it came about that I did not see the capture and release of the famous Cowan-Carpenter tourist party in Yellowstone Park, which was such a good part of our Nez Perce memory, and that I did see the murder of Richard Dietrich, the friendly little German piano teacher at the Mc-Cartney cabin, which was such a very bad part of it.

33. Canyon Creek and Cow Island

It was night when we came into camp. I sought out the fire of Beaver and the Asotin grandmother, two places from that of

Joseph. Meanwhile, Yellow Wolf went up to see our chief and
tell him what we had done. Perhaps I should have gone with him
but I was not that brave and I wanted, also, to have some food
and rest.

The tall sister of Coyote was waiting for me.

"*Taz ziketin*, Heyets," she greeted me. "It has been a long time
since we said good-bye."

"Not so long," I said. "It's good of you to work for me and
watch my horses, though, Meyui."

"Thank you for not calling me that other name, Heyets. You
remembered. That's nice."

"It's nothing. Where's the old woman?"

I did not get my answer from Beaver but from inside the dis-
graceful hut of sticks and cowskins which sat beyond the fire
and which was all that remained to Heyets, the Wallowa, of his
father's fine lodge.

"I am in here!" croaked the Asotin, in that frog's voice which
I knew so well by then. "I thought you might have sense enough
to want to do something interesting to that girl when you came
in. But I might have known. I wasted my time squatting in here.
You're a fool."

Tired as I was, I had to grin.

"Come on out," I said. "Get some air. Help Meyui with the
supper. Don't be so polite. This girl and I are old friends."

"Old friends, *hah!* A girl like that? With that body?"

"Her brother was my blood-brother. It is as though we had
grown up in the same tipi."

"It is time you grew up and got back in the same tipi, then.
Bah! You're a fool, boy."

"And you are an old bag of wind," I told her. "Come out of
there and help with the supper."

"*Enimkinikai*," she told me back. "Go to hell."

Now I had learned hard and early in my childhood that men
do not win fights with women. I remembered very well how my
father used to disappear when my mother began to look for him.

"*Nakaz*," I said, "at least come out and take care of the horse."

"Eh," she said, "the horse? Ah! That is another matter entirely." She popped out of the lopsided little tipi, bright eyes beaming as she saw Mankiller standing with me. Seizing the reins away from me, she put her arm around the evil brute's neck as though he were a weanling filly. "Come on, little one," she croaked. "The grass here is very poor, but I have saved you a secret place, never fear."

"Thank you, *Nakaz*," I called after her. "At least you know a good horse when you see one."

"I know a good man, too!" she snapped back. "And stop calling me *Nakaz*. I told you to begin with that I was not your grandmother. No child of mine would bear a manchild of such —well, let us look it in the eye, boy—you're not—ah, that is to say—*zittt!* Why talk around it? Damn! You're ugly as a newborn bird. *Taz ziketin.*"

"Good evening," I echoed her, and sat down wearily to the fire.

"She doesn't mean it," said Beaver, giving me some boiled horse meat on a slab of pine bark. "She loves you, too."

"Don't say that," I ordered angrily. "Just be quiet."

For some reason I did not want to think about Beaver loving me. I had forgotten it in the hard work of the trail and it could never seem right to me, anyway. She was Coyote's sister. How could she love me? As for myself, there was my lost Meadowlark. How could I ever love anyone else?

"Meyui," I said, "forgive me. I am very tired."

"What is to forgive, Heyets? It was wrong of me to say that. I know you can never be my man."

I nodded, really too weary to talk of it further. Soon I put down the pine-bark plate.

"I am going off in the brush and lie down," I said. "Will you call me before first light?"

Before she could answer, a shadow fell between us and I looked up to see Yellow Wolf standing there.

"Come on," he said. "Heinmot wants us."

"What's the matter?" I asked.

He shook his head, dark face scowling in the firelight.

"Looking Glass is back. He has been to the Crows and they won't help us."

"*Eeh!* That's bad."

"It's worse than that. The Crows told him that many new soldiers are moving at us from the east. One Hand called them on the telegraph. They are from Tongue River, part of the soldiers of Bearcoat Miles, the one who whipped the Sioux and chased Sitting Bull up into the Land of the Grandmother. That's how bad it is."

I got up to my feet.

"Put out the fire," I told Beaver. "Get some sleep. Don't worry about what I said. I'll sleep with Yellow Wolf; we'll be going again very early in the morning."

Coyote's sister looked at me in a strange, shy way, her head partly down, but her big eyes watching me.

"If you want to say good-bye to me, Heyets," she said, "I will be waiting." She let her head and eyes turn ever so slightly toward the lodge, and I was embarrassed that my uncle might read that glance as I did. But he had already turned away. "You are good to think of me," I said, "but you better not wait. *Taz alago*, Meyui."

She took a step toward me, but I made as though I didn't see her do it, and turned away quick. I heard her catch her breath behind me, then her soft voice saying, "*Taz alago*, Heyets." Then even more softly and thinking I did not hear her, "Ride proud, warrior. I pray for you."

The council was not long. Le Forge, White Crow, the leader of the mountain Crows, had sent along his best scout to support the word of Looking Glass. The Crow scout knew a great deal about those new soldiers from Tongue River. Their leader was an eagle chief named Sturgis. He had with him six bands of Yellow Hair Custer's old cavalry, the Seventh Cavalry, about three hundred sixty horse soldiers. Then he had another fifty horse soldiers under Captain Bandire, and about one hundred Bannack, Shoshoni and river Crow scouts. They were camped at Hart

Mountain, north of the Yellowstone mountains, where they could watch if we came through that range either by way of the Stinking Water or Clark's Fork, the only two known trails going over it south to north. Bearcoat Miles, himself, was still at Tongue River, blocking the way east. "Well, now," said the Crow, who spoke in good English, with me translating for Joseph and the chiefs, "how does that seem to you? What do you think of it?"

What we thought of it was very little. Our own back scouts had told us One Hand Howard was on the move again, coming up fast behind us. We could not turn back west or south without running into him.

"It looks as though we are caught," I said to the Crow.

"Maybe not," he smiled. "Just yesterday Colonel Sturgis broke his camp at Hart Mountain. He is coming south, this way. He must have heard where you are."

"Well," I said, "why are you smiling? If he is moving more south, he will cut us off from coming out either by the Stinking Water *or* Clark's Fork. Is that funny?"

"Only if you know what the mountain Crows know."

"And what is that?"

"The third way over those mountains."

"No!"

"Yes, brother, it's true. I can show it to you, if your people want to go north."

When the chiefs were told this, they didn't know what to do. Could they trust the Crow? Should they turn and fight One Hand? Should they try to run east, hoping to get around Bearcoat Miles? What? Run, fight, hide, surrender? The argument got bitter, part of the chiefs backing Looking Glass, who wanted to turn and whip One Hand again, part of them agreeing with Lean Elk, who wanted to go on east into the Sioux country where we knew our way better, taking our chances with Bearcoat Miles.

It was then that Joseph stood up and raised his hand. "My chiefs," he said, "there is nothing now left for us to do but trust our Crow friend. We must go with him, to the north, and we

must then continue on until we are with Sitting Bull in the Land
of the Grandmother. Neither must we stop on the way longer
than to rest the ponies. You know I did not want to come here.
Neither do I want to stay here. The Wallowa will go north.
Count our total numbers. Thirty-eight warriors? Maybe fifty or
sixty, putting in all the old men who can still ride and shoot?
We can't fight any more, we can only run. And there is but one
way left to run. *North.*"

A growl went up at that. But to the surprise of all of us, both
Toohoolhoolzote and White Bird, who had been sitting to one
side saying nothing, now got up. Stalking over to Joseph, they
stood to his side, one to the right, one to the left. They looked
very old in the firelight, and very grim.

"The Salmon Rivers will go with Heinmot," said Toohoolhoolzote. "And the White Birds also," said his companion.

"That is enough for me," said Lean Elk quickly. "We go
north. How say you, Aleemyah?"

Looking Glass raised his two hands in the give-in sign. "We
are all brothers, we go together," he said.

We had never been in those wild mountains south of the Swift
Water, our name for the Yellowstone, having always hunted
north of that stream. But following the Crow—it is not true, as
has been said, that our own scouts found that trail—we now
drove as hard as we could. It was the roughest march of all the
way, rougher even than the Lolo Trail in that great rainstorm.
With the number of horses we were still carrying along, nearly
two thousand even after all our losses, it left even an Indian to
wonder that we came through at all.

Starting southwest to confuse One Hand and Sturgis, we held
steadily to that way until we came to a large open basin. Here
we milled our horse herd over our tracks, spreading the ponies
farther and farther out so that at last their tracks were all over
the basin, and no scout living could untangle them without quar-
tering the whole country lying about that great stretch of
meadow.

Leaving the meadow at a rocky spur of some nearby hills, we

went up out of the basin along a very high and steep ridge, heading due north. This ridge had heavy dense timber up to its crest, which was grassy and open, very easy to ride. But that would be where our enemies would expect us to travel if we took that ridge, and so we stayed down in the timber, every mile blocked with rocks, ravines, deadfalls and loose slides.

Finally, to our amazement, the Crow led us to the very brink of a deep canyon which cut across the mountain whose south side we were clinging to. There did not appear any way in or out of this black pit yawning at our feet, but the Crow waved us on and we followed him down a trail into the bottom of the canyon, and even after we had done it, we looked back up those huge towering walls above us and could not see where or how we had come down them.

In the bottom, though, there was a good trail. It was all the more amazing because the walls of that canyon were never more than a few pony-widths apart from one another, and in many places were closed together so tight that we had hard work to get the horses through, two and three at a time. After only about four miles of moving in that narrow darkness, however, we saw bright sun ahead. In another few minutes we had broken out into the open valley of Clark's Fork of the Swift Water. We did not stop, save to eat and sleep, but went hurrying on more than ever now, our way almost directly north down the wide valley toward the main river. We could not rest until we had crossed it and were safe upon the familiar plains of the buffalo country beyond it. Such was our anxiety now, that we did not even stop when the Crow laughed and pointed off to the right a little ways and told us that Sturgis's old camp was only ten minutes' ride out of the way, if we wanted to look at it. Nobody did. We pushed on, forcing the tired ponies. We came to the Yellowstone at the old Laurel Crossing, and Looking Glass wanted to camp and rest on the south side. Joseph said, no, we would go over tonight. Toohoolhoolzote and White Bird stepped to his side again and Lean Elk nodded his wise head and said, "*Tasnig*, it's decided; we cross tonight."

We went over the river to a lovely place of deep grass, blue water and small pines that smelled to us like home. All of the people sighed, "*Taz, taz,*" and got down off their horses, almost falling into the grass with their great weariness. Here and there I saw an old one take the time to bow his head and move his lips in thanks to Hunyewat for delivering us out of the South Mountains. I did not see any Too-ats praying, though. They never had the power after Big Hole. Even Naked Head, their chief prophet, talked no more of Smoholla and the Big Dream after Red Nose had torn out our hearts at the bloody Place of the Ground Squirrels. All prayers now were for the old gods. All dreams were held upon the hope of reaching Canada ahead of the soldiers. All Nez Perce eyes closed that last night looking north to the Land of the Grandmother.

It was nearing dawn of the following day when our back scouts came in with startling news.

One Hand Howard was over the mountains and marching toward the Yellowstone. He was close. If we had not done as Joseph said, trusting and following the Crow, we would never have reached the Yellowstone ahead of One Hand. Had we stayed to take our rest on the south bank, we might well have been caught in a morning slaughter as bad as Big Hole. These thoughts came to every mind. Yet not a word was said against Looking Glass. Neither was a word said for Joseph.

But the very stillness talked louder than any tongues. It was there in the blackness of that early autumn dawn, safe on the north bank of the Swift Water, that the hearts of his people began to return to Heinmot Tooyalakekt.

We moved at once up the north bank, going toward Canyon Creek. Here the little side stream had carved a passage from the upper plains down to the river bottom, providing a good road up through the rimrock. A little ways along we came upon a stagecoach going away from us toward Virginia City. At once the young men riding in front of the march gave a whoop and threw their ponies on the run. Being with them, I did not argue, but kicked Mankiller in the small ribs. He had me there second only to Black Eagle, Wottolen's son.

The driver and all the people in the coach went diving into the willow brush along the river when they heard our whoop and saw us coming with rifles banging and feathers streaming. We did not go after them, for they were Eastern people and could not hurt us.

We caught the horses and stopped the stage about a mile along the road, and at once we got down to gamble who would get to drive. I won. However, the game of stick had taken so long that all our riders were now up to us. Nothing would do then, of course, but that the whole tribe should try to get in that coach, or up on top of it. Finally, after seeing Beaver and the Asotin grandmother running to get a place, I yelled at the horses, shot fast over their heads with my rifle, and away we went. That was some ride. Old Toohoolhoolzote had managed to knock aside several young men, and seize the prize place on the seat next to me. No Feet, Smoker, Kowtoliks, Otskai and a fat old woman I did not know, had scrambled up and were clinging to the top behind me. Looking down below I could see Bare Legs, Poker Joe, Yellow Long Nose, Kipkip Owyeen and Swan Necklace leaning out the windows, yelling and firing their guns. But the big surprise was when I heard a wild laugh almost in my ear and turned around to see Beaver—who had somehow caught the baggage trunk and clambered up from the rear as we started—clinging to old Toohoolhoolzote and shouting to me, "Move over, warrior, move over! If there's room for two, there's room for three!"

The grizzled Salmon River chief agreed with her. Before I could answer, he jammed me in the ribs with his rifle butt, nearly knocking me off the seat. Beaver, no heed for me or my danger, slid instantly into the space. I could gladly have thrown her off down between the horses, but the next minute she had flung one slender arm about old Toohoolhoolzote's neck, and the other about mine, and had leaned hard and sudden into me with a lurch of the coach and kissed me and cried out, "*Eee-yahhh! Taz, taz,* that's good!" and I decided I would not throw her down but let her ride with us a little way at least.

That ride made everybody happy. All who could, left the

march line to gallop their ponies with the coach and even our loose horse herd caught the spirit of the fun and began to run as if they were all colts.

It was in this way that we came up over the last rise in the river-bottom road before the Canyon Creek cut-off and ran face to face into a long skirmish line of horse soldiers charging at us full gallop.

We had no choice. They were nearer to the canyon than we were. "*Koimze!*" yelled old Toohoolhoolzote. "We will have to run them for it!" Faster than we had got into it, we got out of that stagecoach. The whole march line broke into a ragged mix-up as every person grabbed horses and ran for himself toward the rocks at the mouth of Canyon Creek. Some of us young men, up in the front, managed to beat the soldiers to those rocks.

Lucky for us, those soldiers did not want to fight very much. When they saw we meant to reach those rocks or ride through them, they slowed up and let us get by their line. In fact, if we had had only soldiers to fight that day, it would not even have been a good race. But they had some Indians along—a lot of them—a mixed bunch of Bannacks, Shoshones, Salish (Flatheads) and river Crows. Those Indians gave us trouble, the worst being the Crows, who got in our rear and cut three hundred horses out of our loose herd.

Nevertheless, we got into the rocks and stopped them, Indians and soldiers alike. It is something the whites do not tell on themselves, that little fight. For ten minutes Teeto Hoonnod, a forty-year-old Wallowa of Joseph's own blood—one single man, mind you—held off all that white cavalry with his lone rifle. This let the first of our people get to the canyon and begin going into it. Then with only one other, Swan Necklace, to help him, he held back the horse soldiers another twenty minutes, by which time all our people had got into the canyon. Meanwhile, the rest of our young men were riding off the Indian scouts, especially the river Crows, who were really trying to hurt us. They did kill three of our people, one old woman and two old men, Fish Trap and Surrounded Goose, and shot three others of our women, which were what they were trying to get at, knowing they could break our spirit that way. Here, too, was killed one of our few remaining real fighters, Teeweeyownah, Over Point of Hill, a "bad Indian" but a very brave one.

I do not know how many Indians we killed in that run for the canyon. I saw four white soldiers dead. We got most of our pack animals into the canyon safely, and seventeen hundred of our loose herd. Twenty of us young men lay up in the rocks waiting for the soldiers or Indian traitors with them to follow in after our people. But they had had enough. We didn't know it at the time, but those were the soldiers of Colonel Sturgis. I don't know if he was brave or not, but he was a poor fighter, worse even than One Hand. We all knew we were very lucky that it was not Red Nose Gibbon who had caught us riding that stagecoach along the Yellowstone River road that thirteenth sun of September, 1877.

Thus, grateful and glad for our good fortune, we went on. Now there remained only one last barrier of safety to put between us and the soldiers of One Hand and Sturgis. It was the great river we called Seloselo Wejanwais, the Missouri. Swiftly we struck toward it, meaning to go over it at the old Cow Island crossing, midway between Fort Benton and Fort Peck. Without further trouble we reached it at eight o'clock in the morning of the tenth day from the Yellowstone, September 23rd.

The weather was turning colder. It was raining and gray. Northward across the Seloselo the clouds lay almost black. There was a bite in the wind and Lean Elk, still our trail leader, said to Joseph, "*Uetu saikiza*, I don't like the weather; we had better keep moving. What do you say?"

But it was not Joseph who answered him. It was Looking Glass. And he made the best speech he had made since before Big Hole.

"Listen," he said, "look at the people. They are cold and wet and hungry. Do we have food? Yes, a little camas, moldy with the damp; some bad tea, the flesh of dead horses along the trail. Do you know what is on that island over there in the middle of the river? Yes, we all do. The big boats which come up from below unload all the winter supplies there. Look through this rain. You can see the stacks and piles of good things over there. We must have them."

"No," said Lean Elk firmly. "It is too dangerous to delay here. How do we know where the soldiers are?"

"Bah!" answered Looking Glass. "We know where One Hand is. Two, three long days behind."

"Damn!" said Lean Elk. "How many times must I tell you that there are other soldiers in the world than those of One Hand Howard? You have a head like a rock, Aleemyah."

"This may be," admitted Looking Glass, "but I know that all the food and good things for Helena, Fort Benton and the other places up the river are unloaded here at this of the year when the water is low. Even the things for the redcoats (Canadian Northwest Mounted Police) are put down here, to go up the Cow Creek road by ox wagon. My head like a rock asks me, why should we go on cold and wet and hungry, when over there are food and fire and warm blankets for us all?"

That was too much, of course, for the listening people. Lean Elk's way might be the safest, but Looking Glass's was the most sensible. The vote of the chiefs went to him, and fast. I cannot say I would have voted against the Asotin either. My own belly was sick of slimy horse meat and moldy camas washed down with muddy rain water and no coffee or decent tea. I was as fast as any to put my horse into the belly-deep shallows of the Cow Island crossing.

They were pretty surprised to see us over there. There were only twelve soldiers and a three-stripe sergeant to guard all those rich things. Some of our young men fired at them just for the spirit of it, but they were wise old bluecoats and never sent a shot back at us, staying quiet as lodge mice the whole time of our visit.

We were on the island all the rest of that day. After all those hard fights, lean suppers and long marches across Montana, the unpacking of that treasure of white man's things was past the power of an Indian to tell about. Everything was there and we took all of it that we could carry, either upon our animals or upon ourselves. My poor people accepted Cow Island as a good luck sign for the future and were entirely overcome by the prospects they believed it bore them.

When at last we went on over to the north side and renewed our journey, starting up the Cow Creek road, a few soldiers from Fort Benton did appear upon our back trail. However, they proved as wise as their brothers on the island. Their officer took one look at the number and spirit of us and waved his hand in the signal to turn around and retreat. He ordered a round of shots to be fired, so that his soldiers could feel like men, and that was the true extent of what the white men call "the Battle of Cow Island."

Oh, Tabador and old White Bird and some others of our double-minded ones got angry about being shot at, went back to the island, piled up all the things we had left unharmed and set fire to them so that we could see the smoke for two days, but we Nez Perce never called that a battle.

Now, with thick new blankets, fine tobacco, white sugar, grain salt, English tea, roasted coffee, milled flour, salt pork, bacon, beans, hulled rice, everything for ourselves and our families which we might need to reach Canada—except fresh meat—was in our possession.

All we had to do was watch for One Hand Howard behind us and somewhere up ahead stop and make a rest of two or three days while we killed that fresh meat, and tanned the warm robes, which would take us through the winter in the Land of the Grandmother.

We were now in the heart of *moosmoos illahee*, the buffalo country. Such a hunting stop would not only furnish us with deep curly robes and juicy hump ribs, but would let us treat our trail-lamed horses. As they had been silently thankful to Joseph at the Yellowstone, the people were now openly praiseful of Looking Glass coming away from Cow Island. The Asotin's judgment was grown keen again. He was the old Aleemyah. Forget Big Hole. Forgive it. From here Looking Glass should have the leadership as before. He had earned it by his wisdom.

Ahead the clouds still hung dark. There was bad weather waiting for us up there on Milk River. It looked especially black over the Bear Paw Mountains, where we had thought to camp and make our hunt. But what was a little early snow to people who had just come thirteen hundred miles through three armies of United States soldiers, and were now within four sleeps of the land into which no American bluecoat could follow them? *Eeh!* Let it snow.

Here in our Nez Perce hearts it was sunshine and fair sky. One Hand Howard? Red Nose Gibbon? Slow Fighter Sturgis? They were all far, far behind. In front there was nothing but Canada and plenty of fat cow. *Taz, taz,* kick up the ponies. Laugh again. Sing. Chant the brave songs. Be happy. Lift up the heart. Don't look back. Tomorrow is the only day that counts.

34. The Telegraph

Takasayogot, the strange soldier machine of the little sparks which talked over rivers and mountains through the open sky— that is what did it.

We thought it was our hard marching from Canyon Creek to Cow Island which had made One Hand slow down and drop so far behind us. It was not. It was a talk he made across the *takasayogot* to Bearcoat Miles at Fort Keogh on the seventeenth sun of September, five days before we even got to Canyon Creek.

Said One Hand to Bearcoat, "I am going to go slow after these Indians. I know them. When I slow down, they will slow down. The distance from your camp to Cow Island, where we think they will cross the Missouri, is less than it is the way they will travel it from Canyon Creek. You should be able to catch them before they cross the river, if you are ready to go at once. Are you ready? Can you do it?"

Answered Bearcoat to One Hand, "I am ready. I can do it."

Bearcoat Miles was not a big talker like Custer, but he was the same kind of an Indian chaser. He knew, as Custer had known before him, that the way to get a star on his coat instead of an eagle was to count a big coup in the Indian country.

Only the winter before, with the help of his great scout Yellowstone Kelly, he had made a big name by tracking down and capturing Crazy Horse and most of the Sioux who had killed the Seventh Cavalry, on the Little Big Horn, allowing only Gall and Sitting Bull, with a remnant of their Hunkpapa people, to escape to Canada.

But that was not enough. He was still a colonel and he wanted to be a general like One Hand Howard.

Now if he could only capture Joseph and the Nez Perce, it would make people forget that Sitting Bull had got away from him. It would make the big soldier chief in Washington say, "Aha! Look here at what Bearcoat has done; something that Howard and Gibbon and Sturgis have all failed to do: he has caught Joseph, and he has done it all alone!" Bearcoat saw his chance and he did not stop to talk about it.

One Hand's message came over the *takasayogot* at sundown. Before midnight Miles had his men put into boats and rowed across the Yellowstone. By earliest light the following morning, with six hundred soldiers of the Second and Seventh Cavalry and Fifth Infantry, with even the foot soldiers riding horses, and with thirty of the finest Sioux and Cheyenne scouts out in front cutting for our trail like wolves running a blood track, he started his drive to take us from our lagging rear.

As Red Nose Gibbon had blown like the wind of death up the Bitterroot Valley behind us, Bearcoat Miles now howled hard across the Judith Mountains to cut us off south of the Painted Water, the Missouri River.

He came to the mouth of the Musselshell River in six suns, one hundred twenty-five miles as an arrow might fly. He was in time to see the steamer *Benton* coming downstream. The chief of the boat told him he had seen no Nez Perces up the river; that there had been no sign of Indians when he left Cow Island that morning.

Bearcoat was pleased. He could see his general's star glittering in the rain mist, as the *Benton* swept on down the river and went out of sight around a big bend. Calling to his scouts, he waved them on along the south bank of the river. He told his officers, "Well, we've got them now. They are not yet at the crossing."

But a little ways along the bank, there bobbed into view a small Mackinaw boat tumbling down the fast current from Cow Island. In it were three white men who had used the heavy rain and the far side of the island to slip away downstream when they saw us put our ponies into the water. What, they asked Bearcoat, no Indians at the Island? There were more Indians at that island than they had seen in seven years of trading there. What? Certainly it was Joseph. What other Indian did he suppose could put his people down such fast water in a storm like this?

Now Bearcoat lost his good humor. What a devil's fate! To have the murdering red men right in his hand, then to have them get comfortably away while he could do nothing but sit on the south bank and curse the rain and the river and his evil luck in letting the *Benton* go on downstream by no more than a matter of minutes. With the big fireboat to help him, he could have ferried his whole army across that swirling water in only a few trips. As it was, one of his best scouts had already been sucked down by that swift-flowing river in seeking to cross it that same morning. His soldiers had watched the poor fellow drown, dragged down by the weight of his cartridge belt and winter clothes, and there was no use even asking them to go into that Water, the Missouri River.

If there was only some way to stop the *Benton!* There she was, still only around the far bend, still so close her wood smoke was rolling up into the sky black as a burning wagon train. Yet she might as well have been clear down to Fort Union on the Yellowstone. No rider could hope to catch her now. Race horses running a level river bottom might have done it. Cavalry horses stumbling up and down all the deep ravines and side gullies coming into the river from the rough hills around it, could never reach that rolling smoke before it faded and was trailed away to nothing down the Seloselo Wejanwais.

Look it in the eye, Bearcoat. Admit it like a man. You were beaten. The Nez Perce had come ahead of you to Cow Island.

You were still on the south bank and you would stay a colonel because you could not stop the steamer *Benton* from going on down the Painted Water.

But there was a young lieutenant with Bearcoat who was not beaten. Bearcoat never told the truth about him either. But we had the story, as we had all the rest of Bearcoat's march, from the Sioux scouts who guided him all the way from Fort Keogh. Here Indians give fairness to a white man that even his own leader would not give him. That young lieutenant's name was Biddle. Honor it, if you are white; curse it, if you are red. But remember it. He was the one who thought of the way to stop that steamer.

"Colonel," he said, "if you will bring up the twelve-pound fieldpiece and explode it against that bluff down there where the *Benton's* smoke is, the captain will know something is wrong up here, and will turn around and come back to see what it is."

That is the way they did it. Shooting cannonballs into a dirt cliff far down the river. Three shots was all it took, The steamer *Benton* came back to Bearcoat and by night's first shadows had put all his men and his guns and his horses upon the north bank of the Painted Water.

Gray dawn saw them mounted and moving northwest into the blackness of the snow clouds building swiftly above the ragged line of low peaks which they could see stretching beyond the badlands before them.

"What mountains are those?" asked Bearcoat of the officers who rode with him away from the river.

One of them, a short fat man with the gleaming metals of an oak leaf chief on his coat, reached into his pocket and spread a wrinkled map on his saddle horn. He scowled at it a minute, squinting hard because of the freezing rain which was setting in to blow against their faces. Quickly he folded the map and put it back in his pocket. "The Bear Paws," he said.

35. Place of the Manure Fires

These mountains stand up all alone out of the great grassland which surrounds them. They have good timber on their flanks and from their rocky tops spring several fine streams of clear mountain water, so dear to the Nez Perce people. South are the roughland "breaks" of the Missouri. North, the high plain stretches away to Canada, no hindrance upon it save for the shallow trough of the gentle Milk River.

The people knew a spot here. We called it Tsanim Alikos Pah, the Place of the Manure Fires, because of the vast amounts of buffalo chip fuel to be had there. It was on one of the best streams. There was plenty of scrub growth for windbreak and for starting-twigs for the cookfires. It lay in a broad grassy hollow thirty feet below the rim of the plains, where they began their steep drop to the southern roughlands. It was below the plain to the north also, perhaps twenty feet of protection there. The grasslands all around were thick with antelope and buffalo in all seasons, and here even the deer ran in droves. It was a perfect camp for hunting meat and resting horses. Toward its shelter Looking Glass now directed the band.

Following the Asotin's advice we did not hurry but took advantage of the freedom from One Hand to cull our horse herd on the way. This we accomplished by taking out all the lame and worn mounts which would not recover with a few days' rest and making a particular cut of ours upon one foot which would make the horse too lame for the soldiers to use but which would not cripple him for our own later use should we find him once again. In this manner we came to the new camp with our herd cleaned out to thirteen hundred horses which were either sound or would be sound with a few suns' rest.

We scouts had been sent ahead to begin the hunt before the people arrived and got up the lodges. From the start we had the finest luck in years. For two days of great running we brought down the shaggy beasts. Then, as the village came up, the women took their robes and butchered the meat. Soon the camp was piled high with curly buffalo hides and great stacks of fresh red hump ribs. Once the lodges had been pitched the people gorged themselves. They could not get enough. They ate and slept, ate and slept. After the first few hours no guard was kept. The last of the back scouts were in from looking for One Hand, and the final word was that he had not yet got across the river at Cow Island.

Later in the morning of that remembered arrival day, September 29th, after open weather for the getting-in of the meat, the black clouds closed together again.

It came on to mist, sleety and cold in the forenoon, growing darker by the hour. Harder and harder the wind drove down from the north, pressing the clouds close to the icy ground. By late afternoon it was snowing up on the mountain above us. It was still rain where we were, and held that way as darkness came on. With the full black of night the wind switched into the northeast where the bad snows came from, and the real cold began to settle in.

Walking out of his lodge about ten o'clock, Aleemyah Tatkaneen sniffed the chilling air and called a council of the chiefs. There was no argument. The pleasant days at Tsanim Alikos Pah were ended. The smell of Imekes Meke, the big snow, was on the wind. Winter was coming. It was time to pack the lodges and make the last two days' ride for the border and for the new home in the Land of the Grandmother. "*Talapozanisa*," we said, "may Hunyewat bless the journey."

The camp was stirring at daylight. The rain had stopped. The wind, even colder now, whistled among the lodges, drove the low clouds across the hills, warned us not to be long.

I went out early with Joseph into the horse herd. It was his request. As he instructed, I brought Beaver with me. With him was his twelve-year-old daughter by his older wife, Heyoom Yoyikt. The girl's name was Kapkap Ponmi, Noise of Running

Feet. She was a pretty little thing, the chief's favorite and a real
Nez Perce horse lover.

The herd was out east of the camp, across Tipyahlanah (Eagle)
Creek, the little stream which watered our hollow. All the horses
were standing rump-hunched into the northeast wind, the wet of
the night's rain frozen into rime frost on their thickening winter
coats. Several family pets among them whickered and pricked
their ears as we passed by toward where we could see Joseph and
Running Feet getting out their travel mounts. Here and there
throughout the herd, other men and women were working to get
out their traveling stock for the day. Not far from Joseph I heard
a peculiar fierce half-stallion whistle which I was certain I knew.
Turning, I saw the black Sioux Appaloosa, Mankiller, moving
toward us through the herd. I was flattered that he knew me so
well. But when he got up to us it was Beaver he was after. He
put his nose on her shoulder, rubbed his fine small head against
her arm and followed us along on the walk, as though Coyote's
tall sister had weaned him from his mother. After I had my
scowl, we both laughed. For some reason I put my arm around
Beaver's shoulder. She moved into me and I could feel the
warmth of her body against mine, and it was very pleasant.
"Well," I said, "I see you have stolen my horse. That's pretty
serious. What shall I tell Joseph?"

"Tell him I will trade the horse for your heart."

"No," I said, looking down and seeing that she was smiling in
a light way, "you keep the horse. I have had it in mind to get you
a good horse anyway. I can walk the rest of the way. I want no
horse that doesn't love me."

"He loves you, Heyets," she said in her simple manner. "He is
like the old grandmother and me. He loves you but you won't
stop long enough to let him tell you about it."

"Hah!" I saw she had lost her smile and took my arm away
from her shoulder. "You think I have had any time to stop?
Where has it been? To this very camp I have been on a horse
day and night looking for soldiers. You tell me where I have had
a minute to talk of anything but war."

She nodded her dark head and looked up at me with those great black eyes which seemed always so shy since she had told me *taz alago* the night crazy Otskai lost us One Hand Howard's horses at Camas Meadow.

"Perhaps," she said softly, "there will be time now."

"Who can say?" I answered, glad to see Joseph just ahead, to be freed of Beaver and her way of looking at me and of my own thoughts of how good her warm body had felt for the little minute she had held it against me.

"*Taz meimi*, good morning, my chief," I greeted Joseph cheerfully. Then, seeing which animals he had caught out of the herd, I frowned and said, "What's this? What are you doing with *those* horses up?"

The mounts were his two great Appaloosas, Ebenezer, his famed war horse, and Ebenezer's half-brother, Joshua, his Sunday or "show-off" horse. I did not like to see Joseph with his war horse up. He sensed this and made a motion for me to say nothing in front of the women. Drawing me a little aside, he said quickly, "Do not question me, Heyets, but do as I say. I want you to take Joshua and go with Meyui back along the trail. You ride the Sioux horse. As a young man with a girl, the people will not take alarm to see you ride back. I do not want to worry them, but I awakened this day with a heavy burden on my heart. Something is wrong."

"Are you seeing the trail ahead?" I asked him.

"Yes, and it is dark."

"All right. What do you want us to do?"

"If you see anything, send the girl back first. Let her wave the slow blanket. You stay, and if you see that it is soldiers coming, then you must give us the fast blanket. *Taz alago*, Heyets. Is all understood?"

"Yes, my chief. *Taz alago*."

"What do you think it is?" I asked of Beaver, shading my eyes and peering hard to the south.

"I see nothing at all," she answered.

"There," I said, pointing. "See? Way south, there."

"You mean where those gullies are? And that thin brush? That's four miles, maybe five. You are seeing only shadows."

"All right," I said. "You go on back and tell Joseph that Heyets sees shadows at five miles on the rear trail."

"How about waving the slow blanket?"

She was talking about the Nez Perce "first signal," the one for which the scout rides in slow circles waving his blanket only four times each round. It means "be alert, something is moving— get ready but don't go yet."

"Yes," I told her. "But don't take long with it. Go on in and tell Joseph about the five-mile shadows. He will still be at the horse herd getting the pack animals loaded and helping the women and old men with the work there. You know how he is about that."

"He is wonderful, yes. The women all say that. We could never have come so far without him. All look to him. Asotin, Paloos, Salmon River, it does not matter. There is no other chief like him among us. That's what the woman say."

"The men should hear them," I said. Then, quickly, "*Koümze*, go on. Those shadows are still moving."

She wheeled Joseph's slender-limbed racer, waved to me, and was gone. Alone on the windswept ridge, I went back to scowling at the long fall of the southern slope.

It was very hard to see in that weather. The constant drive and scudding of the low clouds put shadows across the open land out beyond our sheltered hollow, which made far-looking— even for a mountain sheep—a thing of squinting and guessing and talking unhappily to one's self.

It was almost an hour after I had sent Beaver back with the first warning that a favoring shift of the wind got under the cloud scud to the south and stirred it aside long enough for me to see that my shadows were no longer shadows.

They were soldiers. They were hundreds and hundreds of horse soldiers. They were formed in a long line which would take in our camp from three sides when they struck it, and they were coming, on the full gallop, from four miles away!

That is what gave us the only chance we were given in that

grim camp in the hollow at Eagle Creek: Bearcoat Miles did not have my eyes and he thought, in that gray, wind-driven light, that he was much more nearly upon us than he was. Knowing that this advantage was still very slender, I wheeled Mankiller from the ridge and raced him toward our tipis on the dead run, my red King George signal blanket swirling wildly over my head.

Nearing camp I saw that about a hundred horses stood trail-ready, their packs in place, and I thanked Hunyewat that Joseph had listened to Beaver and the first blanket. My relief was short. Aleemyah Tatkaneen, that Asotin devil, had *not* listened. Even as I dashed up yelling that the soldiers were upon us, he was walking his horse around among the people advising them not to hurry, to take all the time they needed.

I could not believe my ears. I spun Mankiller around, blocking the madman's path. "Fool!" I shouted at him. "*Mimillu!* Idiot! Look up on that south ridge where I just rode from. What do you see up there, Asotin? Nothing? Watch it, watch that high ground there? Then go on telling the people there is plenty of time! *Ukeize!* God will curse you!"

I was screaming now in my fury with him. All around us people heard my raging words and stopped their packing to swing their frightened gazes toward the south ridge.

A sound like a great breath of deep pain went up across the entire camp. On the ridge, for the whole length of its crest and running to its either flank, east and west, there swarmed a solid darkness of horse soldiers. As the people cried out in their heart-fear at the sight of them, officers' swords flashed and bugles blew from one end to the other of the blue-coated line. Far and thin with distance, whipped to us across that final mile by a freakish twisting of the wind, we heard the fatal order: "Charge . . . !"

White Bird and Toohoolhoolzote got behind the edge of the camp hollow before the soldiers struck. They were not seen until the last minute. They had the best of our warriors with them, and when they rose up in front of the charging bluecoats they shot only at officers.

The blaze of their Winchesters withered the middle of that charge. Most of Bearcoat's commanders were stretched on the ground, dead or wounded bad. Without their leaders the soldiers broke away and veered off. We had stopped them in the middle.

But on our west side the Seventh Cavalry came on, and on our east side the Second Cavalry swept on by us, drove squarely into our horse herd and swept it away on the run. Swept away with it were Joseph and most of the loaded pack train. At once the fighting was mixed up all over the camp, and the dead were falling like maple leaves in a snow wind.

In that terrible first wild shooting more Nez Perce died than in all the way from the Wallowa to the Big Hole. The flash and roar of rifles and the clot and stink of powder smoke was too great. No one could see to aim. Everyone fired at anything that moved near him. Each shadow was an enemy; no form was a friend. None of us knew at that time what awful things we were soon to learn about that early madness which took our minds when Bearcoat's cavalry burst among our tipis.

About noon most of the soldiers had pulled back and were potshooting at us from the high ground all around the hollow. An hour before, I had seen Joseph in the fighting and thus knew he had got back through the soldier line. Nowhere did I see Beaver or the Asotin grandmother, however. A little later I met Yellow Wolf, who told me the pack train had been chased five miles but had got away to the north, with about fifty women and men—mostly oldsters—going with it. He said Joseph had told him he had ordered Beaver and his daughter to escape, to go on with the pack train, when he himself had turned to come back to his people who were cut off from it and caught by the soldiers.

Yellow Wolf said our chief was happy for the women and few children who got away but very angry with the grown men who went with them. He called them deserters and shamed them to come back and fight, but about twenty of them had kept going with the women.

Yellow Wolf supposed that the Asotin grandmother was with Beaver and little Running Feet, for he himself had seen the old crone with my lodgeskin ponies packed and standing in line just before the soldiers swept in on the horse herd. When I then asked him if it were true the entire herd was lost, he said that it was. At least, he added, as far as any of us would ever care. When I pressed him about this gloomy remark, he fixed me with his fierce eyes and told me exactly what Heinmot, our chief, had just told him.

There might be, he said quietly, a scant hundred horses remaining scattered in the camp. Another one hundred fifty had surely gone with the pack train. It was a certain thing, therefore, that the soldiers now held over a thousand of our horses. It was as certain, because of this, that our tipis pitched here in the Place of the Manure Fires would never be moved again. *Tsanim Alikos Pah* would be the last camp of Joseph and the Nez Perce people.

36. From Where the Sun Now Stands

Somewhere in the mid-afternoon Bearcoat sent three companies of cavalry to drive us free of the stream, thinking to force our surrender for want of drink. Three companies! And those soldiers rode into us as brave as though they could do it. Before we believed they were serious, or could see what they intended, they were among our very lodges.

After that, of course, they had no chance. We drove them out like village dogs. They killed three of us but left six dead and seven wounded of their own number inside our camp. These wounded were treated fair. We gave them water, cared for them the best we could. Pretty soon two of them were strong enough to stand up. When they could walk we let them go over to Bearcoat with a message from angry old White Bird, who had directed the short fight: "Don't send any more soldiers in here like that or next time we will kill them all. If you want to fight, you had better get ready and fight; otherwise get out of the way and let us go on."

Bearcoat sent in no more soldiers. Neither did he get out of the way. As night came on we saw his bluecoats digging with picks and shovels all along the hilltops and high ground around our hollow. They were making rifle pits. They had decided to sit up there and wait for us to starve. At once a war council was called.

Strangely, it met at Joseph's lodge. This puzzled quite a lot of us. Ollikut had been the Wallowa war chief from the beginning, and the leader of the young men of all bands since White Bird Canyon. Why the war talks, which had been held at his lodge, should now be shifted to Joseph's suddenly, was the question in our minds. We had our answer to it soon enough.

The word had gone out for all remaining able men to attend. Able men by this time meant all of us between sixteen and sixty who were not yet hurt so bad we could not walk, or sit up and aim a rifle. When the last of us had come in, or been helped in, Yellow Bull turned to Joseph and said, "Fifty-five, Heinmot," and Joseph nodded and replied, "All right, Chuslum. Thank you."

He studied the circle a moment, then began to speak, placing all the facts in a straight row, as was the Indian way when a bad time had come.

"My brothers, this morning early I was in the horse herd with my little daughter, twelve years of age. Looking south I saw the soldiers coming. I gave her a rope and told her to catch a horse and join the others with the pack train. Even as she obeyed me, the horse herd began to run and I was there all alone with Ebenezer, my war mount.

"I thought of my wife and children who were now surrounded by soldiers, and I resolved to go to them or die. With a prayer in my mouth to the Great Spirit Chief who rules above, I dashed unharmed through the line of soldiers. It seemed to me that there were guns on every side, before and behind me. My clothes were cut to pieces and my horse was wounded, but I was not hurt. As I reached the door of my lodge, my wife handed me my rifle, saying, 'Here's your gun. Fight.' "

Joseph paused, looking into the windy dark toward the west hill where the soldier tents stood gray and thin-walled against the cold shant of the rain, which had begun again.

"I fought," he went on. "We all fought. You saw this old friend fall; I saw that old friend fall. How many soldiers fell does not matter. They will get more soldiers. Our people who are gone will not come back.

"A great tragedy has come upon us today. In our wildness and fear we killed even our own men. Naked Head shot Koyehkown, Kowwaspo and Lone Bird, all three in the same shelter, thinking they were Sioux scouts. By the same manner Lean Elk was killed. But they are only four of the many who are gone. We mourn all alike who fell by our own or by the soldiers' guns. Yet there are two who went down today, who . . . " Joseph could not go on for a moment. He waited until his voice was steady.

"If you will look about the circle here," he said, "you will see that Peopeo Hihhih, chief of the White Birds, is not among our number. That is because he is at the lodge of his dear friend, Toohoolhoolzote, saying *taz alago* to the companion of his lifetime, who fell in the last shooting this afternoon." He stopped again while the men looked at one another and made the sign of respect for the old Salmon River hero. When they had, he continued in a low voice. "Now I must tell you my own great sorrow. Then I, too, must go to a lodge which is not mine and sit outside it in the dark grieving for the life of one I loved."

I had never seen such sadness on the face of any man. It was as though Joseph had come at last upon a need for strength which his heart of mountain oak could not supply. It was the look of one who has been shot low through the bowels, who wants to die fast but cannot. Then he lifted his head and said it very quietly. "I must tell you now, that Ollikut is dead."

There was a silence in that following moment, and a sight such as will not come again — the last half a hundred wounded, desperate warriors of the Oregon and Idaho Nez Perce sitting with heads bowed deep to their breasts so that they would not have to see the brother of Ollikut crying — and more, so that the brother of Ollikut would not need to see their tears, in return, as all wept with him for the death of the greatest fighting Indian of them all.

That night the women dug trenches facing the soldiers on every side. They worked the whole night using only camas hooks, knives, trowel bayonets taken at Big Hole, and when they had nothing else, their bare fingers. Babies as young as four and five, and old men bowed by as many as seventy and eighty snows, worked with them, carrying away the dirt in saddlebags, pack wallets, kettles, tin cups, anything which would hold the soil. With this dug-dirt and what small rocks could be found along the stream, the open ends of the two main side gullies which drained into Eagle Creek at the center of camp, were filled in and built up as high as a child's head. When these were found to be not enough, dead horses, which lay all among the tipis, were roped and dragged to the gullies, or to whatever other position needed filling or raising to make a rifle-firing place.

Joseph directed this work. As it went along, he was everywhere. The vote of the council had been not to surrender. The deaths of Ollikut and Toohoolhoolzote acted as a goad or quirt on the tired people, and with this fierce sorrow to drive them on they worked like slave Indians through the dark hours doing as Joseph bid them, never stopping to question or complain. The thought that they might be digging their own graves must have come to many of them, as it did to me. Yet so great was the return of their faith in Joseph's power to "see ahead," that they tore at the sleety earth like burrowing animals, and the marks they put into its flinty mountain breast are there to this day, standing mute and still under the Montana sky, a grass-grown testimony to that long-gone night of Nez Perce agony and toil.

It must not be imagined, however, that the people were so innocent they worked on faith alone. They knew they had whipped Howard, Gibbon and Sturgis. They knew some fifty of their fellows had escaped with the pack train and must, even now, be slipping toward the Canadian border and the lodges of Sitting Bull's Sioux. The Crows had told them the old Hunkpapa medicine man had two thousand people up there. That meant as many as four hundred warriors, using the Indian count of one fighter in every five members of a tribe. Those were the Indians who had killed Custer. They were the Indians who owed

Bearcoat for chasing them out of their own country. If our fleeing people could reach them in time, we might see those Sioux warriors looming up out of the gray northern mists at any moment after the fourth or fifth day. When that moment came, the Nez Perce who had beaten One Hand, Red Nose and Slow Fighter *without* help, could, as surely, with the savage Hunkpapa Sioux to aid them, rise up and destroy Bearcoat Miles on Eagle Creek, as the Sioux had destroyed Yellow Hair Custer on the Little Horn.

We were not fools. Yes, we dug hard that night because of the anger and sorrow of our grief. But the real hope which drove us was the belief that our Sioux brothers would come down out of Canada and save us.

So the morning found us ready to fight for the time we needed. True, with the pack train gone on, we had little to eat save the dead horses. We had not too much ammunition and not too many warm clothes to keep out the cold. More than one-half our men, and many of our women and little children, were wounded. We had already found the bodies of forty-nine Nez Perce killed in that terrible first day. There were three of the wounded who must die before another sun darkened. We had only White Bird and Joseph left to lead us. The breath of the wind was growing more bitter with each hour. There was no medicine, no clean cloth for bandages, not even enough dry blankets to cover the wounded. The children huddled four and five each to the few worn buffalo robes. The only warmth for the walking wounded and the women and old ones came from the handful of buffalo chip fires which were kept feebly alive in the most sheltered of the remaining tipis. The few young men and older warriors who waited for that dawn out on the edges of our rifle works had only the warmth of their own bodies pressed together, or, if they were lucky, the carcass of a dying pony which yet held the heat of life, but not its movement, against which to crouch and across which to level their guns at the soldier lines. Yet the vote of the men in council had been against surrender; the bloody fingers of their sisters and mothers had dug the trenches in the frozen ground; with torn and blackened hands their wives had held forth to them their guns and said, as Joseph's wife: "Fight."

Sepekuse. So let it be. We were ready.

The morning dragged on strangely quiet. The soldiers fired very little. We fired less than that, waiting for them to try something. About noon they put up a white flag and Tom Hill, their Delaware Indian interpreter, came out and called over to us in Chinook that they wanted a "dinner truce," so that they could eat. We laughed and let them have the time. Ourselves, we never ate while a fight was on. We just pulled some of the cold wind into our bellies and chewed on that.

There were only two other things about that second day, October 1st, which remain in the memory. One was that it began to snow very light and fine in the afternoon. The other was that, as the shadows grew late, I saw Looking Glass for the first time since the soldiers struck us. He had not been in the war council, though he had fought brave as a bear on the first day. Yellow Wolf, who was sharing my dead horse with me on the west side of camp, said that he thought the Asotin chief was having a dream over his failures. He looked as though this might be so. He sat alone, even farther out on the west edge than we were. He was in front of us, a little to our left hand. Uncovered by coat or blanket, he crouched out there in his shallow pit, never taking his staring eyes from the west hill behind which Bearcoat was camped, his only shelter the high-peaked black horse soldier hat which was his main *wyakin*, or war charm. He was a small man but with a heart like a buffalo. His *simiakia* was the most unreasoning faith among us. His utter vainness of self and his blind, stubborn mind — what Lean Elk had called his "head like a rock" — had cost his people nearly ninety lives at Big Hole and already nearly fifty at the Bears Paws. Still, in that last hour of the second day, I felt sorry for him. I knew, with that power of Joseph's blood which let me see such things, what it was that held him out there in that farthest rifle pit; and I turned to Yellow Wolf and answered softly.

"Yes, you are right, and I know the dream. He is seeing that his people forgive him all that he has done — and because of that he cannot forgive himself any of it."

"It may be," nodded Yellow Wolf. "He see things in a hard, dark way, but always straight. I don't mean his mind works straight, Heyets. I mean his heart."

It was my turn to nod. "That is it, Hemene," I said. "His heart is as good as Joseph's, but his mind is as bad as Otskai's. I am sorry that I cursed him."

Yellow Wolf didn't answer me. He only looked off into the north and said, "It is coming on to snow harder. If it holds like this another day, we might go out by night under its cover, even without the horse herd. What do you think?"

"I don't know," I said. "I feel bad inside. I keep on seeing Ollikut lying there in his lodge where we went to pay him the last respect. I cannot be sure, Hemene, but I think I loved him even more than I do our chief."

"*He was a warrior,*" said Yellow Wolf with fierce pride, and so ended the story of Ollikut and the second day of the fight at the Place of the Manure Fires.

On the third day, October 2nd, Looking Glass was killed as he stood atop the piled earth in front of his rifle pit. It was a long bullet which killed him. It was fired from the rifle of Milan Tripp, one of Beatcoat's chief scouts, and many of our people wanted to believe that it was a thing of only shooter's luck, like the great long shot old Fire Body made on Trumpeter Jones at White Bird Canyon. Yellow Wolf and I knew better, although we never said it: Aleemyah Tatkaneen, chief of the Clearwater Asotins, stood on top of that rifle pit with his arms folded over his breast, his black hat straight on his head, his gun in the trench behind him. His face was turned square to the west and square to the soldiers who raised their rifles over there when they saw him. And he stood there like that with nothing moving on his body save the wind whip of the buckskin fringe on his leggings, until Tripp's long bullet whined across the frozen brown grass from the western hill and laid him dead upon the naked dirt.

With Looking Glass gone, the people seemed to settle into their first mood of real fear. White Bird, seventy-four winters, was the only fighting chief left alive. Of first-rate warriors, any age, there were now fewer remaining than the fingers of two hands and the toes of two feet: Wottolen, Yellow Wolf, No Feet, Naked Head, Otskai, Yellow Bull, Sun Necklace, Black Eagle, Band of Geese, Dead Bones, Ten Owl, Tabador — four or five others, no more. The weather, dropping wind and raising temperature, thawed the snow in our pits, making them a wallow of slush ice and mud.

Big trouble now came. In the afternoon a second white flag was shown over in the soldier trenches and Tom Hill walked halfway over the field and called to us that Miles wanted to see Joseph.

Joseph, suspecting nothing, met with Bearcoat on the middle ground. They talked a little and when our chief understood that Miles wanted him to surrender he said he would do it if Bearcoat would permit the Nez Perce to go on to Canada, or even back to Idaho, without killing any more of the women and children. Miles said he had no orders for anything but a surrender without any conditions of good treatment of captives, property rights or anything. Joseph then said no, very flat and hard. At once Bearcoat commanded his soldiers to seize our chief and they took him and carried him back to their camp.

Fortunately, in that same moment, Yellow Bull, on guard at our north line, caught a soldier spy sneaking around to look at our camp while Bearcoat parleyed with Joseph. He was a lieutenant and a brave man. He asked for nothing, only advising us to give up our guns, since we had no chance.

Chuslum Hihhih, White Bull, a bad Indian, wanted to kill this brave Lieutenant Jerome. Yellow Wolf overrode him with a bitter speech. Jerome's guards from that minute were Yellow Wolf and Wottolen, two very tough Indians and single-minded.

We knew the value of that prisoner and we gave him every comfort we could. On the opposite side, Miles treated Joseph like a dog. He had him hobbled and his hands cuffed behind him and tied up to his hobbles. Then he had him rolled in a dirty horse blanket and left on the ground in the droppings of the pack mule picket line.

Eeh, the shame, the treacherous shame — yes, and the startling swiftness of it then. All came to pass with such brutal suddenness from that time to the end that no Nez Perce can say that he tells it absolutely as it was, that his words are all-the-way fair to the soldiers. But these eyes were there, these ears were there; they saw and heard what was done and spoken.

On the fourth morning, October 3rd, Lieutenant Jerome sent a message on paper to Miles telling of his good treatment by us. Miles then let Joseph up out of the mule droppings. The third white flag came out and there was arranged the exchange of prisoners, Joseph for Jerome. The meeting was once more halfway of the field, and our chief was furious. When he left Miles he told him that he would never surrender to him. When this news was returned to our camp, Kahwitkahwit, that coward who had floated to safety down the river between his wives at the Big Hole, broke down and wept in the open. The silence of all those hungry, wounded and freezing Nez Perce was a fearful thing.

"We have made our decision," said Joseph in the stillness of staring at Kahwitkahwit. "It is now only for us to wait and to pray for the Sioux to come."

But the Sioux did not come. Instead, under cover of the snow, now falling thick again, came a bleeding and bad-wounded old Asotin woman sneaking in from the north where she had fled with the pack train. It was the old grandmother. Thirty miles up toward Milk River the pack train had met some of those Sioux we were hoping would help us. Ten Nez Perce were dead, ten others and the pack train taken captive. The remaining thirty had fled into the hills, scattered Hunyewat alone knew where. *Eee-hahh!* Instead of praying for those Sioux to find us, we had better pray that they did not find us.

After that news the fight went on until dark. It continued to be a sniping, rifle-pit fight. All was long-range firing and of little effect. No attempt at advance was made by either Indian or soldier. But now the Nez Perce mood was blacker than the belly of the blizzard which was at last bearing down upon us. With no help coming from the Sitting Bull Sioux, and indeed possible death waiting for us among them if we broke free of Bearcoat, there appeared but two poor choices left to us. We could leave the wounded here with the women and children, the warriors slipping away with the few horses into the black snowstorm that was coming; we could stay and all of us surrender together as Bearcoat had demanded. There was a third choice, of course, but none of us had wanted to think of that. Joseph, however, made us think of it.

"My people," he said, "we can do neither of these first things. Have you ever heard of a wounded Indian recovering while in the hands of white men? Can you forget the scalping done by the Bannack and Shoshone scouts to every one of our aged, hurt or sick which we have had to abandon along the trail? No, we cannot leave the wounded. Neither can we all surrender to Bearcoat Miles. To One Hand Howard, yes, we could give over our guns in safety. He is not a squaw killer like Bearcoat and Red Nose Gibbon. His scouts do not defile our dead, do not murder our helpless living. But I would rather see my women and children honorably dead in the fighting than to surrender them to Bearcoat Miles and see his soldiers shoot them down like animals."

For a little we clung to this brave speech, trying to believe the third choice it gave us. But on that day the soldiers got the twelve-pound cannon to working. They dug a hole in the ground for its tail, so that its nose pointed up in the sky and they could drop the bombshells into our camp like tossing rocks into a hollow stump. Before, they could not get the big gun pointed down enough to fire into our trenches, but as the fourth night came on, they were hurting us very badly with it.

The fifth morning, October 4th, came and the fight went on. Shortly, a cannonshell blew up in one of our pits which held some women and four small children. All of them were wounded and two of them, little twelve-year-old Atsipeeten and her aged grandmother, Intehtah, were torn apart so much that their own people could not tell who they were until they had cleaned them off and laid them together again.

That cannonburst killed our final spirit. All along, the deaths of our women and children had been the things we could not accept. Now, with the one shell, with the single minute of crying out in the red and muddied snow, we knew we were all finished. What General One Hand Howard, Gibbon, Sturgis, Bearcoat and a thousand soldiers could not do to us, one old Indian grandmother and her little granddaughter had succeeded in doing: now we knew we were beaten.

That same night One Hand arrived in the camp of Bearcoat Miles. He had with him our old friend and white blood-brother, Narrow Eye Chapman; also several Lapwai Indians who were kin of ours. One Hand was wise; he knew us better than Bearcoat. He knew those Lapwai people would give us confidence, and he knew we would talk to Ad Chapman when we would never trust Bearcoat, or talk to any of his white interpreters, or even to Tom Hill or any of his other Indian interpreters. And by this far time in our journey we heard the news of One Hand's coming almost as one might welcome the coming of an old friend. Our spirits lifted up; we lost much of our fear. We had been sure that Bearcoat would kill us if we surrendered. Now we knew that he could not do this with One Hand watching him. On the coat of one was only an eagle; on the coat of the other was a star. We knew the difference, and waited through the night for One Hand to send Chapman over to see his old friends from the Fair Land.

Nothing happened. Then, about noon the next day, the fourth white flag came over. With it were Narrow Eye and two old treaty Nez Perces well known to all of us. They were Captain John, called by us Jokais, Worthless; and Captain George, called Meopkowit, Know Nothing.

Both of these old men had daughters with us, so we listened to what they said. Jokais did the talking.

"Heinmot," he said to Joseph, "you must now realize your true position. Bearcoat has six hundred soldiers. One Hand has four hundred which are no more than one or two day's march behind. The soldier chiefs have been watching you with their spyglasses and they know the number of your dead and wounded, and the fewness of your horses."

"Well," answered Joseph, "I know all of this but we will never surrender to Bearcoat. I have told him that."

"One Hand says you must do it; you must surrender as Bearcoat has told you."

"To Bearcoat?"

"Yes."

"Never."

"Heinmot, think of the women, think of the little ones. My own daughter is here with you, a baby at her breast and two at the knee. You must do it; you must stop the fighting and put down the rifle for the last time."

"I will not surrender to Miles. Not now, not ever." He paused, studying the two old men, his face drawn, his eyes dark with feeling. "Jokais," he said quietly, "I must talk to One Hand. Tell General Howard that I will talk only to him."

Jokais and Meopkowit went back to the soldier lines with this word. They were shaking their heads and saying, "Bad, bad, very bad." But in a little while they came again, waving the fifth white flag. General Howard, they said, wanted to speak with Chief Joseph.

Joseph then called the last council of the nontreaty Nez Perce. To that meeting came White Bird for the band which bore his name, Wottolen for the Asotin of Looking Glass, Naked Head for the Paloos of Hahtalekin, Black Eagle for his people, Band of Geese for his, and so, in that thinned order, to the end. We were fearfully few in number, but all were chiefs or the blood of chiefs. Yellow Wolf and I sat in the circle as nearest surviving blood kin of our chief. With the others we waited, crouched in the icy snow outside the lodge of Heinmot Tooyalakekt, not talking, not looking at one another, only watching the door of the lodge — and waiting. Behind those wind-tattered, bullet-ripped flaps, our leader was taking his final decision. What that decision would be, none of us could guess; yet we knew it must be one of two things: no or yes; fight or surrender; die or live.

The entry skins stirred, moved aside. Joseph stood before us. He looked down at us, his face gray and deep-hurt, like the face of a father who has lost a child and must tells its little brothers that it is gone. Then he lifted his eyes from us, placing them upon Jokais and Meopkowit, who stood in the snow beyond us waiting for his answer to One Hand. When he spoke, he spoke to all of us. It was the last time I ever saw him raise his hand. But the power of it — and of his words — remained with me a lifetime.

"Tell General Howard that I know his heart," he said to the old men. "What he told me before — I have it in my heart. I am tired of fighting. Our chiefs are killed. Looking Glass is dead. Toohoolhoolzote is dead. The old men are all dead. It is the young men now who say yes or no. He who led the young men is dead. It is cold, and we have no blankets. The little children are freezing to death. My people — some of them — have run away to the hills, and have no blankets, no food. No one knows where they are — perhaps freezing to death. I want to have time to look for my children, and to see how many of them I can find; maybe I shall find them among the dead."

He paused for one breath, and we could hear the pain of it as he drew it into him. Then he looked back down at us and said his final words.

"Hear me, my chiefs, my heart is sick and sad. From where the sun now stands, I will fight no more forever."

Jokais and Meopkowit, crying like babies, took his message to Howard and Miles, repeating it to the officers standing waiting on the little hill on their side of the ground. It was shortly after two o'clock in the afternoon of the sixth day, October 5, 1877.

At four Joseph rode slowly up the hill, accompanied by five of his warriors on foot.

One Hand had given his word that we would be sent back to Lapwai and could keep all our horses if we surrendered peacefully. That would be in the spring, since the snows already lay deep in the Bitterroots. We all understood this and accepted it.

Joseph was speaking for all of us save old White Bird when he came at last up to General Howard. Impulsively he offered him his gun. One Hand would not take it but directed him to give it over to Bearcoat Miles. Joseph did this without a word. When he had, the soldiers came in two lines of rifles around him and marched him away. I was permitted to go with him as interpreter. Otherwise he was alone in the last hour of his suffering for his beloved people. He sat in the door of the little tent the soldiers gave him, his eyes far away, his heart crying. *Sepekuse* was the only word I heard him say. *So let it be; it is the end.*

From then until dusk the captives straggled in from the rifle pits across the darkening hollow. White Bird, the only important chief beside Joseph still alive, did not come. In the gloom of twilight he slipped through the slackening soldier lines and fled on our last good horses for Canada. He was accompanied by fourteen men and a number of women and children, including his own adopted son, Little Bird, of long-ago Salmon River memory.

The old chief had planned his escape all along, tricking Joseph into surrendering first by saying that he would stay and look to the rest of the surrender, particularly of his own and Toohoolhoolzote's Indians, who had made so much trouble for Joseph before.

One Hand later put much weight on this treachery of White Bird's. He said it made void the promises he gave Joseph. The Nez Perce said One Hand should have remembered that each chief spoke only for his own band. They said he should have got White Bird's surrender separately from Joseph's. Yet no Nez Perce ever said that General Howard lied to us, or ever denied that White Bird betrayed both him and his own chief, Joseph. No, the Nez Perce were never proud of Peopeo Hihhih and his broken word at the Bear Paws. It marked the *one* time in the seventy and more winters since Old Joseph's father shook hands with Lewis and Clark at Weippe Prairie that the honor-word of the Pierced-Nose People was given over in bad faith to the white man.

In the final count made by the soldiers after feeding us that night, the Indians who had stood to their chief's agreement numbered four hundred eighteen. Of these eighty-seven were men, one hundred eighty-four women, one hundred forty-seven children. There were eleven hundred fifty-three horses, one hundred and three saddles, ninety-eight guns surrendered.

The war was over. Only one question remained. *Who had the victory?*

37. Beyond the Bear Paws

Yellow Wolf, despite his fierce heart, did not go with the White Bird band. He was true to Joseph and came in among the very last that freezing cold October night.

Yet all the same, he came in like a wolf. He put his short rifle down inside the leg of his pants. Around his body, beneath his shirt and blanket, he wrapped two belts of ammunition for it. In a brushy draw north of the tipis, he hid out his pony before coming over to be counted by the soldiers. Nor was that all he hid in that secret place beyond the guard lines. He had not forgotten me, his near-blood brother.

It was almost dawn of the surrender night when I heard the slight sound outside the prison tent and he slid in at the door saying, "*Saus, talig,* be quiet, Heyets. It's me, Hemene Moxmox."

"Hemene!" I cried. "What are you doing here?"

"*Saus!*" he repeated sharply. "Where is Heinmot?"

"Here, I am here." Joseph spoke for himself out of the morning darkness. "What is it, Hemene?"

"Uncle," answered Yellow Wolf, "my heart is growing weak. I do not want to go back to Lapwai. Also I think Heyets should not go back. You know Agent Monteith feels strong against us both. Do I lie?"

"No," said Joseph. "Go on."

"I have a confession, uncle. Before coming over last night I hid out my pony. As well, I hid out one for Heyets. I have the old Asotin woman out there watching them, the one who came back to us bad-wounded. It was her idea about the horses, really. She said she wanted to do it for the ugly boy, the skinny Wallowa. That's Heyets, uncle."

"Yes," said Joseph with his sad, kind smile. "What else, Hemene?"

Yellow Wolf slipped to the tent door, listening for the soldier guard to tramp by. When he had gone past, he came back to us.

"I have my short gun and a lot of bullets under my clothes. I think we can walk out of this camp, if we go now before the light gets greater. I want to know if it is all right with you if we go. I want you to say that it is."

Joseph sat thinking. It was no easy thing for him to decide. He had given his word to One Hand, yet he knew it was true that Agent Monteith might be very vengeful with Yellow Wolf and me. In the end he decided like an Indian.

"I think," he said to Yellow Wolf, "that you had better go look for our poor people who disappeared the first day. They are out there in those hills and it is cold out there. They have no food. Go find them and take them food. One Hand should have let me go look for them, as I asked to do. Now you go. Do you understand me, Hemene? Things have changed."

We understood him. Under the words, in his Indian way, he was telling us that we had better escape. He was saying that he saw trouble and treachery ahead for all our people now. White Bird's bad faith had changed One Hand's good heart toward us. He has already said as much to Joseph earlier, and now Joseph was warning us. He did not say, "Yes, run away, One Hand has lied to us." He said only, "Things have changed — do you understand?" And we knew what he wanted us to know.

"Yes, uncle, said Yellow Wolf quickly, "all is clear to us. We honor you, uncle. *Taz alago.*"

Joseph put out his hand in the graying darkness. We each took it and pressed it hard. I could not speak.

"Good-bye, dear children," said Joseph. "You have been like sons to me. My heart will be smaller when you are gone. Be brave. Never do a meanness. Honor your word and your women. Remember your chief. He loved you."

Yellow Wolf nodded and went to the door. He looked out. "All right," he said to me. "He is going the other way. Hurry up." We went out, moving quick to get away from the tent and the guard soldier. My throat was shut tight. Yellow Wolf's face was hard as knife-blade flint. Neither of us looked back. For myself it was the last farewell. I never saw Joseph again.

"Walk slow," said Yellow Wolf. "Act as though we are just wandering around the camp. Laugh a little. Talk loud." I nodded, obeying him. We both knew soldiers pretty well. We had been to Walla Walla many times with Ollikut and he had taught us well about them. The smart white men were not soldiers. Soldiers hardly dared make dirt or water without their officers to tell them to do it. We didn't think we would have any trouble unless we saw an officer. We were right. The soldiers on the guard line were not very bright that morning. Two of them even waved to us. I waved back at them and called out *"taz alago"* to them in Nez Perce. Yellow Wolf laughed at that, thinking it was a fine joke to say good-bye to the soldiers. We went right on walking slow. In a little while we were over a small hill. In another little while Yellow Wolf said, *"Eeh!* You want to see something pretty, Heyets? Look behind you."

I glanced around. There was nothing back there but falling snow and the faint double line of our footprints. Even as I watched, new snow was swiftly filling up the moccasin tracks, making them white and clean and hard to see. Of the soldier camp there was not a sight or a sound, or even a picket-line smell. Just snow, silence, safety.

"We have done it," I said. "Hemene, we have walked right out of the middle of six hundred horse soldiers!"

"Yes," he said. "Enjoy it. Your grandchildren will never believe it."

"They won't have the chance," I grinned, "if we stand here all winter talking about it."

"Aye," said Yellow Wolf with no smile. "Come on."

We got to the draw where the ponies were. Stopping, we held absolutely still, listening into the snow along our back trail. We heard nothing. Yellow Wolf nodded, and we slid over the edge of the draw, down into the pine and alder scrub of its bottom. We listened again, then let out a deep breath together. Now we were truly safe.

Hearing us, our horses nickered up ahead. We went toward them through the growth, calling softly to the old woman. She did not answer us. When we got up to her she lay, not moving, on the ground, the tether ropes of both ponies wrapped around her body. She lay stiff, the snow caked on her from its night falling. There was a line along the ground where the restless horses had dragged her. We thought surely that she was long dead of the cold. Yet, as I bent over her, she stirred and looked up at me.

"Ah!" she snapped at me very weak. "It's you at last, ugly boy. About time, slowhead. Well, here's your Sioux horse. Get on him and ride. Don't stay for me."

I was surprised, indeed, to see Mankiller there. How Yellow Wolf or the old woman had stolen him out of the guarded few head we had surrendered in the camp, I would never know. But my wonderment could not take my mind from the poor Asotin crone huddled there in that icy place, and I shook my head at her quickly.

"Don't fear, little mother. We wouldn't go without you. Come on now, put your arms here about my neck."

She struck at my hand as I reached for her.

"You're a fool, boy. Get on that horse."

"And leave you? Never."

"Now. Right now."

Yellow Wolf came up and took the horses from her. He looked at her.

"She's right, Heyets. She can't ride far."

"I will carry her."

"Listen, Wallowa," said the old woman, raising up to an elbow. "I have one big legbone broken up near the body. I have the other legbone broken all apart at the knee. I have a bullet trough in my back running through both my kidneys. I am seventy-eight winters. Leave me, do you hear? It is my right to demand it. Go after the girl. She is a better one than the Asotin you had. More sense and a stronger body. *Koiimze!* Damn! Get out of here . . . ! "

Peering more closely, I saw the cold gray growing in her face, and the clouding glaze drawing the sight from her eyes. I reached up and got Yellow Wolf's blanket and put it around her where she lay, patting her and saying small sweet words as one would with a tired child.

"*Taz, taz,* that's a good boy," she nodded gratefully. She let her eyes close and her old head fall against my breast. I thought her asleep, but she stirred again and said, "Boy, you find that tall girl. Tell her I found you as I promised. Do you hear?"

"Yes, old one, I hear."

"You stay with her, too, you understand?"

"I understand, old one."

"And don't call me old one. You know what my name is."

"In truth, I don't," I told her softly. "I never heard your name."

She sighed, a very small smile coming to her lips.

"For you, boy," she said, "it's grandmother."

"Thank you, grandmother. I am very proud."

She did not answer and Yellow Wolf, coming up to peer again, said, "She's in the last sleep. I know that rough way of breathing. Let's go, Heyets. I'm feeling nervous."

I straightened, taking Mankiller's reins which my uncle handed me. "Yes," I said. "So am I. We better hurry."

"*Hold* . . . ! " said the white man's heavy voice. "Don't move a moccasin."

We froze like listening deer.

"Drop them reins and step away from them horses."

We did it, our neck hairs crawling.

"Now then, you red sons of bitches — turn around."

We obeyed his deep growl. Our eyes flinched. Standing alone in our back trail from the soldier camp was a huge broad man with a ragged dirty bandage over one eye. He had in his hands a settlement bird gun with short barrels, what the white man calls a sawed-off shotgun. Over his shoulders was slung his regular Winchester rifle. His dress of buckskin leggings, Sioux winter moccasins and wolf-fur hunting coat said he was a soldier scout. But his lone eye, bushy whiskers and burning look of hate for Yellow Wolf and me said more than that. It was Redbeard Bates.

"*Remember me?*" he asked. He moved toward us, stepping over the old grandmother, bringing the birdgun up to his hip, its two big holes staring at our stomachs. "Think hard now, boys," he said. "It'll come to you."

His fat thumb moved twice, setting the hammers on each side of the birdgun. "You first," he said, shifting the gun so that it looked squarely at my manhood. "That's because I know you better, and you're the one held my arms while your friend worked me over with his rifle butt. Likewise, you're the one give me this." He jabbed his left thumb toward the filthy rags over his eye.

I didn't answer him. Neither did Yellow Wolf. Behind him we saw something we could not believe, and we had to use our lifetime of Indian training to keep our eyes from warning Redbeard. The dying grandmother had stirred one last time. She was up on an elbow again, lying but a single long arm's reach from where the white man's great legs stood spread wide and crouching in the trail. And in her wrinkled hawk's claw of a hand she held a nine-inch Asotin skinning knife.

"You ain't going to go fast, you Neppercy bastards," Redbeard told both of us. "I'm going to give it to you where you can feel it a long time. You're to lay here in this snow till you freeze to death, and every minute you're waiting you'll be suffering your heathen guts out. I'm going to give you this buckshot right in the picketpin, and I'll just tell your friend, General Howard, I trailed the two of you out of camp and you jumped me."

He paused, looking at us with his sick hate.

"I've been follering you two Injun bastards three months and thirteen hundred miles. It's going to pleasure my soul to let you die slow. *You dirty, murdering, red heathen sons of bitches!*"

Behind him, the grandmother writhed on the ground, twisted

forward, struck to the limit of her strength. The knife blade went into the tensed back of Redbeard's great thigh, ripped downward, bone deep, to catch and hang prisoned in the rubbery gristle under his kneecap. His scream was no measure of his courage. The pain of such a wound, received without warning, is beyond any man. His huge body thrashed around like a snake, his hands flew apart, the birdgun went spinning up in the air. Yellow Wolf flashed after it, his speed greater even than that of my eyes. He caught it as it reached the ground, rolled back to his feet with it upswung by the barrels, and crashed its stock down into the side of Redbeard's head, as he bent around in agony to pull the Asotin knife from behind his knee. Redbeard went into the snow without a sound. He fell on his back, thick arms thrown out limp and shapeless as those of a Lapwai cornfield scarecrow, and Yellow Wolf forced the two muzzles of the short bird-gun under his wolf-fur coat deep into the fat of his belly and pulled both of the triggers at the same time.

It made very little noise. Sort of a "*ppurrppp!*" as a gun does when there is a bad bullet in it and only the primer powder flashes and smokes at the breech.

Yellow Wolf reached down and wrenched the Winchester out from under Redbird's great weight. He tossed it to me. "Here's your rifle," he said. "Get my blanket and the old woman's knife. She won't need them anymore."

I gathered up the things, together with Redbeard's belt of ammunition for the rifle, while my uncle caught up our horses. Swinging up on Mankiller, I looked back for the last time at the two bodies lying in the snow.

"It was a close thing, Hemene," I shivered. "We owe our lives to the old grandmother. That's certain."

"Not so certain," said Yellow Wolf, black eyes narrowed at the bearlike hulk of Redbeard. "He helped, too."

"What do you mean?"

"He was a white man.'

"Well?"

"He talked too long."

We went on all that day, north always north. The next day it was the same. We traveled slow because we did not know the way, and all the time we were looking for signs of our people and trying to avoid the wandering Sioux band which had scattered them. We found no sign of either our own, or the other, Indians. On the third day we came to and crossed Milk River and were in the Land of the Grandmother. On that day, too, we came to the camp of the Milk River half-bloods, a part-Sioux band of buffalo hunters. They proved kind, friendly people — and more, they had news of our lost Nez Perce.

Our people had been in this very camp only three days gone. The half-bloods had given them food and some few blankets, all they could spare, to help them on their way to find their own camp. We had a night's sleep and a thin meal there — the hunting was bad and these people were hungry themselves — and next day we went on into the north snow looking for our homeless pack train people.

In four days we found them. There were thirty-eight of them, all fairly well but very hungry. They had had no hunting luck and there was food in the camp for but one more scant meal — the last bones and the boiled hide of a horse which had died one day out of the half-blood camp. They had seen nothing of the White Bird band, or of any enemy Sioux. They still talked of getting to Sitting Bull, since the half-bloods had told them he was ten days' journey north and the Sioux who had attacked them could not have been his people.

Yellow Wolf's mother and Joseph's daughter were in the pack-train camp, but Coyote's tall sister was not. She had gone only that morning, into the back snow, taking my one pack horse and tattered lodgeskins with her. When I asked Swan Woman, Yellow Wolf's mother, why the poor girl had gone, she stared at me with a woman's look and said, "She has gone to be with you. Her heart is yours, Heyets, you know that. She waited, and when you did not come from the camp back there, she said the old Asotin grandmother had not reached you, that there was some trouble, that you needed her. *Sepekuse*, that was all. She just went."

"And you didn't stop her?" I said angrily.

"Why stop her? What is a woman without a man?"

Yellow Wolf nodded in agreement with his mother and looked up at the weather. "The snow's been dead since last night," he said. "No new fall. She can't have gone a great ways with that wolfbait horse. There's still half a day of trailing light left."

I smiled, somehow feeling very good and warm inside. I put out my hand, and he took it. "Hemene," I said, "you have always been my brother."

"*Eeh*," he grunted, "I am glad enough to be rid of you. Nearly four moons I have had to watch out for you almost as much as for Otskai. He's only crazy; you're soft in the heart, like Heinmot. Besides, you don't need a brother. You need a woman. Go and get her."

"Wait," called Swan Woman as I turned to depart, "we have something for you, Hemene and I." She disappeared into a clump of spruce and was back in a moment, leading a slim sorrel horse which I knew at once. It was a prize Yellow Wolf had taken from the Big Hole, a gleaming lovely animal of great quality, an officer's horse of Gibbon's cavalry and a possession which my wild-hearted uncle would ordinarily have died for. Swan Woman had saved him from the herd, just before the pack train fight, and brought him all this way for her son, should she ever find him again.

She now gave his lead rope to Yellow Wolf, who in turn gave it to me.

"For Meyui," he said. "A tall horse for a tall woman."

"But I can't take him, uncle! Not your best horse."

"Go on, don't talk. You can't start a lodge without a good horse for your wife. *Ulekiuse*, ride, Heyets. There's more snow coming."

I looked north and it was true.

"Good luck, Heyets," said Swan Woman. "*Taz alago*."

"*Taz alago*," I answered her. "*Taz alago, Hemene* . . . "

Yellow Wolf said nothing. He only scowled and grumbled something under his breath which sounded like "he always talks too much," and turned around, stalking off toward his mother's lodge. With a last wave to Swan Woman, I turned Mankiller and the cavalry sorrel away from the camp of the pack train survivors.

The tracks lay clear in the old snow. The new snow came on but fell slow. There was no trouble running the trail of Meyui and the old pack horse. Late in the afternoon it blew harder and the snow began to drift. I worried then that I would not come up to them. But just at twilight I found some droppings in the trail, and they were still warm when I got down and held my hand to them. I knew now that neither snow nor darkness could steal them from me.

I was right. Around another bend, in the shelter of an alder thicket in a little cup of ground lying low and out of the wind and hidden so snug I would have passed and never seen it in a few more minutes of the fading light, stood my small lopsided lodge. Its torn and patched skins were laced on short, crooked poles. Its shape was like no tipi ever seen in the Wallowa or along the Clearwater. It crouched there in that quiet hollow like some poor wounded thing which had come so far and could go no farther. Yet it was well set, all the same, pitched smart and just-so to take every advantage of that hidden place. There was wood there for the fire, water from the beaver pond I could now see lying in the alders, and there was red and yellow Indian willow and silver birch mixed in the grove to give live bark for our horses when the snow came too heavy for them to paw out the buried grass. So I nodded my head and smiled and felt a great warmness in me for that homely, crooked tipi; and I clucked to the horses and went down the slope toward it, feeling in my heart as if I had come home, as if I had been there many times before.

At the door I stopped Mankiller and the sorrel. The Sioux pony winded the Lodge and got the scent of who was in it. Throwing forward his ears, he belled his nostrils with a glad snort. It made a warning noise in the stillness of the wooded hollow, and I heard the rustle of startled movement within the tipi.

"Meyui," I called sharply, "come out here and take these horses. *Koiimze!* Do you hear? You want me to sit in this snow all night?"

She was at the entry flap then, her slim figure outlined in its opening by the glow of firelight behind her.

"*Heyets?*" she asked, not believing it. "Is it truly you? I cannot see you — those night shadows — the fall of the snow. Speak again. Say my name."

"Meyui," I said. "Morning Light."

"Oh, Heyets! Heyets! Dear, dear Heyets!"

"Don't weep," I ordered. "Do your work. Here . . ."

I got down off Mankiller, giving her his rein and the sorrel's lead rope.

"That's Hemene's fine cavalry horse he got from Red Nose Gibbon at Big Hole. He sends him to you for your own mount. Treat him like your mother's honor. You will never get another as good."

She took the horses and put them with the old pack brute, in a sheltered place behind the lodge. I waited for her. When she returned I held aside the entry flap for her to go in before me. This was high courtesy from an Indian man, and she smiled, happy as a child. Stooping quickly, I followed her into the rosy warmth of the low-roofed lodge.

Within, she had a snowshoe rabbit she had shot with Coyote's hunting bow. The rabbit was on a green willow spit, fixed exactly as it should be to roast properly without burning. The smell of the crisping meat, all rich brown and juicy, gave me the strength of a bear, the spirit of a song bird. I laughed aloud. Meyui opened her red lips and laughed back at me. I threw my arm about her shoulders.

"*Eeh-hahh*," I cried, "it smells like hump ribs basted in back fat! Praise Hunyewat I found you!"

"Yes," she nodded quietly, "praise him that you did." She flashed her white teeth in the quick, odd way she had of smiling with her head half turned away, and gently let herself free of me.

"Come, warrior," she said, "let me do a woman's things for you. Sit back there by the saddle."

I drew away from the fire and leaned against the pack saddle, glad enough for the moment's rest and for the chance to watch her moving in the firelight. The thought came to me that this girl and I had ridden a long, long trail since the happy days of our childhood in the Wallowa. It seemed to me suddenly that she had always been there just beyond my eyes; something that I saw and needed to see, but which I had accepted without gratitude or appreciation, as we accept the beating of our hearts or the drawing of our breaths. To that pausing moment I had never really looked at her. Now I did. And, as I did, the words of the old Asotin grandmother came back to me. I nodded my head as though to answer her after all this time. Yes, grandmother, I said in my mind, you were right. She is indeed a woman worthy of any man to seek after and to stay with. I have found her, grandmother, as you ordered; and I shall stay with her as you had me promise — forever.

For her part, Meyui was having no such long thoughts. She spread the lone buffalo robe on the far side of the fire, away from the door, in the Nez Perce sleeping place. At its head she put one of our two ragged blankets rolled as a double pillow. The other blanket she brought to me, after instructing me to retire to the robe. There she insisted on wrapping it about my feet, after carefully tugging off my half-thawed moccasins and buckskin leg wraps. This done, she brought me my food, serving the saddle and loin of the rabbit to me, taking the bony shoulders and small-meated front legs for herself.

It was the first feeding of fresh roast game either of us had known for seven or eight suns. We ate all of it save for the main leg bones, the clawed feet and the entrails. Afterward, Meyui cleaned up everything neatly and carefully, as I remembered my mother doing. The likeness, not common to most Indian women, struck my memory. Thinking thus of my mother, I asked curiously, "Meyui, what was it my mother said to you when she gave you this *wyakin*?" I held up the Jesus medal, the war charm Hemene had brought me from Meyui in Yellowstone Park. Seeing it, she dropped her head and did not want to answer me. I insisted. Finally, she replied.

"She told me I was the one her heart wanted as woman for her son. She said the Jesus cross would lead you to me. She put that blessing upon it when she gave it to me back there in the village of Looking Glass. I am sorry, Heyets. You should not have made me tell you."

I saw the fire-glisten of the tears running across her soft cheek. I spoke to her, low and gentle, ordering her to come to me. She hesitated, never having known a man, and fearing, too, to believe what I meant. I called to her again, taking the blanket from around me and holding it wide for her to come bed beside me. Then she knew.

She readied herself with graceful shyness. I did the same, feeling awkward and excited as a boy. In the last moment she put a banking of morning wood upon the supper embers. Then she came toward me through the deepened fire shadows and lay herself down upon the thick curl of the robe, her murmur and sigh of greeting and content as soft and grateful as a summer breeze.

I put the blanket lightly over us and we lay a moment, easing to the pleasant feel of our bodies touching. There was no awkwardness after that.

We let the snowflakes whirl and hiss above the smoke hole. We let the prowling wind tug and whine at the tight-laced flaps. We let the feeding horses stomp and whicker in the sheltered comfort of their picket place just beyond the lodgeskins at our heads. We let the fire pop and smolder low, and we lay and talked soft and caressed one another in the furry warmth of our winter bed.

When it was time the tall sister of Coyote turned her willing body into mine and said, "Will you say my name to me this one more time, Heyets?"

I held her close and touched her small ear with my lips. It was very still, very wonderful, in that moment.

"Meyui," I answered. "Light of the Morning. My woman . . . "

The rest of the Nez Perce story is one of sorrow. After the surrender they were ordered to Dakota Territory by General Sheridan. But General Sherman had them sent to Oklahoma, the dreaded Hot Place, over protests by Miles and One Hand Howard.

They made the trip down the Missouri in flatboats, spending the winter at Fort Leavenworth where the entire tribe suffered from malaria. Many died in Oklahoma in that first year alone, their mountain-bred vitality no match for the humid heat.

General Miles, who called Chief Joseph the greatest Indian he had ever known, finally had the Nez Perce returned to their homelands in 1885—eight years after their defeat. One hundred and eighty-eight were sent to Lapwai; but one hundred fifty, including Joseph, were ordered to Colville Reservation in Washington. Exile was bitter for him, at the hands of those who had called him friend.

White Bird, who with Toohoolhoolzote really started the war, was never punished by the white men but was allowed to return to Lapwai from Canada. The other fugitives, the pack train people, stayed with a band of Canadian Sioux, smaller than Sitting Bull's band which had given shelter to White Bird. In the spring of 1878 a cruel rumor reached this camp from Lapwai, that all would be forgiven if they returned to the Idaho reservation. Later the whites, including Agent Monteith, denied making such a promise. But the exiled Indians, believing its truth, started the long journey. In fifteen days, led by Wottolen, with Yellow Wolf scouting, they reached the Rockies and struck for home. But it was a lost hope for they were ambushed by a prowling cavalry patrol and lost all their horses. They recovered their mounts in a daring night raid on the soldier camp but could no longer risk staying together. The country was acrawl with patrols and the problem now was to reach Lapwai and surrender before the soldiers, who plainly had been ordered to do so, could kill them.

At the Salmon River the band separated. Wottolen and his starving group came in first. Yellow Wolf held out, saying, "I will stay in the prairie like a coyote. I have no home." But finally he and his people joined the defeated ones. At Lapwai Reservation on July 31, 1878, protected by the soldiers they hated from the hostile settlers they had so long befriended, ended the saga of Chief Joseph and his people. When Yellow Wolf bowed his fierce head and said, "I put down the rifle," the finest hour of the American Indian was past.

Joseph's own tragedy was no simple one. Neither the bloody murderer described by the Idaho settlers, nor the noble savage created by the white man's newspapers in the East, he was a man not even properly understood by his own people. Such as he was, quiet, lonely, introspective, unknown to his friends as thoroughly as to his enemies, he died alone and unattended in front of his cowskin tipi on the reservation at Nespelem twenty-seven years later.

"When I think of our condition," he said toward the end, "my heart is heavy. I see men of my race treated as outlaws and driven from country to country, or shot down like animals.

"I know that my race must change. We cannot hold our own with the white men as we are. We only ask an even chance to live as other men live. We ask to be recognized as men. We ask that the same law shall work alike on all men. *If the Indian breaks the law, punish him by the law. If the white man breaks the law, punish him also.*

"Let me be a free man — free to travel, free to stop, free to work, free to trade, free to choose my own teachers, free to follow the religion of my fathers, free to think and talk and act for myself — and I will obey every law or submit to the penalty.

"Whenever the white man treats the Indian as they treat each other, then we shall have no more wars. We shall be all alike — brothers of one father and one mother, with one sky above us and one country around us, and one government for all. Then the Great Spirit Chief who rules above will smile upon this land,

and send rain to wash out the bloody spots made by brothers' hands upon the face of the earth. For this time the Indian race are waiting and praying. I hope that no more groans of wounded men and women will ever go to the ear of the Great Spirit Chief above, and that all people may be one people."